Truth Lies Bleeding

Chris Dolley

Book View Café

TRUTH LIES BLEEDING

Published by Book View Café

Book View Café Publishing Cooperative
304 S. Jones Blvd Suite #2906
Las Vegas, NV 89107

www.bookviewcafe.com

ISBN 13: 978-1-63632-306-0

Cover design by Damonza

First printing, 2025

Truth Lies Bleeding

Books by Chris Dolley

Reeves & Worcester Steampunk Mysteries

What Ho, Automata

The Unpleasantness at Baskerville Hall

Other Books

Resonance

Shift

French Fried

An Unsafe Pair Of Hands

Medium Dead

Chapter One

I stopped dead. My front door was ajar. I always lock up before leaving home. It's my routine - switch off the lights, lock the doors. I *never* forget.

I rocked from foot to foot. Should I call the police? I lived alone. No one else had a key. What other reason could there be for the door being open...

But would the police come after last time?

I took a deep breath. And listened. Not a sound came from inside the house. Whoever had broken in would be long gone by now, wouldn't they?

I reached out, gently applying pressure to the door with my left index finger. I slowly pushed it open, trying desperately not to make a sound.

That's when I saw it - the dollhouse - sitting in the middle of the hall floor. It looked ... it looked like an exact replica of my home!

I crept closer, unable to look away. The attention to detail was uncanny. It even had the same bent weathervane on the roof.

And inside? I had to look. I found a latch and swung the front of the dollhouse open. The interior was a perfect reproduction too - every piece of furniture, the wallpaper, the carpets, the...

I froze. There was a miniature figure of a woman lying in a pool of blood on the spare bedroom floor.

~

I swallowed hard. This could not be happening. It had to be a prank. Surely that was more likely than having a dead body upstairs, but ... this was so elaborate. Kids wouldn't have the patience, and who the hell would think this was funny?

I had to call the police. It was the sensible thing to do.

Back slowly out of the house and call the police from a safe distance.

But if there wasn't a body in the spare bedroom...

I couldn't go through that again. Even if they didn't recognise my name at first, someone would soon ask the question. Are you *that* Mathew Sedley? The one from the Sophie Gallindo case?

And it would all start again. The questions. The hate. The ridicule.

They'd charge me with wasting police time, and leak the story to the press – who'd love every minute of it. A chance to pile in and dredge up all the old headlines. I'd only just found a new job and a new place to live. I couldn't just up sticks and move again!

But if I didn't call the police and there was a body...

They'd charge me with failing to report a crime. They might even consider me a murder suspect!

I slowly backed out of the house, watching the stairs, glancing behind me. Maybe I could call on a neighbour? I didn't know anyone in the village and there were a lot of second homes, but surely someone would be in? Maybe they'd agree to check the house with me, or would that be asking too much? Christ, what if I got a neighbour killed?

That's when the phone rang – not my mobile, not the one I always used, but the old landline inside the house.

I'd never given anyone that number.

~

My heart raced. Was it him? The killer? It always was in films. The all-seeing murderer calling the hapless passer-by to torment and threaten. *I can see you. Do what I say or you're next.*

He could be calling from upstairs. Hiding there, waiting for me to check the spare bedroom. *Yes, the police will find a body here today, but it won't be a woman. It'll be you.*

The phone kept ringing. My mind kept racing. What if it was the police? Maybe they'd already been called and were setting up roadblocks on the edge of the village. Snipers even. This could be them trying to contact me. To get me out of the house.

I had to answer the phone.

I edged back inside, breathing hard, eyes darting from the stairs to the kitchen, and picked up the phone.

"Mr. Sedley?"

It was a woman's voice. Not one I recognised.

"Ye-es," I said, barely getting the word out.

"Are you the owner of Laburnum Cottage?"

I swallowed hard. "Why do you want to know?"

"I need to establish I'm talking to the right person."

"Why?"

"Sorry, I should have said. I'm Lauren from Energy Solutions. One of our consultants is going to be in your area next week and he'd like to talk to you about the huge savings that can be made on your home energy bills. Heat pump technology has…"

A telesales call.

I took a deep breath, closed my eyes and tuned out her voice.

Then I had an idea.

"Wait! Stop. Listen, please. I need your help. I think someone's in my house."

"What?"

"Someone's broken into my house. I've just come home and found the front door open."

"Have you called the police?"

"Not yet. It's complicated, but…"

I told her about the dollhouse.

"Get out of the house *now* and call the police."

"I can't. What if there's nothing up there? I can't risk being charged with wasting police time. I need to find out what's up there first and … I can't go up there alone. I *need* someone to have my back and call the police if … if I can't."

She didn't say a word. All I could hear were faint snatches of conversation in the background.

"Look," I said. "I don't have anyone else. I live alone. Please, just stay on the line. You know my name and where I live so … if anything happens you can call for help."

"This better not be a wind up."

"It's not. I can show you the dollhouse! Let me have your number and I'll text a photo to you."

"If this is a ploy to get my phone number you'll regret it."

"It's not!"

"First hint of a dick pic and I'm calling the police. I've got your name and address."

"Look, please! I'm desperate."

She gave me her mobile number. I ran over to the dollhouse, took the picture as quickly as I could, and sent it to her.

"Have you got it yet?" I asked as soon as I got back to the landline.

"Not yet. Wait. Yes. Got it." She was quiet for a few seconds. "You really should leave the house. Forget about going upstairs. Call the police."

"I can't. I have to do this."

I removed the cordless phone from its base unit. I had no idea what range it had, but it had to have at least ten yards, easily enough to reach the spare bedroom.

I crept to the foot of the stairs and listened. Not a creak. Not a sound. I'd keep to the outside of the stairs, and be ready to turn and run at the slightest movement. And I'd keep my eyes on the landing above.

"I'm climbing the stairs," I whispered into the phone.

One step, two - still no sounds, no movement from the landing above. Slowly the top of the spare bedroom door came into view. It was closed. I never close that door. I've never had a guest in the two months I've lived here.

I reached the half-landing and turned. I could see all the way down the landing now. Every door was open except the spare bedroom. Not a sound came from anywhere.

My imagination was on fire. Any second a crazed axe murderer could come running out onto the landing. Or appear at the foot of the stairs. Shit! Why hadn't I checked the downstairs rooms? He could be anywhere!

I took another deep breath. *Get a grip. You can do this!*

"The door to the spare bedroom's closed," I whispered into the phone. "I'm going to open it."

My heart thudded in my chest. I had to do this quickly. Another five seconds and I'd lose my nerve.

I positioned myself to the side of the door and rose up onto the balls of my feet, ready to spring backwards at the first hint of trouble. I reached out, grasped the door handle, and slowly turned the knob.

I threw the door open and sprang backwards. The door slammed against the doorstop and swung back, juddering to a halt, half-open.

I peered into the room. The body was there, exactly as depicted in the dollhouse – same pose, same clothes, same hair.

"What's happening!" asked Lauren

"She's here," I said. "It's just like the dollhouse."

"Is she dead?"

"There's a lot of blood."

"But is she breathing?"

I squatted next to the body and checked. "No. There's no pulse either."

"Do you recognise her?"

"No. Not at all."

"Get out and call the police."

I took a picture first. I needed proof. Evidence had a habit of disappearing in my world.

Chapter Two

I waited outside for the police to arrive, making sure I always kept the dollhouse in sight. I felt numb. All the adrenaline of earlier had just drained away. Either that or I was going into shock.

Two uniformed constables arrived first. I walked over to introduce myself.

"The body's upstairs," I said. "But you need to see this first."

I showed them the dollhouse. "It's not mine. I found it here when I got home. It's an exact replica of the house – the rooms, the carpets, the … the clothes on the body."

The younger policemen went upstairs. The older one got out his notebook.

"What was your relationship to the deceased?" he asked.

"I have no idea who she is. I've never seen her before."

"Do you live here alone?"

"Yes. I have no family."

"She's not a neighbour?"

"She could be. I don't really know anyone in the village. I only moved in two months ago."

The younger policeman returned. "She's dead all right. I've called it in."

"Did you touch the body?" the older policeman asked me.

"Only to check her pulse."

The detectives arrived next – eventually – a chief inspector, a sergeant and two constables. I went over the events again with them.

"Is anything missing?" DCI Terrell asked me.

"Missing from what?" I said.

"The house. You came home, found the front door open and assumed there'd been a break-in. Did you check to see if anything was missing?"

I hadn't thought to look.

"No. As soon as I saw the inside of the dollhouse everything changed. I haven't checked any of the rooms except the spare bedroom and even there I didn't have a close look at anything except, well, the dead woman."

"Collins, get Mr. Sedley an oversuit. As soon as you get suited up, sir, we'll take you through the house room by room. Tell us if there's anything new, or out of place, or missing."

We walked the house, downstairs first. Nothing looked out of place. The kitchen was as I left it. The washing up from breakfast was still in the sink. No extra cups or glasses had been added.

The lounge was the same. None of the furniture had been moved and all the electrical appliances were where they should be.

And then we came to the hallway.

"Did you move the dollhouse at all, Mr. Sedley?" asked the DCI.

"I opened it up to look inside. That's all."

"And you don't make or collect dollhouses?"

"No."

"Do you know anyone who does?"

"No. No one."

DCI Terrell closed the dollhouse, then walked to the door and turned.

"You can't miss it can you?" he said. "It's dead centre and just far enough back so the front door can't knock it when it swings open."

He swung the front door open to prove his point. The clearance was less than an inch.

"And the front door was ajar when you got home?"

"Yes, about an inch," I said.

"Not enough to be noticed from a distance, but enough to hide the dollhouse," said the DCI.

"You think that's significant, boss?" asked the sergeant.

"I think everything about this crime scene's significant. It's theatrical. I mean, who makes a model of the crime scene and puts it on display by the front door? And the attention to detail. This is someone who plans meticulously."

"So, why leave the door ajar?" asked the sergeant.

The DCI shrugged. "Well ... it would make you stop and think, wouldn't it? If the door had been closed, you'd have opened the door thinking all was well and then – wham – you're confronted with the dollhouse. One big shock. But having the door ajar stretches out the shock. As does having the dollhouse closed. If you wanted the maximum effect, you'd have the dead body in the hall, or the dollhouse open to show the miniature figure in a pool of blood."

The sergeant nodded. "But our killer doesn't want the maximum shock. He wants to stretch things out. So, are we looking for a sadist?"

"It's a reasonable opening hypothesis. Have you got any enemies, Mr. Sedley? Someone who *really* doesn't like you?"

"No," I said.

The DCI gave me a long, hard look. "You answered that very quickly."

~

We went upstairs next, starting in my bedroom.

Everything looked as I'd left it.

"Looks very tidy," said the DCI.

"I'm a tidy person," I said. "And I don't have a lot of stuff."

I looked through the drawers. I couldn't see anything missing or hidden away.

"I can't swear there's nothing missing," I said. "I'd have no idea if someone took a pair of socks."

"I think you can forget about socks. I'm more interested in items of value – either monetary or personal. Something significant or unusual."

I continued my search. The drawers, cupboards and bedside table hadn't been touched as far as I could see.

We checked the bathroom next. Again, nothing looked out of place...

Except the glass with my toothbrush in it. It had been moved.

"That should be on the left of the windowsill. I never put it in the centre."

DCI Terrell leaned over for a closer look.

"Bag them both, Collins. The toothbrush and the glass."

I watched, wondering why the killer would move my toothbrush. Had he cleaned his teeth with it? If so, why move the glass? Unless he took them both out of the bathroom.

Then I had another thought.

"Could the killer have used the brush to clean the victim's teeth?" I asked.

"What makes you think that?"

"Isn't that the sort of thing these crazies do? Wash the victim."

"Is that something that interests you?" asked the DCI. "Crime stories?"

"I like reading them," I said. "Millions of people do."

I quickly turned away and busied myself checking the towels on the towel rail. I could feel the DCI's eyes following me. *Be careful, Mathew. Don't draw attention to yourself. At this point in the investigation, you're just as much a suspect as a witness.*

I checked the bathroom cabinet next – everything looked in order – then the bath. The shower curtain was as I'd left it – drawn back to the edge of the bath. I pulled it across to check. It was bone dry. As were the tiles surrounding the bath, and the bath itself. No one had showered in the last few hours.

"What were you looking for on those wall tiles?" asked the DCI.

"Anything unusual," I said. "Like you asked."

"You were looking very closely."

"I was looking for water droplets."

"To see if anyone had used the shower recently?"

"Yes."

"Very thorough. Sima, have SOCO take samples of all the

traps and drains."

A DC met us on the landing.

"We've checked all the doors and windows, boss. No forced entry."

DCI Terrell turned to me. "How many people have a key to this house?"

"Only me."

"Not family or a neighbour?"

"No. I have no family, and I don't know any of the neighbours. I've only just moved in."

"Did you change the locks after moving in?"

"No. It never occurred to me."

It did now. Loads of people could have keys to my home. The previous owners, their family, close friends and neighbours. Why hadn't I considered the risk?

"Are there any locksmiths you'd recommend?" I asked.

"We'll get you a list."

"Oh, and, boss," said the DC. "The pathologist's arrived. She's next door with the body."

~

I was told to wait on the landing while the others filed into the spare bedroom. I hovered by the door, listening. I had a partial view of the room, but not the body.

"Do we have a cause of death, doc?" asked the DCI.

"We don't," said a woman's voice. "But I can tell you she wasn't stabbed. The blood's fake. Realistic, but fake. You can find hundreds of recipes online. Very popular in the film industry, I believe."

"But she *was* murdered?"

"Probably, but we won't know until the PM. There's no obvious puncture wounds. No trauma. No obvious signs of strangulation or poison."

"And you're not prepared to hazard a guess?"

"You know me, chief inspector. Facts, dear boy. Facts. You'll have to wait until the PM."

The DCI – at least I assumed it was the DCI – sighed.

"What about time of death?" he asked.

"That I can help you with. Definitely less than three hours ago. I'd say around three p.m. give or take thirty minutes, maybe an hour at a stretch."

"Have you found any ID on her?"

"I haven't found *anything* on her - no phone, no keys, no cards, nothing. And I don't see a handbag in here."

There wasn't one downstairs either. The killer must have stripped her of anything that could identify her.

"Sima, get Sedley in here," said the DCI.

I braced myself and followed Sima into the room.

"Take another look at the deceased," the DCI said. "A close look. Are you sure you don't recognise her?"

I looked hard at her face, trying to blot out the blood. Fake or not, it still unnerved me. I tried imagining her as a blonde or with longer hair. Had I seen her around the village? I didn't think so. She was young. Late teens, early twenties. I barely knew anyone in that age group any more. Could she be the daughter of one of my old work colleagues? I couldn't recall anyone looking like her.

I shrugged. "Sorry. I have absolutely no memory of her at all."

There was a noise of someone running fast up the stairs. A DC appeared, breathing hard, in the doorway.

"Boss, can I have a word?"

"Fire away," said the DCI.

The DC looked embarrassed. "Um, outside would be best, I think, boss."

The DCI shook his head and followed his DC onto the landing.

"What is it?" I heard him say.

I couldn't hear everything that was said, but I could fill in the gaps. The snatched glances in my direction, the growing excitement. They'd run my name through their files. They knew who I was.

Chapter Three

The DCI popped his head round the door. "Sima, Collins, bring Mr. Sedley down to the lounge. We've finished in here."

I felt like the condemned prisoner being led to the scaffold. I was shown to a chair while the DCI paced. He looked on the verge of exploding.

As soon as I sat down he laid into me.

"Well, well, well, Mr. Mathew Sedley, the attention-seeking fantasist. I didn't recognise you until now. You've changed your hair and grown a beard, but you can't change what's inside, can you?"

I did what I always did. Sat tight-lipped and let them vent. No point in doing anything else.

"Do you know Mr. Sedley's MO, Sima?" said the DCI.

"No, boss."

"He likes to insert himself into police investigations. Sex up enquiries. Lie, fabricate, embellish. But most of all, he likes to point the finger."

He loomed above me, jabbing a finger at my face.

"You accused a grieving neighbour of abusing his child. You turned a missing person and accidental death case into a murder enquiry. You *destroyed* that family. And all for what? Your fifteen minutes of fame?"

I looked straight ahead, avoiding eye contact.

"The question is – are you now a murderer, or are you still just the window dresser? The pathetic little man who sexes up crime scenes to get more media attention. The fake blood – that sounds like you. The dollhouse too. All to drive up the media interest. Is that why you took her ID? To make it more mysterious. 'Who's the mystery woman?' emblazoned across all the front pages."

There was no point in answering. I'd been in this situation

so many times. Closed minds never listen.

"Or are you the murderer now? Did you get so fed up waiting for the next body to arrive that you had to go out and get your own?"

He shook his head and turned away.

"Sima, get some pictures of the deceased and arrange a house to house. Someone's got to know her. Or was in the area between two and four."

He beckoned DC Collins over.

"Take Sedley down the station and detain him."

"What grounds, boss?"

"Suspicion of perverting the course of justice for starters. We can add the rest later."

"That's ridiculous," I said. "How have I perverted the course of justice?"

"You've interfered with a crime scene. You've fabricated evidence, and you lied to me."

"When?"

"When you said you didn't know anyone who really hated you. I know dozens, starting with the family of Sophie Gallindo."

He pulled me to my feet. "He's all yours, Collins. Get his phone over to tech support and make sure he gives you the password."

~

It took a while to be processed at the station. I spoke when requested, and kept quiet and respectful the rest of the time. I'd had worse days. I'd had *far* worse days.

The cell wasn't too bad either. At least I didn't have to share, and it wasn't as though I had anywhere better to be. My home was a crime scene. The police wouldn't let me back in for at least another day. If I wasn't here, I'd only have to hole up in a hotel room and hope the press didn't find me.

After an hour or two, the door opened and I was escorted to an interview room. Sima and DCI Terrell were already there. The latter looking as though he'd eaten something unpleasant and was looking for a place to spit it out.

Sima read me my rights and asked if I wanted to have a lawyer present. I didn't. I just wanted it all to be over. There was no evidence against me and the sooner the police realised that the better.

The tape recorder started and the questioning began.

"Where were you between two o'clock and four o'clock this afternoon?" asked Sima.

"Mowing grass verges on the B31287, the other side of Bristol. If you've got a map I'll show you where exactly. You'll see it's over an hour's drive from where I live."

"Can anyone corroborate you were there at that time?" asked Sima.

"A couple hundred drivers."

"What were *you* doing cutting grass?" asked the DCI. "I thought you were one of the senior managers at Swindon Borough Council."

"Not any more. Apparently being a public spirited citizen contravenes the council's code of conduct."

It still rankled. The press I understood. They wanted a villain to throw to their readers. They didn't know me. They didn't care. All they wanted was to sell more papers. But my colleagues...

They were my *friends*. They knew me!

"You? Public spirited?" said the DCI, sneering.

"When the police asked for information, I came forward. No one else did."

"For good reason. There was nothing to come forward about!"

"I heard screams. On *three* separate occasions that last week. A young girl, terrified. Not playful screams, not temper tantrum screams, but real scared witless screams."

"Which no one else heard! Neighbours who lived closer to the Gallindos than you didn't hear a thing. Some were even in their gardens when you said Sophie was screaming."

"They were lying! They'd all known each other for years. Their kids went to the same schools. They even went on holidays together. Of course they were going to give their friends the benefit of the doubt."

"So why didn't you report it to the police at the time?"

"Because you don't accuse your neighbour of being a child abuser unless you're absolutely sure of your facts."

DCI Terrell threw up his hands. "*Now* you admit it! You weren't sure what you heard."

"Of course I wasn't sure. Not then. Not enough to involve the police. If I hear a scream I don't immediately think 'murder.' I didn't know *what* I'd heard. Was it a kid having a nightmare or was it something on the TV? But when a child goes missing, everything changes. The screams, the note. They take on a significance. And it wasn't just the one instance. It was the accumulation of things that I couldn't ignore any more."

"Oh yes, the famous disappearing note. You'll like this one, Sima. Young Sophie's with her family at a neighbourhood barbecue when she decides to slip a note into Mr. Sedley's pocket. What did it say, Mathew?"

I knew the words off by heart.

"'Help! He's going to kill me. Help me! Please. Sophie'"

"That's right. Of all the people present at the barbecue, young Sophie selects Mathew, who she doesn't know, as her saviour. Except she doesn't tell him she's slipped a note into his pocket, and he doesn't know it definitely came from her. And he does nothing about it until Sophie's disappearance becomes headline news."

"I told you. You can't accuse neighbours of child abuse unless you're absolutely sure. I didn't know what to think. It wasn't as though the child showed any signs of injury. She appeared happy and outgoing. So, I put the note away in a drawer in case something else happened later."

"But according to you something else did happen! The screaming. Three times. And you *still* did nothing until the cameras arrived. *That's* when you showed an interest. When you could grab your fifteen minutes of grubby fame."

"I came forward when the child went missing. The whole

neighbourhood was searching the woods. No one had any idea where she was or what had happened, and the police were desperate for witnesses to come forward."

"So, what happened to the note? The one you so carefully put away in case it was needed later."

"I don't know what happened to the note."

"It magically disappeared, didn't it? The moment the police asked to see it – poof – it disappears."

"Someone must have seen Sophie put the note in my pocket and stole it back later."

"How convenient."

I didn't respond. There was nothing I could say without sounding like a mad conspiracy theorist. One day the note was there, the next it wasn't. How it disappeared was a mystery.

"Getting back to the case in hand," said Sima. "Have you had anyone stay at your house since you moved in?"

"No."

"What about builders or decorators? Have you shown anyone around the house? Someone who might have taken pictures of the rooms."

I sat up. I could see where this was going. Whoever made the dollhouse had to have access to the house. I'd assumed they'd broken in, but maybe they hadn't needed to. The only trouble was that I was a recluse with no friends.

"I've had no one round since the removal men."

"What firm did you use?"

"Ramsgill's. They're based in Swindon."

Sima made a note.

"Do you have a cleaner?"

"No. No gardener either."

"What about neighbours? Have you had any round? Did you have a housewarming party."

"I haven't entertained for over a year, and no neighbours have been round. No Jehovah's witnesses either. No vicars. No local councillors. No salesmen. No..."

It suddenly came to me.

"What is it?" asked Sima.

"The estate agent. They had loads of pictures of the house. They even had a video of the entire interior and exterior. It was all online – anyone could have watched it."

"Which estate agent was that?" asked Sima.

"Stivell's in Bath. I only moved in two months ago, and I haven't made any changes to the house. All the carpets, wallpaper, fitted units. Everything. It's still the same."

"Who's Olivia Gibbons?" asked the DCI.

"What?"

I was taken aback by the sudden switch in questioning. Had they identified the victim?

"I've never heard of Olivia Gibbons," I said.

"That's odd," said the DCI. "Because two minutes before you called the police, you sent her a picture of the dollhouse. Your priorities haven't changed, have they? What is she? Press or TV?"

I was confused. "She said her name was Lauren."

The DCI shook his head. "You can't trust the press these days, can you?"

I told them about Lauren and the call.

"You expect us to believe that?" said the DCI.

"Check with the phone company. They'll have all the call details for the landline."

"Oh, we're checking, but let's get this straight. Seconds after discovering that there was a strong possibility of a dead body being upstairs – maybe the murderer too – you take time out to discuss heat pumps with a woman from a call centre."

"We didn't discuss heat pumps! I was alone and desperate. And I didn't want to die, bleeding out in an empty house, because no one would have come looking for me. I'd have been there, undiscovered, for months."

"My heart bleeds. Maybe if you didn't accused your neighbours of being child-killers you'd have more friends."

"Why are you taking this so personally? I don't remember you from the investigation. You're Avon and Somerset police, aren't you? The investigating force was Wiltshire."

"I have friends there. Good friends. They told me all about you. You cost that investigation two days."

"How? All I did was come forward with evidence."

DCI Terrell shuffled his chair forward and leaned across the table.

"They were searching that river two days before Sophie's body was found. It had just become the main focus of the search, then in you come with your 'evidence' and the teams are stood down. The missing person case becomes a murder enquiry. Everyone's attention is switched to the Gallindos and their garden is dug up. Two days lost. Two days of publicity for you and two days of agony for the parents."

"It wasn't me hounding the Gallindos. It was the press. They went for the father *relentlessly*, which made them turn on me all the more when they found out Sophie's death was an accident. They had to have someone to blame for the hell *they*'d created."

"There you go again. *I'm the victim. It's everyone else's fault.*"

"I *was* a victim. I'm still a victim. Look at me. Why am I here? There's no evidence against me. I have an alibi. The only reason I'm here is because you blame me for everything that went wrong last year."

"Don't you have any guilt?"

"Of course I have guilt! If I could go back in time, I'd have kept quiet."

"Did you hear that, Sima? If Mr. Sedley could go back in time, he'd keep quiet. Now, me, if I could go back in time, my first thought would be to stop Sophie falling in the river. But Mr. Sedley doesn't think like that. He only thinks about himself."

"That's not true."

"Isn't it? What was your first thought when you found the dollhouse? Was it 'there could be a woman upstairs bleeding out. I'd better call 999?' Or did you take a photograph and send it to your agent?"

"I do *not* have an agent. Do you think I want this attention?"

"I think you *love* the attention. Why else would you take a picture of the dead woman? Normal people don't do that. But killers and attention-seekers … that's exactly what they do."

This was not going to be easy to explain.

"It's not like that. I took the picture in case she … in case she disappeared – like the note. Yes, it sounds stupid now, but when you've had something as important as Sophie's note disappear, and the whole world thinks you're a liar, you start to think that the world's gaslighting you. That's why I took the picture. That's why I waited outside, keeping the dollhouse in clear sight until the police came. I needed proof that I wasn't lying."

"Bullshit. You're a liar. A clever one. You sent the press the photo of the dollhouse, but not the one of the body. You're keeping that back as a bargaining chip, aren't you? Because they're worth so much more as a pair."

~

Well, that could have gone better.

I slept fitfully in the cell that night. I couldn't get his words out of my head. *He only thinks of himself.* Was that true? I'd never considered the woman could be alive. All I could think about was *my* safety and how *I* was going to be affected.

But I *had* ruled out bringing in a neighbour to help in case I got them killed. And I did call the police even though I knew that my life would be made an absolute hell. And I struggled for hours before making the decision to tell the Wiltshire police about Sophie's note and the screams. A self-obsessed person wouldn't have done that. They wouldn't have cared.

Or was my reluctance to come forward more a question of not wanting to be inconvenienced. I liked my quiet life. No fuss, no drama. And definitely no irate neighbours banging on my doors and windows demanding to know what I was playing at.

What I still couldn't fathom, though, was what had been

going on in the Gallindos' house. I knew what I'd heard. I knew what I'd seen. But nothing made sense. *Something* had to have been going on. Not abuse – I accepted that now, the evidence was overwhelming – but ... maybe Sophie had had psychological problems – night terrors and paranoia – something the family had been too embarrassed to seek help for.

Not that any of that played a part in her death. The river levels had been high after a wet summer. The banks were slippery, and there were a lot of submerged weeds that could easily entangle the arms and legs of a struggling child.

And children will always be children. Inquisitive, and easily attracted to something floating or trapped in the water.

I woke early the next morning feeling a little more hopeful. The investigation had to be making progress. Once they confirmed my alibi and identified the body, they'd have to start looking elsewhere. Olivia Gibbons for one. Who the hell was she? The woman from the call centre or her accomplice? The more I thought about it, the more suspicious it felt. What were the odds of being cold-called just as you were about to find a body?

After eleven that morning, everything changed.

Chapter Four

I knew something was up the moment I was taken from the cells. Officers, who'd been indifferent to me the day before, were now staring at me.

Sima and DCI Terrell were already sitting at the interview room desk, waiting. The latter had a folder in front of him. He looked even more wound up than the day before.

I'd barely been read my rights when he started.

"I've just come from the post mortem, Mr. Sedley. How do you think the victim died?"

I shrugged. "No idea."

"Not even a guess? Not a little stab at the answer – and that wasn't a clue by the way."

I shook my head and kept quiet. It was obvious he was building up to some momentous announcement – probably followed by five minutes of venting.

He stared at me. "You already know, don't you?"

"No," I said, hoping he'd just come out with it.

"She drowned," said the DCI. "Just like little Sophie. What are the chances of you being innocently involved in two drownings?"

I was stunned. I didn't know what I'd expected but it hadn't been that.

"Zero, Mr. Sedley. Zero. You may think you're being clever, but you're just digging a deeper hole for us to bury you in."

I felt anything but clever.

"Of all the rooms you took us round yesterday, the one you spent most time on was the bathroom. You had a *long* look round – checking the shower curtains, and the wall tiles. Making sure everything was dry. Is that where you killed her?"

"I didn't kill anyone. I never have."

"And all that crap about your toothbrush being in the wrong place. You were showing off, weren't you? Speculating that the killer might have brushed the victim's teeth, and that he cleaned her up. You *knew*. You knew because you'd seen the foam around her nose and mouth and *you'd* cleaned her up to delay the determination of cause of death."

This was getting worse and worse.

"Why would I want to delay the determination of cause of death?"

"To give you time to pack your things and do a runner. You knew the moment we put your name together with a drowning, you'd be arrested."

"That makes no sense. If I was planning to run away, why would I call the police to report the body?"

"Because you're a cocky little bastard. You wanted to show us your face and look us in the eye. And then disappear, leaving us with egg on our faces. Or maybe the plan was to make it look as though you'd been abducted. The killer coming back to tie up loose ends. You'd smash a window, push over a few chairs, leave a little blood. And then you re-surface a few days later as the daring abductee who escaped from the crazed killer. *What* a story you'd weave. The media would wet themselves, and you'd be rehabilitated. But what you hadn't bargained for was us arresting you yesterday."

"You really have a weird idea about me."

"On the contrary, I think I know you very well. You're an attention-seeking sociopath. No empathy whatsoever. You don't care who you hurt. You don't care what you do. All you crave is attention."

"Attention! You think I want attention? I hate it! It's ruined my life, cost me my job, my friends. All I've ever wanted is a quiet life. And I had that – for thirty years – until I came forward to help you lot. And now, just as I'm starting to rebuild my life, it's happening again. *Well, I ... don't ... want it.*"

"Very fervent. You're starting to get the hang of human emotions, but you haven't quite mastered truth. Put your name in a search engine. You're all over the internet. Interviews, articles, videos. You milked your fame for everything you could take."

"That's not true. Show me *one* interview that I actually gave. Show me! If I was an attention seeker there'd be hundreds. There'd be a book. I'd be all over daytime TV and eating bugs in some reality TV jungle. But there's *nothing*!"

"You can't help it can you? You open your mouth and out come the lies. You were all over the press and TV."

"Not by choice! I *never* gave an interview. I kept quiet. I refused every offer to tell my side of the story. It was the press who wouldn't let it lie. They followed me everywhere, shoving cameras in my face, hiding in my garden, banging on my windows, shouting questions at me."

"It's always someone else's fault with you, isn't it?"

"Can't you see I'm being set up?"

"I follow the evidence, Mr. Sedley. Would you be surprised to learn that there are two CCTV cameras on the B31287? It surprised me. You don't expect these country roads to have cameras, but there are two businesses on that stretch of road you allege you were working on yesterday. They're sending over their security tapes. Do you want to change your statement?"

"I want a lawyer. I'm not saying another word until then."

~

I stewed in the cell, waiting, going over events again and again. Every new piece of evidence seemed to drop me in it further. Why would the CCTV footage be any different? I'd pinned everything on establishing an alibi, but my confidence was shot. A company's CCTV cameras were not going to be pointing at the road. They'd be concerned about protecting their own property. Any coverage of the passing traffic would be secondary. And down to luck. Which I didn't have. The tractor could have passed by on the other side of the road.

And the police would never give me the benefit of the doubt. Anything less than a perfect image of my face would be labelled as inconclusive. They might even call off any further attempt to check my alibi. Collecting footage from CCTV cameras was easy work, but canvassing motorists looking for witnesses – that could take days and tie up numerous officers.

If only Jessups had CCTV. Or someone had been there when I dropped the tractor off and collected my car.

But, then again, wasn't that outside the window for an alibi? I reached Jessups just after four. The police had the death occurring between two and four. It was a good hour's drive home from Jessups. I could have killed the woman at two and had plenty of time to drive back to Jessups by four.

Round and round I went. There were so many cameras these days – CCTV, dashboard cameras, even people's door bells. Surely one of them would have picked something up. Whoever killed that woman had to have driven to my house. He had the dollhouse, possibly the woman with him too. Even if he knew where all the traffic cameras were, he could still be caught on someone's dashcam.

Maybe there was hope.

~

The cell door opened and a smartly-dressed young woman entered.

"Mathew Sedley?"

"Yes, that's me."

She turned to the policeman holding the cell door open. "That'll be all, thank you." Then marched forward, holding out her hand. "Georgia Courtenay, I'm the duty solicitor."

She looked very young, probably just out of law school, but she had an aura of confidence about her, and an accent straight out of the poshest of public schools.

She sat next to me on the bed and started to go through the case.

"The good news is they have no reason to hold you. You've co-operated. You've furnished them with an alibi. You've even given them your phone and password – which you should *never* have done, by the way. Very silly not to ask for legal representation immediately. Innocence is not a defence, *proof* of innocence is. From now on you don't talk to the police without checking with me first. Understood?"

I nodded.

"Good. I've talked to the senior investigating officer. He's been very forthcoming – surprisingly so. I think he's so convinced of your guilt that he considers it only a matter of time before the evidence to back up that confidence appears."

"Is he even looking at anyone else for the murder?"

"He said he had a large team investigating a number of leads."

Which could mean anything.

"I do have the bullet points from the preliminary post mortem though. The most interesting, for us, is that they've narrowed the window for time of death. It's now two thirty to three thirty."

The first piece of good news I'd had for ages. I told her about my CCTV fears.

"Don't worry," she said. "Establishing an alibi is central to our defence. I'll make sure they do a thorough job.

"Back to the PM," she continued. "It looks like the victim was restrained for a short period. Marks were found around her ankles and wrists. Also there were fibres in the victim's nose and throat. The pathologist is having them analysed. Could be from a towel used to clean the victim. Forensics are checking the fibres against the towels found in your house."

All my towels came straight from the supermarket bargain shelves. Common brands in common colours.

"They're still waiting for diatom tests on the water to prove that she was drowned in your bathroom," said Georgia. "I'm not sure how they do that. Presumably the test narrows it down to a property served by a particular water company. Unless every property has its own microscopic flora and fauna – which I sincerely hope not. Anyway, I'll look into that."

"Have they identified the dead woman, yet?" I asked.

"No."

"Isn't that odd? Surely someone would have filed a missing person report by now. She didn't look homeless."

"It is unusual, but not overly so. She might be a foreign tourist travelling alone. Or an illegal immigrant. Or just someone who told her friends she was going away for a few days."

"Any idea when I'll be able to return home?"

"As far as I know they've finished their forensic examination of the property. Unless anything new comes up, there's no reason for them to prevent you returning home, but I have the impression Detective Chief Inspector Terrell is itching to dig up your garden. So, no promises."

"What about the press? Are they covering the case? Have they published my name?"

"Not that I've seen. Though that's certain to change if they don't identify the woman soon. They'll have to go public to ask the media to help identify her. Then it'll be national news."

~

I lay back on the cell bed and waited. And waited. Georgia had said she'd press them to release me immediately, but that didn't appear to be going well.

Hours went by. Wasn't there a limit on how long they could keep a person? And how long did it take to find a tractor on a security tape?

Round and round I went. Was it good or bad news that no one had to come to see me? Surely, if they found evidence to clear me, they'd release me. But, equally, if they found no evidence of a tractor passing by, wouldn't they be dragging me into an interview room?

When the door eventually opened, I was so wound up I nearly fell off the bed.

"Follow me," said the constable. "They want you in the interview room two.

Chapter Five

Georgia was waiting outside the interview room. I braced myself for bad news.

"Your alibi has been confirmed," she said. "There's a clear shot of you in the tractor cab at two forty-one driving by a tyre shop in Bourton. Even the police admit it's at least a seventy-minute drive from there to your home, and that's not factoring in driving part of the way in a tractor."

The relief poured over me. "So I'm in the clear?"

"Not quite. DCI Terrell thinks you may have an accomplice."

"What?"

"He does appear somewhat fixated. His latest theory is that you hired someone to do the killing, and made sure you were working as far from home at the time of the murder as you could."

"That's ridiculous."

And impossible to disprove. Even if he ran down every phone call, email and bank statement, and found nothing suspicious. Even if he checked every contact I'd ever had, he could shrug it all off and say I had a hidden burner phone they hadn't found yet, or a stashed computer linked to the dark web.

"Don't worry," said Georgia. "The Crown Prosecution Service won't see it his way. They deal in evidence, and the police don't have it. Unless they find something substantial in the next twenty-four hours they'll have to release you without charge. I'm hoping common sense prevails and they release you today."

I couldn't see DCI Terrell granting me any favours.

"So, our strategy for now is to answer all questions with 'no comment.' I'll make it clear to DCI Terrell that there's no point detaining you, and that I'd be writing to the CPS and the PCC."

"PCC?"

"Police and Crime Commissioner. I have contacts. And they'd not be at all happy to hear that scarce police resources were being used to search for evidence against a man with a cast iron alibi."

~

It was a very different interview to the previous ones. DCI Terrell sat back in his chair, arms folded, looking more annoyed than angry. And I was relegated to a bit part player, while Sima and Georgia did the bulk of the talking.

Sima looked ready to give up after the sixth or seventh 'no comment.' She started glancing at Terrell, hoping he'd jump in, and either take over the questioning or terminate the interview.

Eventually he spoke.

"What were you doing working miles from home on some minimum wage job mowing grass verges? The petrol alone must have cost you twice what you got paid."

I so wanted to reply. I had truth on my side. I was building a business from scratch, taking any job I could find to get contacts and establish myself. I had savings to see me through a few years, but after that I'd need a decent income.

But I was under orders.

"No comment."

"This isn't over," he said, collecting his papers together and standing up. "Sima, release Mr. Sedley. Inform him we'll be keeping his car for another twenty-four hours, and he's not to leave the country."

"Can my client return to Laburnum Cottage?"

Everyone looked at Terrell. He seemed undecided. And then he actually smiled.

"Yes," he said. "He's free to go home. Just give us twenty minutes and we'll even drive him to his door."

~

It took the police sixty-five minutes to drive me from Portishead House in Bristol to my home. I timed it, willing the journey to take longer in case DCI Terrell ever questioned my alibi again. I didn't want any doubt to linger.

As we approached the bend in the road just before home, I noticed a parked car and my heart sank. There was no reason for anyone to park there. Mine was the only house within two hundred yards. This was a quiet, country road on the periphery of a quiet village.

Not any more.

As we rounded the bend, I saw two ribbons of cars and TV vans stretched out along both sides of the road. And a large group of people milling outside my home.

They had to have my name. A crowd like that wouldn't have gathered for a murder that had happened a day ago. News cycles moved on. Old stories got buried and new stories bubbled up.

It had to be Terrell. A quiet word to the press. *Guess who's going to be arriving at the murder house in an hour's time?*

And where were we going to park? My drive was blocked. The road was packed. No way was I going to walk the gauntlet past a hundred yards of feral reporters.

I looked up and down the road. No other police around that I could see – only the two in the car with me.

"Must be like old times for you," said the officer in the front passenger seat.

'Great,' I thought. A lot of help he was going to be.

We parked in the middle of the road outside my house and the two policemen got out. I followed, the three of us pushing and squeezing our way towards the gate under a barrage of inane questions. *Are you a murderer, Mr. Sedley? Who are you going to blame this time, Mathew? How many others are there?*

Microphones and cameras were thrust in my face. Lights flashed. I kept my head down, and my mouth closed.

Eventually, we made it through the gate and I was free. I thanked the policemen, and hurried to the door, not glancing back once. I just wanted to get inside and shut the world out.

~

The phone started ringing before I'd even closed the front door. I unplugged it, locked the front door, drew all the curtains, and felt sorry for myself for a good hour. Whoever had set me up had really timed it well. I was just getting back on my feet. I had a new house with no neighbours. I had a credible shot at a new career. I was beginning to look forward to getting up in the morning. I had hope.

And then – wham – back to being a pariah.

I'd never get another contract. Not for years. Even after I was exonerated – *if* I was exonerated – there'd still be people whispering behind my back – *there's no smoke without fire.*

I put the television on and surfed the news channels. It wasn't the top story, but it wasn't far off. My name scrolled intermittently along the bottom strap line of the screen. And every fifteen minutes they'd cut to excited reporters camped outside my house.

At least they didn't call me a murderer. But they did re-hash my involvement in the Sophie Gallindo case, and point out the odd coincidence of both victims drowning.

Hours passed. I must have dropped off at some point because I remember waking up with a start and finding myself sitting in the dark, the only light a flickering one coming from the TV.

That's when I heard the noise. Someone in my kitchen.

Chapter Six

I froze, listening intently. It had to be a journalist. I didn't want to think of the alternative.

But I couldn't help it. Journalists knock on doors, bang on windows. They don't break into people's homes.

I turned the television's volume down a little – not enough to warn any intruder that I'd heard them, but enough to let me hear that little bit better.

I slowly rose from the sofa, my eyes focussed on the lounge door. I could see light coming into the hall. They had a torch.

"Hello?" said a woman's voice. She sounded almost as nervous as I was. "Mathew? It's me, Lauren from the call centre. We were on the phone when you found the body."

Relief spread over me. For about two seconds. Then I remembered what the police had told me.

"Who's Olivia Gibbons?" I asked.

Lauren, or whoever she was, appeared in the doorway. She didn't appear threatening. She looked for a light switch and turned on the lounge light. My eyes were drawn to the short length of bramble in her hair.

"How do you know about Olivia Gibbons?" she asked.

"The police traced the mobile number you gave me. Who is she?"

"She's me. Olivia's my real name. Lauren Corelli's my screen name. I'm an actor."

"I thought you worked in a call centre."

"I'm between roles."

I was beginning to calm down. Perhaps she was telling the truth, perhaps she wasn't. But she didn't look dangerous. She was a blonde, short-ish thirtysomething with bramble in her hair.

She dug into her handbag and pulled out a driving license.

"See," she said, leaning forwards and handing it to me. "That's me. Olivia Gibbons. Do an internet search on me. You'll see I'm telling the truth."

"I don't have a computer. The police have got my phone and laptop."

She pulled out her phone and started tapping.

"Look, here's Lauren's website. That's me in *Midsomer Murders*. That's from *Marple*. And this one's from *Shetland*. They're not big roles. I always end up dead, but they're big productions."

It all looked legitimate, but then it wasn't that difficult to knock up a fake website.

"Ooh, and that's me as a giant blackcurrant in a breakfast cereal ad. At least I didn't die in that one. Although, come to think of it, I was probably eaten." She laughed. "Me and Sean Bean have the same problem – they always kill us off."

I handed her phone back to her. She appeared to be telling the truth, but what the hell was she doing in my house?

I asked her.

"I had no choice," she said. "You weren't picking up."

"So you broke into my house?"

"I didn't break in! The door was open."

Had I left the back door unlocked? I thought I'd locked it, but I wasn't exactly thinking straight at the time.

"Anyway," she said. "I'm here to save your life. Pack enough clothes for a couple of days and let's get the hell out of here before it's too late."

I stared at her, wondering if I'd heard correctly. "What are you talking about?"

"What am I talking about? You're on the radar of a serial killer, and instead of running for your life, you're sitting here in the dark waiting to be murdered."

"What serial killer? There's been one murder."

"So far. But there'll be others. Think about it. You found a dead doll lying in a pool of blood in an exact replica of your home. And a real body upstairs in your spare bedroom. Burglars don't do that. Drug gangs don't do that. Mafia hit men don't do that. But serial killers – the really weird ones – they love that sort of shit."

She hadn't finished.

"You do realise there are no police out there?" she said, stabbing a finger at the road. "They left an hour ago. And there's only a handful of reporters. In another hour or two you'll be alone, and you haven't even locked your doors!"

"I locked the front door."

"Did that stop him before? He's been in your house at least twice. Once to take pictures – how else could he make a replica of the inside of your house – and a second time to kill the woman. You're not just on this killer's radar, you're dead centre. He wanted *you* to find the body and *you* to take the blame. What's he going to do to you next?"

She made a frighteningly good argument. But...

"Why do you care?" I asked.

"Because I'm human? Look, *you* brought me into this. *You* dragged me into a murder mystery. I'm invested now. And the more I've heard about this case from the media and the police the more I'm convinced that they've got it all wrong. They see you as a suspect when really you're a victim. Probably *the* next victim. But nobody's looking out for you, even though you're in imminent danger. Now, pack up, and let's go."

"Where?"

"Out of here. Haven't you been listening? This killer has only just begun. He knows where you live, and he really, really hates you. So, time to go off grid. It's the first rule of staying alive – hide. If he can't find you, he can't kill you."

"The police have my car."

"Good. No one will be expecting you to do a runner then. My car's parked half a mile away. We can get there the back way. You'll need better shoes than those, though. The long grass is wet, and there's a lot of brambles."

"I'm not sure."

"Look, you can come back to Bristol with me or I'll drop you off at a B&B on the way. It's up to you. All I want is to get you somewhere safe."

I still wasn't sure. She made such a good case, but...

"Mathew, listen to me, tonight is when you're at your most vulnerable. Tomorrow or the next day the police are going to realise their mistake and provide you with proper protection. But, until then, you are on your own in the middle of nowhere. The killer will know that. He'll know that if he wants kill you or dump another dead body on you, then tonight's the best time to do it. Do you really want to bet your life on this serial killer not coming back tonight?"

I changed quickly, threw some clothes in a sports bag and followed her out into the night.

Chapter Seven

I hung back a few yards as we walked through the wood. I still didn't entirely trust Lauren. She could be leading me to my death.

Or she could be saving my life.

We emerged from the wood, a little scratched and a little wet, but well out of sight of any cars. We hurried along the road, looking back every few seconds until we found Lauren's car. No one was hiding on the back seat. I checked.

"Keep an eye out for any cars following us," said Lauren. "We've got to make sure no one knows where you are."

The first ten minutes of the journey were the worst. Every time I saw a headlight behind us, I'd panic. Luckily there weren't that many. Living in the middle of nowhere had its benefits. And Lauren soon got rid of them – either slowing down to make them overtake, or finding a useful turn off or two. No one showed any discernible interest in us.

I began to relax.

"Do you prefer Olivia or Lauren?" I asked.

"Lauren, I think. Lauren has more about her. She's a 'can-do' sort of person."

"Lauren it is then."

I glanced over at her now and then, trying not to act creepy, but intrigued nonetheless. Who drives through the night to rescue a person they'd never met? A person vilified by the press.

"Why don't you hate me?" I asked. "Everyone else seems to."

"Oh my God, who *are* you? Eeyore? Have I rescued you from your sad and gloomy place?"

"But you must have heard of the Sophie Gallindo case."

"If I believed everything I read on the internet my head

would have exploded years ago. Are you a horrible person?"

"I try not to be."

"Okay then. That works for me. Talking about hate, though, have you thought the killer might be Sophie's father? He'd have the motive, and it's obvious the killer really hates you."

"No, Luis Gallindo is the one person it can't be."

"How come?"

"Because he's the one person I could never accuse. Can you imagine the reaction if I even brought up the possibility that he's the killer? I'd be crucified. The police, the press. And I'd deserve it. That man has suffered enough at my hands."

"That doesn't make him innocent."

"To me, it does. Call me irrational, but there's a part of me that would rather go to jail than have *anything* to do with accusing Luis Gallindo of murder."

She shook her head. "You can take a guilt complex too far, you know? He wouldn't be the first good person to be turned crazy by the death of a child. And then there's all his friends and family – what about one of them?"

It was all possible, and the more I considered it, the longer the list of possible suspects grew.

"I don't think you need to be close to someone these days to be moved to avenge them," I said. "There's always been the potential for extreme anger and vengeance out there. Think of Germany in the 1930s. But the internet has made it far easier for crazies to find the like-minded and feed off each other's hatred. If they're American they take their assault weapon down the mall. If they're British–"

"What? They go full Hannibal Lecter?"

"Sort of. What I'm trying to say – in a rambling, round-about way – is that the killer could be someone who neither me nor Luis Gallindo have ever met. Someone who sees themselves as Sophie Gallindo's avenger."

It started to rain. A sudden shower, the raindrops driving noisily against the windshield.

"I don't think he's an angry killer, though," Lauren said.

"The victim wasn't stabbed dozens of times, or bludgeoned. And angry killers don't build meticulously crafted dollhouses filled with lifelike miniature figures. This is a calculating killer."

She was probably right. The killer could still be angry, but he could control that anger.

"Are you sure you don't know the dead woman?" Lauren asked.

"Positive."

"Only ... they say that if you really want to destroy someone – and this killer gives off that vibe – you don't kill *them*, you kill the ones they love. Which would point to the woman being known to you."

"That only works if you have friends and family. I don't any more, so the killer would have to find someone else."

"Not even a cousin?"

"I might have a second cousin somewhere, but if I don't recognise her, what's the point?"

The rain began to ease off. A line of red tail lights snaked over a bridge in the distance.

"It's just that the killer has gone to great lengths to hide the woman's identity." said Lauren. "Why? Why take all her ID, but make sure she's found? If he wanted to make it harder for the police to identify her, he'd have hidden the body too. But he didn't. Why?"

"You're assuming he has to have a reason. Who knows how his brain's wired."

"But we do know, from the crime scene, that he's calculating. The attention to detail. It wasn't any old dollhouse or any old miniature figure. It was important to him to make exact replicas. After all that, can you *really* see him choosing a random victim?"

~

Lauren lived on the outskirts of Bristol. An upstairs flat in a converted three-storey house.

"It's quite small," said Lauren. "Only one bedroom. But

don't get any ideas. You're either sleeping on the sofa, or the pavement outside."

"I think I'll take the sofa."

"Good choice."

The front door of the flat opened into a combined lounge and kitchen. The walls were covered in old movie posters with the occasional photograph of Lauren posing with famous actors.

"That's from *Doc Martin*," said Lauren, noticing my interest. "I got sepsis in that."

Lauren made coffee while I switched on the TV and surfed the news channels. There was nothing new. Nothing of substance. A couple of former police detectives theorised about the case. A psychologist pontificated about the possible symbolism of the dollhouse. No one had identified the dead woman.

My mind started to wander, thinking about the case, tomorrow, whether I'd ever be able to plan for the future. Then I had an idea.

"Have you still got the picture of the dollhouse I sent you?" I asked Lauren.

"You think I'm the kinda person who deletes clues in a murder mystery?"

I didn't. "Can I see it?" I asked. "I need to take a closer look at the dollhouse?"

Lauren found the dollhouse picture on her laptop and turned the screen towards me.

"What are you looking for?" she asked.

"I want to see if I can date it. The estate agent posted a video of the cottage interior when it was on the market two months go. I haven't made any major changes since then, but I have made some."

I scrutinised the photograph.

"It's not from the video of the house sale. I didn't change the carpets or wallpaper, but those are my beds. And the duvets."

I looked closer. The duvet cover on my bed was the brown

one. I changed them every week, alternating between the blue and the brown. They must have broken in last week, or the fortnight before.

Or one of several fortnights before that. Was there anything else that could narrow it down to a specific date?

I scanned the picture several times, zooming in as far as I could. If only I could examine the real thing.

Then I saw it. There was something propped up against the cooker. It was partially obscured, and difficult to make out. Something rectangular and brown.

"What's that?" I said, pointing at the object. "A parcel?"

"Or a briefcase," said Lauren.

It could have been a briefcase. It could have been a box. Whatever it was it didn't ring any bells. Could it be the killer's? Or a clue, something deliberately inserted into the dollhouse for some sick, serial killer reason.

I'd have to tell the police, not that they'd pay much attention. In their eyes, anything originating from me was tainted evidence.

But I had to tell someone. It could be crucial evidence.

I used Lauren's phone to call Georgia. It was late, but I could always leave a message. The phone rang, and rang. Eventually the answerphone kicked in and I left a message.

I handed the phone back to Lauren, who was still staring at the photograph of the dollhouse.

"This is *really* well made," she said. "It must have taken days to make - weeks, if he has a day job. Look at the detail on that mirror, and that washbasin - look at the tiny taps. Or can you buy this stuff online?"

I hadn't thought of that. If he bought things online, there'd be a paper trail - credit card details, delivery address. But would he be that sloppy? Why not, he was human - at least part of him was - and humans made mistakes. Especially the vain ones. I could see him weighing up the options - do I perfect the dollhouse and take a slight risk, or do I play it safe and make every piece myself?

He'd choose the riskier option. Style over substantive risk.

He'd assume the police were too stupid to follow up.

It didn't take long for Lauren to find furniture for dollhouses on sale online. There were pages and pages of them. Every piece of furniture you could imagine in 1:12 or 1:24 scale. There were cookers, mirrors, staircases, rugs, beds and more – in all manner of styles, even antique.

We spent half an hour matching the killer's dollhouse contents to products on line. Only a few couldn't be found.

"What about the miniature figure?" asked Lauren. "That's got to be the most difficult one to make. It looks plastic."

It didn't take long to find several pages of miniature figures for sale. Lauren scrolled though them all until...

"That's her!" said Lauren.

It was definitely her. She was unpainted, but the pose, the clothes, the hair – everything else was identical.

"Oh, God," said Lauren.

"What?"

"Her hair. You said the dead woman's hair was the same as the miniature figure."

"Yes, the same style, the same colour."

"You're sure about that? The same haircut?"

"Yes. What do you see?"

"That's not a common cut. The odds of both cuts being identical through random chance are huge. I thought he'd made the figurine to look like the victim, but he didn't. He cut the victim's hair to look like the figurine."

~

The clothes looked like a match too. I couldn't swear they were the same. I hadn't examined the body that closely, but I hadn't had to. An image like that burns its way into your brain.

She'd been wearing leggings, like the figurine. And a hip length coat with long lapels, also like the figurine. He'd dressed the woman to look like the model.

We had to tell the police. It could be vital in building a profile.

If they bothered to listen. *It's you again, trying to insert yourself into the investigation, sending us on wild goose chases.*

So Lauren took a picture of the laptop screen instead and sent it to Georgia. I'd explain everything when she returned my earlier call.

I yawned, and looked at my watch. It was past one o'clock.

"I'll find you some blankets," said Lauren.

I slept all the way through to seven thirty. I couldn't even remember having dreamed. Even my subconscious must have been exhausted.

I switched on the TV, picked out some clothes and wandered into the bathroom. When I eventually returned, Lauren was sat in front of the TV. She beckoned me over.

"The police are doing a big press conference at eight," she said. "It's all over the news. They're trailing it as a major development and broadcasting it live."

Chapter Eight

The press conference began five minutes late. DCI Terrell was there. Sima too. The other one I didn't recognise, but judging from the fancy uniform, he had to be the chief constable or his deputy.

They were sitting at a long table on a raised platform. A large screen hung above them on the wall behind.

The room was full.

The Chief Constable introduced himself and got straight down to it.

"We need your help identifying the victim," he said. "This is a police reconstruction of the dead woman's face."

A picture flashed up on the screen behind him. It was incredibly realistic. It looked like she was posing for a passport photograph. Her eyes were open, her hair brushed and free of blood.

"The woman is five foot six, of medium build, and between the ages of eighteen and twenty-five. Anyone who recognises her, or thinks they recognise her, please call this number."

A telephone number appeared at the foot of the screen.

"We believe these were the clothes she was wearing on the day of her murder."

A reconstruction of the woman wearing a white T-shirt under a blue jacket with black leggings flashed onto the screen. The figure began to slowly rotate, showing what she would have looked like from every angle.

"We'd also like to hear from anyone who was in the vicinity of Garstock on Monday, the eighteenth of September. We are particularly interested in the area around Laburnum Cottage between the hours of two and four, but we ask *anyone* – anyone at all – who was driving, walking, or cycling through Garstock that day to come forward. This woman is someone's daughter, someone's sister, someone's partner or friend. We implore you. Look at this picture. Ask your friends and neighbours to look at this picture. Someone knows her."

The Chief Constable invited the press to ask questions.

"Is Mathew Sedley a suspect?"

Shit. I sank down into the sofa. It had to be the first question. And the Chief Constable was looking at DCI Terrell, inviting him to answer it.

"Mr. Sedley has been helping us with our enquiries," said the DCI.

And that was it. No 'Mr. Sedley is no longer a suspect because he has a cast-iron alibi.'

At least the next question wasn't about me.

"Why do you think no one has reported her missing?"

"We don't know," said Sima. "It may be that she lives alone, or told her friends that she was going away for a few days."

"Do you have any suspects?"

"The investigation is at a very early stage," said the DCI. "Identification of the victim is crucial to its progress."

"Is there a serial killer in Somerset?"

The Chief Constable took the question. He looked annoyed. "There is no serial killer in Somerset." He shuffled his papers and stood up. "Thank you, everybody. That will be all."

All three police officers left the stage.

"Why are they always so terrified of admitting there's a serial killer on the loose?" said Lauren.

"They don't want to cause panic."

"But pretending there isn't a serial killer when everyone knows there is a serial killer, just makes people panic more."

She was undoubtedly right. People love mysteries. And if the police fail to feed that need to know, then they look elsewhere. And that's when rumours take off.

"And what was the major development?" said Lauren. "I thought they were going to name the victim."

"That could be the TV stations putting a spin on the event

to get more people to watch."

And the police asking the public for help could be viewed as a major development. At least it showed they knew they needed help. And the sooner they had a name for the victim, the sooner the investigation could move away from me and my home.

Lauren's phone rang. It was Georgia returning last night's call. I told her about the figurine and the mystery object in the dollhouse kitchen.

"I'll pass the information along," she said. "Did you see the press conference?"

"I did."

"They're expecting a large response. I thought the Chief Constable did tremendously well. Very impassioned."

"That reminds me," said Lauren after Georgia had hung up. "I think I should take a sick day. Will you call work for me? It always sounds better if someone else makes the call. I'll cough in the background. I'm good at coughs. I played Beth in *Little Women*. You know, the tragic sister who dies. You're not supposed to cough with scarlet fever, but the director was so taken with my coughing that he insisted we kept it in."

I phoned the call centre while Lauren coughed, poignantly, in the background.

~

At ten fifteen Lauren's phone rang. It was Georgia again.

"We have a problem," she said. "The diatom test on the water found inside the victim has just come back. She wasn't drowned in your bathroom. She was drowned in salt water, and you were working fifteen minutes from the sea."

Chapter Nine

I just could not believe it. We were back at square one. No alibi and a police force convinced I was the murderer. In fact, this was worse – the CCTV evidence now placed me within fifteen minutes of the murder scene.

Had I been fifteen minutes from the sea? I'd been driving a tractor. Had they taken that into account?

Georgia said she had to go, but would ring back as soon as she could. In the meantime I was to refer all requests from the police to her.

"Don't volunteer anything," she said.

Lauren pulled up a map of the Bristol area, and I traced the route I'd taken down the B31827. I was never fifteen minutes from the sea. It was more like forty.

"They'll say you had a car parked nearby," said Lauren. "It's a fifteen minute journey by car."

"Only if the woman was murdered near Portishead. Look at the map. There must be sixty miles of coastline around Bristol, and the Avon is tidal all the way into the city. The police have no idea where the woman was murdered."

And how long would it take them to find the crime scene? Weeks? Months? I'd never be cleared. I'd be the perpetual suspect while months of driving rain and rising tides washed away anything and everything that could have cleared me.

"I thought this was over," I said. "The police bit. I thought I just had a serial killer to worry about, but no."

I threw up my hands.

"He knew where I was working that day, didn't he? The killer. He had to know in advance. No one could have planned a murder like this off the cuff. Too many things could have gone wrong. He'd have had a quiet place marked out for the kill. And he'd have the victim tied up and gagged in the boot of his car. He probably drove along the B31827 to make sure I was there. Then he'd kill her, and drive her back to my house."

I'd been done up like a kipper.

~

Georgia rang back an hour later.

"DCI Terrell wants to interview you. We can fight this. You don't have to come in, but I suspect the detective chief inspector will bypass our objections by arresting you."

What a surprise.

"I think I can negotiate a compromise," said Georgia. "A short voluntary interview for no custody. Come in, talk to the police with me present. Then pick up your phone and car, and leave."

"What can I tell them in an interview that I can't tell them over the phone?"

"I suspect he wants to trap you in a lie – get you to say something on camera that he can later prove to be false. That and hope you spontaneously confess."

We arranged to meet in the Serious Crime Unit offices in Bristol at noon. Lauren said she'd drive – and keep the engine running just in case.

~

Georgia was waiting for me in reception.

"Let's talk over there," she said, pointing to a quiet place over by a window. "It's going to be somewhat of a fishing expedition, I'm afraid. Don't react. Be polite, and give proper answers. No 'no comments' this time – pardon the double negative – and if you're the slightest bit unsure about the question or how to answer it, ask me."

"What kind of mood is he in?"

"About seven on the Richter scale. He is, actually, a very good detective. One of the best. It's unfortunate that he's taken such a dislike to you."

Welcome to my world.

"Have they brought in a profiler to help them get a handle

on the killer?" I asked.

"Not that I've heard. I passed on the information you gave me about the dollhouse to detective sergeant Bhagat. She's very thorough."

Georgia checked her watch. "Time to go. I'm not sure they'll release your car today, but they've downloaded everything they need from your laptop and phone."

I wondered what they were doing to my car. Ripping it to pieces looking for hidden compartments?

I asked Georgia.

"They're taking samples from the tyre treads."

"To see if I've driven to the coast?"

"That's right. I take it you haven't driven it to the coast recently?" There was the merest hint of panic in her voice.

"No. I haven't been to the seaside for years."

I'd barely finished the sentence before a worrying thought occurred. Would the killer have pressed sand into the treads of my tyres? He'd done everything else to set me up.

Other thoughts followed, tumbling over each other. Why stop at the tyres? My car had been parked in an empty yard just outside Bristol for seven hours on the day of the murder. The killer had no problem breaking into my home. What was he like with cars?

He could have swapped vehicles at Jessups. Used mine to transport the victim to the murder scene. Then driven back to Jessups and swapped cars again. If he'd driven behind the big barn he wouldn't have been visible from the road. I'd have incriminating soil on the car tyres, and DNA in the boot. Even Lauren would have a hard time believing in my innocence.

"What's the matter?" asked Georgia.

"Nothing," I said. "Just nerves."

~

DCI Terrell and Sima were waiting for us in the usual interview room. The camera was switched on, and everyone introduced themselves for the tape.

Hi, my name's Matt. I like long walks in the rain and

finding dead bodies in my spare bedroom.

Well, I didn't say that, but I might as well have for all the good this interview was going to do.

"In the light of recent evidence," began DCI Terrell. "Do you wish to alter your previous statements?"

"No," I said.

"Have you ever bought or used GHB?"

"What's GHB?" I asked, wondering where this line of questioning had sprung from.

"Gamma hydroxybutyrate. It's a party drug. Also known as a date rape drug."

"I've never taken drugs."

"Have you ever given drugs to other people?"

"No."

"GHB can be detected in people's hair months after they've taken it."

"Good to know."

"Do you wish to change your answer to any of the previous questions?"

"Not at all."

"Would you consent to giving us a hair sample?"

"I'd be delighted. Do you want to take one now?"

I considered, for a very short second, bowing my head and leaning across the table, but I decided the provocation might be too much. Even having Georgia present might not stop my head being banged down hard on the table, and I didn't want my nose broken. Police interview rooms were notorious for freak accidents.

But I had learned something. The killer must have given the woman a date rape drug, which would have made her easier to subdue.

DCI Terrell began a new line of questioning.

"Have you been to the coast in the last week?"

"No."

"Have you been anywhere near the banks of the Avon."

"No, again. I'm a regular landlubber."

"You think this is funny?"

"Believe me, this is the opposite of funny."

Georgia leaned forward and whispered in my ear. "Dial it back."

"No, this can't be fun for you," said Terrell. "The noose slowly tightening. The drip, drip, drip of new evidence. All of it more incriminating than the last. Much better to get it all off your chest now. You'll feel better, and save days – weeks – of anguish, because you know we're going to catch you. It's just a matter of time."

"Have you identified the object leaning up against the cooker?" I asked.

"What object?"

Sima answered. "It was a miniature briefcase leaning up against the cooker."

"What's that got to do with anything?" asked Terrell.

"It's not mine," I said. "It's an anomaly. It either belongs to the killer or it's some twisted clue he put in the dollhouse."

Terrell smiled. "A clue, is it? You really can't stop, can you? Trying to feed us clues so we run off down blind alley after blind alley."

"What about the figurine?" I said. "You know you can buy her online. And the killer dressed the victim to match the figurine. He even cut her hair. How weird is that?"

"You tell me."

"No, you tell me. Tell me you've at least got a profiler working the case."

The interview dragged on for another ten minutes. Pointless question after pointless question. No, I'd never been to Portishead or Avonmouth, or any of the other places he reeled off. I didn't know any quiet spots along the coast, and I hadn't had the car cleaned recently. As for *my* questions – he was deaf to them. Not interested in the slightest.

"Look," I said. "I've only just moved into the area. I know far more about the south coast than I do about the west."

The DCI didn't respond immediately. He was probably working out how long it would take me to fly to the south coast and back by helicopter.

"Interview terminated," he said, rising to his feet.

~

Georgia and I followed the DCI and Sima along the corridor outside the interview rooms.

"They'll hand over your laptop and phone now," said Georgia. "Then you can leave."

"But don't leave the country," said the DCI over his shoulder.

There was a commotion up ahead – a door slamming followed by running feet. Then an excited DC Collins, the one who'd arrested me on Monday evening, appeared from around the corner.

"Sir," he said, trying to gather his breath. "We've got a witness."

"What?" said Terrell.

"A taxi driver, sir. He drove the victim to Laburnum Cottage at one p.m. on the afternoon of her murder."

Chapter Ten

"One o'clock?" asked Terrell, sounding as confused as I felt.

"Yes, sir. He's a very credible witness. His boss confirms everything. The driver phoned the booking through to him on Monday. It's in their system. Westbury Station to Laburnum Cottage, Garstock. Journey started at twelve thirty-five, ended at one."

"Did he get her name?" asked Terrell.

"No, she didn't give one – just walked up to him at the taxi rank outside the train station."

It was then that Terrell remembered he wasn't alone. "You can go," he said, pointedly, to Georgia and me.

We left in silence. The three police officers waited for us to leave and, I don't know about Georgia, but I was straining to overhear the rest of their conversation.

When we came to the corner, I glanced back. DCI Terrell was leading his team away in the other direction. I'd have to wait to find out what else the taxi driver had said.

"Do I have my alibi back?" I asked Georgia.

"I've been trying to work that out. Certainly it makes it harder to make a credible case against you, but Detective Chief Inspector Terrell could argue – and I'm sure he'll try – that the victim, upon finding you not at home, hired another taxi to take her to where you were working-"

"How would she know where I was working?" I interrupted.

"You might have left her a note on the kitchen table. 'Sorry, babe, had to work, meet me in Portishead by the beach.'"

I would never have said 'babe,' but, apart from that, there was an annoying kernel of credibility about Georgia's theory.

I collected my phone and laptop, and left.

~

I told Lauren everything that had happened, starting with the taxi driver.

"Why would anyone take a taxi to a stranger's house in the middle of nowhere?" I said. "I've never seen her before. Why come to my house?"

"Could she be an old friend of the previous owner?"

"She can't be that old a friend. She's barely out of her teens."

"Kids do have friends, you know? She might be an old school friend who'd moved away."

"She'd have rung first, wouldn't she? Or texted."

"Some people are more spontaneous."

"The killer isn't. He's a meticulous planner. He had a dollhouse ready built and a figurine painted. He had to know that woman would be coming to the house. He must have invited her."

"An escort?" said Lauren.

It was possible – likely even – but...

"Wouldn't she have a car? Or a pimp to drive her?"

"She might work in a city where you can rely on public transport. If the taxi driver picked her up outside a train station, then she could have come from Bristol or Reading. If the killer offered her enough money, she'd probably jump at the chance."

"Wouldn't he have to pay up front?"

"Definitely. He'd have to pay her enough to convince her to make the journey."

Which would create a paper trail. There'd be credit card payments, bank withdrawals, records that could be checked. Would a meticulous planner take that risk?

"Do escorts take bitcoin?" I asked.

"How would I know? I may be between roles, but I haven't had to walk the streets yet."

The conversation continued all the way to Lauren's flat. The pros and cons of using an escort were weighed and dissected. I couldn't see the killer taking the risk. She could turn up at the door with a couple of large men looking to shake him down. *Rich john paying over the odds to invite a prostitute to his leafy home in the country – bound to be an easy mark.*

Lauren disagreed. There was a good reason serial killers chose prostitutes. They were used to knocking on strange doors and climbing into strange cars. They'd be more likely to accept an invitation to visit someone they'd never met.

"But why the taxi?" I said. "That had to be a mistake, surely? It creates an unnecessary witness. She was in his cab for twenty-five minutes. They're bound to have talked – cabbies are famous for it. She might have told him the killer's name – or, at least, the name he gave her."

"What's the betting he gave his name as Mathew Sedley?"

Shit. He probably would have.

"It's still a mistake," I said. "He should have picked her up in his car. Or made sure she had her own car, and was going to drive down herself."

Lauren shook her head.

"If she drove down, he'd then have to get rid of her car."

I hadn't thought of that. If the killer was working alone, which he probably was, then he'd have a hell of a problem disposing of a car. Garstock was in the middle of nowhere. There was no public transport – not even a daily bus into Frome. If he wanted to abandon a car, he'd have to walk back – or call a taxi.

And he was already on a tight schedule. If the victim arrived at one, he had to subdue her – probably with the help of a GHB spiked drink – then drive seventy, eighty minutes to the coast. He'd then have to find somewhere secluded – which wasn't going to be easy at three o'clock on a summer's day in a tourist area – and drown her.

Then he'd have to drive seventy, eighty minutes back to Laburnum Cottage and prepare the crime scene. Which, again, wasn't going to be quick. I arrived home at five. He only had forty-five minutes. First, he'd have to clean her up.

Her hair and clothes had been dry when I found her. He'd have to cut her hair, dry her, wipe away the foam around her nose and mouth, dress her, and arrange the body.

Then he'd have to add the fake blood, place the dollhouse in the hall, bag up everything the two of them had brought into the cottage, leave the door ajar and go.

If he'd had to dispose of her car as well, he'd barely have had time to drive it outside the village.

The more I thought about it, the more the tight schedule bugged me. There was hardly any contingency for things going wrong. I could have come home earlier. He could have been delayed by road works, or a traffic accident. He might have found his quiet, secluded spot by the sea awash with tourists.

And why drown her at sea? The drowning part, I got. The link to Sophie. The link to me. But Sophie had been drowned in a freshwater river. Her death had no links to the sea at all. It was a totally unnecessary complication that added a two-and-a-half-hour drive to an already full schedule. Not to mention the risk of being seen dragging a body into and out of a car.

It did rip up my alibi. There was that, but why not just arrange to meet the victim in a seaside hotel room? That would have removed all the time pressure.

"I can't see it," I said. "The killer had the woman in the cottage – alone, no witnesses – and then he decides to take her on a drive to the coast. It's a totally unnecessary complication that could have got him caught."

"He's a serial killer. What you see as a complication, he sees as an embellishment – something to heighten the thrill."

~

Back at the flat, we surfed the news channels. No one had the taxi driver story, but I couldn't see that situation lasting long. It was the best lead the police had. Even if the victim hadn't given any names to the taxi driver, there was still the Westbury train station angle. There would be CCTV cameras inside the station. The police would be able to work out which train she came in on and, from there, follow her route all the way back to the beginning of her journey. They'd know where she came from, and how she paid for her ticket.

Time ticked on. I debated phoning Georgia. She'd said she'd ring me if she heard anything, but she might have forgot. Or she might be busy with other clients.

When the story broke, it broke fast, interrupting a news story about the NHS.

"We're going live to Kirsty McLean outside the Avon and Somerset Police Station in Bristol," said an excited news anchor.

Kirsty was one of a throng of several dozen reporters and cameramen, all jostling for the best shot.

"Thank you, Tasha," said Kirsty. "I'm talking to Anton Williams, a thirty-eight-year-old taxi driver who has just come forward as a witness in the dollhouse murder."

Anton had the look of a person who'd jumped at the chance of being on TV, but was beginning to have second thoughts. Cameras and microphones were shoved in his face. Reporters jostled for a better position.

"Anton, you say you drove the victim to Laburnum Cottage on the afternoon of her murder?"

"Yes, that right."

"Are you sure it was her?"

"Positive. She was in back of my cab for twenty-five minutes. I saw her face very well."

"Did she give a name?"

"No, she barely speak. She give me address. She pay in cash. She say 'goodbye.'"

"Did she have anything with her? Luggage?"

"She had small suitcase – like for hand luggage on plane."

"What about a handbag?"

"Yes, she have that too."

"Where did you pick her up from?"

"The train station at Westbury."

"And what time did you arrive at Laburnum Cottage?"

"One o'clock exactly."

Kirsty was running out of questions. Another reporter took advantage of the slight pause. "Did you see anything unusual at Laburnum Cottage?" she said, squeezing into a non-existent gap.

"No. Nothing. I saw her walk to front door, ring bell. That all. I had another fare in Westbury so I no hang around."

"Did you see any other cars parked nearby?"

"No. There was one strange thing though."

"What's that?"

"The girl in the police picture, she was brunette. This girl blonde."

"But you're sure it was her?"

"Positive. She wearing same clothes police show at press conference."

Chapter Eleven

It took a while for his words to sink in. *She wearing same clothes police show at press conference.* The clothes her body had been dressed in. The clothes that matched the figurine found in the dollhouse.

We'd assumed the killer had bought the clothes to match the figurine and dressed her post mortem. But she'd brought the clothes with her.

"He told her what to wear," said Lauren.

She had to be an escort. Who else would dress up to order?

"And why the blonde hair?" I said.

"Someone should have asked the taxi driver about her hairstyle. Did the killer have time to cut and dye her hair? Was she wearing a wig? And if so, why?"

None of this made sense. The killer painted the figurine's hair. It wouldn't matter to him whether her hair was brown or blonde. Unless he ran out of paint. Which was ridiculous. The man had gone to so much trouble to match the clothes and colours he wouldn't forget to buy enough paint.

I phoned Georgia. She might know if the victim's hair had been dyed. It was the sort of thing you'd expect to be noted in a post mortem report.

"It's all rather hectic here at the moment," said Georgia. "I haven't heard any mention of her hair being dyed. But what I do know is that the pathologist has ordered more tests, and she spent a good ten minutes this afternoon re-examining the body."

"Any idea why?"

"My source couldn't tell me, but he says it was after the results of this morning's tests came back."

"Do you know what those tests were for?"

"If I remember correctly, there were blood tests, fibre tests and tests on the drains."

"And the new tests she's ordered?"

"Sorry, my source is wonderful, but not omniscient."

"Have any other witnesses come forward," I asked.

"Lots. A few mention the same name, but the detective chief inspector isn't getting excited. He's more interested in tracing the victim's train journey. I think he loves having all the CCTV recordings to look through – much more reliable than witnesses."

"Have they found out where she started her journey?"

"Not yet. They've got back as far as Bristol, but it looks like the trail goes further. She might even have come from Birmingham."

"Birmingham?"

"Yes. Initially they were looking in the other direction, as she came in on the Portsmouth to Bristol train. But then they found that she'd got on that train at Warminster, which is the next stop down the line from Westbury. And before that she'd been on the Bristol to Portsmouth train, getting off at Warminster. So it looks like she missed the Westbury stop the first time and had to get off at Warminster and catch the next train back to Westbury."

"You are remarkably well-informed."

"I have a lot of friends and very good hearing. Having a desk in the same building helps a lot too. I'm around so much people stop noticing me. Also this is *such* an interesting case. I usually get drugs and petty theft. Duty solicitors rarely catch the big cases."

~

I was reminded of the Chinese curse – may you live in interesting times. The same applied to being the chief suspect in an interesting case. There was no end. The more you learned, the more questions you had. What had made the pathologist re-examine the body? What was the significance of the victim's hair colour? Did I have an alibi any more?

The latter was really beginning to worry me. I'm sure I'd read that time of death was calculated in relation to ambient temperature, and that murderers could use that to fool the pathologist by heating up or cooling down the body.

Had the pathologist discovered that that had happened here? The killer could have kept the body in a hot bath or an ice bath for an hour or two. Maybe one of the blood tests showed evidence of freezing which made her re-examine the body.

Or maybe I was overthinking everything. My brain was so fried I couldn't work out if pushing the time of death back or forward was good or bad for me.

"You've got to be more positive," said Lauren. "Remember, you're innocent. However clever the killer is, however much he manipulates and fabricates evidence, you have truth on your side. And the killer's not immune to things going wrong. Look at what happened with the victim missing her station. That must have put his plans back an hour or so."

That was true. And he wouldn't have liked it one bit. A meticulous planner like him. I could see him pacing up and down inside my house, wondering where she was, wondering if she'd decided not to come, running to the window every time he heard a car. He'd be beside himself.

And if she'd phoned to warn him, there'd be a record. A nearby cell tower would have picked up her call and logged their numbers.

But had the missed station really set him back an hour? What if it'd only been twenty minutes?

We searched online train timetables. It looked like she would have arrived at Westbury around 12:22 on a train that left Warminster at 12:13. We switched destinations to pull up the Bristol to Portsmouth trains. The best fit for her earlier train was the one arriving at Warminster at 11:21. Which meant that train would have stopped at Westbury at 11:11.

Missing her stop had cost her an hour and eleven minutes.

Perhaps the killer's original schedule hadn't been as tight as I'd previously thought. He'd given himself a contingency, and kept to his plan, even when his victim had arrived over an hour late.

He was meticulous, but he wasn't averse to taking a risk.

~

I needed a drink. Something to help me relax. Something to turn the dial on my brain down. I was just sitting there – on the sofa – unable to do anything except wait and think.

I should be *doing* something. I had skills. I had time. I could scroll through endless CCTV files for the police. I could collate long lists of telephone numbers from cell towers. I can be conscientious. I didn't mind doing boring, repetitive tasks. It wouldn't be boring to me. It would be therapeutic. And it would speed up getting an answer.

Just put me to work!

"Are you all right?" asked Lauren.

I looked down at my bouncing leg. It wouldn't stop. It was like a nervous tic, my heel tapping continuously on the floor.

"Do you have any alcohol?" I asked.

"I have wine and an extensive collection of cocktails – I'm playing the part of a cocktail mixologist next month for Channel Four."

"Does she get killed?"

"No, I'm the murderer in this one. That's why I went for it. That and the complimentary mixers."

"Cocktails it is then," I said, massaging my right thigh, and attempting to slow my leg down.

"Which one do you want? I've been practising. I can mix dozens."

"Surprise me."

"Ok, this one's my favourite. My character calls it the 'slow, uncomfortable death against a brick wall.'"

It might have been named for me.

I was on my third slow, uncomfortable death when the news was suddenly interrupted. Avon and Somerset Police had called a press conference for three o'clock.

~

This time they were ten minutes late, the Chief Constable hurrying to take his place next to stone-faced DCI Terrell and his sergeant.

A picture flashed up on the screen. It was victim's face. This time she had blonde, curly, shoulder-length hair.

"It's got to be a wig," said Lauren. "He'd never have had time to cut, dye and straighten that hair."

"Do you recognise this woman?" said the Chief Constable. "Note that she has blonde hair in this picture. It may be a wig. This is what she looked like on Monday."

The picture changed to show her full length. It was the same picture they'd showed earlier in the day except that this time they'd given her the blonde and curly hair.

"We'd like to hear from anyone who saw this woman on Monday. You may have seen her at Westbury train station between 12:25 and 12:35, or at Warminster train station between 11:15 and 12:15, or at Bristol Temple Meads station between 9:35 and 10:21."

He held up a sheet of paper. "All the times and places mentioned in this press conference are here in this hand out, which is available from the press officer by the door."

He paused while the press officer identified himself then continued.

"We'd also like to hear from passengers on the 10:21 Bristol to Portsmouth Harbour train, the 10:23 Portsmouth Harbour to Bristol Train, and the 6:03 Manchester to Bristol train. Did you see this woman? Did you talk to this woman? Did you see someone talking to her?"

Manchester? Had they tracked the woman all the way back to there? That had to be two hundred miles away from Garstock.

"We also believe," said the Chief Constable, "that this woman may have been in the vicinity of the Bristol Channel coast, somewhere between Weston and Severn Beach, possibly on the River Avon downstream from Bristol. She may have been on a boat, or by a mooring. This would be between the hours of two and four in the afternoon."

That was new. A boat or a mooring, not a beach or tidal pool.

"Did you see or hear anything unusual? A woman screaming, a tussle in the distance, a woman looking unstable on her feet, being helped by a man. Something that, at the time, you might have thought innocent, or maybe you didn't want to get involved. If you think you may have seen her, please contact the police on this number."

He pointed to the number on the screen above him.

And then, abruptly, it ended.

"We will not be taking questions," said the Chief Constable. "As I'm sure you appreciate, we have a lot of work to do. Things are moving very quickly. Thank you."

I watched DCI Terrell leave the stage. He couldn't get away quick enough. I bet he loved being pulled off the investigation to be paraded in front of the media. A silent prop to provide a bit of background for the Chief Constable.

"Someone's got to recognise her soon," said Lauren. "Her face is going to be everywhere."

I couldn't get over the fact that the investigation had reached Manchester. Was it going to end there, or had she come from even farther afield?

"There's an airport at Manchester," I said. "You can fly in from all over the world. Do you think that might explain why no one has reported her missing? She could have come from thousands of miles away."

And in this modern online world a murderer and his victim didn't have to be in the same country for their paths to cross. It can all happen online.

My train of thought was interrupted by my phone ringing.

It was Georgia.

"There's been a development," she said.

Chapter Twelve

"What's happened?" I asked.

"I don't know. Everyone's become very secretive – lots of small groups huddling in corners and meetings behind closed doors. It's something to do with the post mortem, but no one's saying what. Anyway, it affects you. They want to know if you have a boat."

"A boat?"

"Yes, those wooden floaty things."

Luckily I'd had three slow, uncomfortable deaths to restore my sense of humour.

"I don't think many are made out of wood these days."

"Oh God, don't tell me you *do* own a boat."

"No, I've never had a boat."

"Thank God for that. This is important. They're going to check this extremely thoroughly. Do you know anyone with a boat, or anyone who has access to a boat? Is there any way at all that you could borrow a boat?"

"No."

I was totally baffled. How could a post mortem suddenly point to a boat owner. Engine oil? Did boats use special oil?

"There's more," said Georgia.

I braced myself.

"Do you have, or do you have access to, a trailer?"

"No."

"What about a lock-up? Do you have access to any property or yard? That's not including Jessups – the police have already applied for a search warrant for that one."

That was going to go down well with Martin Jessup. I could say goodbye to hiring any more equipment from him.

"No," I said. "I don't have any lock-ups or access to any yards or buildings."

"Okay, and finally, the police want to search your property again."

"Why?"

"It seems to be the outbuildings, the garden and the roof space that they're interested in this time. They can get a warrant, but they'd prefer to save time and ask nicely first. What I need to know from you is – do you want me to fight this request?"

"No. They can dig up the garden if they want – especially the bit with all the brambles."

~

I swiftly moved on to my fourth slow, uncomfortable death, wondering if Lauren had a suitable cocktail for a washed up, unemployable pariah.

"Why all this sudden interest in boats and trailers?" asked Lauren.

I could see a potential reason for an interest in boats, but trailers – that was beyond me.

"Do an internet search on engine oil for boats," I said. "See if it's different to other oils."

It didn't take long to find out that marine engine oil was a different beast to automotive engine oil. And marine diesel was different to the diesel used in cars. The post mortem could have found trace deposits in the water inside her lungs and stomach. Or on her clothes.

That would explain everything.

Except the interest in trailers.

We searched the internet, trying various keywords and angles, but found nothing. The one piece of good news was that my car didn't have a towbar.

"It's got to be easier to kill someone on a boat than on a beach," said Lauren. "You could take a boat a mile out to sea where no one could see or hear you. You couldn't do that on a beach."

That had been bugging me from the moment I'd heard she'd been drowned in salt water. How do you drag a nearly unconscious woman from a car, across a car park, across a beach and then drown her at three o'clock on a summer's day in a tourist area, without being seen?

I'd never been to the Bristol Channel coast. I had no idea what the coastline was like, but I couldn't imagine there being a secluded spot where you could drown someone unnoticed.

And even if there *was* such a perfect spot it would have to be miles from where you could park a car. Anything less and tourists would have found it, making it no longer private. I just couldn't see the killer dragging or carrying a dead weight over miles of rough ground, and then having the strength to drown her and carry her back.

But was it any easier to carry her on and off a boat unseen?

A marina was out of the question. There'd be scores of boats, boat owners, and boat owners' friends milling around. Probably CCTV as well. Theft would be an ever-present danger with all those expensive boats on show. And carrying a dead woman along a gangway past a line of boats back to a car park would attract serious attention.

A private mooring might work. A quiet concealed spot – lots of shrubs and trees – the only access a single track. Somewhere you could drive right up to the boat. But even that was a risk. People would be more likely to know each other at a private mooring. More likely to ask questions. *Who are you? Is your daughter all right?*

And people would see his face, hear his accent. With the dead woman's face and clothes about to go viral, people would remember and come forward.

Whichever way I looked at it, it was all so unnecessary. Yes, he'd destroy my alibi by moving the murder scene from Garstock to the coast close to where I was working. But he'd risk being seen – being challenged, being caught – having his murder spree ended before he'd even begun.

I just couldn't see how someone could plan something so meticulously, and then suddenly 'go rogue.' But then, I wasn't a serial killer.

Hours dragged by. I think I dropped off at some point, those slow and uncomfortables having taken their toll. Lauren searched and surfed, and, together, we waited.

The breakthrough came just after six.

Chapter Thirteen

"They've identified the victim," said Georgia. "Not officially, the parents have yet to view the body, but everyone's acting as though it's a done deal. Does the name Susan Phillips mean anything to you?"

"No, never heard of her," I said.

"She's nineteen years old and was a second year history student at Manchester University. Do you have any links with Manchester or the Uni.?"

"Not at all."

"What about Lincoln? That's where she was brought up and where her family still live."

"No. Never been there. Never met anyone from there. At least I don't think so."

"Does the name Phillips ring any bells?"

"Not at all. Have the police considered she might have been moonlighting as an escort?"

"It's been mentioned. It's usually the first thing male police officers think when the victim's female."

I considered myself suitably chastised.

"It's just that she did travel 200 miles wearing clothes picked out by a stranger," I said.

"Fair point," said Georgia. "Though we don't know he's a stranger. He could be a boyfriend or an acquaintance, who invited her to some kind of fancy dress party in the country."

I'd never considered that. They could have met online or through a dating app. He could have cultivated her trust over weeks or months, before inviting her to her death.

~

Lauren searched the internet for Susan Phillips while I watched. The pages flashed by so quickly I could barely keep up.

"There are thousands of Susan Phillipses," said Lauren. "Why couldn't the killer have chosen a victim with a less common name."

I imagine Brunnhilde Spinstersdottir would have had a different opinion on the matter.

Lauren tried to cut down the matches by adding extra keywords – Manchester and Lincoln, University and History. That either reduced the hits to nothing or produced thousands of hits that matched the other keywords, but had nothing to do with Susan Phillips.

"I'll try the social media sites," said Lauren.

She logged into all the social media sites one by one. I didn't realise there were so many. Or that they were so specialised. There were video sites, picture sites, chat sites. There were plenty of Susan Phillipses, but not the one we were looking for.

And it took ages to page through. Most had pictures of the account holder and could be quickly discounted, but some were unclear or had no picture of the owner. Which meant scrolling through the user's posts, looking for something that could tie her to the Susan Phillips we were searching for.

After the first hour I left Lauren to it, and surfed the news channels on the TV instead. None of them had the victim's name yet.

"This is weird," said Lauren.

"What's weird?"

"She's not on social media. Or if she is, I can't find her, and I'm good at finding people."

"Not everyone's on social media, Lauren. I'm not."

"Yes, but you're the most hated man in Swindon. She's a nineteen-year-old girl."

There was that.

"Are you hungry?" I said. "I'm starving. I can't even remember the last time I ate."

"There are takeaway menus by the door."

I wandered over. There was a choice of Chinese, Indian or Italian. I felt hungry enough for all three.

"Do you think it might be safer to go out to a restaurant?" said Lauren. "I don't like the idea of opening the door to a stranger wearing a motorcycle helmet."

Good point. Though the alternative wasn't much better for me. Spending an hour in an enclosed public space, waiting to be recognised, was not my idea of fun. But it would be safer to be with people. And we were off grid. I'd take my fake glasses and keep my head down. No one would recognise me in a dimly lit restaurant.

We settled on an Indian. Lauren said the restaurant was quiet, and it was only a short walk away. Off the grid or not, I still kept an eye out – trying to perfect the combination of keeping my head down whilst turning occasionally to see if we were being followed. I didn't see anyone.

Inside the restaurant I chose a table in the back corner where I could sit with my back to the world.

Eventually I relaxed. I couldn't remember the last time I'd actually gone out to a restaurant. It had to be well over a year. It felt good. Normal. Okay I was wearing fake glasses and hiding from the room, but it was a glimpse of what life could be like.

If I survived the week.

I spent an age contemplating what to order. Everything was so tempting in Indian restaurants. Then I did what I always did – begin by deciding categorically that I would not order my usual chicken tikka masala. I would have something different this time – the vindaloo, the jalfrezi, the dhansak. Five minutes of indecision later, I'd order the chicken tikka masala. It was just too good not to order.

"You're very good at all this internet searching," I said to Lauren as we moved onto the second course. "Did you have to learn it for a part? The tragically murdered computer genius?"

"No, it's all part of being a modern actor. You can't wait for an agent to find you work. You have to network – make sure your bio is up to date and prominent in all the places it might be seen. Obscurity is the actor's worst enemy. And good research gives you an edge over the competition."

Perhaps I should try that. If I ever shook off the 'most hated man in Swindon' epithet.

It started to rain when we left the restaurant. A few spots at first, but I could hear distant rumbles of thunder. Neither of us had brought a coat so we picked up the pace, hurrying along the pavement. The rain began to ease off as we approached the door to the house. Lauren quickly unlocked it and we dived inside.

"I enjoyed that," I said as we started the long climb up the stairs to the top flat.

"The run or the meal?"

"Both. I haven't done 'normal' for a very long time."

"I'd say 'you should get out more,' but in current circumstances that's probably not a good idea."

We'd just reached the top step when Lauren grabbed my arm.

The door to her flat was ajar.

Chapter Fourteen

Lauren silently eased the door open with a finger, gradually revealing the main room. We both peered inside on tiptoe.

There was an A4 sheet of white paper in the middle of the floor.

Lauren pushed the door open to its maximum extent. Once we were certain no one was hiding behind it, we crept into the room. Everything was quiet except for the muffled sound of passing traffic.

I crept closer to the piece of paper, keeping an eye on all the doors. Both internal doors were closed. I was certain we'd left the bathroom door open.

Lauren ran to the kitchen area and grabbed two knives. I could see what looked like writing on the piece of paper – four words printed in a very small font. I squatted down next to the paper for a better look.

"Don't touch it," whispered Lauren.

"I wasn't planning to."

The four words on the paper froze my blood.

She's in the bedroom.

"I'm calling the police," said Lauren, handing me one of her knives.

I wasn't sure the police would send anyone soon. They were in the midst of a major murder enquiry. They'd asked the public for help – that had to have eaten up manpower. Would they have anyone left to come out to a break-in?

They would if victim number two was in the bedroom.

I looked at the bedroom door. *Déjà vu*. I'd been here before. The same dilemma. To open the door or not to open the door. The killer could be inside. He wasn't last time, but there was no dollhouse this time. He could have changed his MO.

And if we didn't open the door, we had to spend the next hour or more … where? Here in the flat waiting to be attacked? Or outside in the car waiting to be attacked?

"They're sending a car round," said Lauren. "I pushed the fact that you were here."

I wanted to feel buoyed by that, but was the operator just saying that to make us feel better? It was a break-in. Did the police even respond to break-ins these days?

I couldn't take my eyes off that bedroom door. One push and we'd know. It was like Schrodinger's door. Open it, and the uncertainty would collapse.

"The operator said we should wait outside," said Lauren.

"No," I said.

"What?"

I put my finger to my lips and beckoned Lauren to follow me to the far side of the room.

"The police might not come for hours," I whispered. "They might not come at all. To them, I'm an attention-seeking fantasist, and you're my agent."

"So what do we do?"

"We've got to open the bedroom door. There are two of us. Young, fit, armed with knives. He drowns his victims and has to use drugs to incapacitate them. He won't have a gun or a knife. He's probably not even in there. He'll be long gone."

Lauren didn't look convinced.

"Look," I continued. "If there's a body in there, the police will be here in five minutes. If there isn't, we can barricade the front door and relax. Do you want to spend the next hour in your car, terrified every time you see someone walking towards us?"

"Ok," she said. "Let's do this."

I looked around for some kind of shield or longer weapon, but couldn't find anything.

Where were all the narwhal tusks when you needed one!

So, knives it would have to be.

I positioned myself by the bedroom door, reached out for the handle, and slowly pulled the lever down.

"Ready?" I mouthed to Lauren.

She nodded.

I threw open the door, crouching down and holding the knife out in front of me, ready to spring forward.

No one was inside. But on the bed, on top of some clothes, was another sheet of white A4 paper. And on the paper was a miniature figurine.

~

I quickly checked the room to make sure it really was empty. I looked under the bed, in the wardrobes. No one was hiding anywhere.

Lauren was standing over the bed looking down at the paper and the figurine.

"Is there a message?" I asked.

Lauren's face had turned ashen.

I looked at the paper. There *was* a message, printed in the same tiny font as the one on the lounge floor.

See you soon, Mathew. I like your new friend. Can't wait to give her my special room service.

The figurine was different to the one he'd left in the dollhouse. It was the same general size, but a different pose. And she was blonde, wearing a red speckled dress, and carrying a beige bag over her shoulder.

My eyes were immediately drawn to the dress the figurine was sitting on. A red, floral dress. The bag was there too, next to the dress. A beige straw handbag.

"She's me," said Lauren. "The handbag and dress aren't mine. They're what he wants me to wear."

Chapter Fifteen

I rang Georgia. She'd have telephone numbers for all the senior detectives. She'd be able to reach them far quicker than any 999 call.

I told her what had happened, and where we were. I wanted to say more, but it was imperative I hung up and let her call SCU.

"How did he find us?" said Lauren, still shaken. "How did he know I was blonde? How did he know I even existed?"

I had no idea. We'd been so careful.

"No one followed us from Garstock," said Lauren. "We'd have seen their headlights. There were long stretches of road where it was complete darkness behind us."

"It must have been from the police station," I said. "But how would he know I was going to be there?"

Could he be part of the investigation? A police officer? Or someone passing himself off as a reporter – that would give him a reason to hang about outside police stations. It might have been a complete accident that he was there when Lauren drove me to the SCU headquarters.

"Your phone!" said Lauren. "He might have put a bug on it, or cloned it, or did whatever hackers do to phones to track people."

Shit. I switched off my phone, and then felt stupid as he already knew where I was, and I needed to keep the phone on in case Georgia or the police called.

"That's how he'd know about me," said Lauren. "He'd have my number from when you sent the photo of the dollhouse."

My fault again. I'd dragged an innocent stranger into a serial killer's orbit. What was it with me? I never set out to harm anyone. It's like I was cursed.

I looked at my watch. How long would it take the police to

come? Should we be outside on the pavement ready to meet them?

I took pictures of the bed and the note in the lounge. Old habits die hard. I wanted a record of what we'd seen. Just in case.

"Should we check the bathroom?" asked Lauren, looking at the one door in the flat that we hadn't opened.

I was torn. I was pretty sure the killer had long gone. But ... who knew how his brain worked? He was a risk taker. He might get off on being close to being caught, slipping out at the last minute to rearrange the crime scene before stealing away through a back window.

And I needed to pee. Two pints of lager at the restaurant were beginning to make themselves known.

I talked it over with Lauren. "Knowing the police, they could keep us outside on the pavement for the next two hours. This might be our last chance."

Lauren agreed. He was almost certainly long gone, and, if there was anything in there, it was probably another note – something designed to frighten and unsettle.

We took up our positions in front of the bathroom door, knives out, ready for anything. I reached out, slowly pulled the door handle down ... and pushed.

The door swung open. I couldn't see anyone, but the shower curtain was drawn. I was sure it hadn't been when we'd left.

I hesitated, keeping my distance. I'd seen too many horror films, not to be freaked out by the thought of a knife-wielding killer hiding behind a shower curtain.

"Here, use this," said Lauren handing me a mop.

I considered ramming the mop handle through the shower curtain ... repeatedly, with everything I had. If he was there I could keep him at a distance and hurt him.

But what if he wasn't there? What if he'd propped his next victim up inside the bath. She might be drugged, unconscious, hanging from the shower head. I could end up hurting her, *seriously* hurting her.

Plan B. I'd hook the mop head around the far end of the shower curtain and gradually pull the curtain open while keeping a nice, safe distance.

I liked plan B.

I slowly pulled the shower curtain back.

The bath was empty

~

Five minutes later, the police arrived sirens blaring. I told them where the flat was and what was inside. Another couple of police cars arrived soon after. Then came the detectives.

No DCI Terrell or Sima this time. I assumed they were busy elsewhere. A smartly dressed woman in her late thirties seemed to be the one in charge. She introduced herself as Detective Inspector Lipinski, took our statements, and then went inside to view the crime scene.

Lauren and I hung around outside for ages. On the pavement at first and then, as the crowd of onlookers grew, we moved to the car. The media were going to arrive soon and neither of us wanted our faces plastered all over the news. And the car was parked inside the area the police had cleared the public away from, so we were safe – from both the killer and the press.

I hunched down and tried to look uninteresting.

"Do you think it's significant that my figurine wasn't lying in a pool of blood?" asked Lauren.

I shrugged, and then decided to be supportive. "Could be. He's very precise."

"He could easily have added the blood if he'd wanted to. I've looked it up on the internet. It's easy to make fake blood. You don't need special ingredients."

"Very true," I said.

"So, it could be a warning, couldn't it? 'Stay out of it' rather than 'you're next?'"

"Definitely."

I decided not to remind her of the 'can't wait to give her my special room service' part of the message.

But Lauren could be right. This killer wasn't a maniac straining to kill anyone who crossed his path. He was a sadist. A rational sadist who delighted in terrifying people – mainly me – and he seemed quite happy to keep me alive. Maybe he'd added Lauren to his list.

"I think DCI Terrell had it right," I said. "When he was being insightful, before the red mist of 'Mathew Sedley is guilty' clouded his judgement, he said the killer was a sadist, someone who liked to stretch out the terror. He did it again tonight, didn't he? He left your front door ajar. He didn't let you walk into the flat and hit you with a figurine on a pile of clothes. He did the same as he had at the cottage, slowly ramping up the terror. The door, the note, the clothes, the figurine."

"It's weird though," said Lauren. "If there's no link whatsoever between you and Susan Phillips-"

"Which there isn't."

"Then where does she fit in? The killer chose *your* house. He arranged for *you* to find the door ajar, the dollhouse, the dead body. He drowned her to incriminate you. He chose a location to incriminate you. He followed you to my flat, planted notes and dresses and figurines to freak the pair of us out. It's as though Susan Phillips was irrelevant – collateral damage in a campaign against you. And now me."

"But on the bright side," I said. "He hasn't killed me. And he won't be able to make his frame stick. I'm innocent, and I spent the afternoon of the murder in full public view. Okay, the police have only found two CCTV cameras so far, but they've hardly begun looking. Something will turn up. I'm sure of it."

I almost believed what I was saying.

Lauren looked at me, long and hard. Her eyes seemed to glisten in the half light. "Have you ever considered he's saving you 'til last?"

I hadn't. Until then.

Chapter Sixteen

Well, that was the last time I'd attempt to cheer Lauren up. I thought I was the pessimist of the two of us.

A uniformed constable tapped on the car window. DI Lipinski wanted to see us.

We walked over. I hoped she had good news. A nice, clear fingerprint on one of the notes would have gone down well. Or maybe they'd caught the killer on a neighbour's CCTV. I had a quick look up and down the street. I could see plenty of cameras – all hand-held and pointing our way – but no CCTV.

"Sorry to keep you so long," said the DI. "Just to let you know, you won't be able to move back into the flat until tomorrow. Have you got a place you can go to for tonight?"

"No," said Lauren. "Do you have a safe house you can put us up at?"

DI Lipinski laughed. "We're not the FBI. Bristol has a housing crisis. The PCC would have a fit if we suggested keeping an empty house in case we needed to hide someone. Your best bet is to book into a hotel."

"And wait for my 'special room service?' No, thank you."

"Family then?"

"They moved to Spain years ago. And before you say 'what about friends?' Think how that would go down. *Hi, Fran, I'm being pursued by a serial killer. Can I stay at yours?*"

"I can think of one place we could go," I said.

"You *must* be joking!"

~

"It's all set up," said Detective Inspector Lipinski, walking back over. "The team searching Laburnum Cottage will be finished within the hour, and they'd already arranged for a car to be stationed outside the cottage overnight. You'll be safe there."

Lauren was still not convinced.

"What about the back door?" she said. "We'll need that covered as well."

"I'll see what we can do," said the inspector. "We can set up a panic alarm tomorrow if you want – with a button in every room."

I wondered about nailing the windows and back door shut, but that wouldn't stop the killer smashing the glass to get in.

Still, it was better to be in the middle of nowhere with a police car outside than holed up in a hotel room where every serial killer and his dog could walk up and down the corridor outside or book into the room next door.

"I'll arrange for a patrol car to do an hourly sweep of the nearby roads," said the inspector. "I can't see the killer walking to your house. He'd need a car. And a car driving around a small village in the middle of the night, or parked up on a lane, that will get noticed."

I couldn't shake the feeling that we were bait.

"What about Mathew's phone?" asked Lauren. "Did you find out if your tech team had discovered any tracking apps on it?"

"They said they hadn't, but it might have been cloned. If you'd like you can leave the phone with me and we'll do further tests."

I didn't like the idea of handing over my phone to the police, but the alternative was worse. I needed to know I had a clean, uncloned phone. And until then I didn't want that phone anywhere near me.

I handed it over. I'd buy a cheap, new phone tomorrow.

~

We had a police escort all the way back to the cottage.

"I can't believe you suggested this," said Lauren.

"It's the least worst option. You said yourself you didn't want to stay in a hotel or with friends. What else was left?"

"One of the other forces could have had a safe house. And what about all those grace and favour homes with armed guards that the government keeps for entertaining foreign dignitaries."

"I don't think we're important enough."

"Are you still keeping an eye out for any cars following us?"

"I am. The traffic's easing off now. If anyone's following they'll be easier to spot."

A few cars followed us for miles, but by the time we approached Garstock we had the roads to ourselves.

I wasn't sure what I expected to find back at the cottage. A building site for a garden? A pulled apart garage? Gaping holes in every ceiling? I was partially right. The garden was a mess – the lawn was more mud than grass, and the flower beds had been trampled. The garage floor was covered in tools and the contents of several large boxes that I hadn't got around to unpacking since the move.

But my ceilings were intact, there were no press camped outside, the promised police car was already parked in my drive, and someone had cut back all my brambles.

Lauren had to park in front of the garage. I took one look at the garage floor and decided that making room for a car was a job for another day.

Our escort drove away and our protection team – Bob and Kofi, who resembled a couple of rugby front-row forwards – introduced themselves.

"Don't worry," said Bob. "We'll be here all night."

"You *are* covering the back door as well?" asked Lauren.

"Yes. We'll do a full check of the perimeter every half hour – trying all the doors and windows."

"You're not stationing someone by the back door permanently?"

"No," said Bob. "It's best not to split up. We know what we're doing. We'll be right outside."

"There's a patrol car too," said Kofi. "It's doing a full sweep of the neighbourhood every hour. They've got orders to stop and question anyone they see."

"Trust me," said Bob. "Just having the patrol car outside

the house will be a deterrent. One look at the car and they'll be off."

I had a quick look at the back garden to see what damage the search teams had done then joined Lauren inside.

"You haven't got any bolts on the front *or* the back door," said Lauren.

"I'll get some tomorrow. If the police are installing panic alarms I'll see if they can arrange for bolts and new locks on both doors."

"What about the windows? Do they have locks?"

"I think so."

"You *think* so."

"It wasn't a major concern when I bought the place. I think there are locks, but I haven't opened every window."

Lauren checked every room and every window. Well, what do you know? I had locks on all of them.

"I think we can barricade the back door," said Lauren heading off towards the kitchen. "It's the weakest link. If the killer's coming in, that's where he'll choose."

I followed along behind her. I thought she was overreacting – we did have police protection – and, surely this time, the killer wouldn't know we were back in the cottage. But if it helped her cope, I was happy to go along with anything that made her feel safer.

We started with the kitchen table, pushing it up against the back door, but Lauren didn't think it was heavy enough – even if we piled it high with kitchen appliances and tins.

So we tried the Welsh dresser instead. It was heavy enough – too heavy – which meant taking some of the drawers out and removing the top half. But we managed it, shuffling it across and re-assembling it in front of the back door.

No one was coming through there without expending a hell of a lot of effort and making a hell of a lot of noise.

"Now we need some trip wires," said Lauren.

"Pardon?"

"Trip wires. We're up against a cold-blooded killer who had

no trouble breaking into both of our homes. So, let's assume he's broken in undetected, and lay traps. Trip wires on the stairs will be easiest."

I held up a hand.

"Whoa. What if he's broken in through a window upstairs and we're running downstairs to the front door. I'll never be able to pick my way through a series of trip wires."

"Okay, just the one trip wire on the top step. We can arrange a string of pots and pans under the windows. That'll make a lot of noise if anyone knocks into them. He won't be expecting that."

"You've really thought this through."

"I read a lot of crime fiction. And I swore that if I ever found myself in a situation like this I wouldn't go quietly. I'd prepare. I'd fight. And then I'd go full honey badger on him until he stopped moving."

She looked at me with an intensity that I found disconcerting. Her speech wasn't an act of bravado. She really meant it.

I made a mental note – never get on Lauren's bad side.

~

It was nearly one by the time we'd finished fortifying the cottage. The only time I put my foot down was when Lauren suggested hammering wooden wedges underneath the front door. First, I wasn't confident we'd ever be able to get the wedges out. And, second, our protection was on the other side of that door. If the killer got in I didn't want anything to impede Bob and Kofi from coming to our aid.

"Come on," I said. "It's late. I'll show you where the spare sheets are. Are you going to be okay sleeping in the spare bedroom?"

"The one where the dead body was found? No thank you. We shouldn't sleep alone either. Best we both sleep in your room."

"Okay," I said, suddenly feeling a lot more awake than I had a few seconds earlier.

"And you can wipe that look off your face," said Lauren. "You're not getting lucky."

I'd forgotten the last time I had.

"We'll bring in the mattress and bedding from the spare room and put it on the floor by the door," said Lauren. "That'll make sure no one can creep into the bedroom without being noticed. You choose which bed you want. I doubt if I'll sleep much anyway."

I chose the mattress on the floor. I was a well-mannered host.

"Do you have a baseball bat?" asked Lauren.

I didn't. I had a cricket bat in the garage somewhere but neither of us wanted to go outside to search for it.

"I'll get some knives," said Lauren. "We can keep them under our pillows."

Lauren returned a couple of minutes later with four knives, a mop and a rolling pin.

I fell asleep not long after.

~

I slept like a log. I must have been more tired than I'd thought. I didn't wake up until a quarter to eight. My first thought was to check on Lauren – just to make sure she was alive.

She was. I could see her foot twitching away under the blankets. Hopefully it was a good dream. I didn't want her suddenly waking up and going full honey badger on me. Whatever that meant. I'd have to look it up on the internet later.

I decided to let her sleep. She might have been awake most of the night. I'd go down to the kitchen and make coffee and toast.

And make sure Bob and Kofi were still alive.

I pulled my mattress back a foot or two to make enough room for me to squeeze through the door.

The cottage was quiet. No dead bodies at the foot of the stairs, and the door to the spare bedroom was wide open –

just as we'd left it. I peered inside just in case. No dead
bodies on the floor, and both windows were closed and
unbroken.

I checked the bathroom next, availing myself of the
facilities, then opened the window to look outside.

The police car was still there. I couldn't see Bob or Kofi as
the angle was too steep. But everything looked normal.
Lauren's car was in front of the garage. There were no pieces
of broken wood outside the door or piles of smashed glass
outside the windows.

We'd survived the night unscathed.

I remembered to grab the banister railing and hop over the
trip wire at the top of the stairs. Hopefully I'd be able to
persuade Lauren to take it down soon. One of us was bound
to trip over it eventually. It would be somewhat ironic to
evade a serial killer and die tripping over a wire that you'd
put up to protect yourself.

I didn't notice the lounge door at first. I'd reached the
bottom of the stairs and was just about to turn left towards
the kitchen when it registered.

The lounge door was ajar. Last night we'd left it wide open.

Chapter Seventeen

I tried not to panic. Lauren might have got up in the night, unable to sleep, and decided to go downstairs to watch TV.

It was possible. Unlikely, but possible. She'd have had to pull the mattress back without waking me. Which again was possible. You didn't have to be strong to slide a mattress along a carpeted floor. I didn't weigh that much, and I was spark out. Nothing would have woken me.

I knew I was grabbing at straws, but was the alternative any more likely? The cottage was a fortress. No one could have broken in.

I tried the front door. It was locked. I ran to the kitchen. The Welsh dresser was still in place. All the windows were locked and unbroken.

Should I call Bob and Kofi? Lauren?

I felt stupid and indecisive. The door being ajar could be one of those quirks of living in an old house where timbers shift and groan in the middle of the night. The door could have swung to by itself. Nothing in the cottage was square.

I decided to check on Bob and Kofi. If they were outside in the car then everything had to be well. No one could have broken in with them parked right outside the front door.

I ran to the door, grabbed the handle then stopped. If this were a film, this was the point where the hero would find the police car empty or both officers slumped in their seats, their throats cut.

I took a deep breath, opened the front door, and peered out.

Bob and Kofi were sitting in the front of their patrol car. It looked like they were having breakfast. I waved. They waved back. I closed the door and leaned back against it. Relieved. No one could have got in.

I walked over to the lounge door and gave it a solid push. There was a dollhouse in the middle of the floor.

~

I didn't hesitate. I didn't examine the dollhouse. I didn't open the dollhouse. The killer would have to find someone else to play his sick little games. I was out. I walked straight back outside and called Bob and Kofi over.

"You'll need to call the SCU," I said. "There's a dollhouse in the lounge."

I showed them where it was then ran upstairs to tell Lauren. She didn't believe it.

"How did he get in?" she asked.

"I have no idea. Both doors were still locked. The back door was still barricaded. The only windows I haven't checked are in the lounge."

"What about Bob and Kofi? Did they fall asleep?"

"I don't know that either."

"What about the figurine? There was a figurine wasn't there? Was it the same one he put on my bed? Was it me?"

"I didn't open the dollhouse."

"You're joking. Why not?"

"Because that's what he wants me to do. I'm not playing his games any more."

"Well go down and find out. I'll get dressed and join you. I won't be long."

~

Bob and Kofi were outside by their patrol car. Bob was talking to someone on his radio, while Kofi paced. Neither looked happy. Kofi looked like he was about to punch something.

"Sorry, man," he said. "We fucked up. Did you hear the screaming?"

"What screaming?"

"The girl last night about two thirty."

"I didn't hear a thing," I said. "I was spark out all night."

"We had to respond," said Kofi. "She was screaming and terrified. We thought her life was in danger. What could we do? We was only gone for a minute. There's no way anyone got past us. We chased them past that house there." He pointed to my neighbour's house about two hundred yards away. "Then they got in a car and drove off. We tried to follow but they disappeared. There was no lights. No sound. No nothing. So we called it in and drove back. Couldn't have been gone more than a minute. And we did a full sweep of the house the moment we got back. Checked everything – the doors, the windows. I even looked in every window. Except that room – the one there with the curtains drawn."

The lounge. The one room where we'd drawn the curtains. Was that why the killer had chosen it?

"The killer's got an accomplice," said Lauren from the doorway. "He'd only need a minute to break in through the front door and drop off a dollhouse. The decoy gave him that minute. It was a girl you said?"

"It sounded like a girl."

"But you never saw her?"

"No," said Bob. "We never saw her, the man, or the car. But we heard them. There should be burnt rubber all over the road down there the noise that car was making when it set off. Proper wheelspin."

"Did you hear the man speak at all?" asked Lauren.

"No. Just the girl."

So, one accomplice. Most likely a young woman.

"Matt," said Lauren. "You need to look at this dollhouse. It's not Laburnum Cottage."

Chapter Eighteen

Bob wouldn't let us enter the lounge.

"We're going to get a bollocking for leaving our post as it is. I'm not risking another one for letting you walk all over a crime scene."

We agreed not to enter the lounge. We'd stay in the hallway and look from there. All four of us had already walked on the hall carpet several times that morning.

"Do you recognise the house?" asked Lauren.

I didn't. It was bigger than Laburnum Cottage. It had the same white render, but it had a slate roof and more windows. And two chimneys – one at either end of the house.

"I've never seen it before," I said. "It's nowhere I've ever lived or visited."

"Do you think you could open it, Bob?" asked Lauren. "Just to see if there's a figurine inside. I need to see if it's me."

Bob refused. He'd let us see the house – from a distance – but that was it. We'd have to wait for forensics and SCU.

I looked at my watch. It was five past eight. We were going to be in limbo until the SCU and forensics arrived. Which could easily be an hour if they were all based around Bristol.

Lauren showered while I made breakfast. It was going to be a long morning, and I had no idea if we were going to be allowed to stay in the cottage. Would the whole house be declared a crime scene? It wasn't as though there could be much to find. The killer had been in the house for less than a minute. The house and gardens had been searched the night before, and we'd arrived shortly after with one piece of hand luggage each. It's not as though we could have smuggled a dollhouse in.

Lauren surfed the internet on her phone while we ate breakfast in the kitchen. The police had released Susan

Phillips's name to the press. A few interviews with shocked friends and fellow students were already online, and floral tributes had been laid outside her hall of residence in Manchester.

No one could believe she'd been murdered. Or that she'd travelled down to Somerset.

"She said she was going home for a few days," said one friend.

"She was such a quiet person," said another.

There was a passing mention of her having come from Lincoln, but it didn't look like any reporters had been sent there yet. The family had that hell yet to come.

"Do you think the dollhouse could be a replica of Susan Phillips's family home?" asked Lauren.

It was an interesting notion. He must have known he couldn't keep using Laburnum Cottage for displaying his dollhouses or dumping his victims. He'd be caught. He had to have some plan of where he'd go next. Isolated rural properties made sense. He'd need somewhere on a quiet road with no immediate neighbours or CCTV cameras. Somewhere he could carry a dead woman from his car to the front door without being noticed. This latest dollhouse had the look of a rural property.

And Lincolnshire was a pretty rural county. Could that be why he'd chosen Susan Phillips? Because of her parent's house? Or some grudge he had against her parents? They could be his next target. He'd grown tired of torturing me and had moved on to his next mark.

I had an even more worrying thought. He'd also need to know when the houses were empty. He'd need time to pick the locks, to carry the body inside and arrange it to match the pose of the figurine. Susan Phillips's parents had had to travel to Bristol to identify her body. Had they left their home empty?

The killer was a sadist who loved to stretch out the torment. He'd already taken their daughter away from them. Why stop there when he could twist the knife further? Have them come home to find their front door ajar, then some sick, twisted note on the hallway floor. *She's waiting for you in her bedroom.* Then, when the terrified parents opened the door to Susan's room, they'd be confronted with the horror of another dead girl.

I shared my thoughts with Lauren.

"We've got to tell Bob and Kofi," she said. "If the parents stayed in Bristol overnight, they're probably on their way back to Lincoln now."

~

Bob called SCU and passed on my concerns. Susan's parents *had* stayed in Bristol overnight, and Susan *was* an only child. Their house in Lincoln had been empty since yesterday evening.

Bob was asked to take a photo of the dollhouse from the lounge door and send it to SCU. Someone would then show it to the parents to see if they recognised it.

As soon as Bob had sent the photo, Lauren and I returned to the kitchen. I didn't feel like any more toast. I was feeling guilty about feeling relieved by the idea that the killer might have moved on to another target. No one should have to go through what I had, and no one should feel any relief for someone else being put in that position.

But I so wanted my torment to end. To be able to walk past a room without wondering if there was a dead body inside, or a killer lurking behind the shower curtain.

Or wake up to see your name in the papers.

Lauren nearly spat out her coffee.

"Oh my God," she said. "Look at this! Bristol flat raided by police."

She turned her phone round so that I could see the newspaper story. There was a grainy picture of police clustered around the outside door to Lauren's flat last night. The headlines ran: *Bristol Flat Raided by the Police.*

"Raid! What raid?" said Lauren. "We called *them*. We were the victims, not suspects."

I read the short article below. It was mostly conjecture. They thought it was a raid related to the dollhouse murder, but they had no facts. Other than me being there. Or as the article put it: *It was rumoured that Mathew Sedley was staying at the flat.*

Great. They hadn't actually said that police had raided a flat in Bristol and dragged Mathew Sedley, aka the guilty bastard, off to chokey, but they'd implied it.

I needed to change the subject.

"Can you find out how long it would take to drive from here to Lincoln?" I asked Lauren.

"You're not thinking of driving to Lincoln, are you?"

"No, I was just wondering how long it would take the killer. He was in Bristol yesterday evening some time between seven and nine. Then in Garstock at two thirty this morning. Did he have time to drive to Lincoln and arrive in the dark?"

Lauren checked an internet route planner. It was a four-hour drive to Lincoln. He could have got there by six thirty if he'd set off immediately.

"And sunrise in Lincoln on September 22nd," said Lauren, calling up another set of screens. "Is six forty seven."

It would be starting to get light then, but ... did he really need to arrive in the dark? If the property was secluded enough all he had to do was arrive before the local traffic built up.

~

DI Lipinski was the first member of SCU to arrive. She appeared at the front door a few minutes behind the scenes of crime team, who were already getting suited up.

She interviewed Bob and Kofi first then asked us to step outside. We told her everything that had happened.

"You're absolutely sure you don't recognise the dollhouse?" asked the DI.

"As sure as I can be," I said. "Have you heard from Susan Phillips's parents?"

"Not yet. I want both of you to suit up. I need you to take a closer look at that dollhouse."

We were handed white oversuits from the forensics team's van and pulled them on. Then waited for the SOCO team to finish their initial round of photographs and the search of the immediate area around the dollhouse.

"You can go in now," the DI told us. "One at a time, and don't stray outside the marked area. I want you to take a good look at both the front and the back of the dollhouse. If there's anything remotely familiar, tell me."

I went in first. The house was built to the same exacting standards as the first had been. And had the same little flourishes – such as what looked like a small damp patch in the render under one of the windows, and moss on the slate roof.

But I didn't recognise it. It was possible I'd visited the place years before, but if I had, it had never stuck in my memory.

I moved around to the back. The rear of the property was a little different. There was a large conservatory and what looked like a boiler house protruding from the ground floor. I could even see tiny pot plants inside the conservatory. Again, none of this tripped any memories. It looked like an expensive country property, but not one I had any memory of.

Lauren went next. She didn't recognise the house either.

Then came the moment that Lauren in particular had been waiting all morning for. The opening of the dollhouse.

The scenes of crimes officer did the honours, unlatching the clasp on the side of the house so the front could swing open.

Lauren and I watched from the lounge doorway. I thought I saw a figurine in one of the upstairs bedrooms, but SOCO's body soon blocked my view as he took a series of photographs of the inside from various angles and distances.

"Is it the same figurine as last night?" asked Lauren.

"No," said SOCO. "This one's male."

Chapter Nineteen

Crap. Thirty minutes earlier I'd been castigating myself for feeling relieved that the killer might be losing interest in me. Now I was back in his cross hairs.

Unless the figurine wasn't supposed to be me. He hadn't left a pile of clothes for me, had he? I peered around the door, my eyes darting from the sofa to the dining table. I couldn't see anything.

SOCO made way for the DI to take a closer look at the dollhouse interior.

"The figurine is a young male wearing brown chinos, a dark brown bomber jacket, a white turtle neck shirt and what looks like black desert boots," said the DI. "Do you own any clothes like that, Mr. Sedley?"

"No," I said.

The DI spent a good couple of minutes examining the interior before inviting me to come forward for a closer look.

"You might have forgotten the outside of the house," she said. "But take a close look at the interior. Don't touch anything, but see if any of the rooms or the arrangement of the furniture jog any memories."

My eyes were drawn to the figurine. He was lying on his back in an upstairs bedroom. His head rested in a pool of bright red blood – just as the first figure had. It was an odd pose – a bit like superman, but lying down. His arms were akimbo and his legs slightly apart. He was dark-haired like me. He could have been the same age as me, but then he could have been any age between eighteen and thirty five. And there was no way of gauging his height. He was a scale model. He could have been representing someone six foot six or five foot six.

I examined the rooms next, looking for anything familiar. I

found nothing. Then I checked the kitchen. There was a tiny briefcase sitting on the kitchen table.

I told the DI.

"It looks like the briefcase from the first dollhouse," I said. "The one that was leaning up against the cooker. This one's on the kitchen table. It's got to be significant, hasn't it?"

~

What could the briefcase symbolise? Was it the killer's trademark? Some kind of encoded clue? Was it significant that it had moved from the cooker to the kitchen table?

Or was it all a game? A red herring inserted into the model to misdirect and waste police time?

SOCO picked up the tiny briefcase and looked at.

"Moulded plastic," he said, turning towards the DI. "If you want I could scan it. It might have something hidden inside."

I couldn't see the killer hiding a microchip inside a miniature plastic briefcase. That was more James Bond than serial killer.

"Scan it," said the DI. "But only after you've processed everything else."

"On the subject of scanning," said Lauren. "Can we be scanned? My car, our clothes, the house. The killer knew we were here last night. How? Only a handful of people knew where we'd be and I'm certain no one followed us. So is there a tracking device somewhere?"

"Did you have your phone on?" asked SOCO.

"Not until an hour ago," said Lauren. "I took out the sim card last night before we left Bristol. And Mathew gave his phone to the detective inspector."

"Process the room first," said the DI. "Then look for tracking devices."

"Ma'am," said a voice from the front door. I turned to look. It was Sima. She stood in the doorway. She'd yet to suit up.

"Yes, Sima?" said the DI.

"We've just heard from Susan's parents," said Sima. "They don't recognise the dollhouse."

~

DI Lipinski thanked us for our assistance and suggested we wait outside while her team continued their work.

"Stay on the drive," she said. "We're treating the garden and the road outside as a crime scene. Oh, and hand your oversuits to the uniformed officer by the door. We shouldn't be too long. Have you got your car keys with you?"

"I have," said Lauren.

"Good. We'll start with the car as it's the easiest place for someone to plant a tracker. We'll scan it inside and out."

We changed out of our oversuits and handed them over. There were several police cars parked outside, but none on the stretch of road leading up to my neighbour's house where Bob and Kofi had heard the screams.

And there were no press cars or groups of curious locals. It looked like the police might have closed the entire road.

We decided to wait in Lauren's car. A cold wind had started to blow and I had the feeling it could be hours before DI Lipinski came to find us.

"I was convinced the dollhouse was going to be Susan's parent's house," said Lauren. "The killer wouldn't choose a random house, would he?"

"I have no idea. He might have voices in his head who tell him which houses to pick."

"I don't think he's psychotic," said Lauren. "Or if he is, he's a high functioning one. There's far more method than madness in what he does. I think the house will link to Susan somehow. She wasn't selected at random. Do you think the male figurine could be her boyfriend?"

As long as it wasn't me. The thought slipped out before I'd had time to censor it. I felt bad. For a second or two, then accepted the fact that I was a flawed individual who didn't like the idea of being murdered.

"The house might belong to the boyfriend's parents," said Lauren. "That would make sense. It would connect two of the figurines with one of the houses. All you need..."

She stopped mid-sentence.

"What is it?" I asked.

"The connection to you," she said. "What's that saying? Everyone's connected to everyone else by six degrees of separation. What if you and Susan Phillips *are* connected, but not directly. And the killer is working his way through the chain of acquaintances, starting at the ends and moving inwards. You won't see the connection until the last victim is identified."

~

I was intrigued by Lauren's theory. Intrigued, but far from convinced. Nor could I see it helping the investigation. If there were only two degrees of separation, then you could start drawing up lists of acquaintances and look for a match. But anything beyond two degrees and the connection was as good as random.

I could see it explaining the killer's motivation after the case had been solved, but I couldn't see it being a useful tool in catching him before he'd finished. It would be a time sink.

"I wonder if the killer is the final link," said Lauren. "That would make a weird sense. Maybe his life has gone to shit and he decides it's all the fault of this malignant chain of acquaintances who he needs to destroy."

Our theorising was interrupted by a car approaching at speed, followed by a screeching of tyres and a door slamming.

Ten seconds later DCI Terrell was striding up the drive. If this had been a cartoon he would have had steam venting from both ears. The man was a walking heart attack. God knows what his blood pressure registered as.

I sank lower in my seat, hoping his anger wasn't about to be directed at me.

It wasn't. Bob and Kofi had that honour.

I didn't hear all the conversation, but I heard all the shouty bits. Terrell was mad at the two policemen for abandoning their post, for letting the killer slip past them, for not realising they were chasing a decoy and for not searching the inside of the house the moment they'd returned from their wild goose chase.

"You had him!" shouted Terrell. "He was there for the taking."

I didn't hear a lot of what Bob or Kofi said. I imagine they'd decided the best approach was to let the DCI vent and wait until he'd calmed down. It hadn't really been their fault. If they'd waited for back up before leaving their post, a girl could have been killed. You can't assume that every scream you hear is a potential decoy. And I knew what it was like to have the silence of the night rent by a young girl screaming. Your first reaction is to rush to investigate. Everything else is forgotten.

Lauren opened the car windows a little, just enough so we could hear more of the conversation now that the DCI was calming down.

"You're sure it was a girl screaming?" asked the DCI.

"That's what it sounded like," said Kofi.

"It could have been someone impersonating a girl," said Bob.

"Just before the car drove off," said the DCI. "How many car doors did you hear slam shut?"

"One?" said Bob.

Kofi agreed. "It was definitely one."

"Did the car engine start up before the door slammed or after?"

"After," said Bob.

"How long after?" asked the DCI. "Fractions of a second, or more than a second."

"More, I think," said Kofi.

"Definitely," said Bob.

"So it could be one person. It could be more," said the DCI. "Did you hear anything before the screaming – like the car pulling up by the neighbour's house? Presumably it didn't drive past you?"

"No. Only one car drove by the house last night and that

was the other patrol car. Every hour on the hour," said Kofi.

"Didn't hear the car pull up either," said Bob. "Or see any headlights. They must have switched them off after the last bend."

"So the car would have been facing Laburnum Cottage when it made its getaway," said the DCI.

"I expect so. We couldn't actually see it. It was parked beyond the bend in the road there," said Bob pointing up the road.

"Did you ever catch a glimpse of the car?"

"No."

"But you heard it?"

"When it first started up. Yes. There was a lot of screeching tyres."

"So, the car would have set off in reverse, gone into a quick handbrake turn and then sped away?" asked the DCI.

"I guess so," said Kofi.

"But you couldn't catch it?"

"It disappeared."

"Did you hear it in the distance?"

"We had the siren on. You could hardly hear anything else," said Kofi.

"We did turn the siren off though," said Bob. "It couldn't have been on for more than twenty seconds. I turned it on when they drove away and turned it off after we lost them. I opened the windows as well to see if we could hear the car."

"Did you hear anything?"

"No," said Kofi. "Couldn't see no lights neither. The road's all bends, high banks and hedges. You can barely see fifty yards ahead and there's a couple of crossroads up there as well. They could have gone anywhere."

"All the trees and bends muffle the sound too," said Bob.

The car probably doubled back onto the main road and picked the killer up on the bend the other side of the cottage.

"Has anyone interviewed the owner of that house?" asked the DCI, pointing at my neighbour's cottage.

"Not yet," said Bob. "But they would have heard

everything. It was right outside their house. No one could have slept through all that screaming and shouting."

"Shouting?" said the DCI. "Who was shouting?"

"The girl," said Bob. "In between the screaming she kept shouting 'Help, he's going to kill me.' We had to intervene."

"She said what?" said the DCI, his tone changing.

I felt the hairs on the back of my neck bristle. It couldn't be...

"This is important," the DCI continued. "Tell me *exactly* what you heard her say."

"Er … Help. He's going to kill me. Help me," said Bob.

"Help me, please," said Kofi. "It was 'Help, he's going to kill me. Help me, please.' She said it after the first two screams then I think she shouted 'help' and 'help me' a couple more times after that."

"What is it?" asked Lauren. "Why are you and Terrell looking so weirded out?"

"Because those are the words I heard Sophie shout. The ones she put in her note to me. The ones I heard her scream on three separate nights."

Chapter Twenty

He was playing with me every chance he got. It wasn't just arranging for me to find the dollhouses, or showing me he could find me wherever I hid. He was using Sophie. Drowning his first victim. Using Sophie's words to create a decoy. Everything designed to point to me, to knock me off balance, to terrify and destroy me. What the hell had I ever done to this man? Or was there no personal connection at all? Did he just come across me on the internet and liked the way I never fought back? The quiet sap with the perpetual 'rabbit in the headlights' expression. Was it a personal challenge for him to break the most hated man in Swindon?

Good luck with that. I was already broken. I was just very good at hiding it.

But not so good at hiding from DCI Terrell. I'd watched him disappear into the cottage shouting my name. "Sedley! Where's Sedley?"

Lauren had offered to call Georgia, but what was the point? The DCI wanted someone to shout at, and I'd been shouted at by the best. Maybe if he offloaded some of that anger, he could start becoming that very good detective that Georgia had told me about.

Terrell burst out of the house and headed straight for the car.

"I really think you should call Georgia," said Lauren.

"It's okay," I said, opening the passenger window to its maximum extent.

Terrell leaned into the car and spoke in a quiet, barely controlled voice. "You may have fooled some of my team, Sedley. But you don't fool me. Where were you at two thirty last night?"

"In bed, asleep."

"Can anyone besides your girlfriend confirm that?"

"I'm not his girlfriend," said Lauren.

"What *are* you then? Accomplices with benefits?"

"I'm a witness," said Lauren. "Who can confirm that Mathew never left the bedroom until seven forty-five. Go check for yourself. His mattress was pushed right up against the door all night. There's no way either of us could have left that room without the other one knowing."

Well, that wasn't entirely true. I'd left without waking her at seven forty-five, but there was no reason to tell Terrell that.

"Accomplices can't alibi each other," said Terrell. "Tell me. Was it always planned for two thirty or were the girl's screams the signal?"

"We were asleep," I said. "In a house we had to fortify because we were in fear for our lives. Have you seen the barricades and the trip wires?"

"Theatrics," said Terrell, dismissively. "You're an actress, aren't you, Ms. Gibbons? And you're an attention-seeking fantasist, Mr. Sedley. I bet you enjoyed all the set building."

His mind was still closed. Nothing we could say was going to convince him of our innocence.

Lauren tried.

"Haven't you worked out yet that the killer wouldn't need any accomplices inside the cottage? He needed *one* accomplice, *outside,* acting as a decoy to draw Bob and Kofi away, while he slipped into the cottage and set up the dollhouse."

"That's one theory," said Terrell. "But I have another. And mine doesn't need an accomplice outside."

~

"It was you, wasn't it, Ms. Gibbons?" said Terrell. "You were the girl. An actress like you could do the voice of a young girl easy enough. And Mr. Sedley could tell you what to say."

"What?" said Lauren, sitting up suddenly.

"You'd be able to slip out of the house no problem. You'd

wait for Bob and Kofi to do their rounds at two o'clock, wait a
minute or two, then slip out the back door."

"The back door's barricaded," said Lauren. "No one could
get in or out that way."

"It's barricaded now, but it wasn't when you went out. All
you had to do was sneak into the back garden, make as little
noise as possible and make sure you kept the house between
you and the police car. From the back garden you can get into
the woods and then you've got cover all the way to the
neighbour's house. You'd get there in no time."

"In the dark without a torch? You're insane," said Lauren.

"It wasn't pitch black though, was it?" said Terrell. "And
it's not as though you're a stranger to those woods. I bet you
familiarised yourself with the path you had to take. Lots of
rehearsals."

"And then what?" I asked. "Where did the car come from?"

"The killer had the car. He was parked by the neighbour's
house waiting for Ms. Gibbons."

"Wait a minute," I said. "If the killer was at the neighbour's house, how did the dollhouse get into the lounge?"

"You put it there, Mr. Sedley."

"What? How?" This was ridiculous.

"You already know how. It was clever. I'll give you that. But
not clever enough."

"Enlighten me then. How did I smuggle a dollhouse into
the lounge? Teleportation?"

"No, you slipped out the front door when you heard the
patrol car race off to investigate the screams. I imagine the
killer left the dollhouse close to the cottage, probably on the
roadside in the other direction to where the Bob and Kofi
were heading. He would have waited for the patrol car to
come by on its hourly sweep of the local roads. So that would
make it about two o'clock. He'd then pull up about four
hundred yards short of Laburnum Cottage, just far enough
away not to be heard or seen. He'd then walk a couple of
hundred yards or so towards the cottage and place the
dollhouse on the roadside for you to collect later. The killer

would then return to his car, and drive around the back roads to where Ms. Gibbons was waiting."

There was a disconcerting logic to the DCI's theory. It was rubbish, but people could believe it, especially if they started from the premise that we were guilty.

"So how did I get back to the house?" asked Lauren.

"The killer would have driven you back. He'd have dropped you off where he'd parked half an hour earlier when dropping off the dollhouse. You'd have made your way through the woods to the back door of the house where Mr. Sedley would have let you in. Then you would have barricaded the back door."

Georgia was right. Terrell was clever. Totally misguided, but clever.

"Now," said the DCI. "Do we continue this charade – which you know is going to come crashing down around your ears any minute now. Or do you come clean and tell me how clever you both were? I bet you're itching to tell people. I can arrange for all the top journalists to have access to the pair of you. Or I can lock you both away in solitary with no TV, no internet, no visitors and let you rot in obscurity. Which is it going to be? It's up to you."

He really was obsessed with the idea that I was this crazy, amoral attention seeker. Being locked up in solitary with no TV, no internet and no visitors sounded pretty good to me. Where do I sign up? There's a ton of books I've been meaning to read for years.

"How about we start with this second victim," said the DCI. "Is he alive or is he dead?"

"I have absolutely no idea," I said.

"We can talk hypothetically, if you'd prefer," said the DCI. "Let's say you're this killer – or an associate of this killer – would you kill the victim before or after you display the dollhouse?"

"I think this killer wants to hurt as many people as he can for as long as he can," said Lauren.

I looked at Lauren, surprised. She'd changed her voice,

slowed it down and altered the inflection slightly to give it a calmer, more menacing feel. What the hell was she up to? Was she playing along with Terrell or winding him up? Neither of which she should be doing! It would only prolong this waste of time. Terrell should be questioning the neighbour about the girl screaming outside his house last night. He might have looked out the window and seen the car, or even the killer.

"So," continued Lauren. "He'd make you believe that the victim might be alive. To give you hope so that he could later snatch that hope away and make finding the body that much worse for everyone involved."

"How would he do that? How would he make us believe the victim was still alive?" asked the DCI.

Lauren shrugged. "I don't know. Maybe by leaving no clue as to which house the dollhouse was modelled on. Or maybe the dollhouse is the clue. Find the house in time and save the victim. Take too long and the victim dies."

The hairs on the back of my neck were bristling again. One, Lauren seemed to find it very easy to slip inside the mind of a sadistic serial killer. Two, she sounded the part. And, three, I could see how the killer could do it.

Drowning. Drug the victim, put him in a box, leave a note in the house with the box's location, and let the tide do the rest. It even fitted the killer's MO. Drowning at sea.

I jumped when the DCI's phone suddenly rang. He answered it gruffly. "What is it?"

His face gradually changed, annoyance being replaced by surprise. I couldn't hear much of what was being said on the other end of the line, but I could pick out the occasional word like 'drowned.'

"Are you sure?" said the DCI, turning away from the car and heading off towards the house, his ear pressed to his phone.

"Sima!" he shouted before disappearing inside.

Chapter Twenty-One

"What was that about?" said Lauren, back to using her normal voice.

I told her I'd heard the word 'drowned' a couple of times.

"Do you think they've found the next victim?" asked Lauren. "Drowned just like Susan?"

I had no idea. I didn't think they'd made any progress finding the house, but a member of the public could have found a body washed up on a beach. Or trapped inside a box.

We'd know soon. If they'd found another body there'd be a sudden exodus of detectives heading off to the new crime scene.

"And what do you think you were doing just now?" I said to Lauren. "Playing along with Terrell like that. You know he's going to see you as a suspect from now on? You were starting to convince me."

"I'm an actor. I'm trained to convince people. Anyway, he already sees us as suspects. There's nothing we can do to change that in the short term, but we can point him to where he should be looking. Which is identifying that house. Find the house, identify the next victim, and things will begin to slot into place."

"In a normal world maybe, but there'll be some 'clue' in the house that will point everything back to me. It's the killer's MO. Implicate Mathew Sedley."

A large police van drove up and stopped on the other side of the road just beyond the gate. Sima came out of the house and walked over to the van. She talked to the front seat passenger for a short while then about a dozen uniformed police officers spilled out of the back of the van.

They were going to knock on doors, and search the roadside for evidence. Two were tasked with finding footprints in the woods behind the cottage.

"Do you think I should tell them my shoe size?" asked Lauren, smiling.

I didn't think Lauren appreciated just how soul-destroying and relentless police attention could be.

We watched Sima set off down the road towards my neighbour's house. Hopefully on the way to interviewing him ... or her. I had no idea who lived there. I knew someone did. I'd seen a car there a few times, but that was all I knew.

"Oh, God," said Lauren, pulling out her phone.

"What is it?"

"I forgot to call work. I should have called hours ago."

She stopped. "I can't keep on phoning in sick. God knows when I'll be able to work again. Do you think I should tell them I'm in police protection or will they think I've just dreamed up the most ridiculous excuse ever?"

"You're asking the wrong person," I said. "I haven't called anyone to explain why I'm not at work. If they've got a TV they'll already know, and won't ever want to speak to me again."

"I know, but people like me."

I had to laugh. Not immediately, and not wholeheartedly, but I managed a stifled chuckle. When she wasn't channelling serial killers, or turning my house into a fortress, she was amusing company.

"I'll tell them the truth," Lauren decided, pressing connect. "Hello. Samantha? It's Lauren. Sorry for not calling earlier, but – you'll not believe this – I'm in police protection! No *protection*, not custody. What? It's not? Oh. My. God. No, of course it's not true. There was no raid. My flat was broken into by the Dollhouse murderer. Yes, him. He left his calling card on my bed – a figurine dressed up to look like me. I know! Totally. So I'm in police protection at a secret location until they catch him. I'll let you know when it's safe for me to come back to work. Got to go. Love to everyone. Bye."

Lauren disconnected the call and immediately started tapping on her phone.

"My name's all over the internet," she said. "And they're still calling it a raid."

Lauren spent the next ten minutes surfing and exclaiming 'Oh, my God.' I hadn't realised anyone could say three single-syllable words in such a variety of different ways.

Sometimes she was named as a potential suspect, sometimes she was described as a friend, usually in quotes, of the prime suspect in the dollhouse murders – the infamous Mathew Sedley. Occasionally she was mentioned as a victim.

"At least they don't have any pictures yet," said Lauren. "I bet they'll drag up that one of me dressed as a blackcurrant. From cereal girl to serial girl. I'll never live it down."

"I wouldn't worry about it," I said. "You'll be old news very soon. Finding the second dollhouse will suck the air out of all the other news stories."

"I should still ring my agent," said Lauren. "She'll have to be told in case she gets a call from a producer. Production companies can be anal about image. And I've got that big series with Channel Four next month."

Lauren called her agent, who assured her that no one had called, and that, as long as she hadn't actually killed anyone, a bit of notoriety could be beneficial for her career.

Lauren wasn't convinced.

"Things are different these days. If Susan Phillips's parents picketed Channel Four, they'd drop me like a stone."

Lauren's phone rang.

"Oh, God," said Lauren. "She's calling back. No, wait. It's Georgia."

Lauren handed me the phone.

"Hello," I said.

"Good news," said Georgia. "Your alibi is back."

~

"What? How?"

"Because Susan Phillips wasn't drowned in the sea," said Georgia. "She was drowned in your bath."

My head started to swim. I was relieved, and confused.

"What about the diatom tests?" I asked.

"That's what clinched it. They did a diatom test on the water in your bath's waste trap. It matched the water they found in Susan's stomach and lungs.

"That's ... brilliant," I said.

"I must warn you that the detective chief inspector isn't entirely convinced. He's clinging to the idea that the sea water in the trap was a result of the body having been washed in your bath. But the pathologist is adamant. The concentration's too high to be a result of washing. Couple that with all the other evidence, and it's the only logical explanation."

So, it had all been one gigantic red herring. Just to incriminate me. But how had he transported a bath full of sea water to my home? He must have filled his car with water containers. He'd need gallons. And it would be cold. How did he get Susan Phillips into a bath full of cold water? Wouldn't that wake her up? Even if she was drugged, wouldn't she come to the moment her body hit the cold water? She'd put up a fight. There'd be water everywhere, and bruising, even if her wrists and ankles had been bound she'd have lashed out.

I raised my concerns with Georgia.

"He didn't need gallons of water," she said. "Do you remember me telling you that the pathologist had a second look at the body yesterday? Well, that was after the diatom tests came back on the water in the victim's body. She wanted a second look at the lividity and see if any more bruising had appeared. Did you know that bruises that weren't initially visible can appear a day or two after death?"

I didn't.

"Anyway," said Georgia. "She found new bruising on the victim's heels, back, thighs, arms and shoulders that were consistent with her being strapped down on a hard flat surface and waterboarded."

"Waterboarded?" I said.

"Put the phone on speaker," said Lauren, grabbing for the

phone.

I wrestled the phone away from her and put the phone on speaker.

"Yes," said Georgia. "Couple that with the large number of fibres in her nose and mouth and waterboarding becomes by far the most likely cause of death. The fibres come from the towel placed over the nose and mouth apparently. No need for a large amount of water either. The pathologist thinks five litres would be sufficient. According to her, one keeps recycling the water when one's waterboarding, pouring it over the towel, collecting it in a bucket and then repeat."

"Could one person do that alone?" I asked. I couldn't see how. It sounded like the victim would have to be strapped to something the size of a door. Could one person manipulate that in a small bathroom with a struggling body strapped on top? I couldn't see it. He'd need to have the board pointing down into the bath, and he'd need at least one hand free to pour the water. And all the while the victim would be fighting for their life. You'd need two or three people.

"The pathologist consulted a colleague who knows about this sort of thing. He said the bruising indicating that heavy strapping was used is the clincher. One only needs strapping if one doesn't have anyone to help pin the victim down. But it does mean that the killer had to have a custom-built board. There are designs for these on the internet."

"There's a surprise," I said.

"Quite," said Georgia. "I looked one up. It's quite a simple design. A tilting board on a trestle. Some have wheels. One places the victim on the board, strap them in, wheel them into position, and then tilt."

"That's a lot of bulky equipment he's got to bring with him," I said. "A board the size of a door with a trestle table attached. A large dollhouse. A five-litre container of sea water. He's got to have a van or SUV."

"That was another reason for ruling out the coast as the murder scene," said Georgia. "It's difficult enough to carry a drugged woman into the sea and back again without being seen. Add a waterboard and it becomes practically impossible – even if they had a boat. Then there was the lividity. That clearly showed that the body had been kept on its back, in a flat horizontal position, in the hours after death. She couldn't have been transported in a car boot. There wouldn't be room. She'd have to have been laid out flat in the back of a van or in a trailer. Or, far more likely, on the floor of your spare bedroom."

That made far more sense than driving Susan all the way to the coast to implicate me, when it was far simpler to use a five litre container of sea water to achieve the same result.

"So he tortured her," said Lauren, her eyes unfixed, and staring into the distance. "He didn't just drown her. He waterboarded her. Over and over again."

Chapter Twenty-Two

"Susan's not just collateral damage, is she?" said Lauren after the phone call had ended. "Torture is personal. Waterboarding is personal. He wanted to hurt her even more than he wants to hurt you."

A group of people emerged from the house and started peeling off their oversuits. Both DI Lipinski and DCI Terrell were in the group. It didn't look like forensics had found anything. No one was in a rush or talking excitedly.

"They'll want to scan the car," said Lauren. "We'd better get out."

DI Lipinski walked over to us. "We're ready to start scanning now. If you'll both stand over there by the side of the garage, one of our officers will pass a small device over you. It won't take long."

DCI Terrell approached. He spoke to DI Lipinski as he walked past. "Natalia," he said. "Keep those two separate. If the search teams find anything, I don't want them conferring."

I watched Terrell leave by the gate and head towards his car. He was never going to believe I was innocent.

I waited for the DI to tell us to move further apart, but she carried on as though nothing had happened.

"If you have any phones on you," she said, "could you please turn them off and hand them to me."

"You're not going to separate us?" I asked.

"The search parties haven't found anything yet," she said.

One of the forensics team started scanning the underneath of Lauren's car while another started to scan Lauren.

"Hold your arms out straight to the side like this," he told her. "And stand with your feet two foot apart."

The scanning device looked like a television remote control. He passed it over her body like the standard security checks at airports.

Nothing flashed or beeped.

I was clean too.

"We can check your phone for trackers if you want," the officer said to Lauren. "But we'd have to take it back to the lab. If you say you took the sim card out last night, then no one could have tracked you. Have you noticed any strange apps on your phone?"

"No," said Lauren.

"What about battery problems? Unexpectedly high data usage? Strange messages or background noises? Unexpected reboots?"

"No, none of that."

"Then your phone is probably okay."

"Has *my* phone been checked yet?" I asked. "I gave it to DI Lipinski last night."

"Not yet," said the tech. "We were going to do it first thing this morning, but then all this happened. We'll try and get it done later today, but, obviously, things could change."

The car was pronounced clean as well – inside and out.

Next came the house. I followed DI Lipinski and the two forensics officers, stopping at the door, unsure if I was allowed inside. Lauren pushed past me. "You're not a vampire," she said. "You don't have to ask permission to enter a house."

"Technically," I said, "as owner of the house, I wouldn't have to ask permission anyway even if I was a vampire."

I knew my vampire lore. I'd watched enough television series over the years.

"Actually," said one of the forensics team. "If you were a vampire, our scan would have picked it up."

"Start in the lounge," said the inspector. "Mathew, could you and Lauren wait in the kitchen? I'll be with you shortly. A cup of coffee would be much appreciated."

Lauren and I went into the kitchen. It still looked like a

fortress with the Welsh dresser blocking the back door. And I had to use the filter coffee maker as the kettle was still upstairs with all the other metal pots and pans – all tied together under the windows as our primitive early warning system.

I'd barely switched on the coffee machine when the first call came from the lounge.

"We've found one," said one of the forensics team. "There's a camera in the light fitting."

~

Both Lauren and I rushed to the lounge door. Everyone was looking up at the ceiling. One of the forensics team was placing a dining chair under the ceiling light. No need for a step ladder in Laburnum Cottage. All the ceilings were low. Low enough for a tall man to reach up and touch with an extended finger.

"I want pictures and I want the light fitting and camera dusted for prints," said the DI.

One of the forensics officers left while the other climbed on the chair for a closer look at the camera. It had to be pretty small. I couldn't see anything from where I was standing.

"Was this light fitting here when you bought the place?" asked the DI.

"Yes," I said. "I didn't change any of the lights. I barely changed anything."

"Think carefully," said the DI. "Are you sure that's the same style of light fitting that was here before? Could someone have changed it – installed a similar model – in the weeks since you moved in?"

"I couldn't swear to it. It looks the same, but – it's a light fitting – I never really paid much attention to it."

The forensics officer returned with a camera and his boss. Lauren and I were ushered out of the way. I looked up at the hall ceiling light. It was a similar model to the one in the lounge. And not just that one. I was pretty sure the ceiling lights were the same in every room – an inverted, flattened glass dome about a foot in diameter mounted in a wooden surround flush with the ceiling.

They all worked, and none were caked in dust or cobwebs. That was all the attention I'd paid them.

"Inspector," I said. "The estate agent took a video of the house interior when it went on the market. That'll show the light fittings."

Not in any great detail, but it might show something. It might also show that I had the observational skills of a blind mole. The cottage furnished with a mishmash of light fittings that looked nothing like the ones I had now. But so what? Light fittings hadn't featured anywhere on my list of requirements for a new home. All I wanted was something I could afford that was habitable and had no neighbours.

The search continued from room to room. Lauren and I were told to stay in the hallway.

"We won't be long," said the inspector.

They weren't that quick either. Every ceiling light fitting had a camera – even the hallway, upstairs landing and bathroom. And every one of them had to be carefully removed, photographed, dusted and bagged.

We listened from below, hearing the steady stream of beeps from the bug detector and calls of 'It's another camera' from the forensics team.

"Tell me there wasn't really one in bathroom," said Lauren when the inspector and SOCO came down the stairs.

"Sorry," said the inspector. "Every room had one."

"Were they being streamed?" asked Lauren. "I had a shower there this morning. Is it on the internet?"

We all looked at SOCO.

"I wouldn't worry about it," he said. "Yes, the cameras are almost certainly transmitting via the internet, but I'm sure it's all encrypted so that only the killer can access the feed. Otherwise we'd know about it."

"How would you know about it?" asked Lauren, far from placated.

"Because the cameras would have shown the murder and the face of the killer. No one who stumbled on that footage would keep quiet about it. Not with all the publicity this case has aroused. And this killer's no mug. If he knows how to bug a house and configure the cameras for remote viewing then he's going to know how to encrypt everything so only he can view the content."

That made sense. A few people might keep quiet if they chanced upon a video feed from a murder house, but most wouldn't. There'd be screenshots posted everywhere. *Look at this! There's another dollhouse! Here's the url to watch.*

I wondered how long the cameras had been there. Days? Weeks? He could have used the cameras to make the interior of the dollhouse. To know when I was going to be out, where I was going to be. That's how he knew I was going to be working the other side of Bristol last Monday. He'd have had time – over a week – to plan the murder knowing the house was going to be empty.

And he could watch my reaction when I found the body.

It was a lightbulb moment. Of course there were cameras! There had to be. The killer was a sadist who liked to see people suffer. He'd want to be there when I found the dollhouse and the body. He couldn't be there in person, so he'd set up a video link. He'd get off on my panic, my fear, my 'rabbit in the headlight' running around.

"You'll have to scan Lauren's flat," I said. "And this new house when you find it. The one the second dollhouse is modelled on. The killer feeds on terrifying people. He'll need to watch the body being found, and he'll need to overhear the conversations of whoever lives there so that he'll know when they'll be out and for how long."

"How could he have bugged my flat?" said Lauren. "There wasn't time."

"He'd have known who you were on Tuesday evening. You told me your name and showed me your driving license. That would have had your address in Bristol on it." I turned to face SOCO. "Would the camera in the lounge have been able to read a driving license?"

"It's a high-resolution camera, but it would depend on how far away the license was and if it was in the field of view. That camera was set up to point at the door."

Positioned to catch my reaction when I opened the lounge door. The killer had planned leaving a dollhouse in the lounge for me to find from the very beginning – before he'd even installed the cameras.

"I walked from the lounge door to the centre of the room holding the card out in front of me," said Lauren. "A hi-res camera would have had no problem reading that."

"Were all the cameras pointing at the doors?" I asked.

"Yes," said SOCO. "Except the landing which was pointing at the top of the stairs, and the bathroom which was pointing at the bath."

"So he could have a video of the murder to watch later," I said.

"That's what we thought," said the inspector. "It'll make him easier to convict when we find him. I can't see him deleting that footage."

But first you had to catch him.

We'd thought we were being so careful. Sneaking out the back door of the cottage, running through the woods, making sure we weren't followed, hiding in a flat with no connection to me whatsoever. And all the time he'd had Lauren's name and address. He hadn't needed to follow us. He could take his time to prepare and plan.

"He could have watched your flat Wednesday morning," I said. "Waited for us go out when you took me to the police station. Broken in, planted his cameras, then went back to his car to wait for his next opportunity."

"When we went for a curry," said Lauren.

"Exactly," I said. "That gave him time to plant the notes, the clothes and the figurine."

Lauren looked confused. "Why didn't he plant the second dollhouse in the flat?" she asked. "You were there in the flat. He knew you were there. He even wrote the notes to you so he knew you were going to find anything he left there. Why wait five, six hours to plant the second dollhouse?"

"Perhaps he didn't have the dollhouse with him," said DI Lipinski.

"But this killer is such a meticulous planner," said Lauren. "He'd have planned the second murder days earlier – maybe weeks. He'd have known he had to plant the dollhouse where Mathew would find it. He'd have known time was running out. And he'd have known that the police were all over Laburnum Cottage, even planning to leave a patrol car outside there all night. So the sensible course of action is to seize the opportunity presented and plant the dollhouse in the flat."

It was the easiest option too. No need for an accomplice to distract the police guarding my front door.

"Serial killers rarely change their MO," said the inspector. "His MO is having the dollhouse found at Laburnum Cottage."

"But that's got to change, hasn't it?" said Lauren. "You're going to lock this cottage up so tight that no one will be able get near the place. He'll have to give up killing or change his MO. Won't he find it easier to change his MO than give up?"

"Perhaps he's an obsessive," I said. "Perhaps he finds it really difficult to alter his plans once he's formulated them."

"In which case," said Lauren. "He must have been really pissed when I took you off to Bristol. Up until eleven o'clock last night you weren't going to be anywhere near Laburnum Cottage this morning."

That was true. We would have been in Lauren's flat. Even after finding the figurine Laburnum Cottage wasn't seen as an option. Lauren wanted a police safe house. I thought we'd book into a hotel.

"Do you think that's why he left the clothes and the figurine?" said Lauren. "To scare us out of the flat and make us go back to Laburnum Cottage?"

I had another lightbulb moment.

"It wasn't just the clothes and the figurine," I said. "It was the note."

Chapter Twenty-Three

"I thought at the time the wording was odd," I said. "How did it go? 'See you soon, Mathew. I like your new friend. Can't wait to give her some special room service.'"

"*My* special room service," said Lauren. "It was 'my special room service.' I'm never going to forget those words."

"Exactly," I said. "And because of it, you wouldn't entertain the thought of staying in a hotel or B&B. He was manipulating us, Lauren. First, he had to remove your flat as an option for us to spend the night. Which he does with the figurine and clothes. Next, he had to make sure we didn't book into a hotel. So he writes a note – which he hasn't done before. There are no notes in the dollhouse. And the words he uses. 'Room service' to make us think of hotels. 'See you soon' and 'Can't wait' to make us think it could be tonight. And 'My special room service' to set your imagination dredging up every nightmare and horror that has ever terrified the life out of you."

No one spoke for a while, then the inspector turned to SOCO. "Can you send a team to Lauren's flat to check for recording devices?"

"Will do," said SOCO.

"I take it that's okay with you, Lauren?" said the inspector.

"More than okay," said Lauren. "Here's my keys. The smaller one's for the outside door."

~

The forensics team scanned the outside of the cottage too. The inspector wanted both doors checked.

"If he gets off on watching people squirm then he's going to want one on the front door," said the inspector. "It's important to him. He always leaves them ajar."

She was right. There was a camera in the wooden door

frame just below the lintel.

It would have given him a good view of Bob and Kofi too. He'd know they were parked outside the front door. He'd know their routine – when they left the car to check the perimeter. How long they took. He might even be able to see the other patrol car when it drove by on its hourly sweep.

He wouldn't have to observe the cottage from a nearby hiding place, risking detection every time the police patrol car drove by. He could have stayed inside in the warm watching all the camera feeds on his computer.

Forensics checked the back door too, but there was nothing there. Planting a dollhouse in the kitchen couldn't have appealed to him. Or maybe he'd didn't think I'd use the back door when coming home – which I wouldn't. The drive went to the front door. The garage door opened onto the drive. The only time I used the back door was when I was home and wanted to nip into the back garden.

Lauren buttonholed SOCO as he came back inside, reminding him he'd agreed to check the clothes she'd worn the previous night and the contents of the bag she'd brought with her from the flat, just in case the killer had slipped a tracking device into a pocket or a seem.

His team found nothing.

"Could you check Matt's things?" Lauren said after they'd finished. "Please. I just want to know we're safe. I'll make you coffee."

I ended up making coffee for everyone. It's amazing how many people can suddenly appear out of nowhere when there's a promise of a hot drink. I had to use paper cups when I ran out of cups and mugs. But I wasn't complaining. There were nearly a dozen police officers in my kitchen and none of them wanted to arrest me.

Not only that. Now that the contents of every drawer, cupboard and wardrobe had been scanned thoroughly, I was living in a bug-free house. Maybe now I was finally free of that sick, torturing bastard. The cottage was going to be a fortress – the police would make sure of that. And I wasn't going within a million miles of any house that resembled that dollhouse.

The killer was going to have to look elsewhere.

~

The house began to empty. The DI told us the cottage was no longer an active crime scene. We could move back in. There were men searching the woods and the road, and there'd be a permanent police presence on the property for at least twenty-four hours.

"We'd like to station two officers inside the house," said the DI. "If that's okay with you. They'll be firearms officers. I was thinking the kitchen would be the best place. They'd be largely out of your way, and they'd be able to see both outside doors."

I had no objection. I was open to a small tank taking up a position in the back garden.

"Okay," said the DI. "They'll be here sometime late afternoon and will stay until about seven tomorrow morning. We'll re-evaluate the situation then to see if we need to extend the cover or not."

"Will there be a patrol car by the front door as well?" said Lauren.

"Yes," said the DI. "And two more patrol cars tonight doing half-hourly sweeps of the neighbourhood. It's highly unlikely he'll risk coming back tonight, but if he does, we'll be ready for him."

"Am I still getting new locks and bolts fitted to the doors today?" I asked.

"Yes," said the DI. "We've contacted someone we use a lot. He's accredited by the national security inspectorate and by Avon and Somerset police. He'll be here midday to do the doors and install the police response panic alarms. You'll be safer than the crown jewels tonight."

"Any progress locating the original of the new dollhouse?" I asked.

"Not yet. I think there's going to be press conference

soon."

~

We had the house to ourselves. Three police cars and a police van were parked outside but, inside the house, we were on our own.

I locked both external doors. I knew locks didn't appear to stop this killer, but it made me feel better. Next we moved the Welsh dresser away from the back door, and dismantled all of Lauren's window alarms, carrying armfuls of pots and pans back to the kitchen.

Then we watched the news channels on the TV.

There was no mention of the second dollhouse, but all the channels carried the news that there had been an important development and more would be revealed in a press conference at twelve.

I looked at my watch. It was eleven twenty.

They all had news teams in Garstock too, reporting that the roads around Laburnum Cottage had been closed all morning by police roadblocks.

There was the usual speculation. A second murder? An arrest? A hostage situation? My name came up several times.

And there were a number of interviews with Susan Phillips's friends. Most followed the same line – she was a lovely girl, everyone liked her, she cared passionately about the environment, always ready to help others, quiet.

But a few painted a different picture. One female student said that Susan had become more secretive recently, more withdrawn. She told the reporter that the previous year Susan had been very sociable, joining in with everything, even going on demonstrations. When asked what kind of demos, the girl listed several – Just Stop Oil, Black Lives Matter, Extinction Rebellion, Reclaim the Night, Trans Rights, Women's Rights. If there was a march, Susan was on it. If there was a cause, Susan was campaigning for it. And it wasn't just the more left-wing causes that interested Susan. She was involved in anti-vaxxer and anti-5G groups. She even got rid of her smartphone and bought an ancient Nokia. Her friend said it was like she was searching for a spiritual home. She was trying out everything.

Then, during the summer term, something changed. Her friend said it was like she threw a switch. She got on with her work, kept her head down and walked away from any kind of confrontation. She was never rude. She never blanked anyone. She just wasn't interested in conversation any more. She spent most of her time in her room, or the library, or off campus somewhere. Her friends thought she might have a boyfriend, but they never saw her with anyone.

As the news channels started recycling clips we'd already seen, Lauren switched to the internet.

Susan Phillips was trending everywhere.

"A lot of this will be rubbish," said Lauren. "Bat-shit crazy opinions, speculation, and tearful accounts from 'best friends' who've never met Susan in their life. But you'll find good stuff here as well – unfiltered, unvarnished material that never makes it to the mainstream news. It's just a matter of recognising the difference."

If you can recognise the difference. It sounded a bit like a rabbit hole to me. A way to lose an hour or two of your day, sloshing about in other people's fantasy worlds.

I muted the television, so that Lauren could listen to the various videos and podcasts that she was finding on her phone, but I kept the TV tuned to a news channel so I wouldn't miss the press conference at twelve.

Lauren sampled scores of sites – forums, podcasts, video logs – tapping in keywords to refine her search in an attempt to home in on the ones that were the most trusted and most likely to be relevant.

It didn't always work. One tearful American influencer claimed that Susan was one of her most loyal followers. "Susan was family," she said. "We've lost one of our own. I'm setting up a fundraising page."

Another blamed her death on the 'Wokist Elite.' They didn't say why the 'Wokist Elite' had targeted Susan, but who else could it have been? The 'Wokist Elite' controlled everything from the weather to VAR.

I had to laugh. I'd long suspected that there was something suspicious about the way the video assistant referee appeared to favour the bigger teams.

But some of the sites Lauren found were very interesting – interviews with real friends and pictures and videos of Susan on demos and at parties.

It was strange to suddenly see her, to hear her talk and laugh. A real person. Not the lifeless body on a bedroom floor, or the police photofit. There she was. A vibrant fun-loving young woman.

"She's got long hair," said Lauren. "I almost didn't recognise her."

It was definitely her though. There was nothing fake about the footage. There were close ups of her face and scores of selfies with friends. She had the same hairstyle in every shot – long, wild, brown hair. A lot different to the short hair she'd had when I found her.

There was also a video of what appeared to be a wake held for Susan last night at a pub. It had been posted by a video blogger called Nastya News who was interviewing anyone who'd talk to her. The quality wasn't that good. It was dark and difficult to hear people talk above the background music.

But one of her interviews had me riveted to the screen.

She'd cornered a slightly drunk goth girl.

"Do you think Susan knew her killer?" Nastya had asked her.

"Definitely."

"What makes you so sure?"

"Because he hasn't come forward. What boyfriend doesn't come forward when his girlfriend is murdered?"

"You think she had a boyfriend? No one else mentioned one."

"She cut her hair," said the girl, swaying a little and almost losing her balance. "The day before she was killed, she cut her hair. She wouldn't do that. Not Susan. She loved her hair long. *He* must have told her to do it."

"Her boyfriend?"

"Right. Who else could make her do that? No one. He'll be one of those mind controller types. What do they call them?"

"Coercive controllers."

"That's right. He got into her mind. Then he killed her."

Lauren and I looked at each other. The killer hadn't cut Susan's hair. She'd done it herself the day before.

Chapter Twenty-Four

"It fits his profile," said Lauren. "He's a sadist. Why not a coercive controller as well? It's all about dominating someone else, making them feel worthless, breaking them."

She was right. But...

"The next victim's male," I said. "Is the killer bi-sexual?"

"Or he never meets them," said Lauren. "If he only talks to them online, he could pretend to be anyone – male, female, young, rich."

I noticed the face of the Avon and Somerset chief constable suddenly fill the television screen. I quickly turned the volume up. The press conference had started.

"A second dollhouse was found at Laburnum Cottage this morning," he said. "This dollhouse is *not* a replica of Laburnum Cottage. We need your assistance in locating where this house is. It could be anywhere in the country. We are going to show you the front and rear elevations of the house. If you recognise it, please phone us immediately. A person's life may be at risk."

Photographs of the dollhouse appeared on the large screen above the Chief Constable. The phone number to call filled the bottom strap of the screen.

"Was there a figurine inside?" shouted one of the journalists.

"I will not be fielding questions," said the Chief Constable. "But I can confirm that a figurine was found inside."

A barrage of questions erupted from the floor. *What room were they in? Was it another girl? How was she dressed? Was there a body in Laburnum Cottage? Have you arrested Mathew Sedley?*

The Chief Constable tried to quieten them down, restating that he wasn't taking any more questions, and that handouts showing the dollhouse from every angle were available from the press officer by the door.

It almost worked, but a handful of journalists persisted. *Is there a serial killer in Somerset? Is the victim another student? Will there be another one tomorrow?*

In the end he just walked off the stage.

"Do you think they'll find the house today?" asked Lauren.

"I would think so," I said. "Once the house is all over the news and internet, someone's going to recognise it. They'll be postmen, neighbours, estate agents, dog walkers, joggers. Unless the house is set way back from the road behind a high hedge, someone will have seen it."

~

"What is his fixation with these figurines?" Lauren said. "It doesn't fit with the rest of his profile."

"How so?" I asked.

"Well, he's a sadist who needs to be in control, but it looks like he's ceding control to the model figures. Why the obsession with making the victims resemble the figurines?"

"Perhaps they talk to him? Wasn't there a famous serial killer who killed because his dog told him to?"

"Do we think he hears voices? I don't see him as schizophrenic. I see him as someone far more rational than that. Someone who has no empathy, no conscience, and no boundaries."

"Maybe that's it," I said. "His lack of empathy makes him see people as puppets. And arranging his victims to look like plastic figures is some kind of statement."

"I think there's more to it than that," said Lauren. "There's something about the figurines themselves."

She plunged back into the internet, calling up the page where we found the first figurine for sale. There were pictures of other figurines on that page too. All were unpainted, but I recognised the male figure standing with his arms akimbo and the one we'd found in Lauren's flat. They were part of a set. Six male figures and six female figures. They wore different clothes, struck different poses. Some carried bags or briefcases, others were empty-handed. Nine were standing, and three were sitting

Twelve figures. Was that significant? Was that his target – to kill six men and six women? And then what? Would he stop at twelve or move on to the next set?

~

There was a knock at the front door. Even with half of the Avon and Somerset police force roaming about outside it still made me wary. I opened the door slowly and peered out. A curly-haired man with glasses, a bushy beard and a florid complexion smiled back at me.

"Afternoon," he said. "Gary Turner. I've come to fit your police response panic alarms and secure your doors. Here's my card."

He looked more like a farmer than a security expert, and had the thick West Country accent to match. I took his card and looked at it.

"Take a good look at the photo," he said. "You can't be too careful in your situation."

I had another look at the photo and checked it against his face. They matched perfectly.

"Right," said Gary. "Shall we do the doors first?"

He scrutinised the front door and the surrounds, grimacing and shaking his head as he did so. I wasn't sure if this was his usual ploy to prepare the customer for an unexpectedly high bill. Neither was I sure who was paying for the work – the police or me.

"There's a back door as well?" he asked.

"Yes. Through here."

I showed him the back door. That didn't meet his exacting standards either.

"Ideally, we'd be looking at replacing both doors with modern reinforced ones," he said when he'd finished. "But these old houses are never standard. We'd have to order custom doors, which'll take days. Best bet is to work with what we've got – upgrade the locks, put in some heavy-duty bolts. Won't be a proper job, but it'll slow the bugger down."

I took back all I'd thought about Gary Turner. He wasn't looking to gouge me after all.

"Now, where do you want these panic buttons?"

Lauren joined us and we toured the house.

"First thing you need to decide," said Gary, "is do you want these panic buttons easy to reach or hidden so you can press them without alerting the intruder?"

I looked at Lauren. "We don't want them hidden, do we?"

"No. If the killer gets in, we want to hit the button as quick as we can."

"All right," said Gary. "Now you need to work out where to put them. Most people put them close to where they spend the most time. So in a bedroom you put it on the wall where you can reach it without having to get out of bed."

That made sense. Not so much when your mattress was on the floor up against a door, but I was hopeful that that situation wasn't going to become permanent.

We went round the house choosing locations for panic buttons in the two bedrooms, the bathroom, the lounge and the kitchen.

"Course," said Gary after we'd finished the tour of the rooms, "these panic alarms ain't much good if you're on the other side of the room staring down a gun barrel, or you're out in the garden, or alone in a car park. If you really want to be safe wherever you are, you need a personal alarm. You know, like the ones they have for old folk. The ones you hang round your neck or keep in a pocket. Doesn't matter where you are, it's always within reach. Some even send an alarm automatically if it senses you've had a heavy fall – like being whacked on the back of the head from behind. The police get notified, *and* they get your GPS location."

"Doesn't that mean you can be tracked?" said Lauren

"Not if you don't want to be. Most alarms have a power saving mode to prolong battery life. The biggest drain on the battery is the GPS, so in power saving mode the GPS is switched off until needed."

"Why have the GPS on at all if you don't need it?" I asked. It sounded like a no-brainer to me to leave the GPS switched off when not required.

"Because there's a lag while the alarm connects to the GPS," said Gary. "It varies from a couple of seconds to maybe twenty seconds. That could give an assailant time to wrestle the alarm off you. So if you sense danger, I'd come out of power saving mode to give the alarm time to connect to the GPS."

We decided to get one each. You can't put a price on peace of mind. And, hopefully, this was temporary.

"Do you think you can get all this work done today?" I asked.

"No problem," he said. "I've got all I need in the van. It's going to get a bit noisy though. I've got a fair bit of drilling to do for those doors."

"That's fine with us," I said. I just wanted the work done.

Gary paused at the front door and turned back to talk to me.

"I've been doing this job a long time," he said. "Liasing with the police, advising witnesses on security. I tell you. It's not now you need to worry about. You'll be fine for the next few days. The police are going to protect you like you're one of their own. But next week, next month, when the case stalls and their attention is drawn elsewhere ... you'll be on your own. And, if I were you, I'd vary my routines, be unpredictable, and trust no one."

Chapter Twenty-Five

Gary took three hours to fit the alarms. Lauren and I spent most of that time in the lounge or the kitchen, waiting. Waiting for news, waiting for a knock on the door, waiting for Gary to finish. There was little else we could do. We couldn't leave and neither of us wanted to miss out should any news break.

It was a relief when Gary asked us to test our new panic alarms. At last we were doing something productive.

We started with the fixed panic alarms. Gary phoned the police first to warn them and stayed connected as we moved from room to room hitting buttons. They all worked and they all made one hell of a noise – enough for two police officers to come running in from outside to check on us.

We tested the personal alarms next. They looked like key fobs and came with a chain to put around your neck. Gary showed us how to use them, and how to switch off the GPS tracking by pressing the power saving button.

They were as loud as the police panic buttons.

"One hundred and thirty decibels," said Gary after I'd switched off my alarm. "To be honest, the noise from that alarm going off can be a better deterrent than the police being called out. It's instantaneous, just when you need it. Anyone within a hundred yards is going to hear that alarm and look round. And criminals don't like witnesses. You can mute the alarm, too, if you don't want to draw attention to where you are. Which is handy if you're hiding."

Gary cleaned up after himself, hoovering up all the mess created when fitting the door bolts, and left.

We weren't alone for long. Our firearms officers – Keith and Amrit – arrived just after five. They told us they'd be with us until seven the following morning when another team would take over. They had no idea what would happen after that. The situation was apparently fluid.

They wanted to see all the rooms and know where we were sleeping. I looked at Lauren, I was quite interested in knowing that too.

"What do you think of the window in the spare bedroom?" Lauren asked Keith and Amrit. "Could someone break in without you seeing?"

Amrit unlocked the spare bedroom window and looked outside. "That's the kitchen immediately below this room, isn't it?" he asked.

"Yes," I said.

"You'll be safe then. There's nothing for an intruder to climb up. The downpipe from the gutter is too far away. He'd need a ladder and we'd see that from the kitchen window.

"What about the main bedroom windows?" I asked. "They're over the lounge."

"The windows lock don't they?" said Keith.

"Yes, both of them."

"And you've got a panic alarm by the bed, a squad car out front and firearm officers in the kitchen. I'd say you were safe even if he brought a SEAL team with him."

~

With Keith and Amrit making themselves at home in the kitchen, Lauren and I returned to the lounge. We sat at either end of the sofa, Lauren surfing online, me cycling through a hundred TV channels looking for some mindless distraction that didn't have serial killers, endless adverts, or celebrities I'd never heard of.

How long did it take to identify a house? Wasn't it about this time yesterday they identified Susan Phillips?

I was just getting into a program on GPs – one of the patients had symptoms very similar to ones I get occasionally – when someone started hammering on the front door. It didn't sound like good news.

By the time I reached the hallway, Keith had already

opened the door. It was DCI Terrell.

"Where is he?" he said, pushing past Keith.

"Here," I said, raising my hand like the startled schoolboy I felt.

"We've found the house," said Terrell, far from happy and standing a good deal closer to me than I'd have liked. "And guess what? It's in bloody Garstock!"

"What?" I was shocked. I thought it would be miles away. I thought he'd moved to another locality.

"You swore to my officers you didn't recognise that dollhouse," said Terrell. "It's only over the top of the hill behind your garden. You're practically neighbours!"

"I've only lived here two months! The only houses I'd recognise are the ones I drive by on the way in and out of the village. I don't know my neighbours. I don't socialise. I didn't even know there was a road over the hill behind me."

"You've never heard of a house called Hillside?" asked Terrell.

"No."

"Have you found a body?" asked Lauren, appearing behind me.

"We're on our way there now," said Terrell. "Don't leave! And you," he said, looking at Keith. "If he does try to leave, don't be afraid to shoot him."

Terrell left, slamming the door behind him.

I looked at Keith. He did realise Terrell was joking, didn't he? Keith held my gaze, his face impassive.

"I'm … going back into the lounge," I said, swiftly closing the door behind me.

~

"They are all joking, aren't they?" I asked Lauren, keeping my voice down even though the lounge door was closed.

"Of course they are," said Lauren. "But it's police humour. There's a reason cops don't do stand-up. You see plenty of doctors and lawyers doing stand-up, but you never see a cop. Now you know why."

I slumped onto the sofa. I couldn't understand Terrell's presumption that I had to know every house in the village.

It was ridiculous. Garstock wasn't a town with houses lining every street. It was a mishmash of country lanes snaking through a rolling countryside of wooded hills, fields, and high hedges. There were clusters of houses by the church, and smaller clusters by road junctions and the larger farms. The rest was a loose collection of isolated cottages randomly dotted throughout the parish, often separated from their neighbours by hundreds of yards.

You could live a quarter of a mile, as the crow flies, from a neighbour, but face a three-mile drive if you ever wanted to visit them.

Was it any wonder I didn't know every house in the village?

It didn't take Lauren long to find Hillside on her phone. Terrell was right, we *were* practically neighbours. It was less than half a mile away. A five-minute walk, probably less, up the hill through the woods.

Had the owner discovered the body? Or was the owner the victim?

I surfed the TV news channels to see if it had made the news. The media had to know that something was happening. They'd had reporters stationed at the police roadblocks all day. They must have seen a police convoy suddenly drive by heading off to Hillside.

But none of the channels mentioned a thing. Perhaps Terrell had chosen a different route, deliberately bypassing the media encampments. It was the sort of thing he'd do. And Garstock was a warren of minor roads.

"I think you should call Georgia," said Lauren, handing me her phone.

"Why?"

"Because she's the only one likely to tell us anything. The police are only going to tell us what they want us to know. And with the investigation moving to Hillside, we're going to be sidelined, reliant on the police to protect us when we need to be able to protect ourselves."

"We are protecting ourselves. We've got a houseful of alarms."

"Which, as Gary said, is not going to be much help when we're out of the house. Even the personal alarms won't be any good if someone creeps up behind us and chloroforms us. But if we knew what the killer looked like or what car he drove we'd know what to look out for. Your neighbours could have seen him last night. The police must have interviewed them by now, but has anyone told us what they saw or heard. No, nor will they, as they work on a need-to-know basis and, for them, we don't need to know. Ever."

It was a compelling argument. We did need to know what to look out for. The police presence on the property wasn't going to last forever. Food was running low. I'd either have to go shopping soon or arrange for a delivery. Either way it would mean interacting with strangers, any of whom could be the killer. A killer who'd shown himself to be both obsessive and persistent. He wasn't going to leave me alone. All he'd need was a moment's inattention on my part and – zap – I could be tasered and bundled into a van.

But was Georgia still my lawyer? She was a duty solicitor. Her job was to help unrepresented defendants who'd been arrested or charged. That was no longer me.

Lauren disagreed.

"Mathew, five minutes ago DCI Terrell threatened to have you shot if you left your own house. That's house arrest. What do you think he's going to do if he finds anything remotely connected to you at Hillside?"

I rang Georgia.

"I think I may need a lawyer."

"What's happened?"

"You know they've identified the second house? It's in Garstock."

"Is it? I knew they'd found it, but no one was saying where. It's not a house you should have recognised, is it?"

"DCI Terrell thinks it is. But I've never seen it. It's not on a road I've ever been on. But it *is* close. A five-minute walk up the hill through the woods."

"Is it just the proximity that's the problem?"

"No, I think there's a very good chance that the police will find something linked to me at Hillside. Not because I'm guilty, but because it's what this killer does. And DCI Terrell will be looking for it. He's already told me I'm under house arrest."

"He what? He doesn't have the authority to place anyone under house arrest."

"He was probably joking, but he did tell one of the firearms officers not to be afraid to shoot me if I tried to leave."

"Unbelievable. Was anyone laughing?

"No, but I'm sure it was a joke. I'm not in fear of being shot or anything like that. I just wanted to give you a heads up that something could be found at Hillside and DCI Terrell will jump on anything that he thinks will incriminate me."

"Okay," said Georgia. "Assuming your worst fear materialises, my first piece of advice is not to wind him up. Answer his questions calmly and politely and, if in the slightest doubt about how to answer, refer him to me. Never volunteer information. It's not up to you to build their case. If you are arrested, call me immediately."

"Thank you," I said. "Another thing we were wondering about was my next-door neighbours. We heard they might have seen the killer or the car he was driving. There was a big disturbance outside their house last night. Have you heard anything about that? The police haven't told us anything."

"Was that the screaming girl diversion?"

"That's the one."

"I heard that no one was at home when Sima called this morning. Looks like the owner had left for work. She's calling round again this evening. They did find a very good boot print though in the general area where they think the killer's car was parked. Size eleven. You're not a size eleven, are you?"

"No, thank God. I'm a nine."

"Well, that's one less thing you can be accused of."

"Did anyone pick up a trace of the killer's car?" I asked. "Bob and Kofi called the incident in, and there was at least one other patrol car in the vicinity. Did anyone catch sight or sound of the killer's car?"

"No. It disappeared into the night. It didn't even leave any discernible tyre tracks on the road."

Lauren tapped me on the shoulder. "Ask about cameras in my flat. Did they find any?"

I switched the phone to speaker phone and asked Georgia.

"Hello, Lauren," said Georgia. "Yes, they did. They found one camera outside your front door, one in the lounge and one in the bedroom."

"Nothing in the bathroom?" asked Lauren.

"No."

"Have they all been removed?" asked Lauren.

"Every one of them has been tagged and bagged and sent to the lab. I'm getting one of those bug detectors myself. They're quite inexpensive and awfully simple to operate. The thought of someone watching me in my apartment makes my skin crawl."

"Talking of bugs," I said. "Did they find anything on my phone?"

"I haven't heard anything about that. Do you want me to follow up and get back to you?"

"If you could. And have they finished with my car yet? They've had it for days."

I'd almost given up hope of ever seeing my car again. The last I'd heard they were checking the tyre treads for sand. Given that the theory of Susan being murdered by the coast had long been scrapped, there was no reason for the police to keep my car.

"Haven't they returned it to you yet?" asked Georgia.

"No. You don't think they've lost it, do you?"

It was meant as a throwaway remark, but an unsettling thought came to me as I was speaking. What if they really *had* lost my car? Or, more to the point, the killer had taken it. It was the sort of thing that would appeal to him. Steal my car and use it to incriminate me. Like using it to create a diversion last night.

~

An hour or so later there was a loud banging on the front door. It had to be Terrell. I was beginning to recognise his knocks. It wasn't one of his angry 'Jack Nicholson in *The Shining*' knocks, but it was far from friendly.

I let Keith open the door. I stood by the lounge door, bracing myself.

DCI Terrell entered. This time he had a colleague with him. A detective constable if I remembered correctly. Did that mean he was about to arrest me?

"I want to see you and your girlfriend in the lounge," said Terrell.

"She's not my girlfriend."

DCI Terrell breezed past me into the lounge. I followed.

"Did you find a body?" asked Lauren, rising from the sofa.

"You know we did. I have a picture of him here. Do you recognise him, Miss Gibbons?"

Lauren scrutinised the picture for several seconds. "Never seen him before. Was he dressed like the figurine?"

She handed the phone to me. I stared at the victim's lifeless face. I didn't recognise him either. I tried to imagine him alive. I tried to imagine him smiling, or with different hair, or a beard. But there wasn't the slightest recognition. He was young, and from the little I could see, had no obvious wounds. Or foam around his nose and mouth. He'd probably been cleaned up like Susan had.

"I don't recognise him," I said. "Did he drown?"

"What shoe size are you, Mr. Sedley?" asked Terrell, looking at my feet.

"Nine," I said.

"Do you mind if DC Collins confirms that? It won't take long. He'll just take a quick look around the house checking on footwear."

"Feel free."

"I'm a size five," said Lauren.

DCI Terrell ignored her, signalling to Collins that he should begin his search.

"Your main bedroom has a window on the north wall, doesn't it?" Terrell asked me.

"Yes, it has windows to the north and south."

"Did you hear anything around four o'clock this morning – give or take an hour or two? Hillside's not that far from you."

So, they had a provisional time of death. Four o'clock. That was cutting it fine if he was breaking into Laburnum Cottage at two thirty to drop off the dollhouse. He must have had the victim bound and drugged beforehand and driven straight back to Hillside after picking up his accomplice.

"No," I said. "I didn't hear a thing. I was out like a light until seven forty-five. And we had all the windows closed."

"What about you?" Terrell asked Lauren.

"The same. I didn't hear anything."

"Does the name Onslow mean anything to you?" Terrell asked me.

"No."

"You don't recall a Derek Onslow? You might have worked with him or met him in the village."

"Sorry, I have no recollection of ever meeting anyone called Onslow."

Neither did Lauren.

"I have some more photos to show you," said Terrell. "Tell me if you recognise any of them."

We were shown photos of a smart-looking couple in their late thirties and two teenage girls. I didn't recognise any of them. Was this the family that lived at Hillside? The Onslows? And why was Terrell showing them to us? The victim, I could understand, but the family...

"Oh, my God," said Lauren. "How many bodies did you find?"

Terrell didn't answer at first. He just stared at Lauren.

"How many do you think we've found, Miss Gibbons?"

"I don't know. You're the one searching the house."

I waited for Terrell to say something. I had no idea where this line of questioning was heading. Had there been a bloodbath at Hillside? Was Terrell playing mind games?

A sudden hammering on the front door made me jump. Moments later a breathless detective sergeant opened the lounge door.

"Boss!" said Sima.

"What?" said an irritated DCI Terrell.

"I've just interviewed the next-door neighbour. The one whose house last night's disturbance was outside."

"Can't it wait? I'm in the middle of an interview."

"No, boss. It can't. You have to hear this."

Chapter Twenty-Six

Sima entered the room.

"Go on," said DCI Terrell.

"The neighbour says he was wide awake last night at two thirty," said Sima. "He was reading and had his bedroom window open. He heard the police car. He heard the sirens. But he didn't hear the girl screaming or the second car."

"What?" said DCI Terrell. "Was he sure?"

"Positive, boss. I pushed him on it. He remembers hearing the patrol car speeding towards his house. He confirmed that the patrol car put its siren on as it passed by. And he remembers hearing the siren receding into the distance for about a minute. The only other car he heard was shortly afterwards – that would have been the patrol car returning to Laburnum Cottage."

I could feel the blood draining from my face. He hadn't heard the girl screaming. The girl screaming the same words that Sophie had. The same words and screams that a year ago I'd heard but other witnesses – much closer witnesses – hadn't. It was happening again.

"How old is he?" asked Terrell. "Did you ask about his hearing?"

"He was in his forties, boss. He had no problems hearing me. His bedroom window opened onto the road."

"He might have nodded off," said Terrell. "It's easy to fall asleep reading. Especially at two thirty in the morning. The siren probably woke him up."

Terrell looked like a man desperately clinging to a failing argument.

"I don't think so," said Sima. "I pushed him on that very question. He was adamant. He often wakes up in the middle of the night and has to read for an hour or two. Last night he woke around two, spent twenty minutes trying to get back to sleep then picked up his book at two twenty. He remembers it clearly as he checked his alarm clock. He was wide awake at two thirty."

"Do you believe him?" asked Terrell. "Is he a credible witness?"

"I do believe him, boss. He's a very credible witness. He's a solicitor. He's not making this up."

Terrell looked at me. I could see confusion, anger, even a little fear. He knew what this meant.

"Get me officers Cooper and Wambua," he said. "I want them here. Now!"

"Do you really think Bob and Kofi made it all up about hearing a girl screaming?" I said.

"You can be quiet," said Terrell. "I'll bet you're loving this, aren't you?"

"Of course I'm not loving this, but I see the connection. As do you."

Terrell stood up and stabbed a finger at my face. "You will *not* drag Sophie Gallindo into this case!"

"I'm not! The killer is."

How, I had no idea. But I could see the why. He wanted to hurt people and he wanted to hurt the investigation. Reminding me of the hell I'd been put through the previous year. Reminding the police and the media that I was the hated Mathew Sedley. And, after watching the hidden camera footage of DCI Terrell's reaction to me, he'd know it would wind up the senior investigating officer.

Stick the knife in and twist – that was this killer's MO.

"Convenient for you though, isn't it?" said Terrell. "You think this is going to rehabilitate your reputation. Vindicate yourself. Make people believe you really did hear a girl screaming in the middle of the night. It won't work. I know what you're doing."

"And what are you doing? Denying inconvenient facts. You should be looking for ways the killer could play with sound. There are directional microphones. Why not directional speakers? Is there a way to block out sounds reaching specific locations with a noise cancellation device?"

"That's exactly what you and the killer want us to do, isn't it? Waste time and resources chasing noise cancellation devices."

"You could at least look!" I said. "How else can you explain Bob and Kofi hearing screams that a closer witness didn't."

"People fall asleep without knowing they've fallen asleep all the time," said Terrell. "Even solicitors."

"Bob and Kofi both said they heard tyres screeching, but there were no tyre marks on the road. How do you explain that?"

"Not by re-writing the laws of physics. Witnesses can be mistaken, and tyres can screech without leaving rubber on the road." He paused for an instant. "How do *you* know there were no tyre tracks on the road?"

Shit! I didn't want to drop Georgia in it. She was our only inside source of information. "I read it on the internet," I said, trying to sound convincing.

"Er... Excuse me," said Lauren, raising her hand. "I've just looked it up online and there is such a thing as a directional speaker. Look."

She held her phone out for people to see.

"They use them in museums," she said, "to send sound to specific locations without interfering with other sounds being broadcast to other parts of the same room at the same time."

I read the description. It wasn't just museums. They used them outside for all kinds of events. Some could be focused into a tight beam that would send the sound to a small target area whilst leaving the surrounding area free of any kind of noise pollution.

I turned away, staring into space as the full realisation hit me.

"He was there," I said. "In Rayford. He was there before Sophie went missing. Deliberately targeting me. Faking the screams. Faking the note."

"No!" shouted Terrell.

"Yes!" I said. "I heard the screams *before* Sophie went missing."

"Only according to you. You never told anyone at the time. You never said a word until *after* Sophie went missing."

"I *know* what I heard. I just haven't been able to explain how other witnesses didn't hear the screams. But now I can. It wasn't Sophie I heard. It was this serial killer using a directional speaker. He targeted me then like he's targeting me now, knowing that I'd have to come forward and accuse Sophie's father when she went missing."

"Sophie's death was an accident," said Terrell.

"Are you sure?" I said. "A serial killer who drowns his victims shows an interest in a girl who later drowns – how can that not be suspicious? You have to at least take another look at Sophie's post mortem."

"You really want us to do that? Knock on the Gallindos' door and tell them we're reopening their daughter's case? Sorry, Mrs Gallindo we know we put your family through hell last year, but Mr. Sedley now thinks your Sophie was waterboarded by a sadistic serial killer. Is that what you want?"

"Of course not."

"But it's what *he* wants," said Terrell. "Your friend. Can't you see that? He's a sadist who gets off on people's pain. Reopening the Gallindo case would be like Christmas to him. The media would be all over the Gallindos. They barely survived last year. This would open up all those old wounds and then some. Because this time they wouldn't be able to get the thought out of their heads that their daughter had spent her last minutes being tortured by a sadistic serial killer."

"Couldn't you investigate without telling the Gallindos?" I asked.

"There's nothing to investigate! *He* knows that. *You* know that. He's trying to derail the investigation and create more pain. You, you're looking for rehabilitation. That's why you're helping him, isn't it? He promised to restore your reputation."

"Why are you so blinkered?" I said. "You could be missing vital clues. If Sophie was his first victim, then isn't that when he's most likely to have slipped up? Don't serial killers get more careful with practice?"

"You are *really* pissing me off," said Terrell. "There was no evidence of foul play in Sophie's post mortem!"

"Boss," said Sima. "Directional speakers will be specialised equipment. Most of the purchasers will be companies and institutions. If we contacted the manufacturers and asked for a list of purchases in the last two years by private individuals–"

"No!" said DCI Terrell. "You don't know Sedley like I do. He sounds plausible. That's what makes him so dangerous. People believe him. Next thing you know you're digging up his neighbour's garden."

Chapter Twenty-Seven

Terrell and his team left soon after. They were wanted back at Hillside. The family that lived there still hadn't been located.

I was still reeling from the news about the directional speakers. I'd spent a year questioning my own sanity. How could I have heard Sophie screaming when people far closer hadn't? Had I imagined it? Were the neighbours lying? Was there a huge conspiracy against me? I thought I was going mad.

And then there was the missing note. It made me sound like a complete fraud. Vital evidence going missing the moment I'm asked to produce it. But it all made sense now. The killer had no problem with locks. He could have broken into my house when I was at work. He might even have installed cameras so he could see where I kept the note. In fact, he was certain to have installed cameras. He'd want to watch me fall apart, see my torment grow as the police and then the press turned on me. He'd have months of entertainment. The fall and fall of Mathew Sedley. Despised, sacked, shunned and deserted. He'd probably want a camera covering the outside too – so he could see the local kids egging my windows, the neighbours shouting abuse, the press trampling my front garden, banging on the windows, shouting idiotic questions through the letter box.

He'd have loved it. Watching the pain, watching me toss and turn every night unable to sleep, unable to even read a book – I'd just stare at the same page, reading the same paragraph over and over again, unable to comprehend, unable to concentrate, every word slipping through memory like sand though fingers.

And the nightmares. Even when I managed to sleep, I found no peace.

I'd been alone. As alone as anyone could be. No one to talk to, to confide in, to listen. Abandoned by everyone I'd ever called a friend. No family. No support.

Not even from me. I'd hated myself as much as everyone else had. I couldn't see a doctor. I didn't *deserve* to see a doctor. Instead, I bottled it all up.

I couldn't even commit suicide. I'd thought about it several times, but I'd reached a level beyond suicide. I'd reached a level of self-loathing that regarded suicide as the easy way out. I had to stay and suffer.

Perhaps that was why the killer had chosen me for this year's show? I'd provided him with so much entertainment that he had to have me back. Last year had been an audition.

Thinking about it, wasn't what he was doing to me very much like waterboarding? The continual rounds of torture – not physical pain, but psychological – keeping it at a level that terrified, but didn't kill. Threatening death, threatening incarceration for a crime I didn't commit. But not actually killing me, or having me charged. He wanted to keep me in play and off balance – not knowing what the next attack was going to be, but knowing it was coming. Just like now. He'd have left something at Hillside. Something I wasn't expecting.

~

"Why the gap of a year?" said Lauren.

"What?" I'd been miles away.

"Between murders," said Lauren. "If he killed Sophie, which I agree with you looks likely, why wait a year before killing his next victim? He only waited two days between the last two victims."

"Who says he waited a year? There could be other murders out there he's got away with."

"Someone would have noticed. It's the first thing the police do – check their computer for similar cases. A serial killer drowning his victims is going to stand out."

"Not if all the deaths are classified as accidents. Like Sophie's."

"Okay, but what about the dollhouse? That's such an integral part of his MO. When did he start leaving them at the crime scene? Sophie didn't have one, did she?"

"I never heard it mentioned. It might have been hushed up if the police didn't think it relevant or regarded it as an unnecessary complication. But even Terrell wouldn't keep that quiet once a dollhouse played such a major part in Susan's murder."

"So when did he start using dollhouses? It's such an unusual prop someone's going to notice. Even accidental deaths have inquests."

"He might have spent the year abroad."

"True. But this is a high-profile case. Foreign police forces would have heard about it and come forward."

"The killer could have been in gaol for a year. That would explain the gap. Or he had another outlet for his sadism."

Like watching me. The 24/7 reality show mess. Tune in any time to watch the reviled Mathew Sedley slowly fall apart. You could even re-watch the best bits in slow motion.

"So the killer might have experienced a trigger event that set him off on this latest killing spree?" asked Lauren.

"It's possible." Another thing that could be down to me. I'd been getting better, starting to sleep through the night, beginning to see a possible future. I'd become less entertaining to sadistic serial killers.

"What about the family that lived at Hillside?" asked Lauren. "Where are they? The killer's MO is to leave the body where someone innocent can find it. Wouldn't he have wanted the family to find the body? Do the whole 'door ajar, freaky note paper trail' routine all the way to the body in an upstairs bedroom. He wouldn't want the police to find it."

He wouldn't. It was an opportunity missed. He'd left the dollhouse for me to find, but he'd made no attempt to lure me to Hillside. Had he been planning to, but the increased police presence at Laburnum Cottage had forced him to change his plans?

Or had something else unexpected happened?

"What if the family changed their plans?" I said. "He could have chosen Hillside because he knew the family was away. But then they changed their plans and came back early. Or decided to extend their vacation. Either way it would throw him."

"If they did come back early, what's he going to do?" said Lauren. "He drugged Susan. There's no evidence that he carries a gun or a knife. Will he be able to subdue two adults and two teenagers?"

"Don't forget his accomplice with the size eleven boots. They could threaten to kill the youngest daughter and make the others tie each other up."

"And then what – they abduct them? I can't see him wanting the complication. He likes his victims drugged and tied up. Easy to manage. He doesn't want a kicking, screaming family in the back of his van – even if he does have an accomplice with him. No, I can see him drugging them and tying them up, but then he'll wipe down the house and bolt. The police would find the family the moment they entered the house."

"Which they didn't," I said. "So odds are the family are alive and well and about to get a huge shock when they get a phone call from the police."

Lauren grabbed her phone and started tapping. "What was the name of the family?" she asked. "Onslow?"

"That's right. The father was called Derek."

"Derek Onslow of Hillside, Garstock."

"What are you doing?" I said. "Don't phone him. Terrell will check his phone records, and if he sees your number in his call list, he'll assume the worst. He already thinks we're accomplices."

"I'm not phoning him. I'm searching for him. He might not be on social media, but his teenage daughters will."

It didn't take long for Lauren to have the names of the entire Onslow family. It was impressive to watch. She traced the father using his address, found the wife, Katya, via the electoral role for that address, and then found Katya's

Facebook page after scrolling through pages of various Katyas and Onslows. Katya posted a lot. She was a very sharing person, chronicling pretty much every event in her life – her daughters' birthdays, pictures of her garden through the seasons, restaurants she visited, meals she ate, and holidays.

The Onslow family had spent the last two weeks in Bodrum, Turkey. They were due home tomorrow.

"So they were never going to discover the body?" I said.

"No," said Lauren. "Either the killer thought it would take longer to identify the house or he had a different plan."

~

I was amazed that people posted details of when their house was going to be empty. Admittedly Katya hadn't posted her actual address, but she'd provided enough information for someone with a modicum of detective skills to track it down. It had taken Lauren five minutes.

I wondered what other properties in Garstock were empty. I knew there were a lot of second homes. Would the killer take the risk of staying in the village – moving from empty house to empty house?

"I think you should phone Georgia," said Lauren.

"Why?"

"She might be able to get hold of Sophie's post mortem. Terrell's not going to reopen the case. I doubt he'll even have another look at the police files. So we've got to do it."

It was worth a try. I could tell her about the directional speakers and the strong possibility that there were still cameras installed in my old house. Would the killer have bothered to take them down or would he have left them there, just in case the new owner was as entertaining as I'd been?

I phoned Georgia and told her everything.

"I doubt I'll be able to see the post mortem report," she said. "It all depends on the coroner. I believe that 'properly interested parties' can apply to see inquest reports –

including post mortems. Whether you or I are regarded as properly interested parties, though, is very much up to the coroner."

"I don't suppose you have any contacts who might be able to take the tiniest of peeks to see if there was ever a suggestion of foul play?"

"Why Mr. Sedley what *are* you suggesting?" said Georgia, sounding like a character straight out of a Jane Austen novel. "Unfortunately, my web of contacts doesn't stretch that far. Sophie Gallindo's inquest would have been conducted by the Wiltshire and Swindon Coroner. I'm more of an Avon and Bristol girl."

It didn't sound promising. The coroner at Sophie's inquest had taken a real dislike to me. If he was still in charge, he'd never view me or anyone acting on my behalf as a properly interested party.

"I do have some news though," said Georgia. "Greater Manchester and Lincolnshire police have been in touch concerning their enquiries into Susan Phillips."

"Did they find anything?"

"It's more a case of what they didn't find. They searched her room at Uni and her bedroom in Lincoln. They found no phone, no computers, no letters, and no recent photographs. Either someone had cleaned out her rooms or she had. Both her roommate and her parents said she definitely had a phone and a laptop."

"Did she have *any* personal belongings in her room in Manchester?"

"Only clothes, toiletries, and books. Nothing of note was found. The books were mainly for course work or light reading. She had a thing for fantasy novels apparently."

"Did the roommate mention anything particular that had been removed?"

"Just the phone, laptop and a small suitcase that Susan always kept locked."

"Had the roommate ever seen what was inside the suitcase?"

"No. She said Susan had become increasingly secretive and withdrawn during the summer term. Susan's parents mentioned that too. Though they thought she was being more private and guarded than secretive and withdrawn. Her mother put it down to a bad experience with a boyfriend."

"I don't suppose she ever met this boyfriend?"

"She did not. She said she'd been worried about her daughter and had tried on several occasions to talk to her, but Susan had always changed the subject. I think the mother blames herself terribly. She thinks she should have been more insistent, but as Susan never showed any outward signs of being depressed or upset, she thought it best to let her daughter work through whatever it was in her own time. Hindsight's a bugger."

"Did the mother say anything about what was taken from Susan's bedroom?"

"All her bank details. She's not sure when they were taken. Susan never said anything about it. She may have taken them with her or thrown them out. But all Susan's bank statements and every letter she'd ever received from the bank have gone."

"Did she have a lot of money in the bank?"

"Her father didn't think so. And it's silly, really. If someone was trying to hide the bank account from whomsoever might search her room, they forgot about her parents. They knew where Susan banked – Lloyds Bank in Lincoln. It was hardly a secret, and they knew her account number."

"Have the police checked her bank account?"

"They've put in a request with the manager. They should have everything by tomorrow."

Why would anyone want to hide the existence of a student's bank account? Was she involved in money laundering? Or had she paid for a meal out with her boyfriend? A payment that would have shown the restaurant, the date, and the time. If the police had that, they could check the CCTV cameras and, maybe, put a face to the killer.

~

An hour or so later there was a loud knock on the front door. It had to be Terrell. I was surprised he'd waited so long. I looked at my watch. Nine o'clock. His team had had three and a half hours at Hillside. They must have found everything the killer had planted by now.

Lauren and I stood in the lounge doorway while Keith opened the door. In walked DCI Terrell and Sima. For once Terrell didn't look angry. If anything he looked pleased with himself – which was probably worse.

"Yes?" I said, bracing myself for whatever hell the killer had cooked up for me this time.

Terrell walked right past me. "Miss Gibbons," he said. "I'd like a word."

"Me?" said Lauren, pointing at her chest.

"Yes," said Terrell. "Sima, read her her rights."

"What? What are you doing?" I asked.

"Our job," said DCI Terrell.

We all followed DCI Terrell into the lounge. I hung back, expecting to be excluded.

"Come on, Mr. Sedley," said the DCI. "Don't be shy. You'll want to hear this."

I was pretty sure I didn't. Terrell had made it perfectly clear what he thought of me only a couple of hours ago. I had no wish to watch him do the same to Lauren. I fetched one of the dining chairs and sat near the back of the group.

"Mr. Sedley," said DCI Terrell. "Didn't you find it strange that your phone rang seconds after you found the first dollhouse?"

"Me? I thought you were interviewing Lauren?" I said.

"Do you have a problem with the question, Mr. Sedley?"

"No, not at all. What was the question again?"

"Didn't you find it strange that your phone rang seconds after you found the first dollhouse?"

"I found everything about that evening strange."

"I find it strange that you stopped to pick the phone up at

all," said Terrell. "A normal person would have got the hell out and called the police. But not you. You thought it was the murderer on the phone, didn't you?"

"It crossed my mind. I've seen enough crime thrillers, but I also thought it might be the police."

"But your first thought was the murderer. It would have been mine too. You thought he was watching you. How else would he know the exact moment to call? It had to be the murderer. Or…" He paused and turned to look directly at Lauren. "His accomplice."

"That's ridiculous," said Lauren. "Matt's number was chosen by the call centre computer."

"Was it? Or did you pause the system and tap in the number the killer gave you?"

"The system doesn't work like that."

"But you do, Miss Gibbons. You're one of those serial killer groupies, aren't you? All the really notorious murderers have them. And the job our killer gave you was to get close to Mathew Sedley. But how? Sedley's a loner who never goes out, and has no online presence. So, how do you get close to him?"

"This is total bullshit," said Lauren.

"It's not bullshit, Miss Gibbons. It's a lesson in perseverance and timing. You phone him at the exact moment he's at his most vulnerable. You'd know the approximate time that Sedley would find the dollhouse. All you'd need was a signal from the killer. And the killer had cameras planted all over Laburnum Cottage, so he'd know exactly when to signal you.

"You checked my phone. I received no call."

"We checked the phone you gave us, Miss Gibbons. But how many other phones do you have? We didn't search you at the call centre. We had no idea you even existed back then. We were as surprised as Mr. Sedley here when you suddenly turned up at his house uninvited. Tell me, did he take a lot of convincing? What did you have to do to get him to leave his house and run off with you?"

"This is ridiculous," I said. "The killer spent the next day doing everything he could to get us back to Laburnum Cottage."

"Did he? Whose idea was it to go out for a curry last night, Mr. Sedley? Yours or Miss Gibbons?"

"I can't remember. I think it was a joint decision."

"Are you sure? Who vetoed the idea of staying in a hotel or B&B last night?"

"That was Lauren, but I'm the one who suggested Laburnum Cottage. Lauren was dead set against it."

"And yet she acquiesced."

"This is all conjecture," said Lauren. "You haven't come up with one piece of evidence."

"You want evidence? We have evidence."

He took out a clear plastic evidence bag with a small square piece of paper inside it and handed it to Lauren.

"Do you recognise the numbers on the notepaper?"

"The top one is Matt's landline number," she said.

"And the bottom one?"

"No idea."

"Would it surprise you to learn that it's the landline number for Hillside?"

"Nothing would surprise me."

"Really? Do you recognise the handwriting?"

"No."

"How about this?" He hands her a large photograph. "This is a photograph of that same note taken using oblique light. Oblique light highlights the indentations in the paper caused by whatever had been written on the note above. We've come a long way from pencil rubbing."

I couldn't see what was on the photograph, but Lauren looked worried. She looked at me then at the DCI.

"It's the address for an audition I went to last Saturday."

"Do you recognise the handwriting?"

"It's mine – which I can explain. Obviously this has been torn off the notepad I keep by the phone in my flat. We already know the killer broke in there. This is what he does.

Plants evidence at crime scenes to incriminate others."

"Not all evidence is planted, Miss Gibbons. Most of it is the result of sloppiness. Guess where we found it?"

"Somewhere incriminating," said Lauren. "You know the killer's MO better than I do. He'll plant it where it can do the most damage."

"You see him as a heroic figure, do you? Someone omniscient and incapable of making mistakes?"

"I see him as a high functioning sadistic killer who'd be better off dead."

"Perhaps it was you who made the mistake, Miss Gibbons. Perhaps it was you who dropped the note and didn't notice it slip under the dining room sideboard. You have been staying at Hillside, haven't you?"

"What? Of course not."

"Are you sure?"

"Positive."

"Sima, pass Miss Gibbons her underwear."

Sima took two evidence bags out of a holdall and passed them to Lauren. It looked like a bra and matching pants.

"Do you recognise them, Miss Gibbons?"

Lauren looked flustered. "They ... could be mine. They're almost certainly mine. I wore them on Monday. They would have been in my clothes basket in the flat. He must have taken them."

"You said nothing was missing from your flat."

"I didn't check my laundry basket!"

"You didn't check the bed in Hillside's main bedroom very well either. We found these items stuffed down between the headboard and the mattress. Very easy to overlook. I expect you were in a rush. When you took them off, *and* when you were packing to leave."

"Is that all you've got?" said Lauren. "Evidence that was undoubtedly stolen from a burgled flat and innuendo."

"Ah, yes. The burgled flat. That worried me at first. It seemed so incongruous. What was the killer playing at? Why the excursion to Bristol? Then it came to me. He needed to protect you. He knew there was a chance you'd left something behind at Hillside. You weren't as careful as he was. That's why he had to stage the break-in at your flat. So you could claim that any evidence we found at Hillside had been stolen from your flat. Which is exactly what you've just done."

"You really have a twisted mind, Chief Inspector," said Lauren.

"Tell me, Miss Gibbons," said DCI Terrell. "Do you feel lucky?"

Oh God, I thought. Was Terrell about to channel Clint Eastwood?

"Not at the moment," said Lauren.

"You see, there are some things you can explain away saying they were taken from your burgled flat. And there are some things you can't. Fingerprints, for one. DNA for another. How careful were you cleaning up after yourself at Hillside? Did you miss a spot? You missed your underwear. Did you forget to wash the bed sheets and the quilt cover? And let's not forget strands of hair. We've taken samples from all the waste traps. Did you wash your hair while you were there, Miss Gibbons?"

"I've never been to Hillside, and as for hair, the killer could have taken some from a hairbrush in my flat."

"Well, lets see. Sima, would you take Miss Gibbons's fingerprints and DNA? Do you have a problem with that, Miss Gibbons?"

"Do I have a choice?"

"You always have a choice, Miss Gibbons. As do we. If you refuse to let us take your fingerprints and DNA, we will arrest you, take you to Bristol, and take your fingerprints and DNA there. The choice is yours."

"Let's do it here," said Lauren.

And that was it. As soon as Sima had taken Lauren's DNA and fingerprints, the police left.

"I'm sure you two have a lot to talk about," said Terrell just before he closed the lounge door.

Chapter Twenty-Eight

We sat in silence until we heard the front door close. I wasn't sure what to say.

"I'm not who he says I am," said Lauren in a rush. "I've never been to Hillside, and it was the call centre's phone system that called you, not me."

"I know," I said. "Terrell's an expert at getting under people's skin, and the killer's an expert at planting evidence. We knew something like this was going to happen. We just thought it was going to be me being skewered, not you."

"You're not the tiniest bit suspicious? Because you should be. You're in the cross-hairs of a devious serial killer. You shouldn't trust anyone."

"I admit it *was* a bit odd you turning up at my house."

"Exactly! But that's me. You know that now. I don't do things by halves. You wouldn't pick up your phone. I knew where you lived. What's an hour's drive when a life's at stake? It's not the things you do that you regret, but the things you don't do. That's my mantra. I could save a life and, maybe, I could be *that* person. You know, the plucky amateur in the Agatha Christie novels who finds herself thrown into a puzzling mystery. I was born to play that part. Here was my chance. I couldn't walk away from that."

Her eyes had filled with tears. I knew she was an actress, but her passion seemed real to me.

"It's all right," I said. "I understand. I'm not someone who should judge others. When we first met I asked you why you didn't hate me. You said you didn't believe everything you read on the internet. I don't believe everything Terrell or serial killers tell me. So, we're good."

"Really?" she said, brushing away a tear. "You don't want me to leave?"

"Really. You can stay as long as you like."

"You realise you're still sleeping on the floor?"

"I'm getting used to it. But don't worry about Terrell's accusations. When the DNA and fingerprint evidence comes back, you'll be cleared."

~

We almost missed the Avon and Somerset police press conference. We'd been watching another channel trying to immerse ourselves in something light and amusing when I'd switched to a news channel during an advert. The first thing I saw was the strap line – Dollhouse Murders Press Conference at 9:30. It was nine twenty-seven so I left the TV on that channel.

"Do you think they'll have anything new to announce?" asked Lauren.

I couldn't see them announcing anything that would be new to us.

"It'll be a request for help identifying the second body," I said.

"As long as they don't ask for help identifying my underwear," said Lauren.

The press conference followed the same format as earlier. The Chief Constable ran the show. A couple of uniformed officers, neither of whom I recognised, sat alongside him. He announced that they had found the house in Garstock, and that a body had been found in an upstairs bedroom. The cause of death hadn't been established yet, but it was likely that he had been drowned.

The victim's picture appeared on the large screen above the Chief Constable. First, they showed just the face – the same picture that Terrell had shown us earlier. Next, they showed the clothes.

"We're not sure if these were the clothes he was wearing yesterday," said the Chief Constable. "But it is likely that they are. Do you remember seeing this young man? If you do, call us on the number at the bottom of the next screen."

The screen changed to show the victim's face and the number to call.

"The young man was killed in the early hours of today. We have no indication of when he arrived in Garstock or by what means. If you were in Garstock yesterday, we ask you to look at this man's face and clothes. Is it possible you saw him? He may have been in a car or a lorry. We also ask members of the media – if you were in Garstock yesterday, and recorded any footage, please take a look for this man."

I wondered if we might have seen him. We were driving through Garstock around midnight last night.

"Do you remember seeing any cars around Garstock when we were driving back from your flat last night?" I asked Lauren.

"No, the roads were deserted for the last couple of miles."

"I will take a small number of questions from the floor," said the Chief Constable. "If you'd raise your hand first."

One reporter was very quick, and didn't wait for an invite.

"Why did it take so long to find the house if it was in the same small village as the first murder?"

"The house was invisible from the road with no close neighbours. Next question. Yes, Stephen, isn't it?"

"Do you think the victim might be a student from Manchester?"

"We are keeping an open mind."

"Could he have arrived by taxi?"

"We are actively canvassing taxi drivers in the area."

"Are you getting any closer to finding the killer?"

"We are making significant progress. I'm sure you realise this is a very complex case. There is very little physical evidence for us to work with. Both victims have had all their ID removed, and we believe this killer is forensically aware."

"Are Mathew Sedley and Lauren Corelli suspects?"

"They are helping us with our enquiries."

Lauren almost bounced off the sofa. "Helping with our enquiries! He might as well have said suspects. It's what everyone's going to think. I can't let that stand. I'll be blacklisted."

"I thought you said your name was already all over the internet after the police raid story."

"That's different. Lazy journalism from an obscure local paper that can be easily disproved. But this one's on prime time TV in front of all the main media outlets. A chief constable, for fuck's sake, in charge of one of the highest profile murder cases *ever*. This won't go away on its own. I've got to do something.

Lauren's phone rang. Several times. Calls and texts from concerned friends and colleagues. *Are they talking about you? What's going on? Are you all right? What have you been up to?*

"Shit. Shit. Shit!" Lauren paged through the messages, replying to some, passing on others. She could barely keep up. "Why didn't he just say 'no, they aren't suspects?' He didn't have to elaborate!"

I tried to keep an eye on the press conference. It looked like it was wrapping up, but it was hard to hear with Lauren melting down next to me.

"Don't you think you're overreacting?" I said.

"Overreacting! The biggest part of my career to date starts filming next month. You don't know how lucky I was to get it. Or how easy it would be for them to recast. All it would take is for one person to have second thoughts. A producer, a director, some PR person at the production company or Channel Four. I've got to get in front of this before it's too late."

The press conference ended. I muted the sound on the TV while Lauren rang her agent. I asked her how it went, but Lauren wasn't sure.

"I think she was trying not to upset me."

Lauren paced and stewed. Occasionally she bounced ideas off me, but didn't seem to like any of my suggestions.

"You have no idea how the entertainment industry works," she told me.

She considered contacting the production company, but

what if they hadn't seen the press conference? She'd make things worse for no reason. But if she let them find out for themselves, how would they take that? Wouldn't that be far, far worse?

I tried to put things in perspective. Compared to being threatened by a serial killer, this was all pretty minor stuff.

"Pretty minor stuff!"

I held my hands up. This was not a time to offer advice. "Sorry," I said. "Do you want coffee?"

"No, I think I'll go to bed. I'll take the spare room. It's silly you sleeping on the floor when we have armed police in the kitchen and panic alarms in every room."

I watched her leave. I'd never seen her so rattled.

~

I slept reasonably well. I woke up a few times and spent an uncomfortable ten minutes or so listening intently – convinced I'd heard a sound outside or on the landing – but I soon dropped off again.

Just after seven I switched the bedside radio on to listen to the news. There was nothing about the identity of the latest body. I was surprised. I thought there would have been. Someone must have recognised him. His face would have been all over the evening news.

I heard the faint clink of cups and saucepans from the kitchen. Someone was making breakfast. I wondered if Lauren was in better spirits this morning. Knowing her, she'd have bounced back by now.

I waited another five minutes before getting up. I noticed Lauren's door was closed on my way to the bathroom. Ten minutes later it was still closed. I thought about knocking, but she was probably downstairs already, cup in hand, eyes glued to her phone.

I got dressed and ambled downstairs. I could hear the two firearms officers talking in the kitchen. I opened the lounge door and peered inside. I couldn't see Lauren. I went to the kitchen. No Lauren there either. And the firearms officers were different. Keith and Amrit had been replaced by the next shift. They introduced themselves as Aaron and Bradley.

We shook hands. I'm rubbish at shaking hands. I try to go for firm and manly, but always worry I might overdo it, and end up presenting a grip like a wet lettuce. I smiled apologetically and left. I'd knock on Lauren's door. She had to be awake by now.

I knocked. No answer. I knocked again. Still no answer.

"Lauren," I said. I tried again louder. She had to have heard me. Unless she was out like a light. She might have been up all night worrying about that press conference.

Or maybe she was in the bathroom.

I checked. She wasn't.

I went back to her room and slowly opened the door. "Lauren, are you awake?"

I peered around the door. The room was empty and the bed made. I was confused. Where was she? That's when I noticed the sheet of white A4 paper on her pillow.

Chapter Twenty-Nine

Déjà vu. I could feel my heat thumping in my chest, my mouth drying up with every step I made towards the bed. He couldn't have broken in again. There were armed police in the kitchen!

There was writing on the paper. Handwritten this time, not printed. It read:

Sorry. I had to do it. I'll explain everything later.

Was it Lauren's handwriting? I couldn't recall ever seeing anything she'd written. Terrell hadn't showed me the handwritten note he'd found at Hillside.

Could it be the killer's?

I ran to the bathroom and threw open the window. Her car was still outside the garage. The patrol car was there too.

It didn't make sense. Was she in the patrol car? Had she gone for a walk? Had the killer whisked her away without anyone noticing?

I ran to the kitchen.

"Excuse me," I said. "Have you seen Lauren? She's not in her room."

"She left about forty minutes ago."

"She left? To go where? She never said she was leaving."

Both officers shrugged. "We weren't here at the time. The night shift told us she left when we relieved them. They didn't say why?"

I went outside to talk to the officers in the patrol car. I'd hoped to find Bob and Kofi, but found a different team. They *had* seen Lauren leave though.

"She left at six fifty-two," said the officer in the passenger seat. "We thought it strange, but she wasn't under house arrest."

"Our brief was to keep people out, and be on the lookout for anything odd," said the driver. "We weren't asked to keep people in."

"Did you ask her where she was going or why?"

"She said there was somewhere she had to be. She had a rolling pin with her."

"A what?"

"A rolling pin. We thought it odd. She said it was for protection."

Could this get any weirder?

"Did she have anything else with her? A suitcase?"

"She had a small suitcase, yeah."

"And where did she go? Her car's still here."

"She got into a taxi which had just pulled up. It looked pre-arranged. A woman got out of the taxi and called to her. They seemed to know each other. I think she called her Jennie."

"Jennie was the taxi driver?"

"No, Jennie was in the back. The driver stayed in the car."

"We ran the plates," said the other policeman. "It belongs to a taxi firm in Bristol. I took a picture of both Jennie and the driver."

"Can I see?"

"Do you have a warrant card?"

"No," I said.

"No warrant card, no picture. Sorry. Them's the rules."

Oh, well. They'd told me more than they had to. I stepped back and took a long look at Lauren's car. Why hadn't she taken it? Why take a taxi? Did it mean she was coming back, or had she abandoned it?

~

I tried to phone her, but she wasn't picking up.

Had she gone off to talk to the press? Had she called a friend? What the hell was she playing at?

And that note – what did it mean? *Sorry, I had to do it.* Had to do what? Leave? Befriend me? Was her exodus sparked off by the press conference or by Terrell finding evidence against her at Hillside?

I just didn't know any more.

I made breakfast and carried it through to the lounge on a tray. I felt abandoned, lost and angry. She'd been the only person who'd treated me like a friend since Sophie's death. Had it all been an act? I didn't want to believe it. I liked her. She was fun, and clever, and supportive. How could she run off like that?

I surfed the television news. Most covered last night's press conference and repeated the Chief Constable's plea for help discovering the latest victim's identity. But no one had come forward. Or if they had the police were keeping it quiet.

I gave up on the TV and got out my laptop. I wasn't as skilled as Lauren, but I wanted to know who this Jennie was. I found Lauren's website and paged through it hoping to find a mention of someone called Jennie, hopefully with a surname attached and a clue as to what she did. But I found nothing. Lauren would have known a dozen other ways to tease the information out of the internet. But I wasn't Lauren.

I switched off the laptop and slumped back in the sofa. I stared up at the ceiling, then the walls. I contemplated changing the colour scheme. Was white too stark? Perhaps a hint of cream or beige to make it feel warmer?

I sighed, amazed at how empty a tiny cottage with a kitchen full of burly policemen could feel.

After half an hour of feeling sorry for myself, I reached for the TV remote. There had to be something engaging to watch. I cycled through the channels, sampling each for a hint of an interesting story. One that immediately caught my attention was a strap line on *Morning Everybody*, Channel Three's immensely popular morning show.

Coming Up – Dollhouse Murders Exclusive.

My first thought was that it had to be Lauren, but I couldn't see even Lauren snagging an interview on *Morning Everybody*. More likely one of their reporters had found a friend of victim number two. The appeal had gone out last night. Someone had to recognise him. A young man barely out of school. Hundreds of people would have known who he was. And a fair number of those might think that contacting the media was the clever thing to do.

Whoever it was, I had to watch.

I waited, sitting through story after story, wondering if they'd decided to drop the interview. Then, just after nine, it began.

"And now we hear from Lauren Corelli in an exclusive interview about the dollhouse murders," said the female anchor. "You will not want to miss this. Lauren's the only victim of the Dollhouse Killer who's still alive. He's marked her for death, but she's not going quietly."

I stared open-mouthed at the television. What was Lauren doing?

Chapter Thirty

The identity of the mysterious Jennie was soon solved. She was Jennie Graham, a reporter cum presenter for *Morning Everybody*. She was interviewing Lauren in their Bristol studio.

"Here's Lauren earlier today leaving Laburnum Cottage," said Jennie as footage of my house filled the screen. "Yes, *that* Laburnum Cottage. The Garstock murder house where Lauren has been forced to hide out."

Forced? I had a really bad feeling about this interview.

The footage on screen showed Lauren coming out the front door. She exchanged a few words with the officers in the patrol car, then looked towards the camera and waved a rolling pin.

I just stared at the television. What was it about that rolling pin? Presumably it was *my* rolling pin. She hadn't brought one with her.

The screen changed back to the studio. Lauren looked different. I couldn't quite put my finger on how – maybe it was the hair or the dress. I'd only ever seen her in clothes you could wear comfortably while breaking into a house.

Lauren looked nervous as the camera zoomed in on her face.

"Let's start at the beginning," said Jennie. "How did you first get involved in the dollhouse case, Lauren?"

"It was a total accident. I'm an actor who works at a call centre in between roles. I know. I'm the person who phones you up to talk about heat pumps, but I'm very polite. And a lot of my older customers really appreciate a chat. Anyway, I was cold calling when Mathew Sedley picked up the phone. He was in a complete mess. He'd just found his front door open and a dollhouse with a figurine inside lying in a pool of blood.

He was in a total panic and didn't know what to do."

"Did you tell him to call the police?"

"I did. Several times. But he was terrified they wouldn't believe him. He was adamant they'd say it was him. I thought he was being silly, but he was right. The moment they found out who he was, they arrested him – even though he was an hour's drive away at the time of the murder with hundreds of witnesses."

"I hear you were still on the phone with Mathew when he discovered the body?"

"I was, Jennie. He got it into his head that the only way he could call the police was if he actually found a body. He was terrified of calling the police out to a hoax. So he begged me to stay on the line while he checked the spare bedroom. He wanted a witness, and he wanted to know that someone was on the other end of the line in case the killer was still up there, waiting for him. He didn't want to die alone in his own house knowing it would be months before anyone would bother to check on him."

"That's terrible. How did you feel when he found the victim's body?"

"I felt sick, Jennie. I thought I was going to pass out, but I knew I had to stay strong. I had to get Mathew out of that house, but first I had to see if Susan was still alive."

"Of course."

"So I told Mathew to check for signs of life. He didn't want to. He was terrified. He thought the killer might be behind the door waiting for him to enter the room. But I persuaded him. Talked him through it. Told him to push the door back. Make sure no one was hiding. To move slowly, looking left and right. Listening. Listening for the slightest creak of a floor board or a door. And then, when he felt safe, to reach out and feel for a pulse. I'll never forget that long, long wait. Was she alive? Was she dead? And then I heard Mathew's voice. She was dead."

It may have been embellished – and I was sounding like a total wimp – but it was compulsive viewing. Lauren could certainly sell a story. Her face was so expressive.

"I then had to get Mathew out of there – fast. We didn't know if the killer was still on the premises. I had to make sure that Mathew was safe, and that he called the police the moment he was out."

"When did you next meet Mathew?"

"The next day. I'd been watching the news and reading everything about the murder. I felt invested in the case, because I'd been there at the very beginning. But... it was being reported all wrong."

"How so?"

"Everyone thought there had been *one* victim. Susan. No one had realised there'd been two."

"Who was the second victim?"

"Mathew, of course. The killer was obviously obsessed with him. He'd chosen *his* house to commit the murder in. He'd modelled the dollhouse on Laburnum Cottage – which means he must have broken into the house weeks before to get the internal layout and furnishings correct. And he didn't just *leave* the body in the house, he created a trail designed to maximise the psychological terror."

"How do you mean?"

"I mean this killer is so sick, so sadistic, that his idea of fun is to watch people suffer. You're not going to believe this, but we now know that he installed hidden cameras in both Laburnum Cottage and my flat. And not only that, he had the cameras pointing at specific locations in the rooms so he could catch our expressions when we found his ... little presents."

"Little presents?"

"Yes, I'm not sure what else to call them. He likes to start off by leaving your front door ajar. That's not frightening in itself, but it starts you thinking. Have I been broken into? Is he still inside? What am I going to find? It puts you on edge. Then he hits you with the dollhouse. Again, not frightening in itself. But this one's of your house. That's not normal. And look at the craftsmanship – someone's gone to a hell of a lot of trouble. That's no prank. Then you open it. See the perfect replica of your home – the wallpaper, the furniture … and the figurine of a young woman lying in a pool of blood in your spare bedroom. *That's* frightening. And he's watching. Back at home on his computer, feet up, watching the big screen on his wall. Replaying the scene over and over again, watching the blood drain from your face. Then you find the real body."

The camera cut back to Jennie who looked visibly shaken.

"Wow," she said. "That's terrifying."

And Lauren had made it more terrifying, the way she could make the viewer feel that they were there, seeing through her eyes. It was unnerving. As was the ease in which she could switch between light and chatty, and slow and atmospheric.

"A killer like that doesn't stop," said Lauren. "I knew it. The police knew it. But they couldn't come out and say it as they're terrified of creating a panic. So the Chief Constable, when asked by a reporter if there was a serial killer in Somerset, says 'no.' Meanwhile, Mathew Sedley is released and sent back to Laburnum Cottage without any form of police protection. I couldn't believe it. A serial killer had singled him out. Watched him for weeks. Built an incredibly detailed scale model of his house. Turned his home into a murder scene. Did the police really think this killer was going to move on? He was obsessed with Mathew. He wasn't going anywhere. So I drove down to Garstock to rescue Mathew. My plan was to take him off-grid. The killer wouldn't know about my flat in Bristol. More fool me. I never dreamed he'd have a camera in Mathew's lounge. But he did. He overheard everything. He knew where we going before we even left the house."

"I believe the killer broke into your flat in Bristol."

"He did. He didn't have time to make a dollhouse, so he improvised."

"Talk us through it. What did you find?"

"We'd gone out for a curry. Mathew and I. When we got back to the flat, the first thing I saw was my front door ajar. I knew what that meant. I couldn't believe he'd found us. We'd been so careful. The previous night I'd spent the entire drive up from Garstock looking in the rear-view mirror. No one had followed us.

"I pushed the front door open. I wasn't going to run. Even though I knew that whatever was behind that door was going to scare the crap out of me, I had to look inside. So I did.

"What did you see?"

"A sheet of A4 paper in the middle of the living room floor. I let Matt read what was written on it. I went straight for the kitchen knives."

"What was written on the paper?"

"Just four words, written in a tiny font." Lauren paused and looked straight at the camera. "She's in the bedroom."

"What did you do?"

"I called the police. Then we waited. We had no idea how long the police would take. We knew they were stretched. The Dollhouse murders were eating up their resources, and what did we have? A suspected break-in. Would we be a high priority? Would the police even believe me when I said it was linked to the Dollhouse case? So we decided to open the bedroom door."

"What did you think you'd find?"

Lauren's eyes had filled up. And she'd slowed down her speech. She really was mesmerising to watch.

"I knew it was going to be bad. I thought ... I thought it was either a body ... or the killer. I thought maybe that I was the 'she' the note referred to."

"But you still went in?"

Lauren wiped a tear from her face.

"We were two young, fit people. We had knives. I don't know about Mathew, but I'd already made up my mind. They say the biggest problem a member of the public has when confronted with a stone-cold killer is hesitation. A good person hesitates. A killer doesn't. I wasn't going to hesitate."

"Wow, you really thought you were about to fight for your life."

"I did. Luckily there was no killer or body in the bedroom.

But there was something almost as bad."

"Right. We have a picture of what you found. Can you talk us through it?"

The screen was filled by Lauren's photo of the figurine on a pile of clothes.

"This is what we found on my bed. A pile of clothes, a beige bag, another sheet of paper, and a figurine. It was me. The figurine. We had the same colour hair, and ... look at the clothes. The figurine is wearing the same clothes that are on the bed. They're not my clothes. It's not my bag. They're the clothes *he* wants me to wear. He's laid them out on my bed for me to put on."

"How did that make you feel? To see the figurine and the clothes laid out like that."

"It made me feel sick, Jennie. Violated. He'd been in my home. He'd chosen the clothes that he wanted me to wear for him. The clothes that he was going to torture and kill me in. And ... look at the note he left for me."

The screen flipped to show the close up of the A4 sheet of paper. Lauren read out the killer's message.

"See you soon, Mathew. I like your new friend. Can't wait to give her my special room service."

The screen flipped back to a horrified interviewer.

"What do you think he meant by 'special room service?'"

The camera switched back to Lauren who shrugged.

"That's what he does. He knows it's far more frightening to hint at what he might do than to spell it out. Because we're all different. We all have different fears. He knows that our imaginations will fill in the blanks. And then there's the uncertainty factor. What if we've guessed wrong? What if he's planned something even worse?"

"He really is a sadist," said Jennie.

"The worst you could imagine. He's also very clever. He was desperate to get Mathew back to Laburnum Cottage because he had his next murder planned back in Garstock. He wanted Mathew to find the new dollhouse. So he hunted us down, violated my flat to make sure we couldn't stay the night there, and used the term 'room service' in his note. He knew that, with the flat a crime scene, we'd most likely choose a hotel or B&B to spend the night. But by mentioning room service he'd planted a warning. Where do you get room service? How could I stay the night in a hotel or B&B? I'd spend the entire night wide awake listening for the killer's footsteps. So we returned to Laburnum Cottage."

"Did you consider staying with friends?"

"I couldn't take the risk, Jennie. I was being hunted by an obsessed, sadistic killer who always seemed able to find me. Can you imagine what he might have done to my friends? They say that if you really want to destroy someone you don't attack *them,* you attack the people they love. This killer knows that. He would have followed me to my friend's house and…"

Lauren paused to compose herself before continuing.

"Sorry, I can't get the images out of my head. Imagine waking up at your best friend's house and finding a note on your pillow. *She's in the bathroom. You killed her.* You'd never forgive yourself. Whatever anyone told you, you'd always know that you'd brought a killer into your best friend's home."

"Didn't Mathew have any friends?"

"No. His friends disowned him last year. He's been a recluse ever since. Hiding, alone, in his house."

I hadn't been hiding. Or a recluse. I talk to people, sometimes. I'm just wary around people – with good reason.

"So you went to the Garstock murder house."

"We did. There was nowhere else to go. The police gave us protection though. They knew our lives were in danger. They stationed a patrol car right outside the front door and arranged for another car to do a sweep of the village every hour. But it wasn't enough. They didn't know the killer like I did. They thought the presence of a police car would put him off. I knew it wouldn't. He doesn't think like that. He doesn't see two policemen on guard as a deterrent. He sees it as a challenge."

"Did you tell them your concerns?"

"I did. I begged them for another two officers to guard the back door, but they knew best. I can't really blame them. They were over-stretched and the killer had only just struck in Bristol. Was he really going to stage another attack a couple of hours later thirty miles away?"

"So, you arrive at Laburnum Cottage. You have a police car outside the front door. What do you do next?"

"I fortified the house."

"You fortified the house?"

"Yes. Mathew didn't think it was necessary. After last year he prefers to take a more passive approach and leave everything to the police. If they say it's fine, it's good enough for him."

"But not for you?" .

"No."

I wouldn't have described myself as passive. DCI Terrell certainly wouldn't. Was this all part of Lauren's strategy to big up her involvement by reducing mine?

"Top of my list was to blockade the back door. So, we slid the Welsh dresser across. And we strung lines of pots and pans under each window to give us a warning if anyone got in that way. Then I criss-crossed the stairs with trip wires. I wanted to hammer wedges underneath the front door but … Mathew didn't think we'd be able to get them out again. And there *was* a police car on the other side of the door only a few feet away."

"But it wasn't enough."

"No, it wasn't. We didn't know about the cameras then. There was I thinking I'd been clever and all the time he'd been watching. He knew where all the traps were. He knew that if he could trick the police into leaving their post, he'd only have the front door to negotiate. And he'd done that several times before. He probably had a key."

"How did he get the police to leave their post?"

"He created a diversion. I don't blame the two officers at all. I want to go on record about that. The two officers did what anyone else would have done in their position. They believed someone's life was in danger, and raced off to save them. They were only away for a minute, but that was all the killer needed to slip inside the house, to set the dollhouse up in the lounge, and to..."

Lauren paused. She looked to be having trouble holding it together. Jennie reached out and touched her hand.

"Take as much time as you need, Lauren."

Lauren sighed a couple of times and smiled nervously before continuing.

"I think ... I think I woke up around then. I remember having this premonition. A feeling that something terrible was about to happen. A feeling of being watched. A certainty that I wasn't alone. I thought I was being silly, but now I wonder if somehow I'd sensed him. He might even have been in the room. He knew where all the trip wires were. He could have made his way to my room. He could have been standing there, in the doorway, watching, imagining all the things he wanted to do to me."

Lauren's eyes stared, unfocused, into the distance. She didn't say a word. Neither did Jennie. The camera froze on Lauren's face. I think I held my breath for a good five seconds. And jumped when Lauren started speaking again, her voice slow and reflective.

"I remember sliding my hand under the pillow where I'd kept my weapons. Two kitchen knives and this." She held up the rolling pin. "My fingers curled around this rolling pin. You might not think it much of a weapon, but to me, that morning, it was a lifeline. I could feel the strength returning to my body. I may have been terrified, but fear was not going to paralyse me. I was going to fight. I lay there, like a coiled spring, listening for the slightest sound, gripping that rolling pin, waiting for the signal to jump up swinging.

"It never came. If he had been there, he'd left. But that moment taught me a valuable lesson. Waiting to be killed is not a strategy. It was time to take the initiative. Have you heard about honey badgers, Jennie?

"I've heard of them, Lauren, but I don't know much about

them."

"They're small furry animals. Friendly, peaceful, no trouble to anyone. Unless they're cornered by a much larger animal. You see, if a honey badger reaches that point where death is a certainty, they don't play dead. They don't go limp and accept their fate. They don't make one last attempt to escape. They turn, they face their would-be killer, and then they attack with everything they've got. Everything! No animal on this planet can match them for ferocity. Well, that's me now. I'm the honey badger. And this honey badger isn't running any more."

She turned to face the camera. "I know you're watching. Yes, you. You sadistic, murdering bastard. If you want me, come and get me. I'm not going anywhere. The time has come to end this once and for all. Are you man enough? Because I'm woman enough. And when I start swinging this." She paused while she held up the rolling pin. "I'm going to keep swinging until there's nothing left to swing at."

Chapter Thirty-One

I just sat there staring at the screen. She was both magnificent and deranged. Calling out a serial killer may be great TV, but it was madness. He could choose the time he attacked. Lauren would have to be watching out 24/7.

And he could go for her friends. In fact, wasn't that more likely? She'd even alluded to the possibility in her interview. As good as told him how she'd feel if she thought she caused the death of one of her friends.

I thought the interview had ended, but it hadn't. Jennie was inviting viewers to phone in and ask Lauren questions.

I hoped Lauren knew what she was doing. Her interview couldn't have gone better. She'd got her story out and then some. She should have dropped the mic and walked off set. Why risk everything with a phone-in? The public could ask anything.

The first batch of callers were all supportive of Lauren. *You're amazing. Such an inspiration. How do you manage to cope? Do you have family who could help? A boyfriend? What films have you been in?*

Lauren answered them all with ease. The camera really did love her. She came across as everyone's best friend and favourite daughter. Self-deprecating, funny, supportive, indomitable.

Then came a question about me.

"How can you live in the same house as that piece of filth Mathew Sedley?"

"I speak as I find," said Lauren. "The Mathew Sedley I know isn't anything like the monster he's portrayed as online. He's broken. I don't know everything that happened in his past, but I know he never defended himself. He's a private person. He thought if he kept quiet and avoided people then everything would go away. He didn't realise that if you don't say anything, someone else will step in and say it for you. One day, I'm sure, the real story will come out and it won't be anything like what's out there now."

"You really believe that?" sneered the caller.

"I do," said Lauren. "And, believe me, I know what it's like to encounter a real piece of filth."

"Next caller," said Jennie.

Very professional. I had thought she might mention the directional speakers, perhaps hint that there was proof that I hadn't been making things up. But that would have invited difficult questions. If I hadn't been making things up, did that mean that Sophie Gallindo's death wasn't an accident? It wouldn't take long before the Gallindos' house was besieged by the press.

The next caller, Jade, was upset. She was a student like the first victim. Maybe the second victim too. She was terrified to go out alone.

"Do you have any advice?" she asked. "Is there something else I should be doing?"

"I do have advice, Jade. For everyone. Let's start with what to look out for. This killer is a sadist who likes to watch people suffer. He chooses isolated properties so he can torture and kill without being seen or heard. First, he hides cameras in every room so he can watch you and find out when you're most likely to be out. Then he lures his victim to the house, drugs them and tortures them. So, if you live in an isolated property, get it scanned for hidden cameras. You can buy a bug detector online. They're not expensive and they're easy to use. Even I can use one.

"Next, and this applies to you Jade, if you're invited to an isolated property by someone you've barely met in person, take a friend with you. Don't go inside alone. And don't accept a drink unless you've tested it for a date rape drug. You can buy a date rape wristband for a few pounds."

"Good advice," said Jennie. "Next caller."

The next caller sounded like something out of a horror

film. They must have been using some kind of voice changer. And the delivery – it was slow and laboured. It didn't sound human.

"Hello, Lauren," they said. "Always a pleasure to see you."

Jennie looking shocked. "Take him off air. Now!"

I was stunned. Surely the production staff vet calls before allowing them on air.

"No. Let him speak," said Lauren. "Come on, you sick bastard. I've got a few questions for you. Why do you have to drug your victims first? Aren't you strong enough? Aren't you a real man?"

"Who said I was a man?"

That was a surprise.

"What are you then?" said Lauren. "A louse transitioning to human?"

"I'm someone who catches honey badgers and ties them up for later."

"Is that supposed to frighten me? You're not the Dollhouse Killer. You're a pathetic wannabe. If you're the real killer, tell me something you couldn't have read in the papers."

There was a long pause. Had he hung up?

"There are two of us," said the distorted voice. "My friend has size eleven feet."

Chapter Thirty-Two

The program went straight to a commercial break.

I sat there staring at the screen. Had the police told the press about the footprints they'd found outside my neighbour's house? I didn't think so.

And as for there being two killers...

No one had ever mentioned that. There'd been speculation about an accomplice. The use of a decoy to lure the patrol car away from the cottage had pretty much proved that, but no one had thought they might be equal partners.

I froze the TV and rewound the program to the point the 'killer' called in. I wanted to listen to his exact words.

I played it back several times. He didn't actually say there were two killers, but he didn't refer to his partner as an accomplice either. He left it open to interpretation.

Which, as Terrell would undoubtedly point out, was what this killer did. Drop hints and misdirect. Anything to waste police resources, and divert the investigation.

But had the killer made a huge mistake? Technology was always making advances. People were no longer as anonymous as they thought they were. The police might be able to trace his call or strip away the distortion from his voice.

It was about time there was a major breakthrough.

I wound the TV program forward to the end of the adverts. The interview had been terminated. The presenters in the London studio apologised for the abrupt ending and the last caller.

"We are so sorry," one said. "We don't know how that call got through. It should have been screened. But *what* an interview, what an amazing person."

The program then segued effortlessly into the next story.

I wondered if I should record the interview for Lauren. It would look good on her show reel. But then I wondered if I'd ever see her again. I really had no idea what her plans were. She'd ended her interview saying she wasn't going anywhere. Did that mean she was coming back to Laburnum Cottage, or had she decided to stay in Bristol?

I tried calling her again. She didn't pick up and she didn't call back. She could have been busy. She'd have wanted to talk to the production staff about that last call. Did they have the number he'd called from? Did he say anything else? He must have spoken to someone first – you don't patch callers through to a live interview without doing some kind of screening.

I recorded it anyway. It had been a real *tour de force.* It may not have been true, but it wasn't that far removed from the truth. It was more a re-interpretation of events – the movie version of what had had happened with a famous actress playing the part of Lauren. A more exciting version with Lauren's role pushed to the fore.

The question was though, had this been Lauren's plan all along? To use her tenuous connection to me to insert herself into the investigation. And then, when she deemed the moment right, to take her story to the media and milk it for as much as she could.

If that had been her plan, it had certainly worked. That interview was going to go viral. She'd have invitations from talk shows, casting directors, everybody.

As long as she survived the week.

That's where my theory fell down. Any plan that involved deliberately making yourself a target of a serial killer was insane. No matter how much you craved fame, it just wasn't worth it. Or was I hopelessly out of touch? Young people were always taking stupid risks in pursuit of fame. And Lauren *was* impulsive. But she wasn't stupid. She may have just called out a serial killer on live TV, but she'd already been a target. She was a calculated risk-taker.

At least, that was what I thought. But did I really know

her? She was a consummate liar *and* an actress.

I still regarded her as a friend though, despite the doubts. She could have spiced up her story this morning considerably by painting me as the evil Mathew Sedley, but she hadn't. She'd humanised me. A slightly broken, ineffectual human, but after a year of being portrayed as an evil, manipulating fantasist, that was progress. It showed what could be done. If only I had someone like Lauren to represent me. It wasn't that I couldn't speak for myself. I've always considered myself a good public speaker – albeit in a dry, factual style – but Lauren had presence. I could recount facts. Lauren could sell them.

~

It was nearly ten thirty when Lauren eventually phoned.

"Sorry," she said. "It's been chaos here. Did you see the interview?"

"I did. You were amazing."

"I know. Did you hear the phone-in afterwards?"

"Yes. Have they managed to trace the call?"

"They're trying, but they're not hopeful. What is interesting though is they have a recording of the killer's voice. The caller sounded normal when they first phoned in. She said she had a question about the figurines. Then when she was put through, she suddenly starts talking like a creature out of a horror movie."

"The caller was a she?"

"Possibly. There was something off about the way she spoke. Had that computer generated feel to me. But then it might have been a double bluff. I could do a computer generated voice. I'm sure the killer could too."

"But you think it was the killer?"

"It's exactly what he'd do. I've spent half an hour looking and I can't find any reference to the police finding a size eleven boot print outside your neighbour's house. If it wasn't the killer then they're very well informed. Anyway, I'm just about to set off, so I'll be with you in an hour. Oh, and don't worry, I've sent you and Georgia a picture of my driver just in case he murders me."

~

So, she was coming back. I was both relieved and angry. Had she any idea what she'd put me through? Finding her room empty and an A4 sheet of paper on her pillow. I thought the killer had her!

I made a cup of coffee and watched the news channels. Lauren and the 'horror' caller were prominent. Most stations were treating the call as probably genuine. The police were expressing doubts. And stonewalling any questions about shoe sizes.

Then, just after eleven, a new story broke. They had a name for the second victim. He'd been named locally as Mark Weatherly, a twenty-year old bicycle delivery driver from Southall, West London.

Information was sketchy. It was mainly coming from former school friends and some of their accounts differed. Some reports had Mark living in Hillingdon now, or Hayes. And his job varied from delivery driver to bike courier. But everyone was adamant that the young man in the picture released by the police last night was Mark Weatherly, former pupil at Queen Mary's Secondary School in Southall.

First Manchester now London. This killer certainly got around.

~

Lauren arrived at Laburnum Cottage clutching her rolling pin. She noticed me staring at it.

"It's my trademark," she said. "I can't be seen in public without it. Do you think the manufacturer would pay me to endorse it?"

I wasn't in the mood for banter.

"Do you have any idea what you put me through this morning? When I saw that white sheet of A4 on your pillow I thought the killer had taken you!"

"I'm so sorry. I was in a rush. All I could think about was

the interview and the only paper I could find was the stack by your printer. It was either that or lipstick on the mirror, which I think would have been worse."

"But why didn't you tell me what you were going to do? I thought we were a team."

"We are. I tried to talk to you last night, but you didn't get it. The entertainment industry is all about image, and I was about to have mine trashed. That's not a temporary setback. That's terminal. Something radical had to be done, and done quickly. You'd have tried to talk me out of it, and we'd have wasted time arguing when I should have been planning."

"I would have helped."

"I know you would have tried, but I'm the one who knows the media. It abhors a vacuum. It always needs feeding. And if *you* don't feed it, someone else will. So get out there quick and be interesting. People love the plucky underdog. So give them the plucky underdog on steroids. And whatever you do, don't be boring. Boring stories get forgotten. Exciting lies get believed."

"Well, for the record, you still could have told me. I might have thought you were insane, but I would have come with you."

"I'm not sure the police would have let us both go. Are they guarding us or the house? They'd probably have insisted that they followed along behind, then as soon as Terrell found out, he'd tell them to pull us over and bring us back. He'd find some pretext. 'I thought they were doing a runner' or 'I did it to protect them.' I did think this through, you know? I did nothing else *but* think this through. All night. Hours of going through every scenario. I couldn't take the risk. I had to go to the studio alone."

"You took the risk of getting into a strange car. How did you know it wasn't the killer's?"

"By insisting Jennie came along. Jennie's a well-known presenter. I'd recognise her anywhere. I pitched her the interview, explained the situation, and she was happy to come down to Garstock. The driver was someone they've been using for years. She vouched for him. It didn't stop me from taking his picture though. I sent you a copy just in case."

"The police still have my phone, Lauren. It could be days before I get it back."

"Oops. Still, all's well as they say. You will not believe how many offers I've had since the interview aired. Talk shows, news channels, podcasts. I've had to switch my phone off and pass everything to my agent. It's a shame I've got to turn so many down, but you have to be careful. It's a fine line between feeding a public need and outstaying your welcome."

"Lauren, listen to yourself. You called out a serial killer. You made yourself an even bigger target than you were before. He's going to be watching you. And if you keep climbing into the back of strange cars, he's going to notice. You know he will. He'll set a trap. One you don't see coming. He doesn't have to impersonate the driver. He could sabotage the car and wait for it to break down. He could litter the road with tyre spikes. He's cunning, resourceful, and he won't stop."

"I know. I've already considered that. I'll do it all online. That way I don't have to leave the house. Which room do you think has the best acoustics?"

"Probably the bathroom, but that won't go down well with a TV audience. Hi, I'm Lauren broadcasting from the very bathroom that poor Susan was tortured in."

"You're right. Though a good backdrop would go down well. Most people go for a bookcase, but I could have firearms officers."

"You'd have to pixelate their faces. I think it's a rule to keep them anonymous."

"They could wear those balaclava masks. I'm sure they've got them. They could lurk in the background, stripping their machine guns. It would make brilliant TV. Do you think they'd be up for it?"

"They might, Terrell wouldn't."

"True."

"Lauren?"

"Yes?"

"Why did you embellish your role in recent events, but play down mine? Couldn't we both have been heroes?"

"Not easily. I did think about it. A lot. But the problem with making you a hero is that the audience are predisposed to thinking of you as evil. You can't go from the most hated man in Swindon to national treasure in one go. People would have questioned what I was saying. And if they didn't believe what I was saying about you, then they'd start to question everything else I was saying. My goal was to humanise you first. Present you as this broken, vulnerable person. Then as soon as Terrell accepts that the killer was responsible for Sophie's murder, we go in hard with Mathew Sedley was right all along."

It sounded so credible. It was probably even true. But I had absolutely no idea how to tell.

~

Lauren went upstairs to shower and change. When she came back down, I told her about the second victim being identified. She was just about to scour the internet for more information when Terrell pounded on the outside door.

I wondered if he'd ever had the ability to knock quietly. I looked at Lauren. "Your trip to Bristol won't have gone down well."

"I'm more worried about him finding traces of me at Hillside. If the killer stopped to steal my underwear, he probably took hairs from my hairbrush as well. That could be enough to arrest me. Terrell would think so. And I wouldn't put it past him to leak news of my arrest to the media. I'd have to schedule another interview to try and rescue my reputation."

The lounge door opened. Terrell was on his own this time. Was that a good sign? He usually brought a constable with him if he was arresting anyone.

He looked smug. That was never a good sign.

"Well, well, well," he said. "Miss Gibbons. Or is it Miss Badger now?"

"Lauren will do."

"Miss Gibbons it is then. I hear you took a taxi to Bristol this morning. Refresh my memory. Wasn't it you who insisted we provide four officers on permanent guard duty at Laburnum Cottage to keep you safe? And yet you ditch your guard and climb into the back of a strange taxi. Don't you want your police guard anymore?"

"I took every precaution before climbing into that taxi. The driver had been vetted and the other passenger was a well-known TV presenter."

"A well-known TV presenter? That would certainly frighten off any serial killer."

"Anyway, it was your chief constable who forced me into this. Did you see his press conference last night? He was asked if Matt and I were suspects and, instead of saying no, he said we were helping police with their enquiries. My phone didn't stop ringing. Even my friends assumed 'helping with enquiries' was synonymous with being a suspect! My career was being destroyed. I couldn't leave that unanswered."

Terrell turned to me and said: "She's very good, isn't she? Must have put your nose out of joint, though. Your girlfriend getting all the attention. She doesn't need you now. You do realise that? You've served your purpose, Mr. Sedley."

I knew what he was doing. Trying to drive a wedge between us. Presumably in the hope that we'd turn on each other.

"She did tell you about the interview, didn't she?" continued Terrell. "I was surprised she didn't invite you along."

"You should be thanking me, Chief Inspector," said Lauren. "I flushed out the killer. Did you manage to trace the call or strip out the voice modifications?"

"I'm always suspicious of so-called killers phoning in. Ever hear of the Yorkshire Ripper? The police were so convinced the caller was the ripper they ruled out the real killer because he didn't have the caller's accent. I'm not letting that happen, besides, who was the main beneficiary of the phone call?"

"You," said Lauren.

Terrell shook his head. "My tech people tell me it's impossible to trace the call's origin. The caller knew how to hide themselves. You're a very techy person, aren't you, Miss Gibbons?"

"I'm not *that* good."

"But you are the one who benefited the most from the phone call. It was exciting. Great television. A real ratings booster. And it cemented your credibility as someone the killer pays attention to. Lauren Corelli's the real deal. That's the message the call sends."

"I was also in the studio when the phone call was made. I couldn't have been in two places at once."

"*You* could. A clever person like you. An actress used to learning lines. You could have scripted the entire conversation. Put a timer on the message and filled the gaps in with your live replies. You could make it appear seamless."

"You just do not get it," said Lauren. "If I'd really wanted headlines, I'd have told them about Sophie and the directional speakers. That would have been headlines for days."

Terrell shook his head. "No, you wouldn't. The directional speaker story would have benefited Mr. Sedley more. He'd be the one the media would want to talk to. Not you. You'd be old news."

He was very good. Blinkered, but very good.

"You also seem remarkably well-informed about this case, Miss Gibbons. How did you know the killer used a date rape drug? We've never released that."

"I told her," I said. "After you told me."

"I never told you."

"You did – as good as – when you questioned me about GHB."

"What about the size eleven feet that the caller mentioned. I watched your response several times, Miss

Gibbons. You reacted. You either knew it was important or you wanted to convey to the viewers that the foot size was something only the killer and the police would know. Either way, you knew that we'd found a boot print."

I looked at Lauren. Was she going to drop Georgia in it? Terrell would ban her from the SCU offices.

"I didn't know you'd found a boot print," said Lauren. "I just thought it likely. I'd challenged the killer to tell me something he couldn't have read in the papers and he mentions foot size. Why? If it was a red herring, he'd have been better off saying nothing. So it had to be true. Didn't it?"

A nice save. She really could think on her feet.

"Does the name Mark Weatherly mean anything to either of you?" asked Terrell.

We both shook our heads.

"Have you any links to Southall or West London?"

"No," we said in unison.

"You're quite the little team, aren't you," said Terrell. "Well-oiled. Covering for each other. Of course, it can't last. Egotists soon get bored with being a team player. Do you want to hear my latest theory?"

I didn't think we had a choice.

"Go ahead," I said.

"This case is all about misdirection," said Terrell. "We thought the accomplice staged the diversion at two thirty so the killer could slip in and plant the dollhouse. He then picks up his partner and drives away. But now we know he was at Hillside around four. Suddenly, there's no need for a car. They could have both walked there. Which got me thinking. What else could we have got wrong? What if the dollhouse wasn't planted at two thirty? What if there was another reason for staging the diversion."

"Do tell, Chief Inspector," said Lauren. "I'm all ears."

"What if the diversion was to reinforce the idea that the killer wasn't one of you?"

"You don't give up, do you?" said Lauren.

"No, I don't. You see, the need for a diversion makes you think that the killer needed a minute to gain access to the cottage via the front door. You two wouldn't need that. You're already inside. I'd thought that maybe the killer had stashed the dollhouse on the roadside for Mr. Sedley to retrieve. But now we know that the killer was hiding out in a nearby property, it opens up the possibility that the dollhouse was at Hillside."

"How does that change anything?" I asked.

"It changes everything. We know the dollhouse wasn't in Laburnum Cottage at midnight. The house had been searched that evening. The garage and grounds too. And there was no way you two could have brought it with you from Bristol. So the only way the dollhouse could have been brought to the house is via a third party. The so-called killer."

"You've lost me," said Lauren.

"I very much doubt it, Miss Gibbons. I think you see exactly where I'm going. If the dollhouse was at Hillside, then either of you two could have slipped out the back door and retrieved it. The need for a third person disappears. In fact, I think the most likely scenario is that the two of you staged the diversion, then walked to Hillside, murdered the second victim, then returned to Laburnum Cottage carrying the dollhouse."

"That's rubbish," I said. "We'd been in Bristol the whole day. When would we have had time to abduct someone and stash them at Hillside?"

"Exactly," said Lauren. "Or do you think we went cruising around Garstock in the early hours looking for dog walkers to abduct?"

"Hillside was empty for over a week," said Terrell. "A sadistic killer wouldn't balk at imprisoning someone for several days. You could have kept him drugged. It makes sense really. That way you'd have him on hand to kill when it best suited you."

"Ten out of ten for effort, Chief Inspector," said Lauren. "But really. Yesterday you accused me of being a serial killer groupie. Now I'm the serial killer. Make up your mind. Next you'll be saying I was the honey trap for the victim, enticing him away from London with the promise of a free heat pump."

"Do you think this is funny?"

"I think it's ridiculous."

Terrell left soon after. His parting shot was a warning.

"In light of today's little trip to Bristol, we'll be reviewing the need for a police presence on the premises."

"You can't be serious," said Lauren. "I challenged him to come and get me."

"I said we'd be *reviewing* the situation. We might remove officers. We might not. It depends on events, and it depends on you. If you stage another stunt like this morning, there'll be consequences."

Chapter Thirty-Three

"I suppose that was to be expected," said Lauren after we heard the front door close. "Payback for the TV interview. Behave or else."

I couldn't see Terrell removing any officers. If he really suspected us, it made more sense to have us under close surveillance. Unless the plan was to make us think they'd pulled out. To watch us from a distance and wait for us to move onto the next victim.

"You know at some stage someone is going bring up the possibility of using us as bait," I said.

"I know," said Lauren. "I'm not averse to the idea. It might be the only way to smoke out the killer."

"Would you trust the police to get to us in time, though? The killer's not stupid. He's going to expect a trap. He'll observe from a distance, look for weaknesses, and probably throw in some kind of diversion to pull the police away from where they should be."

"It would help if we knew more about the killer. What's his weakness? Is he vain? Can we goad him into taking one risk too many? He reacted very quickly to my TV interview. Which makes me think that's the way to get to him."

"You didn't answer the question," I said. "Would you trust the police not to be outwitted by the killer?"

"I wouldn't. But I don't think we should regard this killer as infallible either. We just need to lure him in and make sure we have a plan B and a plan C."

"You'd really do it?"

"I think it might be the only way. Some of these serial killer investigations go on for years. Especially the ones where the killer chooses the victims at random. If Susan and Mark didn't know each other then this is looking like one of those. Do you want to spend the next two or three years waiting to be killed? I don't."

~

Information about the second victim increased rapidly from midday onwards. All the networks had reporters in the area, and every lead was being run down and checked. There was still some confusion about his job. Some witnesses were adamant he was working as a bike delivery man, but others said he'd changed jobs the previous month and was working as a car mechanic for a garage in Hillingdon.

Everyone agreed about his family though. Mark's childhood hadn't been an easy one. His dad had never been on the scene, and his mum had a drinking problem. He'd had a succession of stepfathers, none lasting more than a year and, when one of them had taken a strong dislike to him, he'd been kicked out of the family home. Sixteen years old and homeless. Initially, his uncle took him in, but that didn't last. They fell out when Mark got in with the wrong crowd. No one was quite sure where he went after that. Some thought he was living with his new friends. Others thought he was at a hostel.

No one really wanted to go into detail about what Mark got up to with this 'wrong crowd' either. Which wasn't a surprise. Who wants to speak ill of the recently dead on national TV? The boy had only just died. Feelings would be raw.

So a consensus formed that Mark was a likeable lad from a broken home who'd fallen in with a bad crowd, but then had moved away and turned his life around.

Away from the mainstream media the story was different.

"He was a racist thug," asserted Chandan Patel on an alternative news site. "He and his friends terrorised my aunt and uncle. Going into their shop telling them to go back to India. Spraying racist graffiti all over the shop front."

Tamara Okonkwo held a similar opinion. "He was a fascist. You'd see him at all the counter demonstrations, taunting and yelling at anyone remotely left wing or black."

He was a football hooligan according to another source who didn't want to disclose his name: "One of the Chelsea mob. A bunch of white supremacist homophobes."

A longer interview on another independent channel expanded on Mark's activities.

"He always seemed to have money," said a man who appeared on screen in silhouette. "He was never short of cash. I know bike couriers can make good money, but ... Mark was never that good at anything. I couldn't see him making that kind of money legally."

"You think he was involved in criminal activities?" asked the reporter.

"Don't get me wrong. Mark wasn't a bad guy. He was just easily led. And the crew he was running with were hardcore. Not just football violence, but all the right-wing stuff too – English Defence League, Football Lad's Alliance, Britain First. And there were rumours. They always had money, and most of them worked as bouncers or bike couriers. if you were supplying drugs to dealers or making sure dealers had access to the big pubs and clubs, they'd be handy jobs to have."

Lauren tried to find Mark on social media, but gave up after half an hour. She couldn't even find anyone who called themselves a close friend.

She tried some more alternate news sites and various local forums and groups. It looked like Mark hadn't had a close friend since he left school. He had plenty of acquaintances. He was a regular at several pubs. But he was always on the periphery. A follower.

"How did he get out of this gang he was in?" I asked. "*Did* he get out?"

Lauren tried to find out. I was amazed how fast she could read. I'd barely get halfway down a page before she'd moved onto the next screen. Plenty of people agreed that Mark had moved to another borough and cut all ties with his former friends, but there were no details as to why he'd moved or how his departure had been received. Perhaps I'd watched too much American TV, but I'd thought gangs took a dim view of people leaving.

"This is interesting," said Lauren.

"What?"

She pointed to a paragraph half way down the screen. "It's an exchange on a local bulletin board between two people who knew Mark."

I started reading.

"I disagree," said Frankie97. "Mark totally turned his life around. He stopped all that nonsense two years ago."

"No, he didn't," said TerminallyPoor. "Not all of it. He stopped the racist shit, but he was heavily involved in those other fringe movements. He used to hand out leaflets Saturday mornings at the Hayes Shopping Park."

"What leaflets?"

"Anti-vaxxer, anti 5G. He was a real believer. You couldn't walk past him without getting a leaflet shoved in your face."

We both looked at each other. Susan was heavily into the anti-vaxxer and anti-5G movements. Was this the link?

~

"I'll phone Natalia," said Lauren. "The police need to know this."

"Who's Natalia?" I asked.

"DI Lipinski. We got talking this morning at the studio. Jennie knows her from the Clifton murder. You know, the nurse who was abducted in the car park?"

I vaguely remembered the case. I was more intrigued by Lauren being on first name terms with DI Lipinski.

"She gave you her number?"

"I'm an important source. And she's the only senior SCU officer who actually listens to us."

I watched while Lauren phoned. I half-expected DI Lipinski not to pick up, or to end the call while Lauren was in mid-sentence. But she didn't. From the bits I could hear, it all sounded very congenial. Lauren told her what she'd found, and gave her the address of the bulletin board conversation.

"She's going to look into it," said Lauren when the call ended. "It's the first link between Susan and Mark they've found."

Lauren continued tapping and swiping at her phone. "I've got a ton of messages. Oh, there's one here from Georgia. It might be for you."

She put the phone on speaker and called Georgia.

Georgia answered on the eighth ring.

"Hello, Lauren," she said. "Why did you send me a picture of a strange man?"

"Didn't I say? Oh, sorry, he was my driver. I thought it best to send a picture to you and Mathew in case I got murdered."

There was a slight pause.

"You do lead an exciting life," said Georgia. "Congrats on the interview, by the way, I haven't seen all of it, but the excerpts I've seen were excellent. Watch out for Detective Chief Inspector Terrell though. He really *does* want to murder you."

"Too late. He's already been here. He accused me of being the serial killer. Are you available for hire, or would I have to be arrested first?"

"I do have private clients, but my law firm insists I charge considerably more. The economic option is to be arrested first."

"I'll bear that in mind. Have you heard any more about Susan's bank account? Yesterday you thought the police would have access to it today."

"They're going through it now. Lots of online payments. It's going to take a while though, as most of the payments are to the big multinational online retailers. They don't tell the bank what's been bought. They just mention the date and the amount. Warrants have been issued, though. It will be next week before access will be granted, but when it is, the police will have complete access to Susan's online accounts, including purchase history *and* delivery addresses. Let's hope she had a birthday present delivered direct to her boyfriend."

"Was there a lot of money in her account?" I asked.

"Hello, Mathew," said Georgia. "No one mentioned an unusual sum of money. I haven't actually seen the bank statements of course. I just happen to hear things."

"You'll soon hear that we've found a link between Susan and Mark," said Lauren.

"Have you?" said Georgia. "Do tell."

"They were both in the anti-vaxxer and anti-5G movements."

"Really? How odd. Aren't they the ones that think 5G masts cause Covid and the Covid vaccination injects microchips into everyone's brains?"

"That's them," said Lauren.

"I have some odd news too," said Georgia. "But first the good news. Mathew, I've arranged for the police to deliver your car this afternoon. Your phone too. They found no indication that it had ever been cloned."

"Well, that *is* good news," I said. "They're actually going to deliver the car here? I don't have to pick it up from anywhere?"

"No, I was most insistent. They've had both items far too long. It was the least they could do."

"What's the odd news?" asked Lauren.

"Have you heard of the Sherlock Holmes short story, 'The Adventure of the Solitary Cyclist?' The one where a young woman is followed by this strange cyclist with a long, black beard?"

"Yes, I've heard of it," said Lauren. "Why?"

"He was seen in Garstock at nine forty-five on Wednesday evening. One of the journalists caught him on their dashcam. I've seen the footage. It looks like Mark Weatherly cycled to Garstock wearing a long, black beard."

Chapter Thirty-Four

It took a while for me to process. A long, black beard? Why?

"Like fancy dress?" asked Lauren. "A false beard?"

"That's what the police think. They're convinced it's him. There's a particularly good shot of his face when he turns to look at the car."

Fancy dress again. We'd speculated that Susan might have been lured to Laburnum Cottage to attend a fancy dress party. It made sense. How else could she have been persuaded to wear the exact clothes the killer wanted? It wasn't as though the clothes were anything special. But Mark's figurine didn't have a beard. There was no reason for him to wear one.

"Was he wearing the clothes he was found in?" asked Lauren.

"No, he was dressed in jeans and a long jacket."

"They don't think he cycled all the way from London, do they?" I asked.

"No," said Georgia. "They're collecting CCTV footage from all the local train stations."

That made sense. Susan had come by train. You could transport a bike on a train, too.

"Was it Mark's bike?" I asked.

"They don't know. They haven't found his last address yet. It appears that Mr. Weatherly did not like staying in the same place for too long."

~

Why on earth would Mark wear a false beard? It must have been dark at nine forty-five. None of the roads near Garstock had street lights.

But they *were* crawling with police and journalists.

It still seemed odd.

Lauren switched on the TV and started surfing through the news channels.

"If a journalist has footage of Mark, it's not going to be long before all the channels have it."

She handed me the television remote while she surfed the internet on her phone.

It didn't take long before she found it. The footage was only eight seconds long, but Mark's face was clear. It did look like him. I couldn't quite place the stretch of road the car had been driving down. One twisty country lane flanked by hedges looks very much like all the others. There weren't any buildings in the footage or helpful road signs that could be used to identify the location. And it was dark.

Lauren was not so easily defeated. She went to a mapping site where she could toggle between a standard road map and a street view. She used the latter to simulate driving through Garstock, looking for a section of road that had the same topography as the journalist's footage.

It took a while. For such a small village Garstock had a large number of twisty country lanes. But she found it. The road the cyclist was heading down led directly to Hillside.

He would have arrived around nine fifty. We knew the killer had been in Bristol that evening. He'd planted the figurine in Lauren's flat sometime between eight and ten. If he'd broken in during the first half hour, he'd have had plenty of time to lay out the clothes and notes, *and* drive back to Garstock in time to meet Mark at Hillside.

"He's got a bag on the back of his bike," said Lauren.

She tried to freeze the picture for a better look, but it made it worse. The dashcam footage was not high resolution. But you could definitely make out some kind of sports bag on the bike's rear luggage rack.

So, both he and Susan arrived in Garstock carrying luggage. Were they expecting to stay for several days? That's what it looked like. And you don't do that unless you know the person who invited you.

~

"At least that destroys Terrell's theory of us keeping Mark drugged and imprisoned at Hillside for several days," said Lauren.

"It won't stop him suspecting us," I said. "He'll say we arranged to meet Mark later that night. That we left Hillside unlocked or we told him we'd left the key under the mat. Terrell isn't going to stop suspecting us until he catches the killer in the act."

Lauren checked her messages again.

"I've got to take this," she said. "It's my agent. I'll be a while. We've got to work through all these offers and finalise a strategy."

I left Lauren to it. I had a garage to clean up. My car could arrive any minute and the only place left to park it was in the garage the police had wrecked the previous evening.

I grabbed a coat. I hadn't been outside the house since breakfast. The press contingent had certainly increased. They shouted the predictable questions at me. *Have you found any more dollhouses? Are you under house arrest? Are you expecting another visit from the serial killer? Have you anything to say?*

There were also a few shouts I hadn't expected. *How's Lauren? Is Lauren inside? Can Lauren come and speak to us? We love you, Honey Badger!*

I kept quiet and stared ahead. I could see I was going to have to tidy the garage with the door shut. If I didn't I was going to have the nation's press filming everything while desperately looking for anything incriminating. *Mathew Sedley has woodworking tools that could be used to build dollhouses!*

I opened the garage door to the accompaniment of a dozen camera shutters. Then slipped under as soon as I could, closing the door behind me. It was dark. The only light came from a line of small, dirty windows along one side. I switched the single light bulb on. There was a slight improvement.

The police had certainly made a mess. Their idea of searching was to empty every box and drawer onto the floor. And then to remove every tool from its hook on the wall and strew those over the floor too. It took ages to clear up.

I debated whether to take the cricket bat I'd just found and wave it at the crowd outside. It worked for Lauren. I could call it my Big Basher.

Reality didn't take long to knock that idea on the head.

The press would have crucified me. *Out of control Sedley threatens bystanders! Sedley loses it! Media threatened with cricket bat!*

I hurried back to the house, avoiding all eye contact.

Lauren must have finished her call. I found her lounging on the sofa watching TV.

"Have you looked outside recently?" I asked.

"No. Why?"

"Take a look. A crowd's gathering. I think your fan club has arrived."

"Really?"

Lauren picked up her rolling pin and went outside. I watched from the front door. The shouting erupted the moment they saw her – far louder than the shouts that had greeted me. I think someone actually screamed.

"Are you here for me?" gushed Lauren, slipping into her Honey Badger persona. I really should have taken notes. She spent the next fifteen minutes out on the road chatting with her fans, making sure they took priority, telling the media not to worry, she'd talk to each of them in turn, but not quite yet. She wanted to thank all her fans first and hear their stories.

She absolutely nailed it. She came across as genuine and caring. No airs, no swagger. She was the ordinary person thrown into unimaginable danger. And when she talked to someone, she treated them as though they were the celebrity. She listened to all their stories of why they'd felt compelled to come and support her. She laughed with them. She cried with them. I watched on in awe.

Then I became concerned. Several of the fans started

talking about forming a human shield to protect Lauren.

"I'm sure we can get the numbers," said one of the superfans. "If the media puts the word out, we can get thousands here tonight. We'll surround the murder house. That'll keep the killer out."

I looked at the two police officers in the patrol car. They were watching this too. I imagined they had a similar thought to mine. Several thousand people gathered together on the lookout for a serial killer was a potential disaster. Someone could get hurt. Badly. All it would take was one loudmouth pointing the finger at someone he thought looked like a serial killer, and suddenly you have a mob of vigilantes.

And the real killer was a clever opportunist. He could manipulate the crowd. He had directional speakers. He could make the crowd think that a young girl was being attacked outside my neighbour's house. Or even *inside* my neighbour's house. The police wouldn't be able to stop a crowd who'd heard that. They'd be forced to leave Laburnum Cottage to protect my neighbour from being dragged out by the mob.

Lauren and I would probably be okay. We'd still have the firearms officers and the bolted doors, but, in the dark and the confusion, the killer might be able to abduct someone. An urgent request for assistance. *Help! Someone's hurt. Quick! She's behind here. Give me a hand.* Then, when their back's turned, out comes the chloroform.

Maybe I was too much of a pessimist, but, after the year I'd had, I felt entitled to be one.

Thankfully, Lauren, wasn't in favour of the human shield either.

"I'm so touched," she said, clutching her heart. "But this killer is the nastiest piece of work you could ever imagine. He's crazy, and he's vindictive. You do *not* want to get on this crazy man's radar. Which could easily happen if he sees you in a human chain protecting me. Leave this fight to me. Please. I'm already on his radar. There's no going back for me. I'm in a fight for my life. And I'm not backing down."

Cue the cheering and applause. She really was good. The

cheering morphed into chanting – Lauren! Lauren! Lauren! – which went on for a good minute. I looked at the media contingent. They were recording everything. This was going to be all over the news. Again. How was the killer going to react? He'd phoned the *Morning Everybody* show within minutes of the last interview ending. What would he do this time? He was theatrical – like Lauren. Would he feel upstaged? Would he feel compelled to outdo her?

I looked again at the media contingent. There were about twenty of them. Were they all who they purported to be? Anyone could hold up a camera phone and stand with a group of reporters. Was the killer amongst them? Hiding in plain sight?

The chanting died down and the media interviews began. Should I do something? Lauren could be about to be attacked. Not an obvious attack. Even the killer wouldn't assault someone surrounded by witnesses and the police. But there were lethal substances that could be administered through the skin and not take effect until hours later. Delayed killers like strychnine, cyanide, thallium, and loads of others. It would take the slightest of touches. Shaking hands, giving Lauren an object to hold – a present or a microphone – something innocuous. The killer would have to be careful. It would be equally fatal if it touched his bare skin. But he could wear gloves, or make sure he held the object away from the doctored area.

I walked over to the fence for a closer look at the reporters. I couldn't see anyone wearing gloves. It was a late September afternoon. It wasn't cold. No one needed to wear gloves.

Several had hand held microphones. They all held them normally. But their hands didn't cover the entire microphone.

I hovered by the fence, almost in touching distance of the reporters, peering into the crowd for anything remotely suspicious. I didn't want to ruin Lauren's big moment, but maybe I should stop the interviews? People were very close to her. Not just the press, but her fans too. There was some pushing and jostling as people tried to get that ideal position.

Soon it would be too late. If something happened, and I could've prevented it...

I had to *do* something!

"Thallium! Thallium!" I shouted, waving my arms.

Everyone stopped and looked at me.

"We've ... had a thallium threat," I said, desperately trying to think of something to say. "A threat to kill Lauren with thallium administered by touching her bare skin. Would everyone please stand away from Lauren."

People began to shuffle backwards, looking confused and worried. I heard both police car doors open behind me.

"What thallium threat?" asked the first policeman.

Good question. This should have been the moment a clever idea presented itself. I looked at Lauren. She'd have clever ideas to spare. My best one was to hit the ground and feign losing consciousness.

Why had I said we'd received a threat? The police will want to see it. They'd regard it as a potential lead they could trace back to the killer. But there was nothing to give them – no phone call, no email, no letter. I couldn't invent a phone call as there wouldn't be a matching entry in my phone records. The same for emails. And as for letters – as DCI Terrell was always reminding me, I was the man who 'lost' the vital letter from Sophie. No one would believe me. I'd be caught in a stupid lie on national TV.

"You mean the one on that website you showed me earlier?" said Lauren.

"Yes!" I shouted, snatching at the straw. "That one. Sorry, everyone. We're under extreme pressure. And suddenly I remembered that threat to get Lauren to touch something which had been treated with thallium. It's a delayed action poison. She wouldn't show any symptoms until it's too late. Her killer would be long gone and she'd be dead. Sorry, I didn't mean to startle anyone. Could you please just give Lauren a bit more room?"

I was about to flee inside when I noticed my car coming

down the road. I hurried over to the gate, keeping my head down. Lauren, meanwhile, addressed the crowd.

"I'm sure you can all appreciate the stress we're both under. We're up against a serial killer who thinks outside the box. He's not going to use brute force against us. He's going to trick and scheme. Which means we have to be prepared for anything and everything. Sometimes paranoia is just common sense."

I wasn't sure if she'd just labelled me paranoid, but I didn't care. I'd got my warning across. It hadn't been elegant, but it had worked.

After retrieving my phone and overseeing the garaging of my car, I hurried back inside the cottage. In future, I'd leave the media and the general public to Lauren.

~

"Good catch regarding thallium," said Lauren, when she eventually came back in. "I hadn't considered the possibility, but, you're right, it's a credible threat."

"You don't think I went over the top?"

"My old drama teacher would have said so. 'Thallium! Thallium' was a bit reminiscent of 'The Bells! The Bells!' And you had Quasimodo absolutely nailed."

At least I could laugh.

"Did you finalise your itinerary with your agent?"

"I did. I'm going to do a daily video blog. Not sure what to call it yet. It's either *Life in the Cross Hairs* or *Honey Badger's Murder House*. You can be in it. Later."

Much later, I thought. I wasn't the kind of person the camera loved. I came across as too wooden. I don't know why. I didn't think I was particularly wooden in real life, but put me in front of a camera and I'd tense up.

"I'll be doing one big interview every day as well. I've had enough offers to do ten a day, but it's important I don't become overexposed. So, we're just doing the prestige programmes. And varying them so I don't do just one channel or demographic."

She had it all worked out.

"You're going to be busy," I said.

"I'm going to be crazy busy."

Lauren took over the dining table. And my laptop. I watched TV, turning the volume down as low as I could so as not to disturb her. Hours passed. I felt as though I was in limbo. Everyone else was beavering away on the case or their PR while I was waiting for other people to report back.

I thought about cooking dinner. I was a pretty good cook. A year spent under virtual house arrest, terrified of being seen in public, had given me a lot of time to practice.

But that would mean spending an hour or more in the kitchen. Which would mean I'd either have to attempt small talk with the firearms officers or try to ignore them. Neither appealed.

I didn't use to be so anti-social. I'd always been a bit shy around strangers, but I'd grown out of it. Mostly. I'd been a confident, well-balanced individual who enjoyed having friends round. Until the killer took away that Mathew Sedley and replaced him with a frightened husk.

Perhaps therapy was the answer? I'd shied away from it earlier as I didn't think I deserved help. But now I knew that I hadn't been making things up about Sophie, maybe I could start. I'd have to vet the therapist first. Which would make for an interesting first session. *Excuse me, doctor, do you mind if I take a photo of you first? I need to send it to my solicitor in case you're a serial killer.*

In the end I decided on a simple dinner. Pizza from the freezer. Tasty, with the minimum of social interaction.

At seven fifty-five, my phone rang. It was Georgia.

"Heads up," she said. "There's about to be a major announcement."

"What have they found?" I asked.

"No one's saying, but I think it has something to do with the train CCTV. They've called a press conference with only fifteen minutes notice. Something's afoot."

Chapter Thirty-Five

I switched the television on and found a news channel. The screen showed the familiar shot of the conference room in Bristol. Eventually the police began to arrive, and this time DCI Terrell took the middle seat.

"That's either a good sign, or a very bad one," said Lauren.

"We have traced the movements of Mark Weatherly on Wednesday, the twentieth of September," said Terrell. "He took the train from Southall to Frome. Details of the specific trains and times will be available on the screen above and in a press leaflet. We are anxious to hear from anyone who was on the same trains or the same platforms. Here is CCTV footage of Mark at Paddington station at 18:25. Do you remember seeing him? Do you remember a man wearing these clothes?"

I noticed he didn't have a bike with him in the video.

"Mark took the 18:35 train from Paddington to Exeter, getting off at Westbury at 19:55. Here is the CCTV footage of Mark getting off the Exeter train."

The footage showed Mark, still without a bike, walking along the platform.

"Note how he keeps looking behind him."

Terrell was right. Mark did keep looking over his shoulder. No one else was, and I couldn't see any sign of a disturbance or someone calling to him from behind.

"Now Mark walks over to the wall," said Terrell. "And stands there watching everyone getting off the train. When the train pulls out of the station, Mark disappears into the gents' toilets, reappearing a minute later wearing a long, black, false beard."

"What is he doing?" asked Lauren. "I thought the false

beard was some kind of fancy dress joke. This looks like he's trying to disguise himself. Really badly."

"Now we see Mark as the Frome train comes in. This is the train he should have caught. It's the one on his ticket. The 20:11. Watch."

Mark didn't move. He watched. He watched everyone get off. He watched everyone get on. He deliberately let the train leave without him.

I immediately thought of Susan. She'd done the same. Not exactly the same, but similar.

"Susan didn't miss her stop at Westbury," I said. "She did it deliberately. She got off at Warminster to see if anyone was following her. Just like Mark."

"But why?" said Lauren. "Who'd be following them? The killer's not on the train, is he? He's in Garstock, waiting for them."

Terrell showed Mark getting on the next train for Frome. Again he was wary, watching everyone around him, not boarding the train until the very last second.

Terrell then brought up footage of Susan at Warminster and Westbury stations. She wasn't as blatant as Mark, but she was definitely watching her fellow passengers. She waited until the last second to board the Westbury train, and made sure she was the last to leave the platform at Westbury station.

"We appeal to anyone who was on these trains with Mark or Susan to come forward. Did you see them? Did you see anything odd or anyone behaving suspiciously? Did you see anyone taking an unusual interest in their fellow passengers? Did you see any incident – it may not have involved Susan or Mark – but any incident that made you feel uncomfortable?"

Terrell was pushing the idea that something had happened on those trains. The fact that both of them were wary ruled out anything random. The coincidence would have been too great. They must have recognised someone, or been on the lookout for someone.

"Next, we have footage of Mark leaving Frome station.

Note he does not have a bicycle with him."

He was still keeping a good look out though. He stopped by a flower seller. He didn't buy anything, but he used the opportunity to have a good look around him before walking on.

The screen changed.

"Here we have footage of Mark walking along Lock's Hill in Frome. Still no bicycle. But somewhere between Lock's Hill and Garstock Mark obtained a bicycle. He may have hired it. He may have been given it. He may have stolen it. Here's a picture of that bicycle."

The grainy dashcam footage from the journalist's car flashed on screen.

"If you've recently lost a bicycle like this one, or loaned it, we'd like to hear from you. Similarly, if you've found a bicycle like this in the last two days, we want to hear from you. This bicycle has not been seen since Wednesday night."

Terrell glanced at the Chief Constable. "Do you have anything extra to add, sir?"

"No, I think you covered everything admirably, Chief Inspector. We will take a few questions – with the emphasis on 'few.' As you can imagine the investigative team are working extremely hard at the moment. Time is precious."

The first questions came firing in.

"Do you have a cause of death for Mark?"

"We do," said the Chief Constable. "He was drowned."

"In salt water?" asked the journalist following up on his earlier question.

Terrell got in a whisker before the Chief Constable. "We prefer not to divulge that information at this juncture."

"If anyone asks if I'm helping the police with their enquiries I'll scream," said Lauren.

"Surely you've done enough today to counter anything the police might say now?" I said.

"That's Terrell up there," said Lauren. "He's clever, and he hates me."

The questions continued. "Did you find hidden cameras at

Hillside?"

"We did," said Terrell.

"Do you have a make for the bicycle?"

"We don't at the moment," said Terrell. "It's a drop-handled road bike. That's all we could tell from the dashcam."

"Have you found out where Mark was living?"

"We have. We'll release full details tomorrow."

"What about his job? There was talk he'd given up working as a bike courier and had become a car mechanic."

"That's true," said Terrell. "He quit his last job a month ago to become a trainee car mechanic at a garage in Hillingdon."

"Are there two killers?"

"We are considering all possibilities."

"Is it true you found a size eleven footprint at the crime scene?"

"Footprints were found at the crime scene."

"Size eleven?"

"Footprints were found at the crime scene," repeated Terrell.

"How much danger is Lauren Corelli in?"

No quick fire answer this time. Terrell and the Chief Constable looked at each other.

"Oh, God," said Lauren.

"I'll take this one, sir," said Terrell. He looked directly at the camera. "I can truthfully say that Lauren Corelli is in far more danger than even she realises."

He said it with feeling. I couldn't quite place what kind of feeling, but it bordered enigmatic smug and passive aggressive threat.

"He can't resist having a dig, can he?" said Lauren. "Not that it matters. I can use 'Lauren Corelli is in far more danger than even she realises' as a quote. Much better than 'She's helping police with their enquiries.'"

The Chief Constable wrapped up the press conference.

I sat back in the sofa, deep in thought. Why were Susan

and Mark so interested in their fellow passengers?

"I think we've been looking at this all wrong," I said. "We thought the killer groomed his victims. Enticed them to meet him at Garstock. Maybe told them it was for a big fancy dress party."

"That could still be true," said Lauren.

"But it doesn't explain Susan and Mark's behaviour on the train. They thought someone was following them. Was it the killer playing games with them? It's the sort of thing he'd do. But he couldn't physically be on the train with them as we know he was elsewhere at the time."

"An accomplice? We know there's an accomplice because of the directional speakers. The killer could have sent him to watch the victims."

And give them a fright? It was possible, but it felt like too much of a complication. The killer had everything set up. He didn't need to frighten his victims on the train. That was very small beer compared to what he had in store for them. And if his accomplice frightened them too much they could turn round and run home, ruining everything.

And then it came to me.

"What if Mark and Susan's behaviour on the train had nothing to do with the killer?" I said. "Mark was a bike courier, suspected of being a drugs courier. What if Mark and Susan were part of a county lines drug gang?

"Not Susan, surely?"

"Why not? She became secretive and withdrawn. She could have been groomed by a drugs gang. It's what these county lines gangs do, isn't it? Get their hooks into innocent looking kids and use them to carry drugs from the big cities into the countryside? It explains Susan's and Mark's behaviour on the train. They were carrying drugs. Of course they were wary."

"Where does the killer come into this?" asked Lauren.

"I think he targets drug couriers. Think about it. Drug couriers, like hookers, would accept knocking on strange doors in the middle of nowhere as part of their job. The killer wouldn't have to groom them. They're already groomed. And both Susan and Mark were carrying large bags with them. We thought it was for clothes. Why not for drugs?"

"So what happened to the drugs? Drug gangs would expect to be paid. If not, they'd be straight round to collect. They'd have the addresses."

The implication of what Lauren had just said hit us both at the same time. The drug gangs would have the addresses of where the couriers had been sent. Laburnum Cottage and Hillside. It wouldn't be the killer who would have to deal with them. It would be us and the owners of Hillside.

"No," said Lauren. "A drug gang are not going to send tens of thousands of pounds worth of drugs to someone they don't know. Especially when they find out their first courier was murdered."

Reluctantly I let go of my theory. It explained a lot, but Lauren was right. No criminal gang would act like that. And, the more I thought about it, I couldn't see the killer wanting to involve a gang either. He liked control. He liked to dominate his victims. Involving a gang would be a huge risk. He wouldn't be able to trust them. And they'd have the numbers, and the weapons, to do whatever they liked.

Chapter Thirty-Six

Half an hour later there was a knock on the lounge door. It was Keith, one of our firearms officers.

"Just to let you know," he said. "We've had confirmation that this shift will be the last. We'll be here until seven tomorrow morning then firearms protection will be withdrawn. You'll be fine. You have panic buttons in every room, and a patrol car outside."

"The patrol car's staying?" asked Lauren.

"For now. There'll be regular threat assessments, but I can't see anyone removing the patrol car while there's still so much press interest outside the house."

Not to mention the serial killer.

We thanked Keith and wished him a quiet night.

"Well," I said. "We knew it was going to happen soon. And I can't see the killer trying to smash his way inside. He's far more likely to try to trick his way in, or find a way to get us outside. All we have to do is keep the doors locked and stay put."

"What if he sets fire to the house?"

"We have smoke alarms and panic buttons. And, if we did need to get out fast, the roof of the patrol car is handily placed under the bathroom window. Anyway, shouldn't you be recording your video blog? If you want footage of Keith and Amrit to use as background, you've only got tonight now."

"Already done. It only took one take. Keith and Amrit were brilliant. They put on their balaclavas and looked menacing while I talked."

"I didn't hear anything."

"You were engrossed in some ancient black and white film."

"It wasn't that ancient. It was quite good too. A couple of

amateurs thrown into a murder mystery in post war Kent."

"Looked a bit wooden to me."

"Says the woman who usually plays a corpse. So, what did you say in your video blog. You didn't call out the killer again, or name any more kitchen implements?"

"I did not. I thought the first episode should be an introductory one. Show off the cottage. Show people how we were living with patrol cars outside the front door, press at the gate, firearms officers in the kitchen, great big bolts securing the doors, panic buttons in all the rooms."

"Tell me you didn't show them where Susan's body was found?"

"I didn't! I was very tasteful. I made it clear at the outset that there'd been a murder in the house, and I wasn't going to show or talk about where the body was found."

I was impressed. And relieved. I'd had serious doubts about the whole idea of a video blog from a murder scene.

"I also strung up some pots and pans to recreate our old alarm system."

"You didn't rig up the trip wire, did you?"

"I've taken everything down now, but yes, I may have rigged up half a dozen trip wires all over the stairs and landing."

"Half a dozen? We only had the one."

"Artistic license. One looked a little sad on its own. Six looked like we *really* meant business."

~

At nine o'clock things took an unexpected turn.

Lauren picked up her phone to check for messages and found ten from her agent.

"Oh. My. God," she said.

"What's happened?" I asked.

"Stepan Balusek wants to meet me," she said excitedly. "Me! Can you believe it!"

"Who's Stepan Balusek?"

"Tell you later. I've got to speak to my agent. Hello?

Joanne? Did Stepan Balusek really call?"

I heard snatches of the conversation. Joanne was as excited as Lauren. Every now and then one of them would squeal in excited disbelief.

I didn't know who Stepan Balusek was, but it sounded like he was some kind of legendary film director who wanted to talk to Lauren about a new project he had.

It also sounded like he wanted to meet her for lunch tomorrow at a hotel near Heathrow Airport.

I shuffled closer, listening even more intently. This did not sound right. A famous director, out of the blue, inviting Lauren to a meeting far away from her police protection.

I tried to get her attention, but she shushed me. "Later," she said.

I ran over to the dining table, grabbed a pen and paper, and hastily scrawled down some questions. *How do you know it's really him? Is it a trap? Find a number for him on the internet and call him back.*

I held them out in front of Lauren's face. She nodded and gave me a thumbs up sign, before batting my hand away.

"Sorry, Joanne. Could you repeat that. Mathew is having a meltdown next to me. Which airport was it? Charlotte Douglas? And the announcer definitely had an American accent?"

I couldn't work out where Charlotte Douglas came into the equation. Was Lauren being invited over to America now? I simmered for another five minutes, trying to make sense of the conversation from the fragments I heard. It sounded like Lauren was asking the right questions, but it also sounded like she was intending to meet this Stepan Balusek. Had she forgotten everything we'd talked about earlier? We said the killer would try to trick us into leaving. This was exactly that!

Eventually, she finished the call.

"Well?" I said.

"Stepan Balusek wants to meet me. I know it sounds too good to be true, but everything checks out so far. His assistant made the call to my agent. He said he was at the airport about to board a flight to Heathrow, and Joanne heard a flight announcement in the background. It said flight AA731, Charlotte Douglas to Heathrow, was boarding at gate D3. Let me just check that."

"The killer's clever," I said. "He could fake a call like that."

"Could he? Both the assistant and the announcer had American accents. The killer may be clever and resourceful, but he can't be good at everything."

"Faking an American accent isn't that difficult."

"Doing it well is more difficult than you think. Joanne's no dummy. She thought they were genuine. Look, the flight number checks out." Lauren held out her phone for me to look. "Flight AA371 Charlotte to Heathrow," she said. "It boarded at gate D3 and is due in at Heathrow nine o'clock tomorrow morning."

"So track down this Stepan on the internet and phone him back to confirm," I said.

"It's not as easy as that. He's a very private person who doesn't give out his contact details. When he's between projects he's a virtual recluse."

"Contact his assistant."

"I'll try, but he didn't give a name. He just referred to himself as Mr. Balusek's assistant."

"Doesn't that ring any alarm bells for you?"

"A few, but this is Stepan Balusek. He is seriously weird. I heard he calls all his assistants Mario, irrespective of what their real names are."

I couldn't believe that Lauren was still entertaining the idea that the call might be genuine.

Lauren tried tracking down Stepan Balusek and his assistant on the internet. He was certainly popular. There were loads of websites about him or dedicated to him, but no hint of how to contact him – not even a mention of an agency or an assistant.

Lauren was also right about him being weird. One article said he had to move house every time he finished a film. His artistic temperament was so attuned to the vibrations around him that he couldn't work in a house that he'd already been inspired by. He needed new vibrations for new ideas.

"It's no good," said Lauren. "I've tried all the usual places you'd find directors listed. His name's there, his filmography, but no contact details."

"How does he get work without contact details?"

"I think I read somewhere that *he* prefers to initiate contact. He's suspicious of, if not paranoid about, being pitched ideas. He thinks everyone is out to sue him, alleging he stole their stories. So he prefers to find his own ideas then look for a producer to handle the logistics while he controls the artistic side."

"Did the assistant give Joanne a contact number?"

"No, but he didn't hide his number when he phoned. So we could call him. And the number was American. If it's a hoax, it's a damn good one."

I was reluctant to call this 'assistant' on a number the 'assistant' had supplied. The whole point of looking for an official contact number was to make sure we weren't talking to an impostor.

But then I had an idea.

"If you did ring that number," I said. "And it was the killer on the line, could we use that to our advantage?"

"How?"

"Think of a question that any assistant of Stepan Balusek should know. Test him. If he fails then you know it's a scam."

Lauren spent fifteen minutes compiling a list of questions. The killer may have been clever, but I doubted even he would have done more than a cursory background check on Stepan Balusek.

"Here we go," said Lauren. "It's ringing now."

We waited. The phone continued to ring.

"He would have had to turn his phone off before take off," said Lauren. "Airlines insist upon it. Maybe he forgot to switch it back on?"

"Not if he was expecting an important call," I said. "His boss would need to know if you'd agreed to have lunch with him. Stepan sounds like the kind of boss who'd sack an assistant who forgot to switch his phone back on."

Lauren gave up waiting and terminated the call.

"He *is* expecting an important call, isn't he?" I asked.

"Not exactly," said Lauren, looking sheepish.

"Don't tell me Joanne accepted on your behalf?"

"She had no choice. It was a take it or leave it offer. Stepan was only going to be in the UK for a few hours. He was on his way to Europe, then on to the Middle East. He could do lunch at one, or not at all."

"Tell me you're not going."

"I'm undecided."

"But it's classic scamming, Lauren. Offer the victim something amazing, then put them on the spot. Tell them they have to agree now or it's all off. The added pressure makes it more likely the victim makes a rash decision."

"I know that. Of course I know that. But this is Stepan Balusek. It's not unusual behaviour for him."

"He sounds a total prick to me. Why would you want to work with him?"

"Because he's a genius. You must have heard of his films. *The Coconut Seller, Three Graves, The Wall.* Absolute classics every one of them."

The Coconut Seller rang a bell, but only a very small one. I didn't have any premium channels. All the films I watched were on the free channels. It could take years for a popular film to air there.

"I don't think I can turn it down," said Lauren. "This sort of opportunity is once in a lifetime. Actors dream of situations like this. Today I'm hot news, tomorrow I could be nothing. I don't want to be an embittered old woman dreaming of what could have been."

"This is ridiculous, Lauren. It could be the killer. Most likely, it is."

"It could also be the real deal. I'm not going to go through life as the actress who turned down a role in a Stepan Balusek film!"

"You don't have to turn him down! Ask him to reschedule, or have a virtual meeting on your laptop."

"You really do not know the entertainment industry. Everyone wants a hit movie, but no one knows how to make one. You can bring together the best actors, the best writers, the best directors and still have a flop. Then every now and then someone comes along and makes a film that blows everyone away. And follows it up with another. No one knows how they did it. But everyone wants more. And no one cares if this amazing new director is bat shit crazy. That's the price of genius, isn't it? If he wants to be a recluse, let him. If he makes unreasonable demands, indulge him. He is the golden child, the money maker, the career builder. Right up until the moment he crashes and burns. But until then, he gets whatever he wants. And Stepan Balusek is famous for replacing actors who question him. If the first thing I do is ask to reschedule, most likely he'll walk away."

"So suggest a virtual meeting on your laptop."

"He hates video conferencing. He finds it artificial and intrusive, and doesn't think you can connect with another person on an emotional level via a small screen and tinny speakers."

"Look, the chances are it's not him. And even if it is, you're doing brilliantly without him. You'll get far more fame and offers being the rolling pin wielding, serial killer baiting Honey Badger than you'd ever get from being in a Stepan Balusek film."

"You don't understand. I'm not looking for fame. I'll use fame – I'll use the hell out of it – but only as a means to an end. I want to see if I can create a body of work that I can be proud of. I want to fulfil my potential. I want to be stretched. That's what Stepan Balusek can do for an actor. He can bring out performances that you didn't even know you had inside you. He can create moments of pure cinematic genius. Scenes that people will still be talking about in fifty years time. He's that good. If there's a one in a million chance that he wants to meet me for lunch tomorrow, I'm taking it."

I could tell that Lauren meant it.

"Look," she said. "Joanne knows this restaurant. She says it's quite popular and big. There'll be hundreds of witnesses. If it is a trap, the killer is going to be very restricted in what he can do."

"Okay," I said reluctantly. "I'll come with you. You'll need a second pair of eyes."

Chapter Thirty-Seven

We spent the next hour planning, taking turns in being the killer. How would he use this situation to the maximum advantage?

I thought he was more likely to strike before Lauren entered the restaurant. The restaurant was too public. And, unless the killer was Stepan's twin brother, he was not going to fool Lauren into having lunch with him.

"He knows two places we're going to be," I said. "Here and the Hotel Cardinale. I don't think he'll attempt anything within half a mile of here. We've got alarms and a patrol car that could reach us in seconds. But a couple of miles out, if he can predict the route we're going to take, he could set up an ambush. Have his accomplice lie down in the middle of the road looking like he'd been knocked off his bike – which we know the killer has. The killer then flags us down, spins us some story to get us out of the car, then the next thing you know there's a knife at your throat and we're being bundled into the back of a van."

"So we take an unpredictable route," said Lauren. "Head off in the opposite direction to Heathrow and gradually circle round."

"That's what I thought. The more problematic one is the hotel car park. I think he'd wait for us to get out of the car, then drive alongside us in his van. His accomplice then appears from behind a parked car, puts a knife against your throat and we're bundled into the back of that van."

"So we don't park in the hotel car park," said Lauren. "We find a place to park nearby then make our way on foot to the Cardinale, keeping away from the roads as much as we can. I can scout out a route using online maps."

Which brought us to the hotel itself, which was far more

unpredictable. We didn't know the internal layout. Did you have to go through reception to get to the restaurant? Were there narrow corridors you had to walk down?

I thought it best to avoid crowds. Wait by a nice protective wall until the route ahead – be it across a foyer or down a corridor – was clear. Lauren preferred the protection of a large group.

"If we attach ourselves to a large party of diners and get in front of them, they'll protect our backs. All we'd have to do is watch out for people coming towards us."

I was starting to feel more confident about this lunch. We might actually pull it off.

"So, we get to the entrance of the restaurant. You tell the head waiter you have a reservation under the name Balusek-"

"Rosebud."

"Pardon?"

"The reservation is under Rosebud. Stepan never gives his real name at restaurants. Joanne told me it was booked under the name Rosebud. It's a reference to *Citizen Kane*."

"Right. So the head waiter then shows you to your table, and if Stepan's there we can all stop worrying. If it's not Stepan, I suggest you tell the waiter the man's an impostor and get the hell out. And if Stepan hasn't arrived yet, then you take your seat."

"There is another option," said Lauren. "We find out there's no reservation. I'll check."

Lauren pulled up the Cardinale's website and eventually found a telephone number for the restaurant. A minute later she'd confirmed that there was a booking for a party of two at one o'clock tomorrow under the name of Rosebud.

"So, said Lauren. "I'm sitting at a table waiting for Stepan."

"Don't accept any drinks."

"Definitely not."

"And watch out for people walking by your table. If anyone suddenly bends down, pretends to pick something up off the floor, and hands it to you saying 'I think you dropped this,' don't touch it. Just say it's not yours."

"Thallium?"

"Thallium. Basically, assume that everyone coming towards you is a serial killer."

"I suppose I'm not allowed to pre-emptively stab people. Purely as a precautionary measure."

"I think not. Meanwhile, I'll look for a place outside the restaurant where I can get a good view of your table. And we'll need to keep our phones on in case anything urgent happens."

"I'll have to turn mine off when Stepan arrives. He'd go ballistic if it rang in the middle of lunch."

"If Stepan arrives, we can relax."

"You can. I won't be able to."

~

I checked the journey time on a route planner. Heathrow was two hours away by the fastest route. I added on another hour for taking the circuitous route, and another one for contingencies. I added a further twenty minutes when I saw Lauren's planned route from a nearby car park. She had us hiking through shrubbery and climbing a six-foot-high chain link fence.

"You're going to turn up for this lunch covered in twigs."

"Better add another ten minutes for running repairs in the ladies."

We'd have to set off before eight thirty.

I yawned and stretched my arms. I was knackered and ready for bed. Tomorrow was going to be a long day. I had a final sweep through the news channels – just in case something momentous had happened – but found nothing other than speculation.

That and the Honey Badger. Lauren was everywhere – her interview on *Morning Everybody,* and the scenes outside the cottage. Luckily my thallium intervention hadn't been deemed newsworthy.

I left Lauren surfing through the internet, and headed

upstairs.

~

The next day I came down to find Lauren already up and making breakfast. It was nice to have the kitchen to ourselves.

"I think we should leave as early as possible," said Lauren.

"Why? Has anything happened?"

"No, but I have this feeling that it might. I don't want Terrell rocking up at the door just before we're about to leave. It would be so like him to arrest me on the day of my big lunch date."

I was happy to leave early. I'd only be sitting in front of the TV, checking my watch every two minutes. All I wanted was to get this trip over with.

"You look nice by the way," I said.

"Do you think so? I borrowed the top and scarf from the *Morning Everybody* set. They have racks of clothes for the presenters to wear. I gave the stylist a sob story about how I was unable to get into my flat and was running out of clothes."

A quick breakfast later, we were ready to leave. I was going to drive so Lauren could concentrate on what she was going to say to Stepan. Assuming he turned up, that is. Lauren still thought there was a chance. I didn't.

"You have to think positively," said Lauren. "Never underestimate the power of positive thinking."

Or the well-crafted lie.

We'd agreed we had to say something to the officers in the patrol car. If we didn't, they might contact Terrell or chase after us. I left it to Lauren to come up with the words.

As I opened the garage to get my car out, I heard Lauren telling the officers that we were going to her flat to pick up clothes, and would probably stop off on the way back to shop at the supermarket as we were running out of food.

Total bollocks, but eminently plausible. Nothing to set off any alarm bells, and if they did inform Terrell, he'd be looking for us in the wrong place.

Lauren repeated the same story to the gaggle of reporters outside the gate. There weren't as many as yesterday, but I still counted six cars. Lauren chatted to all of them, playing down our road trip, and promising a round of interviews when we came back.

I had a nasty feeling that some of them might follow us. We hadn't considered the possibility last night, but now… What if there were some hardcore paparazzi in their ranks?

I edged the car through the gate and out onto the road. Lauren got in.

"Drive," she said. "Don't hang around."

I headed left, away from the quickest route to the main road.

"Two cars are following," said Lauren, looking behind her.

I wasn't too sure where the road would take me. My plan had been to drive randomly in the opposite direction to Heathrow, then switch the sat nav on after twenty minutes or so and let it sort out the route from there.

I hadn't expected a car chase.

"Can't you drive any faster?"

"Look at the road! It's all blind bends."

Not to mention really narrow. I watched the two cars in the rear-view mirror. They were gaining on us.

"Are they press?" I asked.

"God knows," said Lauren. "If you can't lose them, slow down and let me get pictures of them.

I slowed down.

"There are two of them," said Lauren. "A single man in each car. I don't recognise them from yesterday, and neither of them asked me a question this morning."

"Have you got pictures?"

"I've got one. The other guy's too far back for a decent shot."

Not for long. The second car accelerated, overtaking the first car and looking to come alongside us. I swung the car into the middle of the road to block him off. How the two cars behind didn't hit each other I had no idea. Their side mirrors were practically scraping the steep banks that flanked the narrow road.

And God knows what would have happened if we'd met oncoming traffic.

"Shall I double back to the cottage? Let the patrol car sort this out?"

"Let's try and find a main road first. They'll back off if there are other cars around."

She hoped.

I wasn't so sure. And where the hell was a main road! For all I knew I was driving straight towards a disused quarry.

I swung left and right blocking off all attempts of the cars behind to come alongside. Was it the killer and his accomplice? I'd assumed he'd have a van. Something large and windowless he could hide a body in.

"Take a left in one mile," said Lauren. "That should get us to a main road."

I glanced over. Lauren had a road map on her phone. Hopefully it was up to date.

It was a long mile. I hogged the centre of the road, praying all oncoming traffic could wait another five minutes. At last the turn off appeared – a small crossroads. I indicated right, feinted a right turn, then braked hard and swung left. Tyres squealed. The car juddered. But we made it. I accelerated hard, looking in the rear-view mirror hoping to see a car wedged in a bank or slewed across the road, but they were both still there. A bit farther back, but still following at speed.

"Have you got your personal alarm handy?" I asked Lauren.

"It's in my bag."

"I think you should have it in your hand."

I locked all the car doors. If we were coming up to a main road, we'd have to stop. We'd be vulnerable. There might be witnesses, but would anyone stop to help?

"How long before the main road?" I asked.

"Two and a half miles."

Shit! This road was wider than the others and the high banks had been replaced by grass verges. I was having to work harder to keep the cars from coming alongside.

A lorry appeared out of nowhere, coming round the bend towards us. I swung back into the correct lane. The lorry driver flashed his lights and sounded his horn.

A series of bends followed. And then more oncoming traffic. This was good. It kept our pursuers wondering and made it easier for me to keep them behind us.

Then I saw the junction with the main road up ahead. Our road was a lot wider there, and there was heavy traffic on the main road. I'd have to stop the car. We'd be vulnerable.

I accelerated, hoping I could judge the optimum moment to hit the brakes, hoping a gap would suddenly appear in the line of cars on the main road.

"Brace yourself," I said, hitting the brakes.

I really thought we were going slew out into the main road, but I somehow kept the car together, screeching to a stop a few yards short of the white line. One of the pursuing cars pulled alongside. We were blocked in. One car behind, one alongside. The driver on our right opened his door. He was getting out.

"Shit! Shit! Shit! What was he doing? The car alongside was impairing my view of the traffic on my right. Was that a gap? Was it large enough for me pull out? I went for it, accelerating hard, staying in a lower gear until the rev counter hit the red. Watching the car in the rear-view mirror get larger and larger, its lights flashing, horn blaring.

Don't hit! Don't hit! I willed the car to go faster, bracing myself for impact. I'd never been in a car accident before. I had no idea what to expect.

Seconds ticked down. I was still alive. The car behind was farther back, lights still flashing and horn blaring, but no longer about to crash into the back of us.

"I can't see those two cars," said Lauren. "I think they must be six or seven cars back."

The driver behind me was irate. I could see him in the

mirror shouting and gesticulating at me. Great, I now had three drivers who wanted to kill me.

"Do you think you can lose them?" asked Lauren.

I looked across at her in disbelief.

"Strangely, Lauren, Swindon Housing Department never sent me on a defensive driving course. Look at me! I'm a sweaty, shaking mess."

"You did pretty well back there."

"I almost got us both killed back there. I'm not a getaway driver. I'm a naturally cautious driver who gives way to other drivers and rarely breaks the speed limit."

"They're not going to give up," said Lauren.

"So call the police. You've got pictures of them. Did you get their number plates too?"

"I did."

"Brilliant. Send it all to Natalia and arrange a time and place for us to meet. We'll keep to the main roads and lead them into a police trap."

"I think they're paparazzi."

"You're joking. They were not trying to take pictures. They were trying to run us off the road!"

"The one behind us at the junction was taking pictures. He had a high-end camera."

"But why run us off the road?"

"Paps are a rule unto themselves. They might have wanted to pull alongside for a better shot, or wanted a close-up of me looking terrified. Think of what they did to Princess Diana."

"So what do we do?"

"I'll think of something. In the meantime, stay on the main roads and head towards London. If they try anything, I'll call the police and report them for dangerous driving."

"And if they don't try anything? You can't turn up for a meeting with a reclusive director with a couple of paparazzi in tow."

"I'll think of something."

A gap appeared in the oncoming traffic. The car behind accelerated quickly and pulled alongside. The driver shouted and gesticulated wildly at me. I tried to look apologetic. I tried desperately to think of a gesture for contrition. Why wasn't there one? There were plenty denoting anger and contempt. I mouthed sorry and raised my right palm. I hoped it conveyed contrition and acceptance of blame. The other driver didn't think so, but another car appeared behind him, flashing its lights. So he gave me one parting shot with his middle finger and sped away.

It didn't take long before the two paparazzi cars were back. They took it in turns to overtake, then slow right down, forcing me to overtake them, and start the whole process again. They didn't appear threatening, and, occasionally, they even took pictures. But there was an underlying menace. They were playing with us, and letting us know they were playing with us. Behaviour that reminded me of the killer.

Lauren tried to put them off by draping a coat over her head. I felt like doing the same. We were two hours from Heathrow and my car told me we had petrol for one hour forty-five.

Chapter Thirty-Eight

"I've got it," said Lauren. "There's a service station in another ten miles. We can lose them there."

"How?" Motorway service stations were busy, but they weren't so busy you could lose a couple of determined paps.

"I'll head for the ladies. Even a pap wouldn't follow me in there."

"No, they'll wait for you to come out. There's only ever one entrance to the toilets."

"Exactly. Meanwhile you're disabling their cars."

"What? How? I know nothing about cars."

"You let their tyres down. One should be enough to slow them down. Two would be better. I don't suppose you have a knife in the car?"

"No, I don't."

"A bradawl or a sharp screwdriver?"

"No, I don't have a harpoon either, but I'll make sure I have one next time I give you a lift."

I spent the next five minutes trying to think of a better plan. Service station car parks were busy places. People were always walking back and forth between the car park and the main concourse. Someone would see me. Loads of people would see me.

"The trick is to act confident," said Lauren. "If you believe you're only checking your tyre pressure, everyone else will too."

"I'm not you, Lauren. I've had twelve months of being told that no one believes a word I say. If anyone recognises me, they're not going to think I'm checking tyre pressures. They're going to wonder what Mathew Sedley is doing to that car."

"Look," said Lauren. "You are not that person any more. You never were the person the media portrayed you as. Just concentrate on the tyres. Keep your head down. Don't look anywhere else. Don't think about anything else. You can do this."

~

I turned off the motorway, following the long slip road into the service station car park. The two paparazzi followed.

"Don't park too close to the main concourse," said Lauren. "We want the paps to take two parking places next to each other. It'll make your job easier. There! There are three spaces. Take the far one."

I obeyed. Lauren had her door open before the car had stopped. And then she was off – not exactly sprinting, but not hanging about either. I quickly locked her door. The entire plan rested on both paps following Lauren. If one stayed behind, we were done.

I sank down in the driver's seat, watching the two men out of the corner of my eye, willing them to follow Lauren. I was last year's news, not worth wasting a photograph on.

They didn't even glance at me. They grabbed their cameras, slammed their doors, and ran.

I gave them a few more seconds, then took my tyre pressure gauge, and climbed out of the car.

The car park wasn't that busy, but a steady stream of cars was arriving. I stopped looking, turning my attention to the first pap's car. Nothing to see here. I'm just a motorist checking tyre pressures.

I listened to the steady hiss of the escaping air. I could do this.

Seconds ticked by. Long seconds. This was taking ages. I couldn't see any difference in the tyre at all. How long did it take to deflate a tyre?

I checked my watch. Lauren hadn't told me how long she'd be. What if she came back and I'd only done one tyre? Should I tell her to go back and have a meal?

I could feel the sweat breaking out on my forehead. I was not cut out for this. It was all right for Lauren to say 'act natural,' but my natural state when out in public was to be anxious.

And anxiety went straight to my stomach. I could feel it now – a sharp, stabbing pain in the lower right quadrant. Probably stress related, but it could be appendicitis. It was in the same general area. Knowing my luck, I'd have both.

I took a deep breath, and tried to calm down. Next time I'd bring a bradawl. Come on! Come on! How much longer was this going to take?

Eventually, I could see a difference in the tyre. I checked my watch. It had taken three and a half minutes.

I moved onto the next car, keeping my head down, trying to act confident – which for some reason my brain interpreted as humming the only bit I knew from the 'Ride of the Valkyries.'

I really was not cut out for this.

I knelt down between the two paparazzi cars, convinced the world and his dog were watching me, but past caring. I was a red faced, sweaty, tyre-tampering, Valkyrie hummer. Who in their right mind would question what I was doing? I'd accidentally stumbled upon the other way of ensuring invisibility in British society. Acting weird. People would far rather walk by than risk a confrontation with a weird person.

Two minutes passed. I risked a glance towards the concourse. No sign of Lauren or the paps. Was she all right? What if the paps weren't paps?

I looked again ten seconds later. Still no sign of Lauren. She had her personal alarm with her. If anything had happened, she'd have pressed it. There would have been hundreds of witnesses. 130 decibels in an enclosed area – no one could have failed to hear that.

I checked again every ten seconds, wondering when I should start to really panic.

As soon as the tyre looked deflated, I stood up, staring anxiously at the entrance to the concourse. Should I stay with the car or look for Lauren? I tried her phone. It was either turned off or she couldn't answer.

Then I saw her coming out of the concourse in a group of about a dozen people. The two paps were circling the group trying to take pictures, while the group members – mainly women – blocked and fended them off. Lauren had recruited her own bodyguards.

And there was the rolling pin, which she swung at any pap who came within swinging distance.

I quickly climbed into the car and reversed it towards Lauren. I reached over and threw open the passenger door, expecting Lauren to leap in, but she insisted on thanking her helpers first and waving goodbye.

The two paps didn't hang around. They ran for their cars.

"Come on," I said.

Lauren jumped in and I sped away as fast as I could without running over pedestrians or hitting cars pulling out of parking places.

Lauren kept her eyes on the paps.

"How many tyres did you do?"

"Two."

"Two on each car?"

"No, just two. It takes three and a half minutes per tyre, you know?"

I pulled onto the slip road.

"They're not following," said Lauren. "I think they've stopped, but I can't quite see."

We were approaching the motorway. I accelerated.

"Still can't see them," said Lauren. "It's not going to delay them long. A couple of minutes at most."

I picked a gap in the line of traffic and merged into the nearest lane.

"I'll take the first exit and head across country," I said. "Can you plot a route north away from the major roads? Aim for the M4. We can take that direct to Heathrow."

We took the first exit, both of us looking behind to see what other cars were turning off. There were only a handful. I couldn't see the paps anywhere.

We then followed Lauren's scenic route through Berkshire,

stopping off at a small garage near Bracknell to fill up. I couldn't see any pap guessing this would be our route.

I started to relax. We could take it easy now. We weren't that far from Heathrow. It was all a matter of how early did we want to arrive.

We decided to continue with the back roads and look for a café. Somewhere quiet and relaxing. We'd evaded the paps. Now we had the killer to deal with.

~

I parked the car at the nearby hotel that Lauren had selected. We had plenty of time. Now it was a question of how long should we wait? We didn't want to arrive at the restaurant too early, and we didn't want to wait anywhere in or around the Hotel Cardinale.

So we sat in the car, waiting, and, in my case, trying not to hum 'The Ride of the Valkyries' which for some stupid reason I could not clear from my head.

Eventually it was time. Lauren handed me a plastic bag.

"Can you carry this? It's got my shoes in it. I'll change into them when we get to the restaurant."

I looked down at Lauren's feet. She was wearing trainers. I hadn't noticed before, but it made sense when, any second, you might have to run for your life.

Or climb a six-foot high chain link fence. I knew we wanted to avoid the roads where possible, but climbing high fences could draw peoples' attention. Especially when you're crap at climbing, and fall from the top into a bush.

We made it, though, approaching the Hotel Cardinale from the rear corner. We just had to negotiate a steep grassy slope and we'd be there. I could see a couple of doors on the side of the hotel. One was a fire exit, and the other looked like a staff entrance.

"What do you think?" I asked. "Should we try the staff entrance?"

"I don't know," said Lauren. "I don't want to do anything that might jeopardise this lunch."

We followed the building round towards the front, keeping close to the wall, keeping an eye on the car park in front of us. I could see a few cars arriving, but no menacing vans.

We reached the corner of the building. The hotel entrance was only twenty yards away. There were a few people coming and going, but no one waiting by the door, no one observing who came and went.

We could do this. We moved fast, trotting up the steps, keeping an eye out for anyone taking an interest in us. It was looking hopeful. We were through the door, slowing down as we entered the spacious foyer. Where was the restaurant? Lauren grabbed my arm.

"Over there."

She pointed at a wide corridor off the far left of the foyer. There was a large sign above it. *Restaurant La Cardinale.*

The foyer wasn't crowded. It was busy, but most of the people were around reception and a seated café area. The path to the restaurant was almost clear. Only a handful of people heading that way. None of them looked like a serial killer.

"Do you want your shoes?" I asked.

"Not yet. Wait until we see the entrance to the restaurant."

We made it to the corridor. The entrance to the restaurant was only ten yards away. There was a small queue. Only four people.

I kept a look out while Lauren changed shoes. Still no one taking an unnatural interest in us. We were going to do this. I really didn't think we would. I wondered where the killer was. Waiting inside his van outside the car park? Checking his watch every five minutes? Wondering where the hell we were?

"How do I look?" said Lauren. "Do I need to do any running repairs?"

"You look fine to me."

"No twigs or leaves?"

"Only a caterpillar, but it suits you."

"You are joking, aren't you? It wouldn't be funny if I had

lunch with the director of my dreams, and he spent the entire meal staring at my caterpillar."

"Sorry. There is no caterpillar. You look great. Break a leg."

Lauren joined the queue. I stood behind her so I could see which table they gave her. And protect her back. I turned side-on so I could keep an eye out for anyone approaching from behind.

Soon it was Lauren's turn to be seated.

"Good afternoon," she said to the head waiter. "Table for two under the name Rosebud."

"Ah," said the head waiter. "Are you Miss Corelli?"

"I am."

"Your dining companion's assistant left this message with me."

He took a folded piece of paper out of his jacket pocket and handed it to Lauren. She read it then handed it to me.

Sorry, Lauren. Change of plans. Let's meet in my room. I'm in 834.

Stepan

Chapter Thirty-Nine

We never considered this possibility.

"What did he look like?" Lauren asked the head waiter.

"Sorry, I didn't pay that much attention. He was American. Mid-thirties. Average height. Casually dressed. Is there a problem?"

"No, just a surprise, that's all. Thank you." Lauren grabbed my arm, and led me over to our safe spot by the wall where she'd changed shoes earlier.

"You can't go," I said. "It's a trap."

"Probably, but what if it isn't?"

"Even if it's not the killer, it could be a randy director. What if he opens the door in his dressing gown?"

"I haven't heard any rumours about Stepan."

"Nor would you if everyone's been covering up for him."

"Someone would have spoken out."

"Not every victim *can* speak out. Some are too traumatised."

"There would have been talk. You don't go from normal to rapist without spending some time in between. He would have creeped someone out. Word would have got around."

"You're considering this, aren't you?"

"Yes, I am. I know it sounds pathetic and stupid. If the roles were reversed, I'd tell you to get the hell out. But this is a once in a lifetime opportunity. If there's just a *chance* of this being a real meeting to discuss a real project, I'm not going to walk away."

She was not going to be persuaded. I glanced towards the foyer. We'd have to walk through there again. We weren't going to be safe until we were back in the car.

"At least let me come with you," I said. "If Stepan Balusek opens the door with his trousers on, I'll leave."

"I wasn't going up there on my own. I may be a hopeless optimist, but I'm not stupid. I have a plan."

Lauren's plan was to assume it was a trap.

"The killer will expect me to take the lift to the eighth floor. If I was him that's where I'd strike. I'd pose as someone waiting for the lift, stand aside to let me out, then hit me from behind."

"So how do we counter that?"

"We take the lift to the seventh floor, get out, press eight to send the lift up a floor, then take the stairs. That way, if anyone's up there waiting, their attention is going to be on the lift. We can open the stair door a crack and see exactly what's waiting for us."

"And if it's someone acting suspiciously then what?"

"We *could* close the stair door quietly, walk down a couple of flights, and call the police."

I sensed an implied alternative.

"Or what?" I asked.

"Well, if the killer was on his own, and he wasn't that big, maybe he was relying on surprise and a hypodermic needle to overcome us. But if *we* surprised *him…* "

I had so many objections it was difficult to work out which one to lead with.

"How would we know he's the killer? He could be a hotel guest waiting for the lift. We can't grapple innocent people to the ground, and accuse them of being a murderer. Believe me, I know all about wrongful accusations."

"So we take his picture and see how he reacts."

"You're making so many assumptions. Small does not equal weak. He could be a black belt. He could have a knife. He could have a gun. He might have an accomplice waiting by the door to 834."

"You're probably right. It's just that I've read so many true crime stories where opportunities to apprehend the killer are missed, and he goes on to kill again."

"And I've read stories where have-a-go heroes get killed."

"Okay, if we see someone waiting by the lift and they don't

get in when it arrives, we close the stair door slowly and call Natalia as soon as we're far enough away."

"Agreed," I said. "And if there's no one in the corridor, we find room 834, knock on the door, and stand well back, personal alarms at the ready."

~

We waited by the lift doors. Lauren watched the lights of the floor numbers switch on and off as one of the lifts descended. I watched the foyer. It wasn't as busy I'd expected. Maybe lunchtime was their quiet time? It didn't look as though anyone was going to ride the lift with us.

The lift door opened and two people got out. We stood back to let them pass. My eyes did a final sweep of the foyer. Then we got in. I pressed the buttons for floors seven and eight and watched as the lift doors slowly closed.

"I think this meeting might be legit," said Lauren. "This is not the killer's usual territory. He likes quiet, out of the way places. This is a busy hotel near Heathrow Airport. Look! There's even a CCTV camera in the lift. There'll be CCTV cameras everywhere in this hotel. He'd never risk that."

Lauren had a point. This was not the killer's natural habitat. Had he run out of empty houses?

The lift bell rang for the seventh floor. I stood back, bracing myself for any attack, clutching my personal alarm in one hand and the bag containing Lauren's trainers in the other.

The lobby was empty. We jumped out and took the stairs. I stayed behind to make sure the stair doors closed silently – I didn't want any noise to reach the eighth floor – then ran after Lauren, our shoes virtually silent on the carpeted staircase.

I joined Lauren by the eighth floor stair doors. She'd opened it a crack. I peered through. I couldn't see anyone.

The lift bell rang. Lauren opened the door a tad wider. I could see the lift doors starting to open, but that was all. If there was anyone waiting, they were stood a good yard or two back.

We waited. I could barely breathe. Was no one there? Were they waiting for the last second?

The lift doors closed.

Lauren opened the door wider and poked her head out.

"There's no one here," she said.

We both slipped through the door into the corridor, following the signs, *Rooms 821- 836 to the right*, checking the room numbers. The corridor was empty and silent except for the constant low hum from the overhead lights. The corridor turned through ninety degrees. Still empty. Still silent. Natural light coming from the large window at the end of the corridor. Almost there. Room 832. Room 833. Room...

The door to Room 834 was ajar.

~

I stood there, frozen. I should have expected this.

Lauren knocked on the door.

I looked at her in surprise. "What are you doing?" I whispered.

"People do sometimes leave their doors ajar if they know someone's coming up."

She knocked again. "Hello? Mr. Balusek?"

She pushed the door open wider. "Hello? It's Lauren."

I looked over her shoulder. I couldn't see anyone. It was one of those 'L' shaped hotel rooms with a bathroom on the right, a corridor on the left and the bedroom beyond, half of it hidden.

Lauren crept into the room. "Hello?" she said.

I checked the corridor, then followed Lauren inside, clutching tightly to my personal alarm. The bathroom door was open. I looked inside. Empty.

"Crap," said Lauren. "There's a dollhouse."

I hurried to join her. The dollhouse was sitting in the centre of the double bed. I stared at it in disbelief.

It was my old house in Rayford.

Chapter Forty

"Are you sure it's your old house?" asked Lauren, taking a picture of the dollhouse.

"Positive. I lived there for six years."

Lauren rang Natalia and gave her the news.

"I'm sending you a picture of the dollhouse. Matt has the address. It's …"

She looked at me expectantly.

"Nine The Close, Rayford, near Swindon," I said.

Lauren repeated the address for Natalia.

"And the dollhouse is in Room 834, The Hotel Cardinale, Heathrow. We haven't touched a thing."

Natalia told Lauren the Met police would have officers at the hotel in ten minutes.

Lauren mentioned the phone call her agent had received, the flight announcement at Charlotte airport, and the note delivered to the head waiter.

"He really has screwed up this time," said Lauren. "He's let himself be seen. He'll be on CCTV, and he must have left a paper trail booking a hotel room."

I checked the room while Lauren was on the phone to her agent. Had the killer left anything behind? It didn't look like it. No toiletries in the bathroom, nothing in the waste bins, nothing unexpected on any of the surfaces. The bed didn't look like anyone had even sat on it.

Lauren finished her phone call.

"Okay," she said. "Let's have a quick look inside the dollhouse before the police arrive. I'll use this scarf to make sure I don't ruin any fingerprints."

I thought about objecting – momentarily – but I wanted to see inside that dollhouse as much as Lauren did. And this might be our only chance.

Lauren took off her scarf and used it to carefully unlatch the front of the dollhouse and swing it open.

There was a figurine of a dark-haired woman lying in a pool of blood on the floor of the main bedroom. She was wearing a nurse's uniform.

"Well, it's not me," said Lauren. "Does it look like the person who bought your house?

It could have been. The figurines were pretty generic. It was the hair and clothes that you noticed, not the faces.

"It could be," I said. "I don't think she was a nurse. I can't remember what she did. I know the estate agent said she was recently divorced. It could just as easily be another student duped into turning up at a house the killer knew was empty."

I wondered if the police had checked my old house for cameras. I'd told them the killer was almost certain to have bugged the house. If the cameras were still there, he'd have been able to spy on the new occupant and know when she left the house empty.

"A nurse's uniform would be easy to get hold of," said Lauren. "All the fancy dress shops would have them."

I looked closer at the furniture and the duvet covers. They were all mine. The layout of each room was mine.

"This is a replica of what the house looked like when I lived there."

I looked for the strange briefcase. And there it was – on the kitchen island this time. Three dollhouses, three briefcases in various kitchen locations. I still had no idea what it meant.

"Why wouldn't he update the furniture?" said Lauren. "He's such a stickler for detail. And he's had two months to make the changes."

"Perhaps he's running out of time. It must take him weeks to make these dollhouses, and he's killing people every other day."

"He might have a day job as well," said Lauren. "Though, thinking about it, he must have very flexible hours. He killed Susan in the afternoon. He spent another afternoon and evening watching us in Bristol."

"He can take days off. He can also work nights."

"Mark was killed at night. I think he's self-employed. It would give him the freedom to set his own hours."

I looked at my watch. Ten minutes was almost up. "I think we should close up the dollhouse."

~

The police arrived soon after. Lauren and I showed them the dollhouse, and told them what had happened. Lauren emphasised what would have to be done next.

"You've got to find the head waiter before he goes off shift. He saw the man who booked this room. The same for the receptionists. They'd have seen him up close and will have seen his ID."

The two uniformed officers listened politely, but I could tell they were getting a bit fed up about being told how to do their job.

"They know what they're doing, Lauren." I said, putting my hand on her arm. This was going to be a long afternoon, and by the time it was over we'd have told our story several times to several people.

More uniformed officers arrived, then the detectives and forensics officers. We were moved out of Room 834 and asked to wait at the end of the corridor.

I spent a lot of the time looking out of the window. I could almost make out where my car was parked. Annoyingly, I couldn't see the hotel car park. I'd have liked to have seen what was going on out there. The killer might have still been in the area when the police arrived. Unlikely perhaps, but if he was starting to make mistakes...

And we knew he was a voyeur. Did that extend to a fascination with his crime scenes? Would he be sitting in his van at the back of the car park watching all the police arrive. Getting off on the attention.

Two detectives were the first to question us. They introduced themselves as DS Cox and DC Sanchez. They'd been involved in the search for Mark Weatherly's flat. We told them our story from the moment Lauren's agent received the call from the fake assistant.

"The flight announcement in the background is probably fake," said Lauren. "But you never know. I did check it out. The flight code was valid and the time was spot on. So it's worth checking the passenger list of flight AA371 Charlotte to Heathrow getting in at Heathrow at nine o'clock this morning."

I watched to see if either of the detectives noted down the number. DS Cox did. They were taking Lauren seriously.

"Here's the note he gave the head waiter," said Lauren, opening her handbag to show the slip of paper inside. "Sorry about the fingerprints. We both touched it. The head waiter too, and I assume the killer."

DC Sanchez gloved up before carefully removing the note and sealing it inside an evidence bag.

"Have either of you heard of the name Hiram Colescott?" asked DS Cox.

"No," I said. "Who is he?"

"He's the man who booked the hotel room."

They had a name!

"Do you recognise this man?" DS Cox showed us a picture on his phone. It wasn't a clear picture. It looked like a photograph of a photocopied passport picture. Was this the killer? I didn't recognise him.

Lauren didn't recognise him either. "Is this Hiram Colescott?" she asked. "Is he really American?"

"His passport's American," said DS Cox. "And he spoke with an American accent."

This did not make sense. Was the killer American? Or was this another accomplice?

~

We'd asked a few times if they'd found a body at my old house, but no one would say. It wasn't until a detective inspector came to talk to us that we found out.

"Do you recognise this woman?" he said, showing us a picture of a lifeless face on his phone.

"I think so," I said. "I only met her twice, but it looks like Phoebe Leycroft, the woman who bought my old house."

I was surprised. We'd mentioned the possibility of her being the victim, but I'd quickly dismissed the idea. The killer lured his victims to the houses. He didn't kill the house owners.

Until now.

What had changed?

"Was she drowned?" asked Lauren.

"Too soon to tell," said the inspector. "Mr. Sedley, when was the last time you talked to Mrs. Leycroft?"

"It would be about three months ago. I only talked to her twice. After that all communication was between our solicitors."

"Did you ever talk to her, Miss Corelli?"

"Never."

"Have they looked for hidden cameras in the house?" I asked. "I did mention it to the police a few days ago. The killer was almost certainly bugging that house when I lived there."

"I haven't heard anything," said the inspector. "I'll pass the information along. In the meantime, Mr. Sedley, we'd like you to look at the inside of the dollhouse."

I was given a white oversuit to put on and taken into the hotel room. The forensics team had the dollhouse open and were photographing it meticulously.

"Do you recognise any of the furniture?" asked the inspector.

I played along, feigning surprise that the dollhouse interior was an exact replica of the time when I lived there. I couldn't be more specific about the date. I'm not the kind of person who buys a lot of new furniture or decorates. The replica could have been made any time in the last two years.

I made sure I pointed out the briefcase on the kitchen island.

"That briefcase has been in all three dollhouses," I said. "It's always in the kitchen, but it's never in the same place. I have no idea what it signifies. I haven't owned a briefcase for years."

I was thanked for my assistance and asked to remain outside in the corridor.

"It shouldn't be for much longer," said the inspector. "We've almost finished processing the scene."

Seeing as the inspector was being friendly, I thought I'd risk a question or two.

"Have you found any CCTV footage of someone carrying the dollhouse?"

"I'm not at liberty to say. But we are making good progress."

Well, I tried.

I climbed out of my oversuit and rejoined Lauren by the window.

~

"I've been digging into Hiram Colescott," said Lauren. "I can't find anything. Doesn't look like either name is remotely common. Though I am getting hits for historic figures in the Ku Klux Klan. Apparently James Colescott succeeded Hiram Evans as head of the KKK in 1939. Hiram Colescott could be a KKK fan inventing his dream alias."

"The KKK don't go in for drowning, do they?"

"Not that I've read. I think we should tell the inspector Hiram Colescott could be a false name."

I wondered how well that would go down.

"You could mention it," I said. "But I'm sure they'll be checking with the US authorities anyway. They'll be looking for everything the Americans have on him."

"There might be more murders," said Lauren. "We did wonder why there was such a long gap between Sophie and Susan. If he was in America that would explain it."

It would. And also the change in MO from a simple drowning to waterboarding and dollhouses. It might be possible to trace the evolution of his MO.

"But why kill Phoebe Leycroft?" said Lauren. "He's never killed anyone in their own home before."

"He might be running out of his usual source of victims. It must take a lot of time to groom someone online. And with all the publicity this case has garnered people are going to be far more suspicious."

"Showing his face is new too," said Lauren. "Why take the risk? He didn't have to. He could have found another empty property, and invited us there with some anonymous online message that we couldn't resist."

"Would we have gone though?"

"If he'd made it sound tantalising enough. Yes."

"I don't think we would. The only reason we even contemplated coming to this hotel was the public nature of the meeting. Yes, Stepan Balusek was the lure, but it was the busy public restaurant that clinched it."

Lauren looked lost in thought for a while.

"You know, I think you're right," she said. "But it's not so much how *we'd* react as how *he* thinks we'd react. If he thinks he needs to take more risks to get us to play his games, then he's willing to take those risks. Which tells me that our presence – most likely *your* presence – is really high on his list of priorities. Susan, Mark, Phoebe – they're collateral damage. You're his main target."

Chapter Forty-One

Just after three o'clock we were told we could leave. The police gave us a lift to my car, and tailed us for ten minutes to make sure no one was following us.

"Are you hungry?" asked Lauren. "I never did get my lunch."

We stopped off at a supermarket and bought sandwiches and a bottle of water. I thought of stocking up the freezer, but I didn't have my Keep Cool Bag with me. We'd stock up nearer home.

It was an uneventful trip back to Garstock. Lauren surfed on her phone, looking for any updates on the case. All the news channels were reporting that there was significant police activity at my old house in Rayford. Many were saying that a body had been found. No one mentioned the Hotel Cardinale or Hiram Colescott.

I threw in a couple of short detours just to see if anyone was following us. I couldn't see anyone. Nevertheless, I still approached Garstock from the opposite direction. Even if no one was following us, they'd know where we were going.

The press contingent was still encamped outside the cottage. I counted a dozen cars. More than earlier, but at least the patrol car was still there.

"Pull up outside the gate," said Lauren. "I better say something. I did promise them an interview."

The shouting started the moment Lauren opened the door. Reporters swarmed around the car, holding out their cameras, jostling for position.

Lauren! Lauren! Is it true the Dollhouse Killer has struck again?

Did you find another dollhouse?

Have you come from the murder scene?

Where have you been?

What happened at the Yateley Heath service station?

Lauren quietened them down. "Thank you," she said. "I'll be making a statement soon. I need to talk to the police first to make sure I don't disclose anything they need holding back. It's been a hell of a day. A lot has happened, but I can tell you this: the killer has made a huge mistake."

That almost seemed to satisfy them. A few still shouted questions at Lauren, but they began to disperse enough so that I could drive through the gate.

Lauren opened and closed the garage door for me. I collected the shopping bags from the boot, and we headed up the drive to the front door. One of uniformed police officers was waiting for us.

"I thought you were driving to Bristol," he said.

"Sorry about that," said Lauren. "I had to make something up. There were a couple of hardcore paparazzi listening in. I was trying to mislead them. Not that it stopped them from following. Did you see them set off after us? They nearly ran us off the road a mile from here."

I stopped myself from smiling. Lauren's relationship with truth was a very tenuous one.

~

Once inside, I put all the frozen food in the freezer.

"I'm going to call Natalia," said Lauren. "Do you want to listen in?"

I did.

"Let me put the shopping away first."

Natalia didn't seem as chatty as she had earlier. I wondered if Terrell was close by. He'd probably classify any contact with us as consorting with the enemy.

"I thought I'd better check with you first," said Lauren. "To make sure I don't mention anything to the press that you need holding back."

"Do you have to talk to the press?"

"There are a couple of dozen reporters outside the front

door now baying for news. And my agent tells me she's had upwards of a hundred requests for interviews today alone. If I don't say something soon, they're going to start making stuff up."

"Okay," said Natalia, sighing. "Don't name the American, the victim, or the contents of the dollhouse. There's going to be a press conference very soon which will cover all that."

"Got it. So finding the dollhouse and recognising it as Matt's old house is okay. Also the general events of what happened at the hotel, but no mentioning Hiram Colescott."

"That's it."

"You do know the name's most likely fake? I couldn't find any trace of him online, but the name got a lot of hits on KKK sites. I think the killer might be a white supremacist."

"I can't comment, Lauren. Watch the press conference."

That was interesting. It sounded like DI Lipinski knew more about Hiram Colescott than she was prepared to say. Did the Americans have a file on him?

"Have you got a time of death for the latest victim?" asked Lauren.

"We have."

There was a long pause while we waited for Natalia to elaborate.

"But you're not going to tell me?" asked Lauren.

"You'll be told very soon. It's all covered in the press conference."

I could tell we were not going to get much more out of Natalia.

"Why didn't you come to me when your agent called you about meeting that director?" asked Natalia. She sounded put out.

"Because you'd have told me not to go," said Lauren.

"We could have sent officers to watch the hotel. We might have caught him."

"Oh, come on, Natalia. You know exactly what would have happened. DCI Terrell would have said it was a publicity stunt we'd dreamed up to divert the investigation. He wouldn't have sent anyone to the hotel."

"Well, next time – if there is a next time – call me first. DCI Terrell isn't the only one who can make decisions."

"That's good to know. I'll do that. I promise. You were the first one I called the moment I found the dollhouse."

~

None of the TV news channels had any mention of an impending police press conference. I wondered if Natalia had made it up to fob us off.

There was one interesting bit of news I hadn't heard though. The BBC had an interview with Mark Weatherly's employer – the garage owner. He said that Mark had told him his father had died, and had asked for two days off as the funeral was in Cornwall.

"He'd been a good worker," said the garage owner. "So I okayed it."

Mark had expected to be gone for two days. And he hadn't felt able to tell his employer the real reason for needing the time off.

It hadn't been a spur of the moment decision either. The garage owner said Mark had asked him for the time off on Monday morning – three days before his murder. Was that the timeframe the killer was working to? Planning each murder several days ahead?

If so, had he already contacted his next victim?

I muted the television when Lauren started recording her video blog.

"I think I need a different background," said Lauren. "Now Keith and Amrit have gone, I need something a bit more exciting than your curtains."

I considered suggesting she make a batch of fake blood and spatter it all over the curtains, but she'd probably have jumped at the idea.

"I know," said Lauren. "I'll use the view out of the front window. It has the patrol car and the press encampment. Help me move the dining room table."

I helped. And then watched Lauren let her imagination loose on the events at the Hotel Cardinale.

It was mesmerising. I'd been there, and I still wasn't sure what was she was going to say next. There was a kernel of truth in her account, but it was a truth that had been taken out for an extensive makeover. Everything was more dramatic, the odds against us greater, the fears more visceral, the potential rewards more compelling.

But it was Lauren's performance that held it all together. She made you feel that you were there, at the hotel, seeing though her eyes, feeling elated one minute, terrified the next, expecting any second to have to fight for your life.

I did get the occasional mention. I wasn't a total bystander. I was the cautionary voice, counselling restraint.

Lauren did not do restraint.

I had the feeling that another couple of re-tellings of the story she'd have us climbing the lift shaft with home-made weapons clenched between our teeth.

And she had to end her vlog with another go at the killer.

"Today," she said. "The killer made his second biggest mistake. He let himself be seen, and he paid for a hotel room with a credit card.

"His biggest mistake? That's easy. He should never have threatened me. So, if you're watching, Miniature Man. You don't have to worry about where I am any more. I'm coming for *you*."

~

"Are you sure goading a sadistic serial killer is a good idea?" I asked.

"If it pushes him into making mistakes, yes. He's a planner. So put him under pressure, make him act more recklessly. That's how he's going to get caught. If we keep our heads down and hide, we hand him the initiative."

Lauren went outside to spend some time with the press contingent. Her plan was to try and wean them off camping outside the cottage by pushing her vlog as the place to go for information.

"Feel free to download and broadcast any excerpts you want," she told them. "I'm making the site totally free. No adverts. No subscription required."

I watched from the window for a while, then decided to move the dining room table back to its usual place. When I'd finished, I noticed a 'breaking news' banner on the television. *Dollhouse press conference at 7pm.*

Chapter Forty-Two

The press conference started dead on time. The Chief Constable was there, Terrell too. The Chief Constable spoke first.

"A third dollhouse was discovered at one o'clock this afternoon in a hotel room near Heathrow Airport. Mathew Sedley, who found the dollhouse, recognised the house as one he had previously owned in The Close, Rayford, near Swindon. The police were called, and officers were despatched to the house in Rayford, where the body of the householder, Mrs. Phoebe Leycroft, was discovered. She had died some time in the early hours of today."

Not quite Lauren's style of delivery, but factual and concise. A picture of a smiling Mrs. Leycroft was displayed on the screen above the Chief Constable.

"We would like to hear from anyone who was in the Rayford area today or yesterday. Did you see this woman? Did you see anything unusual? We are particularly interested if anyone saw any vans or large SUVs being loaded or unloaded in the vicinity of The Close."

"They're still not mentioning the waterboard," said Lauren. "It can't be easy carrying something the size of a door in and out of a property. What's The Close like? Can you unload a van without being seen?"

"Not easily. Most of the front gardens are lawns or tarmac. There's very little cover."

The Chief Constable handed over to DCI Terrell. A picture of Hiram Colescott appeared on screen. A *good* picture, not the photocopied passport I'd been shown earlier.

"This is Timothy McCord," said Terrell.

That made us both sit up. They had his real name. What else had they discovered?

"He boarded a Heathrow-bound flight last night in Charlotte, the United States of America. His flight arrived in Heathrow just after nine this morning. He hired this car, a blue Ford Mondeo."

Terrell paused, pointing at the car on the screen above him.

"He drove to the Hotel Cardinale, near Heathrow Airport, where he registered under the name of Hiram Colescott. He used a fake American passport as ID, and paid using a credit card in the name of Hiram Colescott. Here is CCTV footage of him arriving at the hotel."

The screen showed him at reception. He had one small luggage bag with him. It was too small to contain the dollhouse.

"He took the lift up to the eighth floor and dropped his bag off at Room 834. He can then be seen exiting the lift on the ground floor and leaving the hotel. He returns a few minutes later carrying a large cardboard box."

I watched him carry the box across the foyer. The box was definitely large enough for the dollhouse.

"We believe the cardboard box contained the dollhouse," said Terrell. "Mr. McCord did not have this box with him when he left Heathrow Airport. CCTV footage shows that it was not in the hire car. Somewhere between the UK Auto Rentals car park and the Hotel Cardinale, Mr. McCord acquired this box. Did you see this man today near Heathrow? Did you see him in conversation with another person? Did you see him picking up a large cardboard box?"

"He's not the killer, is he?" said Lauren. "He was in a plane halfway across the Atlantic when Phoebe was killed. He's an accomplice, told to meet the killer somewhere between Heathrow and the hotel. Undoubtedly far away from any CCTV cameras."

Terrell continued, showing footage of McCord leaving the hotel. The time stamp was 12:10. We didn't arrive until thirty-five minutes later. If we'd driven straight to the hotel, we could have seen him leave. Except we wouldn't have recognised him. But he might have recognised us. Who knows what he might have done?

"We believe this man is still in the country," said Terrell. "If you see him, contact the police immediately. Do *not* approach this man. He is considered highly dangerous, and may be armed. He is a person of interest in three murders in Texas. The FBI believe he owns over forty firearms, including several assault weapons. He also has links to various right-wing militia and white supremacist groups."

"I can't see a person like McCord flying across the Atlantic just to deliver a dollhouse," said Lauren. "He sounds more like a partner than an accomplice. The killer did say there were two of them."

"We think it likely," said Terrell, "that McCord may have been in the country earlier this month. The FBI have informed us that McCord's whereabouts have been unknown for three months. He is known to have several aliases, and may have spent some of that time abroad. Again, we appeal to the public. If you have seen this man in the last month, contact us immediately."

Terrell handed over to the Chief Constable.

"We believe it is too early to determine the exact relationship between Timothy McCord and the killer of Phoebe Leycroft," said the Chief Constable. "I'm sure there will be much speculation. In the meantime, we believe it safest to proceed on the basis that both individuals are suspects in the murders of Susan Phillips and Mark Weatherly."

The Chief Constable then opened up the conference to questions from the media.

"What name did McCord use to enter the country?"

"He used his real name and his real passport," said the Chief Constable.

"Is it significant that Timothy McCord has allowed himself to be seen?"

"I think it's too soon to tell," said the Chief Constable. "It's certainly good for us, and it may indicate a growing desperation on behalf of the killers."

"Does Mrs. Leycroft have any links to Susan or Mark?"

"Not that we have found so far. These are *very* early days."

"Have you made any progress in Susan or Mark's murder?"

"Progress has been made, but it has been difficult as neither Susan nor Mark confided in anyone in the weeks leading up to their deaths. Also both Susan's and Mark's phones and laptops have not been found. We have been proceeding on the theory that both were groomed by their killer and told to bring their phones and laptops with them to Garstock."

"This last killing is only a few yards away from where Sophie Gallindo lived. She also drowned. Are you considering a possible link between the deaths?"

"No. Mrs. Leycroft was killed because she lived in Mathew Sedley's old house. The killer is obsessed with Mr. Sedley."

"Should people who live in other houses he's lived in be worried?"

"We very much doubt that, but we will be contacting the occupants of Mr. Sedley's former residences. We believe that the killer's interest in Mr. Sedley's previous residences does not go beyond his former house in Rayford."

I hadn't considered this at all. How many previous homes did I have? Including the rentals, it must be close on ten.

"The killer wouldn't be *that* obsessed with you, would he?" asked Lauren. "Surely Phoebe Leycroft only caught his eye because he still had cameras in your old house."

I was sure Lauren was right, but this was a twisted serial killer - or killers. Who knew what kind of connections were important to them.

"One last question," said the Chief Constable.

"Have you seen Lauren Corelli's account of how she found the dollhouse?"

DCI Terrell looked as though he was going to field the question, but turned away, leaving it to the Chief Constable.

"I would strongly advise that, should a similar situation arise, Miss Corelli would contact the police first," said the

Chief Constable.

~

"If the police actually listened to me, I'd be on the phone to them every day," said Lauren.

"At least Terrell didn't call you a serial killer groupie," I said.

"You could see him itching to say something cutting, though. I think he hates me more than he hates you."

Lauren spent the next two hours digging up everything she could find on Timothy McCord. There was a surprisingly large amount of information.

The most damning were the three murders he was suspected of being involved in.

"It looks like he was part of a militia group in Texas," said Lauren. "They liked to shoot at illegal immigrants as they crossed the Rio Grande into the US. The police weren't sure if they were trying to scare the immigrants off or kill them. Some reports suggested the militia didn't care. They regarded themselves as patriots in a race war against invading Hispanics, and if the government weren't going to defend the border, they would."

"Was he ever charged?"

"No. Insufficient evidence and a series of alibis provided by his friends."

"What about the victims? Did any of them drown?"

"Not that I can find. But all the reports think three is a very conservative estimate of the number of deaths. Illegal immigrants are going to be very reluctant to come forward as witnesses, and bodies can get washed away downstream."

I wondered if you could classify behaviour like that as sadism. It wasn't that far removed – shooting at people in the water, not really caring if you hit them or not, maybe deliberately missing with the first shots to build up their fear.

"I've also found links to anti-5G and anti-vaxxer groups," said Lauren. "It looks like he's a follower of QAnon. You know, the right-wing conspiracy theorist? McCord's a true believer.

He thinks a secret liberal elite is working with the deep state to control the people, that 5G gives you Covid, that Covid vaccinations inject some kind of mind control device into your body, and that only Trump and a well-armed militia can save the day."

"I don't suppose you found any link to Susan or Mark in the anti-5G and anti-vaxxer groups?"

"No, but outside of social media, most people don't use their real names on the internet. I've found a lot on McCord because he's been in the news and, up until a year ago, he was more interested in pushing his political agenda than hiding his identity."

"Any sign that he might have visited Britain recently?"

"Nothing. No sign of any links to anyone outside of America. That doesn't mean that there aren't any, but unless you know all the user names he posts under, you're not going to find them. You've really got to get hold of his phones and computers."

I wondered if he'd brought his phones and computers with him. And how paranoid he was. Would he have destroyed all his old phones and computers, or was there information out there that the US authorities could find if they raided the right address?

I was deep in thought, wondering what level of priority the US police would assign to a British request for information on Timothy McCord, when someone started hammering on the front door.

My first thought was Terrell. It had his level of urgency. I dragged myself towards the door. What new hell was he about to visit upon me?

But it wasn't Terrell. It was Detective Superintendent Maxton. A big, burly, brute of a man. I froze in the doorway. I hadn't seen him in twelve months. He'd interrogated me, threatened me, physically and mentally assaulted me. Over and over again.

He smiled at me, stepping forward, violating my personal space. I stepped back. He stepped forward, towering over me, hatred in his eyes.

"I told you I'd get you," he said. "Mathew Sedley, you're under arrest."

"On what charge?" I said, my voice sounding small and faltering.

"Perverting the course of justice for starters. The murder charge will follow. We've got you this time, Sedley."

I was too shocked to speak. I looked at Lauren.

"I'll ring Georgia," she said.

Chapter Forty-Three

I was taken away in a daze. I could hear Lauren talking to the police, asking where they were taking me, asking for the name of the officer in charge. Lights flashed all round me. Cameras. Police car lights. People shouting. A hand was placed roughly on my head, and I was shoved into the back of a police car.

I was terrified. I thought I'd got over the trauma of last year, but seeing Maxton had brought it all back. I was shaking. I was cold. I was unmoored in time.

I had no idea where I was going or why. I didn't ask. I didn't say a word. I couldn't. I just wanted it all to go away.

I don't remember much of the journey. It must have taken over an hour. I'd driven the route between my house and Swindon quite a few times when I was moving house. But that night the journey was a blur, time stretching and contracting.

By the time we arrived in Swindon, I was starting to feel a bit more normal. The cold sweats and shaking had stopped, and the fog was lifting from my brain.

I was still confused. Why was I in Swindon and not Bristol? Swindon was a different police force. Surely Phoebe Leycroft's murder was going to be investigated by the Avon and Somerset police not Swindon and Wiltshire.

Or were English police forces fiercely territorial?

I was led from the car into the station. More memories flooded back. I'd spent several days here – first as a valued witness, then as a hated pariah. The latter was the one that scarred me the most. The police had felt so guilty about the way they'd treated the Gallindo family that they had to have a scapegoat they could pin all the blame on. *It wasn't our fault. We were just doing our job. It was Mathew Sedley's lies that made us act the way we did.*

They'd gone after me with everything they had. Perverting the course of justice, wasting police time, interfering with a lawful investigation. In the end they decided to just drop it. The family had had enough. The Chief Constable had had enough. So, they let me go, and set the press on me.

I was led into an interview room. It was probably one I'd been in before. This time I'd remember to hold onto the table if the detective superintendent walked behind me. It was amazing how easily interview room chairs could topple over backwards.

A young constable stood by the door glowering every time I looked his way. I didn't recognise him. This wasn't going to go well. Terrell was bad, but Maxton was an animal.

I waited. I could feel a panic attack coming on. I fought it back, willing the shaking to stop. I'm *not* that person any more. I don't have to question my memory or my sanity. I hadn't been mistaken. I hadn't been evil. I'd been right. I knew that now. I *had* heard a girl screaming, and I knew how the killer had done it. I knew about directional speakers.

I jumped as the door opened. DSU Maxton came in with another detective I recognised – DCI Ponting. She wasn't as bad as Maxton, but she was bad enough.

I took a deep breath. *I am not that person anymore. I was right all along. I can prove it.*

Maxton spoke first. "Well, well, well. Just like old times, Mathew."

No, it wasn't. This time I wasn't waiving my rights in the mistaken belief that the innocent had nothing to fear.

"I want a lawyer and my phone call. Now."

"And you will," said Maxton. "In good time. But this isn't a formal interview. Nothing's being recorded. This is a little chat between old friends. You remember DCI Ponting, don't you?"

"I do. And I don't remember your chats ever being remotely friendly."

"Your memory was never very good, was it, Mathew?"

"Actually, my memory is excellent. Which you'd have known

twelve months ago if you'd done your due diligence and actually investigated my claims."

Maxton was incensed. I braced myself in case he hit me.

"Not investigated your fucking claims?" he said. "We did nothing else *but* investigate your fucking claims."

"Then why didn't you find out about directional speakers?"

"What directional speakers? Is this going to be another one of your rabbit holes you try and send us down?"

"Have a look at the Dollhouse murder files," I said. "You'll see for yourselves. Two witnesses – both policemen – swore that a couple of nights ago they heard a young girl screaming, and shouting the words 'Help, he's going to kill me. Help me, please.' That's exactly – word for word – what I heard being screamed back in Rayford a year ago."

Maxton shrugged. "So? Where do these directional speakers come into it?"

"The two policemen were a hundred yards away from the screams. A far closer witness – a solicitor, absolutely unimpeachable – heard nothing. Doesn't that sound familiar?"

"Still waiting for those speakers."

"Directional speakers are how it was done. Look it up if you don't believe me. Museums use them. Loads of companies do. A directional speaker allows you to send sound in a tight beam to one location but miss out others. That's how I heard the screaming, but no one else did, even though they were closer. So, I wasn't lying when I told you I heard the screaming, and neither were the neighbours. It was someone else –the Dollhouse Killer – deliberately targeting me. You should take another look at Sophie's file. There's a very strong possibility that she was the first victim of the Dollhouse Killer."

Maxton shook his head, rummaged in a trouser pocket, and handed a five pound note over to DCI Ponting.

"It was a bet," he said. "DCI Ponting thought you'd blame it all on the Dollhouse Killer. I thought you'd break like a twig first."

I couldn't believe that they were still not listening.

"But you were right about one thing," said Maxton. "We should definitely reopen the Sophie Gallindo case." He paused. "We've been in your old attic, Mathew."

He looked at me as though that would mean something to me.

"We found it, Mathew," he continued. "We found the shrine."

~

"What shrine?" I asked.

He continued to stare at me. What did he think he had on me?

"Refresh Mr. Sedley's memory, Detective Chief Inspector."

DCI Ponting opened a folder and slid a large photograph across the table towards me. I looked at it. It showed a collection of photographs of Sophie pinned to a board. She looked the same age in every picture. In several she was wearing the same clothes. Were they all taken outdoors? I couldn't see any wallpaper or furniture in the background of any of the pictures.

"You're having a good look, Mathew," said Maxton. "Have you missed having it around?"

"I'm doing your job, Detective Superintendent. I'm examining the evidence. It looks to me like these pictures were all taken outside within a short space of time. I lived a few houses down from Sophie for six years. This looks like the work of someone who only knew her for a short period of time – like the Dollhouse Killer."

"Or someone who became obsessed with Sophie once she'd reached a certain age."

I couldn't think of a suitable rejoinder so I sat there, trying to outstare him.

"Show Mathew the gloves, Gemma."

Ponting produced two evidence bags. Each one contained a single blue, woollen glove. They looked like a child's. Sophie's?

"Take a closer look," said Maxton. "I know you want to. It

must have been a wrench to leave these trophies behind."

"I take it these belong to Sophie," I said. "I've never seen them before, but it's well-documented that the Dollhouse Killer plants evidence at crime scenes."

"It's also well-documented that the dollhouse murders began this week. Do you want to hazard a guess at when these gloves went missing?"

"No idea," I said, though I imagined it was in the week before Sophie went missing.

"We know *exactly* when these gloves went missing. Sophie was wearing them on the day she died. Her grandmother knitted them for her. We assumed she must have lost them on or before falling into the river. But no, *you* took them. You wrenched them from her tiny hands before pushing her into the river. Did you enjoy watching her drown? Did she put up a fight? Did you have to hold her under?"

Suddenly, the incident room door burst open and Georgia appeared. She looked like she'd just stepped out from some society event. Her hair was up. Her dress was long, and her jewellery elegant.

She did not look amused.

"Stop talking!" she demanded. "All of you."

"Who the hell are you?" said Maxton.

"I'm his lawyer. Who the hell are you?"

"Detective Superintendent Maxton. How the hell did you get back here?"

"The more pertinent question is, why wasn't I invited back here? You are interviewing my client without his lawyer being present."

"This isn't an interview. It's an informal chat."

Georgia pointed at the bags containing the gloves.

"They look remarkably like evidence bags to me. Mathew, did you ask for a lawyer?"

"I did."

"Have you subsequently been questioned about your involvement in a crime and shown evidence relating to that crime?"

"I have."

"Then this stops now, Detective Superintendent. I demand to speak to my client alone. Immediately."

Chapter Forty-Four

"Wow," I said as soon as the room cleared. "You were impressive."

"I was, wasn't I? That's what happens when a girl who has been promised chocolate has to walk out before the dessert course."

"Sorry."

"It's not your fault. I chose this profession. Now, Lauren mentioned you were going to be charged with murder."

I told her everything.

"Did they mention anything about fingerprint or DNA evidence linking you to the gloves or photos?" asked Georgia.

"No, though they'd only just started."

"So, potentially, all they have on you is that these items were found in a house that had once belonged to you?"

"That's right, and I haven't lived there for two months."

"Are these more police officers who hate you?"

"They are. Especially Maxton. He blames me for everything that went wrong in the Sophie Gallindo case. Now he thinks he can pin a murder charge on me."

"So, it's personal between Detective Superintendent Maxton and yourself?"

"Yes. He's made that clear."

"In front of witnesses?"

"And on camera. Unless he's deleted all the old interview tapes."

"What about the other death?" asked Georgia. "The owner of the house. Has anyone intimated that you're considered a suspect in that?"

"No. Phoebe Leycroft was killed in the early hours of today. I couldn't have done it. I had four policemen watching my doors all night. They'll all swear that I never left the house.

But whoever did kill her would have had access to the attic for several hours. Add that to the Dollhouse Killer's known penchant for planting evidence to incriminate others, and it's obvious who left the gloves and shrine for the police to find."

"Well, unless they have an actual piece of evidence that implicates you, they have no grounds to arrest you. In fact, given your history with Detective Superintendent Maxton, this borders on wrongful arrest and unlawful prosecution."

"You can get me out?"

"I should be able to. This is a Saturday night though. They might drag their heels."

~

Georgia went off to find DSU Maxton. She was hopeful they'd agree to release me straight away, but told me to be prepared for another session.

"If they have no evidence against you, they'll be looking to trap you into incriminating yourself or wear you down until you're so tired you'll admit to anything. I will *not* let that happen. I can field their questions, and I can stop the interview at any time if you want to confer with me in private. The onus is on them to make a case or let you go. We don't have to prove anything."

When Georgia returned, she was accompanied by DSU Maxton and DCI Ponting. They weren't finished with me.

I steeled myself. It was late. I'd had a very long day, but I could get through this. Georgia could more than hold her own in a battle of wits with Maxton, and as long as the interview was recorded, I was safe.

DCI Pontin switched on the camera and everyone introduced themselves. DSU Maxton opened the questioning.

"When was the last time you visited Rayford, Mr. Sedley?"

"The day I moved house. July 7th."

"Your car was seen in The Close this week. How do you account for that?"

"I ... can't. What day was this?"

I was confused. Was this Maxton making things up, or

another instance of the killer framing me?

"You know very well what day it was. You were seen. Even with your new beard, you can't hide who you are."

I looked at Georgia.

"Do you have a date for this sighting, Detective Superintendent, or are you still fishing for one?" said Georgia.

"I'm seeking the truth, Miss Courteney. What were you doing in Rayford this week, Mr. Sedley?"

"I wasn't in Rayford this week, and if you give me the date and time of this alleged sighting, I'll tell you where I was."

"Wednesday afternoon," said Maxton.

I tried to recall where I was on Wednesday afternoon. Was I in Bristol?

"Are you certain your witness saw Mr. Sedley's car in Rayford on Wednesday afternoon?" asked Georgia.

"That's what I was told," said Maxton."

"Really? This is a ridiculous fishing expedition, Detective Superintendent. My client's car was in a police pound all day Wednesday. And before you reel off a list of other days it could have been, consider the fact that my client has spent most of the week either in police custody or under police observation."

"Your client is a child-killer. He was obsessed with Sophie a year ago, and now we find her missing gloves in his attic along with a shrine to her memory!"

"It is not *his* attic."

"It *was* his attic," said Maxton. "He hid them there. That's right, isn't it, Mathew? You meant to get rid of them when you moved house. You knew that was the sensible thing to do, but you couldn't do it. You couldn't burn *her* pictures or *her* gloves. So you hid them in your old attic just in case you needed to go back for them later."

"Are you really suggesting my client left incriminating evidence where it could easily be found by the new owner or any tradesperson she happened to employ?"

"It's how most criminals are caught. They make stupid mistakes."

"Do you have any crime scene photographs showing where these items were hidden?" asked Georgia.

DCI Ponting handed three large photographs to Georgia who spread them out on the table for us both to see.

The shrine was propped up against the chimney breast in the attic. The gloves were resting on a joist nearby. There was also something else on the edge of the photograph – something large – which I couldn't quite make out.

"This is how the shrine and gloves were found?" asked Georgia. "They weren't covered up or hidden at all?"

"They were in an attic," said Maxton.

"They're in plain sight," said Georgia. "There's been no attempt to cover them with a sheet or put them at the bottom of a large packing case."

"Child-killers are like that," said Maxton. "They think they love their victims. That's right, isn't it, Mathew? You couldn't bury Sophie's things at the bottom of a box. She had to be out in the open where she could see and breathe."

I didn't answer. I was staring at that large object in one of the photographs. Only part of it was visible, but it looked like it had straps. I wasn't sure what they were at first, but now I could see. A large flat object with straps.

"What's that?" I asked, pointing at the photo. "That was never in the attic when I lived there."

"You recognise it, don't you?" said Maxton, leaning forward excitedly.

I didn't say a word. I didn't react. I just kept looking, head down, at the photograph. Thinking hard. I was pretty sure the police hadn't mentioned waterboarding to the media, and I wasn't going to throw Georgia under a bus.

"No, I don't recognise it, but … it looks like a door with straps on it. It's not a waterboard, is it? That's the rumour on the internet. The dollhouse killer waterboards his victims."

"Where on the internet?" said Maxton.

I shrugged. "I can't remember exactly. It was on one of the hundreds of forums I've seen the last few days. There's a lot of speculation out there. People put drowning and sadistic killer together, and got waterboarding. Is that what this is? A waterboard?"

I wasn't in Lauren's class, but I could still lie when I put my mind to it.

"Is it a waterboard, Detective Superintendent?" asked Georgia.

Maxton ignored Georgia and continued with his questioning.

"Where were you between the hours of two and four this morning?"

"In bed. Two firearms officers were inside the house watching the front and back doors all night. Two more policemen were stationed outside. All will swear that I never left the property."

"Detective Superintendent," said Georgia, a little more forcibly than before. "Was a waterboard found in Mrs. Leycroft's attic this morning?"

"I'm not at liberty to say."

"Then I'll say it for you," said Georgia. "If a waterboard was found in Mrs. Leycroft's attic this morning, that means the Dollhouse Killer was in her attic this morning. There is your suspect, Chief Superintendent. Not someone who owned the house two months ago, but someone who was in the attic mere hours before you searched the property."

"The Dollhouse Killer was also in Rayford at the time of Sophie's death," I said. "He set me up with those recordings of a young girl screaming. And did you find hidden cameras in my old house? Examine them. I bet you'll find they've been there over a year."

Maxton and Ponting did not look happy.

"The cameras also explain how the note I thought came from Sophie disappeared. He would have seen where I put the note. We know he's an expert at breaking into properties. He had no problem installing cameras in every room without me noticing. And it would have been him who slipped the note in my pocket, and him that stole it back. Everything is explained. He manipulated all of us."

Maxton looked like a man torn between several courses of action, none of them good. Ponting watched and waited.

"May I suggest," said Georgia. "That you release my client forthwith. My client, in turn, will promise to make himself available to assist with any future enquiries that you may have."

~

I couldn't get out of that place quick enough. Luckily it was a feeling shared by DSU Maxton. He wanted me out of his sight too. Georgia offered to drive me home, which was very kind of her. It was past midnight and, even at night, the drive had to be well over an hour. Plus she'd have another hour on top of that to drive home. I thought about offering her a bed for the night, but who'd want to spend the night at the murder house with a serial killer on the loose?

"Where's your car parked?" I asked Georgia.

"In the underground car park."

"Okay, there's a chance the killer, or killers, know I'm here. They're probably miles away in hiding, but we have to take precautions. You walk on ahead. They won't know you or your car. I'll follow."

I followed Georgia, leaving a gap of around twenty yards. It was dark in the car park. The only light coming from above the exits and those activated by motion sensors as we passed underneath. We appeared to be alone.

Georgia got into her car. I did a final scan of the car park, then hurried over. I climbed into the front seat and bent forward, folding myself as low as possible so I couldn't be seen. I remained like that for the first mile, much to the car's annoyance – as evidenced by the constant beep of the seat belt warning monitor.

"Do you have to do this every time you go out?" asked Georgia.

"I don't go out that much, but, yes, I have to assume that I'm being watched. Could you take a short detour when we get south of Swindon? It's a good idea to turn off onto a minor road for a short while to see if anyone follows."

No one followed. I watched the road behind us, looking for headlights. Nothing. Georgia plotted a route back onto the main road. At last we could relax.

"I can't thank you enough for representing me back there," I said.

"It's my job. And you're my most interesting client. I've never met anyone who has so many alibis and so many enemies. Someone at dinner said there was now an American militia after you."

"Militiaman. Singular. Timothy McCord. He could be an accomplice. He could be a partner."

"That's what's so intriguing about this case," said Georgia. "We know so much, and yet we know so little. There are clues everywhere, but which ones are real? And where do *you* fit in? Are you his primary target or are you a smokescreen? We don't know if his victims are chosen for a reason or if they're collateral damage. Now we don't even know how many killers there are."

That about summed it up. But we were making progress. Weren't we? Although it would certainly help if the police didn't insist on holding so much information back.

"Do you still have your source in the pathology lab?" I asked.

"I may have. Why?"

"It's all gone very quiet on Mark's autopsy. I was wondering if the killer was still using sea water to drown his victims?"

"Not any more. Mark's diatom test came back as tap water. I think the use of sea water was purely an embellishment to incriminate you. There was one puzzling item though. You know they found a size eleven boot print outside your neighbour's house?"

"Yes."

"Well, Mark was found wearing size eleven boots."

"Mark left the prints?"

"Possibly. But when they measured Mark's feet, they found

they were size eight. The killer had dressed him in boots three sizes too big."

"To make it look like Mark was an accomplice?"

"The police aren't sure. The print was an exact match for the boot – so we know the boot made the print – but all of Mark's clothes were on the large size. Our illustrious detective chief inspector believes that this proves that Mark didn't buy the clothes or the boots. The killer did. Which means he bought the clothes before deciding who was going to wear them."

"The clothes were identical to the ones worn by the figurine?"

"Oh, yes. Absolutely."

~

I phoned Lauren to tell her I was on the way back.

"They've released you?" she said.

"Georgia got me out. I'll tell you all about it later, but the big news is they found a waterboard in my old attic along with a pair of Sophie Gallindo's gloves that she'd been wearing the day of her death, and a whole mass of pictures of Sophie pinned onto a large board."

"Was that why they arrested you?"

"That, and their obsession with persecuting me."

"Are there any police forces that don't hate you?"

"I believe I'm looked upon quite favourably in the Outer Hebrides."

"There's still time. They haven't met you yet."

"Anyway, we're about forty minutes away. Is there still a press encampment outside the gate?"

"I'll have a look." There was a pause while Lauren checked. "I can see three cars."

"Okay. Just in case there are any paparazzi out there, can you distract them long enough for Georgia to drop me off and get away?"

"I am the queen of distraction. And if that fails, I have a bradawl."

I can never tell when Lauren's joking.

Lauren was holding court as we approached Laburnum Cottage. I told Georgia to slow down and switch off her headlights. There was sufficient light coming from outside the cottage.

"Pull up about twenty yards short," I said. "I'll be safe from there. The police car can see me. Just you be careful. Get on a main road as soon as you can, and don't stop for anyone."

No one followed her, and no paparazzi tyres were harmed in the process.

Back in the house, I just about had the energy to bring Lauren up to date with everything that had happened. After that I had to go to bed. The adrenaline that had kept me going had been pretty much used up.

Chapter Forty-Five

The manhunt for Timothy McCord was the main story on the breakfast news. There'd been many sightings, but nothing that looked like panning out. I had several mentions. *Wiltshire police question Mathew Sedley, Mathew Sedley arrested in late night swoop.* Some actually added the fact that I'd been released without charge. Most didn't, preferring the story of an arrest being made rather than one of police dragging in the usual suspects.

And they kept running a clip of me being led away from the house looking terrified. I cringed every time they showed it.

"Did I really look that scared?"

Lauren nodded. "You were in shock."

My old house in Rayford came in for a lot of attention. One of the channels was presenting the news from outside the front gate. Others had journalists stationed there giving live reports to camera. None of them mentioned the police finding a waterboard in my old attic.

But several mentioned Sophie Gallindo. No one mentioned gloves or shrine, but they commented on the proximity. Two tragedies in one small road.

I wondered what Sophie's parents were going through. The media were encamped a few doors down from their house. It had to bring all those terrible memories back. And the fears. For the moment, the journalists were being considerate. They were mentioning Sophie's death, but they weren't dwelling on it. How long would that last? Soon someone would knock on their door, or stop them as they came out of their gate. And, even if they didn't, the fear that they might would still be there.

The family couldn't fail to notice the link between the two deaths either. Not just two tragedies in one small road, but two drownings. Two drownings and me – the even bigger link. My house, my testimony that had turned them into murder suspects. How could the deaths not be linked?

Should I talk to them? Tell them what I knew? Was not knowing worse than knowing?

Or was I the last person the family would want to hear from?

"I've been thinking about the waterboard in the attic," said Lauren.

"What about it?"

"The killer would have to have a very strong reason to leave it there. It's a huge risk for him. If he used it to kill Phoebe Leycroft, there'd be trace evidence all over it. Even with all that water being poured over it, there'd still be DNA and fingerprints, hair and skin flakes even. You'd have to be really confident in your ability to remove any traces that could lead back to you."

"Maybe he wears gloves, a full oversuit and sprays the waterboard with bleach?"

"But what does he *gain* by leaving the waterboard there?"

"He links the waterboard to me and to Sophie's murder."

"No, he doesn't. The gloves and shrine link you to Sophie's murder. The waterboard clears you. It links the gloves and the shrine to the murder of Phoebe Leycroft, for which you have the perfect alibi."

"Perhaps the killer didn't know I'd have a perfect alibi."

"He'd have to know. I've blogged about the police protection. I've talked to reporters about it. The media have broadcast dozens of clips showing the patrol car outside the door."

That was all true. The killer was a planner who was obsessed with me, *and* my whereabouts.

"I think he's devolving," said Lauren. "I think that's what they call it. It's when serial killers switch from being organised planners to disorganised risk takers who can't stop killing."

I'd heard the term, mainly on American television series,

but had no idea if it had any basis in fact.

"Look at the way he's changed his MO in this last murder," said Lauren. "He's always chosen isolated properties to stage his murders. It makes his job safer. Less chance of being seen. Less chance of being heard. Which is crucial. He's got to carry a bulky waterboard in and out of the house, plus the clothes he's going to dress the victim in, the clothes he's going to change into, and the towels to clean up with after and to drape over the victim's nose and mouth."

"And torturing someone repeatedly for thirty minutes is going to be noisy," I added.

"Exactly. But in this last murder he chooses a house surrounded by neighbours with no cover to hide his van. If anyone hears a noise and looks out their window, they'll see the van."

I wondered if he could have parked further away. It *would* mean carrying the waterboard along a public road, but The Close was pretty quiet. You could be lucky and meet no one.

"Then there's the other change to his MO," said Lauren. "Killing the householder. He's never done that before. His MO was grooming young, impressionable teenagers and luring them to remote properties miles away from their homes. Why change?"

"Because he wanted the police to find Sophie's gloves and shrine. The murder of Phoebe Leycroft gave the police a reason to search the attic."

"But then he ruined it by leaving the waterboard in the attic."

"Did he ruin it, though?" I asked. "He wants me to suffer. He wants me interrogated, pressured, dragged from my home. But he doesn't want me locked up. He wants me in play, so I can find his next dollhouse. So he plants enough evidence to persuade people like Terrell and Maxton to pull me in, but makes sure the arrest doesn't stick."

It made perfect sense to me.

"And stowing the waterboard in the attic means he doesn't have to risk being seen walking away from a murder scene carrying a great, big door," I said. "He can park down by the river. It's not far away, and there's a couple of secluded spots by the footpath. He can then put all the clothes and towels he's used in a single bag. Far less conspicuous."

"He's still got to get the waterboard into the house," said Lauren.

"But he doesn't have to do it on the day of the murder. Which takes a lot of the pressure off. He's got cameras inside the house so he can pick his time and make sure that Phoebe's out. He can then park on the drive right by the side door and carry the waterboard, gloves and shrine up into the attic. He can be in and out in minutes."

"It's still one hell of a risk," said Lauren.

"I think he'd see it as worth it. He had me hauled off to Swindon, and he's made Wiltshire police re-open the investigation into Sophie's death."

~

Lauren had just finished a short interview for one of the Sunday morning magazine shows when there was a knock on the door.

I jumped. It wasn't as loud or insistent as Terrell or Maxton, but I'd forgotten the last time a knock on the door heralded anything other than bad news.

I took a deep breath before opening the door.

It was one of the uniformed officers from the patrol car outside.

"Sorry to bother you," he said. "But I've been told to inform you that this will be our last shift here. Bob and Kofi will be here for the night shift, but when they knock off at eight tomorrow morning that'll be it."

We knew this was going to happen soon, but I had thought the events of yesterday might have given them a reason to extend the protection period.

"Right," I said. "Thanks for letting for us know. Let's hope you have an uneventful final shift."

I was preparing to close the door when Lauren intervened.

"Who made the decision to withdraw police protection?" she asked.

The officer shrugged. "I expect the decision came from my Inspector or higher. I shouldn't worry. They'd have a done a thorough risk analysis."

Lauren didn't look convinced.

"Do *you* think we're safe here?" she asked the officer.

"Yes, I do. You have excellent locks. You have alarms in every room. These killers are going to be far more concerned about laying low at the moment than going after you. There's a huge manhunt out for them. If they break cover, someone will spot them."

Lauren didn't let it go. There was no point haranguing the constable - he was only following orders. So, she rang Natalia.

Natalia wasn't entirely sympathetic.

"There's nothing I can do," she said. "It's an operational decision. Police numbers are stretched as it is. Especially with the manhunt. Senior management think the officers would be better deployed in the search for McCord. We're getting more sightings than we can process.

"But how can we not be in danger?" argued Lauren. "He's obsessed with Mathew. If you take away police protection, he *will* come for us."

"Will he though? He, or they, have had plenty of opportunities to attack you, but they've never made any attempt to harm you physically. They don't want to kill you. They want to terrify and mentally torture you."

"Until they move onto the next phase. Can't you see we're the eventual victims? If they think the police are closing in on them, they might decide to speed up and move onto us."

"More likely they will lay low and wait for the search to peter out."

Lauren gave up and ended the call.

"They're not going to change their minds," she said. "Terrell said he'd remove police protection if we didn't behave. This is payback for the Heathrow excursion."

"But we did know this was going to happen eventually," I said. "This isn't anything new."

"Yes, but there are two of them now. One we could take – with a bit of luck and a couple of carving knives – but two? The odds would be stacked way against us."

"We have locks on every door and window, and panic alarms in every room."

"The window locks won't stop someone smashing their way in. There are two of them. They could be inside in seconds."

"We'd hear the noise and press the panic alarm. The noise alone could be enough to deter them. If my solicitor neighbour is awake again with his window open, he'll call the police too."

"But he won't come to our aid. No one will. Not for ages. A panic alarm is great in a town where the police are close by. But you live in the middle of nowhere. Where's the nearest police station? I had a look online. I don't think your two nearest stations are manned at night. We'd have to wait for a car to come from one of the larger towns. It could be ten minutes or more. We could be tied up, bundled into the back of a van, and miles away by then."

"Okay, so we sleep in the same room again, and barricade the bedroom door. We could hold out for ten minutes."

"I'm not spending the entire evening and night holed up here waiting to be attacked. We've got to get out."

"Where to? Your flat? He broke into there without much problem. At least here we have the alarms and big bolts on the doors."

"No. We go off grid. Properly off grid. Random, no-one-knows-where-the-hell-we-are – not even us – off the grid. And we do it now, before the killers know our protection is being lifted."

"What, and stay in a B&B waiting for the killers' special room service?"

"The killers won't know where we are this time. The house has been swept. Our cars and phones have been swept. We're bug-free. Plus we have our personal alarms. If we choose a B&B next to a police station, we'll be set."

"What if we're followed like yesterday? I don't want another car chase with the paparazzi."

"I think they've moved on. When I last looked there were only two cars parked outside. Neither of them matched the cars that chased us."

"You're adamant about this, aren't you?"

"Yes, I am. And we keep moving. A different place, a different county, every night. It's not just safer for us. It'll bugger up the killers' plans. If they can't find you, they can't plant a dollhouse for you to find. They might even have to put their killing on hold."

This was an argument I could never win. And, looking on the bright side, if no one could find me, they couldn't arrest me.

Chapter Forty-Six

We decided to have an early lunch then hit the road. We'd pack enough clothes for five days, and make sure we had enough hardware to protect ourselves – two large knives, a rolling pin, a hammer, and a couple of wedges to hammer under doors.

We also removed the SIM cards from both our phones.

"Should we tell the officers outside we're leaving?" I asked. It seemed only polite seeing as they *were* protecting us.

Lauren was torn. "The whole point of being off grid is that no one knows where you are. If we tell the officers outside, they'll tell their boss. The next thing you know your number plate is added to a list of cars to look out for, and we're being monitored."

"And if we leave without a word and don't come back tonight, the police could think we're in trouble and start a search for us."

"There is that."

"You know, we could actually tell them the truth," I said, slightly tongue-in-cheek. "Some people swear by it."

"I don't lie," said Lauren. "I may occasionally interpret reality differently to other people."

"Yesterday you told the police we were going to your flat in Bristol. That's a bit more than a different interpretation. We were driving to Heathrow."

"But it wasn't really a lie. It was more a director's cut – an improved version of the truth that suited the greater good. We *will* drive to my flat to pick up clothes one day, just not that day. You could call it a rainbow lie – that's just like a white lie, but more colourful and multi-faceted."

I had no idea if Lauren was joking or being serious. I

wasn't too sure if she knew either.

But I decided to leave the question of what we told the police to Lauren. She'd handle the press too. Yesterday's paparazzi might have gone, but that didn't mean that others hadn't replaced them.

My job was to stow our luggage in the car without creating suspicion that we were leaving. I was quite proud of my solution. I put both our bags into two black bin liners and carried them out to the garage. Nothing to see here – just a man having a clear out, moving clutter into the garage. As soon as the garage door closed, I loaded both bin bags into the boot of my car where they wouldn't be seen.

I then made a bit of a noise – emptying and re-filling a couple of boxes, banging a few tools against my workbench – doing a passable imitation of a man working in his garage, and definitely *not* loading up his car for a quick getaway.

When I'd finished, I opened the garage door and waited for Lauren. She was in the back seat of the patrol car, chatting. Everyone looked happy.

I never did find out what story she told the two officers. It might have been the truth. It might have been *a* truth. It might have been *her* truth. Whatever it was it smoothed our departure.

Lauren handled the press with similar aplomb, telling them we'd be gone for a few hours, that the case had moved on, that Laburnum Cottage was now on the periphery of the investigation, that Bristol was the new hub, and that if she had any news it would always appear on her blog first.

No one followed us. I slowed down a couple of times to check. The road was always clear.

"Okay," said Lauren. "Head for the main road then it's up to the dice."

I had my doubts about using dice to choose which direction we would take, but it worked quite well – at the beginning. We didn't consult the dice at every road junction, and we modified the rules to avoid motorways, no through roads, and industrial estates. And, later, we changed them again to avoid re-tracing our steps and reduce the number of times we consulted the dice.

Towards the end I suspected that Lauren was cheating as our choice of routes became less circuitous and she stopped showing me the dice after she'd rolled it.

And we started to head towards the coast. Torbay. I'd been there a few times as a child – staying in Brixham one year and Paignton the next. They were traditional south coast seaside resorts. Lots of sand, hotels and seagulls that could spot a bag of chips from a mile away.

The dice was formally retired. We needed to find a B&B in a quiet location. Somewhere that reduced the chance we'd be recognised, but not so isolated that we'd stand out.

"Okay," said Lauren, picking up her phone. "Take the next left, and follow the signs for Exeter."

"I thought we were staying in Torbay?"

"We are, but to find the right hotel I've got to use my phone. So if anyone's tracking it, it'll show us driving out of Torbay towards Exeter."

"Wouldn't it be safer to cruise Torbay looking for a hotel with a vacancy sign in the window?"

"That is so last century. B&Bs don't do that anymore. It's all online."

I wasn't convinced. We should have bought burner phones. Not that I knew *where* you bought burner phones. Or if there really was such a thing as an untraceable phone.

Lauren searched the internet for a suitable B&B in the Torbay area. At least it was no longer high season. There should be plenty of vacancies.

I followed the signs for Exeter, waiting for Lauren to say she'd found something. Twenty minutes passed and still nothing from Lauren.

"What's taking so long? I asked. "It doesn't have to be perfect."

"It's not just about finding a vacant room away from the town centres," she said. "I've got to check the location on the map – see how busy the road looks, make sure it's not too isolated, check there's an off-road car park, and free Wi-Fi. It's not as though we're in a hurry."

"We *are* pinging our location to every nearby cell tower."

"But we're telling them we're heading for Exeter and who knows where after that. The killer, or killers, may be clever, but they don't have infinite resources. There are thousands of B&Bs in South Devon."

Eventually Lauren found a B&B that met her criteria. It was west of Brixham, overlooking the Dart Estuary.

"Are you booking one room or two?" I asked, going for nonchalant, but somehow managing to find a touch of breathlessness, which I hastily disguised with a cough.

"I thought one room would be safer," said Lauren. "Don't get your hopes up. There are twin beds, and yours is going to be pushed up against the door. Mine's going up against the window. If anyone does try to break in, we'll know about it."

I wondered what kind of review Lauren would leave for the hotel. *Excellent room, very easy to fortify.*

Lauren booked the room and took out the SIM card. I swung the car around at the next roundabout and headed back to Torbay.

When we arrived at our destination, I had to admit that Lauren's choice of B&B was a good one. It was quiet, but not too quiet. There wouldn't be much passing traffic as the road ended about a half a mile further on into the woods. But we weren't isolated. There were about thirty properties nestled together on a high promontory overlooking the river Dart. Most of the properties were small hotels and B&B's. The rest looked like second homes. There were no clubs or busy pubs.

I wasn't quite so sure about Lauren's choice of disguise. With a headscarf and sunglasses, she looked like a movie actress from the 1950s. But she assured me it was very fashionable and the easiest way to hide her identity. That, and a very strong Geordie accent, the latter coming as quite a surprise when she began talking to the receptionist.

I kept a low profile – something I'm extremely adept at – standing silently in the background, head down. My only disguise a sun hat and a pair of sunglasses.

Lauren paid for the room in cash, then we took our bags up to our room.

~

I didn't bother unpacking. Our plan was to leave mid-morning then head into Cornwall. It made sense to stay in seaside resorts. They had plenty of B&Bs and a large tourist population. Strangers wouldn't stand out. I would have to withdraw more cash though. We were getting low. A quick detour back towards Exeter to find an ATM might be prudent. If anyone was tracking our debit card usage it made sense to point them in the wrong direction.

I switched on the TV news while Lauren took a shower. The manhunt for Timothy McCord was still the main story. There was quite a bit about Phoebe Leycroft as well. Interviews with friends, colleagues and neighbours. She had two children who were distraught. Helen, her daughter, was at university in Cardiff. Her son, Owen, was on a gap year in Africa. Her ex-husband, Stephen, had even offered a reward of fifty thousand pounds for information leading to a murder conviction.

I wondered how long it would take before someone tried to execute a citizen's arrest on me. My name was getting quite a few mentions. No one was actually accusing me of any wrongdoing, but the killers' obsession with me was being reported as the reason Phoebe Leycroft had been murdered. I was the unwitting catalyst.

I did not like the sound of that. It was true, and the police had said as much at last night's press conference, but I hadn't picked up on all the connotations then.

Phoebe Leycroft would have been alive today if she hadn't bought my house. It wasn't my fault – I wasn't the murderer – but how would I feel towards me if I were a close friend or relation of Phoebe Leycroft?

I was going to become a figure of hate again.

And the killers would have known that.

It was all part of the mental torture. *These victims, and all subsequent victims, they're all on you, Mathew. You're the reason they're dying.*

I couldn't watch any more. I walked over to the window and looked out over the river Dart. So much beauty and so much evil on the same planet.

I was still staring out the window when Lauren came out of the shower.

"I've been thinking," she said. "If there are two killers, why would one of them suddenly fly off to America in the middle of a killing spree?"

"To get something?"

"It would have to be something he could smuggle through airport security."

"Information?"

"You could email that."

"So, something that could only be arranged personally."

I couldn't think of anything. But it had to be important. Serial killers didn't take time off without a reason.

~

I decided I needed a better disguise. I was known with a full beard, and I was known clean shaven. No one had seen me with a goatee. Maybe tomorrow I'd even dye my hair. Anything to become invisible.

Lauren was complimentary about my new look when I came out of the bathroom.

"Very nice," she said. "Have you given any thought to what we might eat tonight?"

I hadn't, but I was suddenly hit by a memory of the last time I'd been in Brixham.

"How about fish and chips from the quayside?" I said.

A reminder of happier, simpler times. I'd have been about ten, without a care in the world. On holiday with my family. Brixham had the best fish and chips in England I'd been told. The fish straight off the boat. The potatoes picked from the local red soil. They'd tasted amazing. The boats might have

all gone now, but if there was a chance of finding some remnant of happier times, I wanted to look for it
I needed to look for it.

"It'll have to be a takeaway," said Lauren. "Spending twenty minutes eating in a packed restaurant is asking to be recognised."

"A takeaway is good," I said. "We never sat inside."

~

We ate on the quay, our backs to the crowds, sitting on a bench looking out across the water. It wasn't quite as scenic as the view over the Dart, but it was near enough. And it looked so familiar. The multi-coloured houses. The boats. The seagulls. The smell.

This was exactly what I needed – to be immersed in memories of what it was like to be truly happy.

We went back to the B&B and found a film where the dog doesn't die, and the happy ending was guaranteed.

Then we fortified the room.

~

I awoke the next day to find Lauren already up and tapping away on her laptop.

"What are you doing?" I asked.

"Booking a room in Cornwall for tonight. Don't worry, I'm using a VPN so it's untraceable. Doing it this way means we don't have to use a phone later and give our location away."

We skipped breakfast as there was no safe way to avoid being recognised. A couple having breakfast in dark sunglasses would attract attention. Lauren suggested we pretended to be hungover, but she'd never seen my acting skills. We'd pick up something to eat at a garage. I'd have to stop for petrol soon.

We pushed the twin beds back to their original non-fortified position, did a final sweep of the room to make sure we hadn't left anything behind, then carried our bags down to reception and checked out.

It was just after nine. The sky was overcast, but not

threatening rain. According to the internet it was a two-hour drive to Newquay, but I thought I'd take a longer, more scenic route over Dartmoor. We could buy a couple of baguettes and a hunk of cheese, and have a picnic on the moor, miles away from anyone. As long as the weather held. Dartmoor was a bleak place when the weather turned.

I carried my bag over to the car and unlocked the doors. As I put my bag down to open the driver's door, I noticed something on the back seat.

A model car.

A large model car – about a foot long – that looked just like my car. The same shape. The same colour. My heart began to race. This could *not* be happening.

I opened the rear door for a closer look. The model car had the same registration number as my car.

"What is it?" asked Lauren.

I moved out of the way so she could see. And quickly swung round, looking up and down the car park. Were we alone? Was anyone watching? I couldn't see anyone close by.

"Do you think it opens up?" asked Lauren. "I can't see anything inside it, but … there's the boot."

Yes, there was the boot. My hand closed around the key fob in my pocket. Should I open the car boot now or wait for the police?

Lauren took a large knife from her bag and used the tip to trip the latch holding the model car's rear hatch closed. It sprang open, revealing a figurine. It was one of the seated ones – male, smartly dressed, lying on its side, its head in a pool of red paint.

I stood back, took a deep breath and pressed the car fob. The rear hatch door slowly opened. There was a body inside, arranged and clothed identically to the figurine. No pool of blood. No obvious wounds. No foam around the mouth or nose.

Lauren rang Natalia.

"Hi, Natalia, it's Lauren. You can call off the manhunt for Timothy McCord. We've found him."

Chapter Forty-Seven

I was shocked. We had been so careful. How had they found us? And what the hell had happened here? Had the killers fallen out? Or had there always been only one killer?

Lauren took pictures of McCord and the model car, and sent them to Natalia.

I wondered how long it would take for the police to arrive. We were in the jurisdiction of yet another police authority – Devon and Cornwall this time. Would Natalia have to arrange everything through them?

I decided it was time to test my personal alarm. It would probably be quicker than waiting for one force to liaise with another.

I pressed it, quickly muting the alarm, and making a note of the time. I'd see how long they took to respond. It was five minutes past nine on a Monday morning on the outskirts of a large town. They ought to be quick.

Lauren finished her call with Natalia and walked over.

"How the hell did he find us?" she asked. "Was it a tracker? My use of the phone to find a hotel? Did the receptionist here recognise us and post a picture on the internet?"

"Could the killer be a policeman?" I said. "Or someone working for the police on the technical side? Someone who could type my number plate and car details into the system and have us tracked by every camera they have access to?"

"Or a spook even. Maybe GCHQ can track SIM cards even when they're disconnected."

We were one step away from speculating that Covid vaccinations had injected everyone with personal trackers.

"And what the hell was McCord's role in all these murders?" said Lauren, gesticulating wildly. "He took an active role in luring me to the hotel. He planted the doll-

house. He must have known he was working with the
dollhouse killer. Everything points to him being an
accomplice, and yet, here he is: victim number five."

"He might have been hired to do a job," I said. "If the
money was right McCord, might have thought it worth his
while. But he didn't bargain on the killer tidying up
afterwards."

"That's possible," said Lauren. "Or, being in America,
maybe McCord hadn't heard of the dollhouse murders. Then,
when he sees his picture all over the TV, he puts the squeeze
on the killer for more money. Which backfires dramatically."

A police siren sounded in the distance, slowly getting
nearer. I checked my watch. Four minutes. Not bad.

~

A succession of police cars arrived over the next hour and
half. We knew the drill. I showed them the body. I showed
them the model car. I recounted our story of why we left
Garstock, and how we came to be in a B&B overlooking the
Dart Estuary.

And then I did it all over again for the next pair of officers.

They wanted to know if we'd noticed anyone following us.
Or phoned anyone. Or put the SIM card back in and forgotten
to take it out. Or noticed anyone taking pictures of us.

Lauren wanted to know if anyone had a bug detector. Or if
you could track a phone with the SIM card removed.

I just wanted it to end.

Eventually, a forensics team arrived. They didn't have a
bug detector, but they had a long-handled mirror used for
checking underneath cars for bombs.

"If someone has planted a device on your car it'll most
likely be in the wheel arch or underneath," said the forensic
supervisor.

He started with the back bumper, passing the mirror
underneath. Nothing. He moved onto the wheel arches,
squatting down, peering into the arch, using the mirror to
check the surfaces he couldn't see.

When he came to the rear wheel arch on the driver's side, he found it.

"Not that professional a job," said the officer. "It's out of sight, but not well-hidden. A rush job, I'd say. Someone walking by the car, sticking it in place without even bending down to check."

"The car was in a police pound until Thursday," I said. "Since then, it's been in a garage most of the time with two policemen parked outside watching it."

"Not all of the time though," said Lauren. "When we came back from Heathrow, there were reporters swarming all around the car. Anyone could have planted a tracking device without being seen."

"There might be others," said the forensics supervisor. "We'll be taking your car in for a full forensic examination anyway. I'll make sure we check for tracking devices as well."

I'd forgotten that the car would be taken away. What were we supposed to do? Stay here? Go back to Garstock?

I broached the subject with Lauren.

"I still think going off grid is the best option," she said. "But not until we've got our own bug detector."

We were very much in the hands of the police. Were they going to provide us with protection? A safe house? Were they going to drive us back to Garstock? One thing I knew – I wasn't going to call a taxi.

~

We went back to the B&B to see if we could get something to eat. It was going to be long morning and we were both in need of food and caffeine.

Lauren dropped all pretence of being a Geordie tourist. Off came the scarf and sunglasses as she walked past the dozen or so people – presumably staff and guests – that had gathered around the entrance to the B&B.

Heads turned. *Is it? No, it couldn't be. Are you? It is!*

Lauren lapped it up. "Yes, I'm her," she said. "And I have my rolling pin to prove it."

I followed along behind, hoping she didn't produce the rolling pin. And hoping the killer wasn't in the small crowd. They all looked pretty harmless, but then serial killers often did.

We all followed Lauren into the reception area.

"Have they found a body?" asked one of the crowd.

"I found a body," said Lauren. "But I can't say much more than that. The police like to keep everything under wraps while they're investigating. I don't suppose anyone knows if there are CCTV cameras pointing at the car park?"

"No," said the receptionist. "We've got one in reception, and one covering the main entrance, but it doesn't cover the car park."

"What about the B&Bs next door?" asked Lauren. "Would they have cameras that might take in part of your car park?"

The receptionist shrugged. "I've never looked."

"Never mind," said Lauren. "Would it be possible for someone to get us a coffee and something to eat? Toast would be brilliant. We missed breakfast, and finding dead bodies gives me an appetite."

One of the kitchen staff volunteered to provide coffee and toast.

"Would you like cereal?" she said. "It would be no problem. I could do a full English if you don't mind waiting."

"That's very kind of you," said Lauren. "I'll definitely take you up on the full English. I don't suppose any of you noticed anyone behaving strangely near the car park this morning? Or late last night."

No one had. They had plenty of questions though. And I noticed several had produced cameras. Whatever Lauren said had a good chance of appearing on the lunchtime TV news.

"Can you tell us why you're here? Were you following the dollhouse killer?" asked one of the group.

"I'm always hunting him. Trouble is he's always hunting us too. He's obsessed with Mathew here."

A dozen pairs of eyes glanced my way. It was probably the first time most of them had noticed I was there.

"Why's he obsessed with Mathew?" asked another of the group.

Lauren shrugged. "It could be something sexual."

I didn't think I could become more self-conscious, but I managed it. What the hell was Lauren playing at?

"Serial killers are often sexually inadequate," continued Lauren. "With weird motivations. I imagine the killer has a very small penis. Miniscule, even."

Well, If Lauren's plan was to piss off the killer, she was doing a bang-up job.

"We know he's a sadist," continued Lauren. "We know he drugs and restrains his victims. That tells me he's not a strong person. He's weak and sneaky, and gets off on seeing his victims weakened and vulnerable. Which is why he's intimidated by me. He knows I'm someone who can't be cowed. When I'm cornered, I fight. I never give up."

~

After our late breakfast and Lauren's impromptu news conference, we found somewhere quieter so that Lauren could call Natalia. We needed to know if police protection at Laburnum Cottage could be reinstated?

I listened in.

"You're going to stay at Laburnum Cottage?" asked Natalia.

"If we have protection, we will," said Lauren. "For a few nights anyway. I still think our best bet is to go off grid and keep Mathew away from the killer. The man's so obsessed with Mathew, I think he might even stop killing if he can't arrange for him to find a figurine."

"He could just as easily speed up his killing spree," said Natalia. "Not being able to find Mathew might cause him to devolve."

"I think he's already devolved. Are you coming down to Brixham to see the body?"

"No, I've got somewhere else to be. In fact, I should be leaving now. Don't worry about police protection. That shouldn't be a problem to reinstate given today's events."

I rang Georgia next. I hadn't been arrested yet – and all the officers I'd talked to so far had been friendly – but, given my track record, that could all change very quickly. We were still in the West Country and DSU Maxton struck me as the kind of person who'd have friends high up in all the adjoining forces.

"Hello, Mathew, I heard about the body in the boot. You haven't been arrested already, have you?" asked Georgia.

"Not yet. Which is why I thought it best to check in. It's obvious to me that the dollhouse killer must have broken into my car last night and planted a dead body and a model car for me to find. But … it could be interpreted very differently."

"Like you drove down to Brixham with a dead body in your boot looking for a place to dump it?"

"That's the kind of thing."

"Well, I think you may be in luck. Your car *is* a Nissan Qashkai, isn't it?"

"That's right."

"Is it white?"

I wasn't sure where Georgia was going with this.

"It is. Why?"

"Because Susan Phillips bought a 1:18 scale model of a white Nissan Qashkai on the fourth of August. I think that rather neatly ties this murder to the dollhouse killer."

Chapter Forty-Eight

I put the phone on speaker.

"Have the police got hold of Susan's online purchase history?" I asked, excitedly.

"*And* all the delivery addresses," said Georgia. "Most went to her parent's home, but several went to other places. Hillside, for one. The police are checking all the addresses now. We may have locations he's earmarked for future murders."

This was a huge breakthrough.

But how did we know it was Susan making the purchases?

"Is it possible the killer logged in as Susan and she knew nothing about this?" I asked.

"Unlikely, I'd think," said Georgia. "All the payments came out of her bank account. Most of the deliveries went to her parent's home during the time she was living with them. She must have known. She must have forwarded them all to the killer."

"What kind of things did she buy?" asked Lauren.

"Hello, Lauren," said Georgia. "Most of the purchases were dollhouse related. Loads of model furniture, and twelve figurines. But she also purchased a drone. Quite a good one, I believe."

"A drone?"

"Yes, it came with a camera, so one suspects that it's for surveillance. Oh, and twelve outfits that matched the clothes the figurines were wearing."

"Were the purchases spread out or did she buy them in large batches?" asked Lauren.

"A mixture," said Georgia. "All the figurines were bought at the same time. The clothes were bought in batches. Looks like three complete outfits at a time. Then there's your car and the drone, which were both single purchases."

"Were all the clothes the same size?" asked Lauren.

"Most were, but he had two on the large side and two on the small side. I think he was preparing for all eventualities."

In other words, when he bought the clothes, he didn't know who his victims were going to be. Or if he did, he didn't know their clothes size.

"You wouldn't happen to have a list of Susan's purchases and delivery addresses, would you?" I asked.

"Strange as it may seem, duty solicitors are not on the SCU mailing list. There's also a limit to how long a person can lurk behind other peoples' desks reading over their shoulders."

"I'm sorry, I shouldn't have asked," I said.

"One may always ask, but one should never expect. Anyway, if the Devon and Cornwall police look like they're about to haul you away to the nearest oubliette, pass them on to me. There's more than enough evidence now to suggest this murder has to be the work of the dollhouse killer."

~

"Are all the victims accomplices?" asked Lauren after the call had finished. "McCord set up my meeting and the dollhouse. Susan seems to have been a quartermaster, buying and forwarding everything the killer needed. Not to mention insulating him from any record of ever having made those purchases. Did Mark operate the directional speakers? Only Phoebe and Sophie appear to be completely blameless."

"Susan and Mark could have been unwitting accomplices. Susan was killed before anyone knew about dollhouses and figurines."

"McCord must have heard about the dollhouse murders. Okay, he was in another country, but it's big news every-where."

"McCord was a conspiracy theory nut," I said. "He'd only listen to the news that fed his obsession with conspiracies. If someone told him it was all fake news, he'd believe them."

"Wouldn't he be the least bit interested about why he was setting me up with a non-existent interview and then luring me into a hotel room with a dollhouse in it?"

"If someone he trusted told him you were a member of the liberal elite and needed to be taught a lesson, he'd believe it. What's the percentage of Americans who believe their country and media is run by a gang of Satan-worshipping paedophiles? Twenty percent? It's somewhere around there."

Lauren went quiet. For about two seconds.

"That's it! They're *all* hard-core conspiracy theorists," she said. "Not casual turning-up-for-the-odd-march supporters, but *real* believers. Susan, Mark, McCord. Remember the way Susan and Mark kept looking behind them at the train stations. The way they broke their journey to make sure they weren't being followed. Their membership of anti-5G and anti-vaxxer groups. The killer didn't have to work hard to groom them because they were already groomed! All he had to do was to channel their paranoia in a direction that suited his needs."

It made sense. He needed to lure victims to isolated properties. Who better to choose than people who were easily led? People predisposed to believing the weirdest things. People he could feed stories to which reinforced their beliefs and prejudices. With the right story, he could even get them to work for him.

All he had to do was be convincing. He probably didn't even need to be charismatic if his target audience had a low bar for prophets.

"The killer will be a member of one those conspiracy theory groups, won't he?" I said. "Anti-5G, anti-vaxxer. He'll have used his position to evaluate his fellow members, looking for the most gullible, the most helpful. He'd be like a wise, friendly wolf in a flock of sheep, cultivating a small band of true believers."

"He'd do it online," said Lauren. "Troll the various discussion groups and forums, looking to see who responds and how. Making a list of potential victims, testing them to see which ones he could manipulate, and how."

"Could you track him down?" I asked.

"It's possible. Some sites only leave posts up for twenty-fours hours before deleting them. Others have archives that go back years. But you'd think he'd have sampled several sites in the beginning to make sure he found enough candidates. He could easily have left a trail, especially if he's still actively looking for victims."

This could work. Lauren was brilliant at finding things on the internet.

"He wouldn't use his real name," said Lauren. "But he might leave enough data in the message header for a computer expert to track his location."

"Could you do it?"

"Not me. I'm an amateur who knows their way around search engines. But the police will have plenty of experts who can."

Chapter Forty-Nine

I thought Lauren might begin her trawl of the internet conspiracy sites, but she was adamant she had to wait until we had a more secure connection to the internet.

"I'll probably have to visit some dangerous sites, and I'm not doing that until I have a secure connection. The last thing I want is some hacker following me back to my laptop."

But there was one thing she could do – buy a bug detector.

"We can't put this off," she said. "The killer's obsessed with knowing where you are. He's bugged your house. He's bugged your car. He's not going to stop. We've got to assume that every time we park a car, or even stop at a traffic light, that someone could plant a tracking device."

It *was* the sensible thing to do. We'd long passed the point where anyone could accuse us of exaggerating the danger of our situation. Or the persistence of the killer.

Lauren spent half an hour comparing the efficacy of various bug detectors. I'd never realised there were so many. And these weren't aimed at businesses. They were aimed at the general public. What kind of world were we living in where people felt the need to check if their hotel room, or changing room, had a hidden camera?

"I think this one will do," said Lauren. "It seems to have everything we want and there's next day delivery."

Our stay in Brixham came to an end soon after. The senior investigating officer – a detective superintendent Jenkins – told us we could leave. Not the car though. That would spend another day, maybe longer, in Exeter, being processed. I'd be informed when I could pick it up.

But we were getting a lift home. An officer had been assigned to drive us back to Garstock.

~

Constable Darren – call me Daz – Cutler liked to chat. To Lauren, that is. Me, he could just about tolerate. He wasn't overtly rude. He just had trouble concealing his contempt. Maybe I was being over-sensitive, but I'd got used to the change in people's behaviour when they realised who I was. People going through the motions of being civil, their voice saying one thing, their face saying another.

I said as little as possible, spending large swathes of the journey pretending to be asleep or looking out of the window.

I also did a lot of thinking. I could feel the nature of the investigation changing. In the beginning everything had been confusing. There was no obvious motive, no discernible pattern, no clues that you could trust. The killer was both omniscient and invisible. He could strike anywhere. Kill anyone. The only constant was me. I was his witness.

But now there *was* a discernible pattern. He wasn't killing anyone. He was killing conspiracy theorists. No, not killing, he was *sacrificing* conspiracy theorists. Was he sacrificing them to me? Were they offerings? Or was I supposed to feel guilty about being the cause of their deaths?

Whichever, his mask of infallibility was slipping. Mistakes were appearing. Susan's list of delivery addresses included properties that hadn't featured yet in his killing spree. The police might even find him – today – hiding in one those properties.

And last night he'd driven to a B&B car park to plant a dead body in my car boot. A B&B on a no through road with plenty of CCTV cameras on the neighbours' walls. I'd noticed that as we were driving away. There had to be over a dozen cameras. And a no through road meant that the killer would have to return the same way he'd come. That would make him easier to identify. The only cars coming and going within a short space of time would be the killer and cars dropping people off. The police would have a small number of suspect vehicles to investigate.

All that was needed was just one of those CCTV cameras to have a good view of the road.

~

As we approached Laburnum Cottage, I noticed the familiar sight of a police car parked outside the front door. We had our protection back. And there was no line of press cars, though I wondered how long that would last.

We said goodbye to Daz, and Lauren chatted with our protection officers while I opened up the cottage and carried our bags inside.

It felt good to be home. Away from strangers, and the scrutiny of others.

I made coffee first then switched on the TV. News of McCord's murder was the lead story everywhere. The press were all over the crime scene. They knew about his body being found in the boot, the model car on the back seat, and that it had been us who'd found the body.

But they didn't mention anything about the police finding footage of the killer's van. And none of the bystanders interviewed mentioned anything about seeing or hearing anything unusual last night.

They did, however, have footage of Lauren's impromptu musings on the size of the killer's penis. And the possible sexual motive for his obsession with me.

I held my head in my hands. I knew what Lauren was doing. There was a modicum of merit in her plan to antagonise the killer into making one too many mistakes, but she didn't have to involve me. The internet was the Wild West. No one could predict how a story would develop. I'd been the victim of its lies before, but at least they'd kept my sexuality out of it. Now, though, I could see myself being labelled as the most hated homoerotic man in Swindon by the weekend.

While I cringed and surfed the news channels, Lauren dived into the world of anti-vaxxers and 5G conspiracy theorists.

She gave up after two hours.

"I think this might take longer than I thought," she said.

"No success?"

"Not really. It's not helped by the fact that the search engines are making it difficult to find information about a lot of conspiracy groups. Type 'How do I join an anti-vaxxer group' into a search engine and you'll get pages and pages of links to sites debunking anti-vaxxer theories. I've had to radically change my approach."

"But you're making progress?"

"Slowly. It's not what I expected. I thought it was all going to be crazy paranoia, but there's plausible science in there."

"Really?"

"Well, plausible to a non-scientist like me. It's like there are two layers. One trying to be logical, quoting scientific studies and providing references to other studies that appear to be carried out by real scientists in real institutions. And then there's a crazy layer tacked on top where people take bits of the science and blend it with their own pet theories to produce a wild concoction of comic book villains and insane conspiracies. But I can see how people like Susan and Mark can get sucked into these groups."

"You're not becoming a convert, are you?"

"No, but the scientific papers they reference both look genuine and raise what appear to be valid concerns. I'm no scientist. I don't know if the papers are real, or if they're flawed, or anomalies. And I don't have the time to follow up all the references or search for papers with opposing views. But I'm left wondering why I haven't heard any mention of this research before. It's a short step from there to wondering if the answer is because '*they*' don't want you to. Where '*they*' is your bogeyman of choice – the scientific establishment, the government, big pharma, the global elite, mainstream media, liberals, intellectuals. And if you start looking for answers, there are plenty of rabbit holes to fall down, and players ready to share their version of the truth. Some sound legit, some are fund raising schemes, looking for donations. Others are political or batshit crazy."

"So you're no nearer to finding any trace of the killer?"

"No. I'm still feeling my way around. It's not helped by various groups using code words for vaccination and 5G like 'dance class' and 'children's TV' to prevent their posts being detected by algorithms. I think I'm going to take a break and attack it later from a different angle."

~

The day dragged by. Lauren had bursts of enthusiasm when she thought she'd found a way in, followed by even longer periods of frustration when she discovered she was wrong.

I let her simmer down before enquiring how she was getting on. I wanted to help, but I knew my limitations.

"If *you* can't find a way in, how did Susan and Mark?" I asked eventually.

Lauren shrugged dejectedly. "They both went on demos. Maybe someone there gave them a scribbled website address to check out?"

She sighed. "But you're right. Either I'm overthinking this or the websites the killer used have been taken down."

"Wouldn't that mean he's run out of victims?"

"Depends. He might have created his own closed group months ago and persuaded his core group of followers to migrate over."

As for me, I spent most of my time watching TV and thinking about the case. Often at the same time. I wondered if the killer had brought in another victim/accomplice yet. Hauling a dead body out of the back of a van on your own was hard work. He'd have to drag it out and carry it across to my car then carefully place it in the boot and arrange it to look like the figurine. To do all that on your own, and leave no trace, was incredibly difficult. He'd know that.

It would make sense to bring in an accomplice, to lift the body out rather than drag it, and use plastic sheeting to minimise any transfer. But the downside of having an accomplice was what do you do with them? How do you

insulate them from the news of who McCord was? The
manhunt for him? The dollhouses? Not to mention explaining
why you're moving a dead body.

And afterwards – what do you do with them then? They
were the next victim. But was the killer ready to kill them? His
MO demanded that I found a dollhouse or model car
indicating where the body was, but it was getting increasingly
harder for him to do that. He wasn't going to get past the
police protection officers again, and I wasn't leaving the
house unless I was in a guaranteed bug-free car with no way
to track my whereabouts.

He might have to wait weeks before he'd get an
opportunity.

So what does he do? Tell his accomplice to stand down,
and hope he doesn't mention anything to his friends? Keep
him locked away as a prisoner until required? Or kill him, and
put his body in a freezer?

Every option carried a risk.

Chapter Fifty

The much-anticipated breakthrough came at five o'clock. The news channels had been trailing the police press conference for over an hour. *Major Announcement Imminent.*

Lauren and I watched from the sofa, coffee mugs in hand.

"It'll be the CCTV cameras," I said. "One of them must have got a good shot of the killer and his van."

It might even show an accomplice in the passenger seat.

Lauren favoured trace evidence on the body.

"The killer's devolving, getting sloppy. He'll have left DNA, fibres, maybe even hair on the body."

Out came the police, their body language completely different to the previous occasions. No stern faces on the dais. Everyone was relaxed and smiling – even Terrell. The Chief Constable looked confident and raring to begin.

Had they caught him?

"At about three thirty this morning," began the Chief Constable. "The Dollhouse Killer left the body of Timothy McCord in the car boot belonging to Mathew Sedley."

I was right. They had a time. An almost exact time. They must have found a CCTV sighting.

The Chief Constable continued. "The killer's vehicle was caught on nearby CCTV cameras."

Yes!

A side-on image of a white van appeared on the giant screen above the Chief Constable. It wasn't a sharp picture. It had been magnified a few too many times, but it showed the van well.

"The vehicle is a white Ford Transit L2H2," said the Chief Constable."

Very little of the killer was visible. He was in profile, wearing a hoodie that obscured his face almost completely.

Only a nose was visible, and that was too pixelated to be of any use.

Another picture came up. This time it was same van coming from the opposite direction. At least it proved there was no accomplice. Unless the accomplice was in the back. There were no windows in the rear of the van at all. There were no logos either. The sides of the van were plain white. Nothing to make this particular van stand out from others of the same make and colour.

"Ten minutes later," said the Chief Constable. "The same vehicle was caught on a traffic camera."

A buzz of excitement went around the conference room as a new picture appeared on the screen. It was a head-on picture of the van. Sharp, good quality. But it was the driver's face that drew the eye.

He was wearing a mask. A bizarre distorted mask that made him look like something out of a horror movie. Barely human. And there was nothing to identify him. His hair was covered by the grey hoodie. His face by the mask. His neck by a black turtle neck jumper. His hands by gloves.

You couldn't even make out his skin colour – there was none on show.

There were no unusual stickers on the windscreen either, and nothing noteworthy in the cab.

But the number plates were visible.

"If anyone believes they have seen this vehicle in the last two months, particularly if you saw this vehicle near Garstock or Rayford, please contact the police immediately. The number plate is at the bottom of your screen now. It's a false number plate, but it may have been on this vehicle for some time."

The Chief Constable moved on to address the question of Timothy McCord's death.

"The post mortem suggests that he was drowned sometime between midnight and six o'clock on Sunday morning. There is evidence suggesting that his body was either chilled or frozen for a number of hours subsequent to that."

That was interesting. Only a few hours earlier I'd been speculating about using a freezer to keep a victim's body on ice.

"I didn't notice that McCord's body was thawing out," said Lauren. "Did you?"

"No, but it was a cold night, and I didn't look very closely."

I didn't look for very long either. One glance to identify it was McCord, and one that he was dead. That was enough.

"We're still analysing trace evidence recovered from the body," said the Chief Constable. "But I can confirm that we have found a significant number of fibres."

"Told you," said Lauren. "He's getting sloppy."

I thought it was more a result of him taking more risks. This was the first time he'd had to transport a body to a different location. The first time he'd had to arrange a body in the open air, knowing that any minute a witness could drive by or step outside from a nearby B&B. He'd have been forced to work quickly. No time to be extra careful.

The Chief Constable threw the meeting open to questions from the media.

"Why would the Dollhouse Killer freeze one of his victims?"

"Our working assumption is that he was waiting for an opportunity to access Mr. Sedley's car. At the time of Mr. McCord's death, Mr. Sedley's car was in a garage in full view of a police patrol car."

"Was there a falling out between McCord and the Dollhouse Killer?"

"We believe that Mr. McCord's killer was using him, and always planned to kill him."

"Why is the killer so fixated on Mathew Sedley?"

I braced myself. *Say you don't know. Move on.*

The Chief Constable shrugged. "We don't know," he said.

Thank God, for that. I looked at Terrell. Was he looking like someone itching to make an observation?

He looked away, smiling to himself.

"Has there been any progress in the other three murders?"

"There has been significant progress," said the Chief Constable. "But I'm not at liberty to elaborate at this juncture."

The questions petered out after that. The police didn't say anything new, and the media didn't press them.

"They didn't mention Susan's delivery addresses," said Lauren. "Do you think they're keeping it quiet so they can stake the addresses out?"

"That's what I'd do," I said. "It would be tempting to break in and take a look around, but, most likely, he'd have the places covered in cameras. Once you go in, you scare him off."

~

Lauren had another go at finding where Susan and Mark met up with their killer online. It didn't go well. A couple of times I thought her laptop was about to be thrown against the wall. She wasn't enamoured with my choice of television channels either.

"Don't you have Netflix? Or satellite, or any premium channels at all?"

"No."

"Why not?"

I shrugged. "I never felt the need."

In the end I had an early night. There was nothing new on the case, and I'd started to drift in and out of sleep.

I awoke the next day feeling almost optimistic. Things were starting to move. Maybe this was the day the killer took one risk too many?

And then I wondered what that risk might be. Lauren had mentioned a few times that I was the last figurine. I didn't like it, but it made a lot of sense. I was his obsession, his perpetual witness. Of course he'd have to kill me, and he'd make it his final act. His masterpiece.

So, what would he do if the police were closing in and his killing spree was under threat?

Would he race to the end? Bring forward his final act?

I was well and truly depressed by the time I started breakfast. This could be my last meal.

~

The bug detector arrived mid-morning. Lauren had just finished her latest online interview, spicing up our adventures in Brixham, when the delivery man knocked on the door.

We read the instruction manual together then headed outside. It looked easy to operate.

I stood back while Lauren passed the detector over her car. It didn't take that long. Lauren spent a little more time around the bumper and wheel arches, and even laid down on the ground to reach as far under the car as she could.

No lights flashed. No buzzer sounded. Everything was clean.

Lauren checked the inside of her car next. Then the boot. Then the engine.

The car was clean.

I thought she looked slightly disappointed.

Then she turned the detector on herself, slowly passing it over her body. Nothing.

I could see I was going to be next, so I assumed the position, standing up straight with both arms stretched out wide.

When the detector reached the top pocket of my jacket, it went off.

Lauren tried it again. The same thing happened. The only thing I had in that pocket was my personal alarm. I took it out.

"Did you turn the power saving mode off?" asked Lauren.

I checked. The power saving mode was on. The alarm shouldn't have been transmitting.

Lauren took out her personal alarm, and held it up against the bug detector. Nothing. She tried mine again. It set off the bug detector.

"Do you remember anyone bumping into you recently?"

asked Lauren. "Or jostling you? You know, like a pick pocket would to distract you while they switched alarms on you?"

"No. I make a habit of avoiding people."

I stared at the alarm in my hand. The only time it left my person was when I went to bed. And even then I kept it on a bedside table. No one, other than Lauren, or a brilliant cat burglar, could have got to it.

Which left Gary, the locksmith who had fitted our alarms. The personal alarm had come from him.

And if it was Gary, the whole house suddenly became suspect.

Lauren rang Natalia.

"Hi, Natalia, it's Lauren. We have a problem."

Chapter Fifty-One

"But it's got to be the man who installed the panic alarms!" argued Lauren. "He's the killer, getting off on showing himself while putting back all the bugs forensics had taken out hours earlier."

"That's impossible," said Natalia. "I've known Ken Holland for years. He's above reproach."

"Who's Ken Holland?"

"The man who installed the panic alarms," said Natalia.

"No, he didn't," said Lauren. "He said his name was Gary."

Lauren looked at me, questioningly, but I couldn't remember Gary's surname.

"He had curly brown hair, a bushy beard, and glasses," I said.

"And a florid complexion," added Lauren.

"That's not Ken," said Natalia, sounding worried. "Did he leave a card?"

"No," I said. "But he showed me an ID card. It had his name and photo on it and it looked official. Society of Master Locksmiths or something like that. He even asked me to look at the card twice to make sure it was him."

I couldn't believe Gary was the killer. He didn't look or act like a sadistic serial killer. He was friendly, and he looked like he knew his job. All the alarms worked. We'd watched as he tested every one of them.

"He had a Bristol accent," said Lauren. "Medium height. Slightly overweight, unless he was wearing padding. Oh, shit! The beard could be false too. He wasn't wearing gloves, though."

Natalia told us to remain outside the house. She was sending a forensics team to us and she'd follow as soon as she'd contacted Ken Holland. There was always the chance that Gary worked for Ken and had innocently deputised for him.

That didn't turn out to be the case.

Natalia rang us twenty minutes later. Ken had been booked to do the alarm installation as she'd said, but an hour and a half before he was due to arrive his office had received a call purporting to come from the police to say that the job had been cancelled.

He hadn't thought any more about it. He'd assumed everything was legit. Clients were always changing their mind.

Natalia had told Ken to meet her at Laburnum Cottage. She wanted him to take a professional look at the installation. Did Gary, or whatever his name was, know what he was doing? Was he a real security technician? And she particularly wanted him to look at an EFit of Gary once Lauren and I had helped the police produce a likeness.

I wasn't as hopeful as Natalia. I was useless with faces, and it sounded like Gary had disguised himself.

But we did know that the killer had no problem with locks. We'd assumed he'd picked up that skill up as a criminal, but why not as a locksmith?

"That was one hell of a risk he took," said Lauren. "To come to a fresh crime scene, teeming with police, and calmly put all the bugs back that had been taken out only hours earlier."

"It shows how desperate he was to listen in," I said.

"And watch," said Lauren. "I bet he put a camera in bathroom."

"He'd know everything we'd planned, everything we knew. He'd know how we were planning to get to Heathrow. How we were going to go off-grid. And where we were staying."

"He'd know I was looking for him on the conspiracy theory websites."

"Should we leave the bugs in place and use them to feed him duff information?" I asked.

"Do we have any duff information to feed him?"

"We could book a room at a B&B and set a trap for him.

Flood the place with police."

It could work. We knew he was obsessed with me. We knew he went to great lengths to know where I was. Even now he'd be looking for the next place to plant a dollhouse. Looking for an opportunity to get in and out without being seen. Why not give him something he couldn't resist?

"Ah," said Lauren. "We might have a problem with that."

"What? Terrell?"

"No. The bug in your personal alarm. It might be just a tracking device, but it might be a microphone."

Shit. The killer would have heard everything we just said.

~

Ken Holland was the first to arrive. Well, that's what he called himself. He offered to take a look at my personal alarm, but I thought it best to wait until forensics arrived. Assuming I could trust anyone who turned up and donned a white oversuit.

My trust in people had disintegrated.

Lauren chatted with the man provisionally known as Ken, pumping him for information about bugs and the efficacy of her bug detector.

"It's a decent model," he said. "For the price. We use a much more expensive model with a wider range of frequency detection and the ability to pick up the weakest of signals."

"You wouldn't happen to have one in your van, would you?" asked Lauren.

It didn't take long before she had him using his state-of-the-art bug detector to re-examine both her car and us.

Everything passed. Except my personal alarm.

"Can you tell if it's a tracker or a listening device?" asked Lauren.

"The frequency it's transmitting at suggests it's a GPS tracker."

Well, that was good news. The killer wouldn't know we'd discovered his bug. Unless his name was Ken, and he was standing right in front of me.

The forensic team arrived next, closely followed by Natalia, who told us DCI Terrell wasn't far behind.

Joy of joys. I wondered if he'd crossed us off his list of suspects yet. I doubted it. He'd have found some bizarre interpretation of the facts that proved we were somehow involved.

Ken, though, turned out to be the real Ken. Two of the forensics team knew him. He told them about the reading he got from my personal alarm, and they confirmed his finding a minute later when they took the alarm apart.

The tracker was removed and bagged.

Natalia then introduced us to a Facial Imaging Officer who, with our input, would create an EFit image of Gary.

"Take as long as you need," said Natalia. "We're going to be processing the inside of your house, so we're going to need you to remain outside until we tell you it's clear."

The EFit picture turned out to be much better than I'd feared. No thanks to me. Lauren had a much better eye for faces than me. Even so it wasn't the kind of image that would be instantly recognisable, unless he really did have a big bushy beard. It completely dominated his face.

The Imaging Officer experimented with other variants – removing the beard, the glasses, changing the hair, toning down the florid complexion. It was surprising how different they looked.

None of the images jogged any memory. I had wondered if I'd met him before in Rayford. One of the neighbours, perhaps? The killer's obsession with me was so personal, you'd think we must have known each other. And the vitriol directed at me by my neighbours had been unbounded.

But I didn't recognise any of the EFit images.

Terrell arrived while we were still refining the EFit. He blanked us, striding straight past on his way to the house. That suited me fine. I'd take an angry snub ahead of an in-your-face rant every time.

Another police car arrived. Two officers got out. They looked nervous. Something that surprised me until I found out who they were, and why they'd been summoned.

They'd been tasked with manning the police roadblock on the morning that Gary had planted the bugs. They'd let him through, even though he hadn't been on their list of approved visitors.

Terrell strode out of the house as soon as he'd heard of their arrival. I kept well out of the way.

"I checked his ID," I heard one of the officers say. "He had accreditation from the national security inspectorate. It was legit. His face matched the ID."

"His name wasn't on the list." said Terrell. "You were told to check the names."

"I did. Ken Holland was on the list. This man had a letter from Ken Holland saying that Gary Turner was deputising for him that day."

Turner! That was it. I remembered now. That was the name he'd given.

"I called Ken Holland to confirm," continued the officer. "But the phone was engaged."

"What number did you call Mr. Holland on?" asked Terrell.

"The one in the letter," said the sergeant sheepishly.

"The one in the letter," said Terrell sarcastically. "Did you try him again?"

"I did, but it was still engaged, and Mr. Turner said he was late and the alarms had to be fitted as a matter of urgency-"

"So you waved him through."

"No. No, I didn't. I got him to open his van and had a good look inside."

That grabbed Terrell's attention.

"You looked inside his van?"

"Yes. It was full of tools, cables, CCTV cameras, locks."

"Did you see anything unusual? Unexpected?"

"No."

"Any doors? Something he could use to waterboard someone on?"

"No. I did get his number plate though. I took down the plates of everyone I let through that day."

"Have you got the number?"

"Yes, it's…" He paused while he dug out a notebook from a pocket. "It's … Oh, it's the number from the press conference last night. HA20 MST."

I thought Terrell was about to explode.

"How did you not notice this last night! We put out a call for info on a white van with that plate number."

"It wasn't a white van. It was grey. And a different model. The one in Brixham was a white L2H2. This one was older and bigger – an L2H3."

The killer had two vans.

~

Terrell sent the two officers to the Imaging Officer to produce EFits of the man. I hoped theirs would be better than ours. Police were trained to remember faces, weren't they?

Terrell glanced our way. He looked like he was about to say something, but then thought better of it, and walked back inside the house.

When he'd finished, the Imaging Officer showed us the police EFits. They looked very similar to the ones we'd produced. Again, the big, bushy beard dominated his face.

People came and went. We waited outside, looking at the house every now and then, wondering what they were finding. The first time an alarm went off, I jumped, looking around in panic.

"They'll be testing the panic alarms," said the Imaging Officer. "To make sure they were fitted correctly. How many have you got inside the house?"

"Five," said Lauren.

All five were tested.

A while later DCI Terrell, DI Lipinski, and Ken Holland emerged from the house.

"We found one device," said Natalia. "A microphone inside the alarm fitting in the lounge."

"No cameras?" asked Lauren.

"No," said Natalia. "He'd have known they were harder to

hide. You can get apps for your phone to find hidden cameras, but a microphone can be hidden out of sight."

"So, everything's clean now?"

"Yes," said Natalia.

"You're sure?" said Lauren.

"As sure as we can be."

"But not 100%?"

"No one can ever say 100%," said Ken. "Spyware technology is always improving. As is detection. Short of taking the place apart stone by stone, it's clean."

"What about the panic alarms?" I asked. "Are they working as they should?"

"They *are* 100%," said Ken. "He did a very professional job."

"So he is a real security technician?" asked Lauren.

"That's enough," said Terrell, cutting Ken off before he could answer. "All you two need to know is that the house is clean and all the alarms work as they should. Now, Ken, we'd like you to look at some faces."

~

Natalia told us we could go back into the house. Forensics were just finishing off.

Lauren took the opportunity to grill the forensics team.

"Are any of you computer experts?" she asked.

"Anil," shouted one of the officers. "You're wanted downstairs."

Anil arrived, looking around inquisitively. "What is it?" he asked.

"This could be your chance to get on TV," said his boss. "The Honey Badger here is looking for a computer expert."

I recognised the look in Anil's eyes. I'd seen it enough times in the mirror. The unease and uncertainty of what the hell was going to happen next.

"I'm having a problem with search engines," said Lauren. "I'm trying to track down anti-vaxxer groups to see if I can find where the killer found Susan, Mark and Timothy McCord, but I'm getting nowhere. I think most of the sites have been taken down."

"Yes, that is likely," said Anil. "Search engine algorithms also block sites they consider untrustworthy."

"So, how would I find where they met online?"

"Without their phones and computers, it is very difficult. Almost certainly they would have used VPNs as well, which means one cannot even use their ISP – that is their internet service provider – should one know it."

"That's what I thought," said Lauren.

"However," said Anil. "I think you may be looking in the wrong place."

"Do you know the right place? asked Lauren.

"I think so. If I were looking for an intersection between the killer and his victims, I would try *all* the conspiracy groups. That is because most conspiracy theorists these days are not single-issue conspiracy theorists. Partly this is because they are predisposed to believe in conspiracies, and partly because interest groups have been pushing that agenda. They see an opportunity to widen their support base by advancing the idea that if one is an anti-vaxxer one should also be anti-5G, anti-liberal, anti-intellectual, anti-science, and pro populist. By widening your search criteria, you will also find the many conspiracy groups that have not had their websites taken down."

"Anil, you are a genius," said Lauren. "You don't have any more tips, do you?"

He did. He gave Lauren a list of platforms and sites that were known for hosting dubious content – all part of the unregulated and unmoderated free speech zones.

~

Natalia dropped in to say they'd finished, and were about to leave. Lauren pounced on her before she could disappear out the door.

"Did Ken recognise any of the EFits?" she asked.

"No. He didn't recognise the name Gary Turner either.

We're getting pictures from the professional bodies. If he's accredited, we'll have him."

I admired her confidence, but that bushy beard was too good a disguise. It completely hid his lower face and jawline. If he was wearing a wig and used make-up to create that florid complexion, it only left his eyes and nose as real. And you could cross those off if he'd been wearing a prosthetic and contacts.

As soon as Natalia left, Lauren plunged into her laptop. She didn't surface for nearly three hours.

"I think this could work," she said, when she finally stopped to eat. "Those websites of Anil's are a mine of information. I'll probably have to have my brain cleansed when I've finished. You wouldn't believe what people are posting. I thought some of them were spoofs at first, but I don't think they are. And there are definite patterns. Someone comes up a with a bat-shit crazy theory, and within days others have tacked on extras to make it fit in with their warped worldview."

Lauren couldn't stop talking. She only paused to bite, chew, and swallow.

"It's a wonder Bill Gates and the Clintons ever have time to sleep. According to these sites they spend most of their time ruling the world, organising under-age orgies and communing with the lizard people overlords who live inside the Earth's crust."

"Have you found anything that might have come from the killer?"

"I don't think so. There's a hell of a lot to sift through. I'm familiarising myself with the terrain at the moment. Getting an idea of what's out there, and where the best places are. As soon as I've done that, I'll think myself into the role of Susan and Mark, and see if I can get a feeling of how they might have approached this, where they might have felt welcome."

Lauren grabbed the last slice of pizza and dived back into the internet.

~

I felt a bit like a spare part. Lauren was busy hunting the killer online. Hundreds of police officers were chasing down leads. And I was sat on a sofa, monitoring news channels and keeping Lauren supplied with food and coffee.

I used to be a senior manager. A real high-flier. Someone who's opinion was sought, a valuable member of every team I ever worked with. A troubleshooter renowned for the calm and efficient way he dealt with crises.

I didn't recognise that person anymore. The killer, the police, the press – they'd eviscerated him, ripping away his confidence and replacing it with an energy-sapping doubt. Even now, when I knew that I'd been set up, that I hadn't been hallucinating, that I wasn't a bad person, or any of those vile, hateful things that people called me, it still didn't take much to puncture that thin veneer of confidence that was slowly growing back.

But it was growing back. And I could be useful.

Lauren rejected my offers of help the first two times.

"It's quicker if I do it," she'd said the first time. "I'm getting really close."

"Maybe later," she'd said the second time. "I really, really need to concentrate on this."

The third time I was adamant.

"Okay," said Lauren. "What I'm doing is compiling a list of users who might be the killer or Mark or Susan. We need their usernames and a URL – an internet address, that is – of the message thread that they posted in. That's so the police can analyse the metadata that accompanies each message when someone posts. If we're lucky they might have got sloppy and left data that gives away their location."

"Why do we need Mark's and Susan's locations?"

"My thinking is that they're most likely to get sloppy, and if we can prove it really is Mark or Susan, then we know we're looking in the right place."

Lauren emailed me the link to one of the message boards

she'd already checked so that I could familiarise myself with the territory, and see if I came up with the same candidates she had.

"It's the most promising site I've come across," she said. "Look for someone who's behaving like the killer would. Someone who's looking to recruit others, or create a following, or set himself up as an expert, or just has that feel of being the killer. Err on the inclusive side. It's easier to remove people from the list later than start again from scratch. Oh, and read the pinned thread first. That'll give you an insight into how these people think."

I read the pinned post. It purported to come from an insider working at GCHQ. He, or she, called themselves GCHQAnon.

They had a lot to say.

The opening paragraphs were familiar. There was a global conspiracy of the elite – big money, big pharma, liberals, intellectuals, the media, the deep state – whose plan was total world domination.

The First Stage in this plan was 5G. Radio masts were erected everywhere. Governments poured money into the project even though there were countless scientific studies that proved the radio frequency they were transmitting on was dangerous to human tissue.

The Second Stage was Covid which, according to GCHQAnon, started in Wuhan when the first 5G tower was installed there. That was the purpose of 5G. To create a so-called pandemic, which the government scientists were told to mislabel as a virus.

The Third Stage was vaccination. The so-called Covid pandemic was an excuse to inject graphene oxide nanoparticles into as much of the population as they could. Once inside the body, these nanoparticles migrated to the spinal cord, where they hid, awaiting activation.

The Final Stage was 6G. Activation. This was where the post deviated from anything I'd heard before. GCHQAnon didn't have all the details yet – only a few trusted insiders were party to all the secret discussions – but he surmised the ultimate goal of this stage had to be some kind of mind control through the activation of the injected nanoparticles.

Follow the money, advised GCHQAnon. All the deep state hedge funds and sovereign wealth funds were piling money into advanced AI and 6G. But no one was talking about it. No one even admitted that 6G existed.

He'd heard from a reliable source that a prototype 6G transmitter had already been built and that, unlike 5G, these transmitters would be underground. People wouldn't even know they were there. Governments would build complete subterranean networks. Then, once complete, they'd switch them all on, and that would be it for humanity. An AI controlled data burst through the 6G network would activate the nanoparticles, and free will would become a thing of the past. The elite would have control over everybody and everything.

After the pinned post came pages and pages of message threads where people discussed 6G. It was a wild ride. Some discussions veered away on totally unrelated tangents. Some were unintelligible. Some were angry rants. But most were from people adding their own ideas about what 6G might be, and how it could be combatted.

GCHQAnon also posted in these threads, adding to his original post, incorporating other people's ideas, refining some, rejecting others. A lot of it was post-truth fantasy and political dogma, but there were also attempts at underpinning the theory with real science. Or what looked like real science to an amateur like me. It could have been pseudo-science. It most probably was.

But there was an interesting consensus developing. The contributors were coming round to the idea that 6G was not being installed in the cities first. It was being rolled out in the countryside. Using isolated rural locations, houses often, where they could sink their shafts, and create their control bunkers without attracting attention. When asked, the 'workmen' would say they were doing renovation work.

Nothing to see here. But the time they were taking, and the type of machinery seen entering the properties, pointed to a very different project.

A number of the later posters claimed to be witnesses.

One poster suggested it was time for direct action. *We need to get our people inside these locations. We need videos to show everyone what's really happening.*

And to do that they needed a map of each location. That went down well, producing a fair number of volunteers who agreed to keep an eye out in their area. Or further afield if required.

I could see Susan and Mark volunteering for something like that. I couldn't see an actual post, and I couldn't see any invite to spend two days in Somerset mapping the countryside. But I could see how easy it would be. And non-threatening. Two days walking and driving through the countryside looking for covert 6G building sites. It sounded fun. It sounded right. A chance to really do something for humanity. Far more productive than marching or giving out leaflets. It was direct action. A chance to make a difference.

What teenage conspiracy theorist could resist that?

I went back over the posts to compile my list of candidates for the Dollhouse Killer. GCHQAnon was an obvious choice. He'd created the 6G theory. And he oversaw its development. He didn't advance the idea that 6G was being installed in the countryside first, but he didn't speak against it. He accepted the idea without comment. I added him to my list.

Psycho1407 was the poster who brought up the rural connection. I added him to my list.

Cwarrior14B was the one who called for direct action and volunteers to map the countryside. I added him as well.

I read out my list to Lauren.

"What did you think about GyGaX76?" she asked.

"Which one was he?"

"The polite one who made a number of suggestions about how 6G might work, and was the first to volunteer to help map the countryside."

"I didn't think he stood out. He came across as a follower, not a leader."

"True, but he also came across as knowledgeable, helpful and trustworthy. The kind of non-threatening persona you could use to hook someone in."

I disagreed, but it was Lauren's list, and, with the exception of GyGaX76, our instincts produced the same candidates.

"Don't forget," she said. "That the killer could be using several names. Here's the next message board," she said. "I'm emailing the link to you now."

This message board was similar to the first except it was more focused on America. The first board had been predominantly UK centred. This one was also more political. The 6G thread started off almost word for word the same as before except the author didn't claim to be working for GCHQ. He was reporting what a GCHQ insider had told him

The big difference came when describing what would happen when 6G was activated. This was far more emotive, hitting every alt right nightmare. The right to bear arms would be struck down. Christianity would be outlawed. Abortion would be made legal right up to the moment of birth. The US constitution would be replaced by Sharia law, and the United States of America would be renamed The Socialist Caliphate of Greater Mexico.

I could see Timothy McCord reacting to that.

It wasn't as though the message had to be credible to mainstream opinion, or backed up with facts or expert witnesses. It just had to appeal to the fears of the target audience. And if one story wasn't working, you made up another until you found something that worked. You could even change your user name every time so no one would know it was you again.

I was sold. These message boards were where the killer was finding his victims.

"How many of these message boards are there?" I asked Lauren.

"Loads. I've only found mention of 6G on a handful of them. He might have experimented with other conspiracy theories. I'll keep looking, but I think we have enough to send to Natalia already."

We continued searching well into the evening. Lauren would send me a link every now and then when she found something interesting. It was a fascinating, if disconcerting, glimpse into a world I never knew existed. I felt useful at last.

And then, just before nine, Lauren made a startling discovery.

Chapter Fifty-Two

"Oh. My. God," said Lauren. "Look at this. There are sev-eral threads on dollhouses. I'll send you a link."

I read the first one. It was about a news story going around that Russia had smuggled twelve battlefield EMP devices into Britain last week in a consignment of dollhouses. The poster said that none of the news agencies would touch the story. They'd all been warned off by some shadowy government figure.

It took me a while to find out what an EMP was. I could tell from the context it was a weapon. It turned out to be an electromagnetic pulse, which could be used to knock out an enemy's electrical devices. The Russians, according to armchair expert DeepThought27, had developed a battlefield version that was small enough to fit in a shoebox and powerful enough to fry every electrical circuit within one hundred yards when detonated.

Much speculation ensued. *What were the Russians up to?*

It didn't take long before someone mentioned 6G. What better way to take out these secret 6G substations than by using an EMP device. Various 'experts' weighed in. You'd have to place the EMP device closer to the 6G transmitter than one hundred yards. You'd have to get it as close as possible. Ideally, inside the building.

But why would the Russians be doing this, asked several posters? JasperD20 thought it was obvious. Russia and NATO had been at war for years. Putin was the deep state's greatest enemy. If Britain was leading the way in building a working 6G network then, of course, Russia would try to slow them down any way they could. Supplying British anti-6G activists with EMP devices made perfect sense.

One poster even gave that help a name – Operation

Dollhouse. He'd heard it called that by an acquaintance he had in 'intelligence circles.'

Operation Dollhouse had its own discussion thread. A secret group of committed Anti-6G activists, with the help of Russia, was tracking down the locations of the 6G substations. They'd successfully broken into one and planted an EMP device inside, destroying the 6G transmitter.

The government were so worried about this information getting out that not only did they block any mention of the story being published on mainstream media, but they created a counter story to make sure anyone searching on 'dollhouse' would find a very different story.

I could see where this was going.

And I was right. The dollhouse murders were fake news, created by an inner circle within government, to prevent the truth getting out. Laburnum Cottage was a 6G substation. That's why there'd been so much police presence on the property. There hadn't been a murder. The only true part of the dollhouse murder story was that the police were desperate to find the other eleven Russian dollhouses.

I read it again from the beginning, adding Paris68 to my lists of candidates for the killer. I noticed the post was dated Friday. Was this confirmation that the killer was having problems recruiting new victims? The publicity surrounding the murders had to be a huge problem for him. Was this his solution?

Murders? What murders? It's all fake news. Dollhouses? They're a symbol of resistance and Freedom. Harmless packaging for the EMP devices that will save the human race.

It could work. In this weird world of conspiracies anything could.

~

Lauren rang Natalia and gave her our news.

"I'm sending you the list of usernames we think he might be using and the links to the discussion threads," said Lauren. "You've got to read them. They show exactly how he's grooming his victims, and if you get your tech people on it, they might be able to find a location for the killer in the message headers."

I was on the other side of the room so I didn't catch Natalia's side of the conversation, but it sounded like it was going well. Though it was difficult to tell as Lauren was doing ninety percent of the talking.

Lauren gave a quick summary of the kind of discussions we'd seen and our take on what he was trying to do.

"I know these websites are probably going to kick and scream if you ask for information on their users," said Lauren. "But you've got to try. They'd probably have all his private messages with the victims. And maybe future victims too."

I'd wondered about that. I'd seen a few posts with 'PM me if interested' – the one calling for volunteers to search for potential 6G sites, for example – but I hadn't noticed any PM button to press.

"I think I got through to her," said Lauren, when the call ended. "I thought she was going to give me a polite brush off at first, but she's not stupid. She knows the potential of this."

"How would you PM someone on those message boards?" I asked.

"It varies," said Lauren. "There's usually an icon somewhere on the post, or you click on the user name."

"So, although only the sender and the recipient would be able to see the message, the message board would store the contents of those messages?"

"That's right, which is why I was pushing Natalia to try and subpoena the message board records. The killer might have moved his later conversations over to a more secure medium, but the initial contact – with the full text – would still be there on the message board."

~

We'd been so engrossed in conspiracy message boards that we'd missed that evening's police press conference. We caught the highlights on a later news broadcast.

If you could call them highlights. They didn't announce anything new. Well, new to us. The Chief Constable showed the EFits of Gary Turner and pictures of the two vans he'd used, but he didn't mention anything about Sophie, or Susan's list of delivery addresses, or the fibres found on McCord's body, or whether they'd found Gary Turner's fingerprints on the alarm fittings. It was just an appeal to the public for help.

Have you seen this man? Have you seen these vans? He may be a security technician called Gary Turner. Has he installed any burglar alarms or new locks for you recently?

I couldn't see anything useful coming out of the appeal. All they really had was his height, build and gender. The EFits just weren't good enough.

But you never know. Sometimes you can get lucky.

~

The next day Lauren was already up, tapping away on her laptop, when I came down. She closed her laptop the moment she saw me.

"What's happened?" I asked, fearing the usual – aka 'the worst.'

"Nothing. Do you think it's too early to ring Natalia?"

It was barely eight. I had no idea if detectives kept normal hours during a major murder investigation. And a phone call from Lauren might not be everyone's idea of a good start to the day.

"Why do you want to call her?" I asked. "Have you found something new?"

"No. I was just wondering if they'd made any progress with the info I gave her yesterday."

Lauren appeared strangely subdued. She'd been such a ball of energy the previous day. Perhaps this was a reaction brought on by the grim reality of our situation. A sadistic serial killer was still out there looking for a way to get to us.

Something that had exercised my brain at four o'clock that

morning as I lay in bed unable to get back to sleep. What was the killer doing? We knew he was obsessed with having me find a model of where he'd left his latest body. He wasn't going to change that MO, but what could he do? I had twenty-four-hour police protection. Bob and Kofi were not going to fall for the screaming girl trick again. And I wasn't leaving the house. Where did that leave him? Was he able to pause his killing spree? Or was he filling his freezers with victims until he found a way to get to me?

Unfortunately, I'd thought of a few ways that he *could* get to us.

"You remember the killer had Susan buy a drone?" I said.

"Yes."

"I think the killer could use it to get us to evacuate the cottage."

"How?"

"By making the police think there was a bomb on the property. It wouldn't have to be an actual bomb. All he'd have to do was create something that *looked* like a bomb. Tape a load of nails to a package with wires poking out of it and drop it from a drone at night. He could drop it round the back of the house so the drone wouldn't be visible from the police car."

"That would work," said Lauren. "The police couldn't take the risk. They'd have to evacuate the house, even if they thought the bomb was a fake."

"And the killer could slip in during the confusion dressed as a policeman and either plant a model inside the house or whisk us away to a supposed safe house."

The fake bomb hadn't been my only worry. I can be a very productive worrier at four o'clock in the morning. A fire would force us out too. The cottage had a thatched roof. If the killer could set it on fire, we'd have to be evacuated. I didn't think a drone could drop a petrol bomb, but it could drop petrol on the thatch. And then return on a second run with something to ignite it.

Lauren thought we should call Natalia.

"You don't need to call now," I said. "Any attack would have to come at night or he'd risk the drone being seen."

"Best not wait," said Lauren, her phone already in her hand.

I listened while she relayed my fears of what the killer might do to get us out of the house.

Natalia didn't think the killer would take the risk.

"The place would be teeming with officers," she said.

"He's obsessed and desperate," said Lauren.

"He's not that desperate, and if there was a fire or a bomb threat, he wouldn't get anywhere near the cottage. We'd block the road like we did last time, but this time we'd make damn sure no one unauthorised was let through."

I thought Lauren might argue the point. After all the killer would be close by. He could slip in and out before any roadblock had been set up. But she changed the subject.

"Have forensics managed to find anything in those messages I sent you the links to?"

"Not yet. I should hear something later today."

"Later today? They do know it's a priority, don't they?" said Lauren. "They've had more than enough time to scan the messages."

"Every job is a priority at the moment, Lauren. Our officers are working all hours and will continue to do so. Now, I have a meeting to go to. Thank you for your call."

I don't think you can slam down a mobile phone, but if there'd been a way, I felt sure Natalia would have found it.

"You do know that people don't like outsiders telling them how to do their job?" I said.

"But that's just it!" said Lauren. "They're *not* doing their job. They should realise that these message boards are *the* top priority. His next victim will be on there. They might have hours to live, a day at the most. The police should be working round the clock on it. I am."

"You didn't work through the night, did you?"

"Not all night. Sorry, I'm not good company at the moment. I'll go upstairs and have a lie down for an hour or two."

I noticed she took her laptop with her.

~

Lauren resurfaced around noon. She didn't look refreshed. She looked on edge.

"Did you get any sleep?" I asked.

"Enough. Listen, sit down, I may be about to do something that will appear stupid, but, trust me, it's not. I've thought this through. I've done little else but think this through. And it's solid. The danger will be minimal, and, if it works, we catch the killer."

Introducing something with the words 'this will appear stupid' is not a confidence-boosting recommendation.

"You want to use us as bait," I said.

"Not 'us.' I'll be the bait. Can I borrow your phone?"

"Yes. Why?" I said, handing it over.

"Natalia's not taking my calls."

She rang Natalia.

"Hi, it's Lauren. I want to go undercover."

Chapter Fifty-Three

Lauren put the call on speakerphone.

"What are you talking about?" asked Natalia

"I want to go undercover. I know how to contact the killer. I've spent two days in those message boards, immersing myself in the culture. I can play an impressionable conspiracy theorist, and I can make the killer choose me for his next victim/accomplice."

"You're being ridiculous. You can't go undercover. He's seen you. Everyone's seen you."

"I'm an actor. We're used to playing people who look nothing like us. I have this friend who's an absolute genius with make-up and prosthetics. She's worked on dozens of movies. She can make me look like anything in this world. No one would recognise me."

"We have undercover officers."

"Who'd have to spend a day or two learning their part and familiarising themselves with the message boards. I'm ready now. In fact, I've already started. I've got five different personas posting on various boards. I'm covering all the bases. One of them will attract the killer. I'm certain."

"You're not trained, Lauren. Undercover work is more than just knowing a part. You've got to be able to sense and react to danger, and work with a team. You're a loose cannon."

"I'm a very controlled cannon. The person I've shown you is only a small part of me. I can do professional. I can do restrained. Remember, I have the ultimate motivation. My life is already on the line."

Natalia sighed. "Lauren, you may think you can talk yourself out of any situation, but you can't. You may have to fight for your life. Do you have any martial arts training?"

"I can fence. My drama school was hot on fencing."

"This is not funny, Lauren."

"I *know* it's not funny. I also know that there is no evidence of any fight between the killer and his victims. He uses stealth and drugs. He doesn't use force. My plan would be to wear a hidden camera with a tracker, get invited to whichever house he's using, get him talking, then have you burst in and arrest him before anything dangerous takes place."

"The risks are just too great. We don't endanger members of the public."

"I'm already in danger! The choice is between sitting here waiting to be murdered or taking the fight to the killer. I vote for the latter every time."

"My bosses would never go for it."

"They will when they've thought it through. I'll sign a waiver. Think about it – using me endangers one less person because I'm already in danger."

"What if there's nothing incriminating at the house the killer lures you to? It could be a test, an interview to see if you're suitable. He might take you to another house. You could be holed up with him for days. Are you prepared for that? A trained undercover officer would be."

"I'm ready to do whatever it takes. But there's no evidence to suggest that the killer spends more than a few hours with his victims. As soon as its dark, all he's thinking about is killing them."

"You're really serious about this, aren't you?"

"I am."

"I'll have a word with my bosses, but I can tell you exactly what they're going to say. In the meantime, pass on any replies you receive to your posts. Don't reply yourself. And don't make any more posts to those message boards."

~

"Natalia's right," I said. "It's too dangerous. It's one thing being able to play a part, and I know you could talk yourself out of just about any situation, but you could be there for several hours, and all it takes is one slip."

"I'm great at improv. I can cover all manner of slips."

"But do you trust the police to come to your aid in time? They could be several minutes away."

"I don't see this killer as a physical threat. I may not know any martial arts, but I work out when I can. I'm stronger than I look."

"But wouldn't it be easier for you to do the online work – make contact with the killer, string him along, agree to meet up – and then hand it over to an undercover cop?"

"In a perfect world, yes. But I don't know this undercover cop. I won't have any say in her appointment, and I won't have any say in what she does or says. I have to trust a stranger to do a job that I know I can do better. And if she messes up, we'll not get another chance like this. We'll be sat here next week, next month, waiting. Our lives in limbo. Do you want that? I don't."

~

Lauren showed me her posts on the message boards. I had to admit they were good. They didn't look out of place or fake. She varied her style, being aggressive and ardent as one character, quiet and reflective as another.

"I've tried to cover all the character types that might appeal to him," said Lauren. "We know he chose Susan, so I've tried to capture her persona – someone slightly lost, passionate about the world, looking for a cause. And I've done a ranty, in-your-face, angry warrior type. And a 'desperate to do something' woman in search of a leader. One of them has got to work."

"Has anyone commented on your posts?"

"There's been a couple of references to what I've posted, but no one's messaged me. That's how the killer will make contact. He'll want to take all future correspondence off onto a secure chat site or email. Then he'll evaluate each candidate before choosing the ones to kill."

"Do you think he'll ask for pictures? He might want to see

which ones look like the figurines."

"Possibly."

"What if he chooses all five of your fake identities?"

"Then I have five chances to be selected. He's not going to ask to meet all five at the same time."

I could see it working. The killer had to be running out of volunteers. However many times he shouted fake news at the dollhouse killings, it was nothing compared to the wall of publicity surrounding the murders.

But I couldn't see the police letting Lauren go undercover. DCI Terrell hated her. And the top management would be more concerned about image. *What if she gets murdered? What if she compromises our case? How do we explain using an untrained member of the public in a covert operation?*

Even Lauren started talking about a plan B.

"I'm sure the police will see sense," she said. "But if they don't, I've got a plan B."

I knew I was going to hate it, but I listened.

"I've bought a pet tracker," she said. "It'll be delivered tomorrow morning."

Well, I hadn't been expecting that.

"I spent over an hour this morning comparing all the tracking devices and this one looked the best. It's got a maximum range of nine miles. I'd carry the transmitter and you'd have the handset. You could hang back way out of sight and always know where I was. The handset screen displays an arrow pointing to my location with the distance in metres."

"You're not seriously suggesting that you meet the killer with me as your back up several miles behind you."

"I did say it was a plan B. And you wouldn't be several miles behind me. You'd be as close as you could get without being seen, ready to press your personal alarm."

"How would I know when to press the alarm? Are you wearing a microphone as well? Am I a one-man, back-up team monitoring your conversations as well as your location?"

"Maybe Natalia would loan us some equipment? Or Ken? He seemed helpful and he's local."

"Listen to yourself, Lauren. You're making this up as you go along."

"So what if I am? Okay, the killer's clever and persistent, but he's not superman. The only reason he appeared one step ahead of everyone else is because he had us bugged. That's over now. He's one man. And he's vulnerable."

"He's a sadistic killer who's used accomplices. There could be two of them waiting for you."

"Not if he has me down as a prospective victim. Susan and Mark never met. He can only cope with one victim/accomplice at a time."

"You don't know that."

"We can never know everything. And we can't allow ourselves to be cowed into inactivity by things that might never happen."

I was about to reply when I noticed the laptop's screen had changed.

Lauren had a private message from Cwarrior14B, the one who called for direct action and volunteers to map the countryside.

Chapter Fifty-Four

It was a short message to Lauren's Susan persona.

Always looking for volunteers. Email me at Cwarrior14B@ZoltanMail.com for information.

Lauren punched the air. "I *knew* he'd bite."

"You really did it," I said, staring at the screen. I'd though she might, but seeing the message suddenly made it real.

If it was the killer.

Lauren brought up a new screen and started tapping away furiously.

"What are you doing?"

"Creating a ZoltanMail account. The killer chose ZoltanMail for a good reason. It's totally anonymous. All the messages are super encrypted and you can open an account without divulging any personal information."

"You're going to reply to him?"

"Of course. Aren't you dying to see what he says next?"

"Natalia said—"

"Natalia hasn't got back to me yet," interrupted Lauren. "The more info I gather on the killer, the more she'll have to take notice."

As soon as Lauren had created her new email account, she brought up the new message screen and started typing.

Thank you for your message. I'd definitely like more information on how I can help.

She signed it with her message board user name – DianaPrince1941 – and pressed 'send.'

We waited, watching the email inbox. Was the killer staring at his inbox too? Waiting for his next victim to reply, thinking of all the ways he could terrify her?

He'd be compelled to reply quickly. He wouldn't be able to

help himself. He might not have killed anyone since McCord.

"Shouldn't you refresh the screen?" I asked. "It might not update automatically."

"I'm sure it does," said Lauren, but she refreshed it anyway. A few seconds later up came a new message.

> *Our next mission is tomorrow night. We have two excellent leads. One of them is certain to be a substation. Where are you based? We're in Wiltshire. Is that too far?*

"It's got to be him," said Lauren. "And he's still in the area."

She started typing again. Wiltshire was quite a large county. He might be a few miles away or way over towards Swindon or The New Forest.

Lauren sent her message.

> *I'm near Bristol. Wiltshire not a problem. Tell me where and when and I'll be there. Can't wait!*

Neither could I. He'd have to give an address. Once he did, we'd have him.

I could barely breathe. For the first time in a week, I could actually see an end to this nightmare that didn't include my death.

Two minutes later his message arrived.

> *I'll give you the address tomorrow. We have to check it's still safe first. The deep state has people and cameras everywhere.*

> *Safest to come by public transport. Take the 21:25 train from Bristol to Warminster, arriving at Warminster at 22:15. There's a taxi rank outside the station. Take a taxi from there to the rendezvous point.*

> *Important: Bring your phone and laptop with you. We have apps we can help you install that will*

make you invisible.

Equally important: Assume you're being watched at all times. Cover your face as much as you can. Wear gloves and come dressed for a covert night-time walk in the countryside.

Lauren replied almost immediately.

See you tomorrow night. Looking forward to it.

"It sounds like him," said Lauren. "It really does. Do you think he's some kind of trainspotter? He does seem obsessed with trains. And did you notice the neat way he's suggesting I bring my phone and laptop with me? That's so he can destroy them after he's killed me, making sure there's no link back to him for the police to find."

I was more interested in his location. Warminster was only ten miles away. That had to rule out Swindon and Salisbury and the more populated areas of Wiltshire. The killer wouldn't want his victim spending a long time in a car with an inquisitive taxi driver. He'd choose the nearest train station to the house he'd chosen for the murder.

That narrowed down the area significantly.

I wondered if it was one of the houses on Susan's list of delivery addresses.

I rang Georgia.

"Hi, Georgia, don't worry I haven't been arrested. I was just calling to see if you knew of Susan using a delivery address in Wiltshire. It would probably be near Warminster."

"No, I haven't actually seen the list, but I have lurked by the coffee machine when the topic was being discussed. There were two addresses that SCU were particularly interested in – one in Somerset, one in Dorset. No mention of Wiltshire. Why? Has Lauren found a clue?"

"You could say that. Well, actually don't say that. Not yet."

Lauren leaned over and put my phone onto speaker.

"Hello, Georgia. What Mathew's struggling to say is there's been a major development. Now, what I want to know is how are SCU reacting to it? Are all the senior officers closeted away in secret meetings, or are they carrying on as though nothing has happened?"

"Hello, Lauren. I haven't noticed any secret meetings. The mood amongst the team has lifted somewhat, but I put that down to a possible breakthrough in the search for those vans."

"Has there been a breakthrough in the search for the vans?" asked Lauren.

"No. Sorry, that was me surmising."

"What about Natalia? Has she been closeted in meetings? Showing any signs of elation or anger?"

"She did have an altercation earlier with your friend the Detective Chief Inspector, but that's not exactly unusual."

"Thank you," said Lauren. "I'm going to phone her in five minutes. You might find it informative if you lurked nearby."

~

Lauren rang her make-up artist friend first to see if she was available. She put the phone on speaker.

"You're in luck. I'm flying out to Budapest on Friday to do a horror film. What do you want done?"

"I want to be totally unrecognisable, but nothing weird. I want to be able to walk down the street without attracting attention."

"Are you *that* famous already?"

"Not quite, but this serial killer is watching me, and I need to get to a secret meeting without him or anyone else knowing it's me. I know it sounds melodramatic, but my life really does depend on it."

"Okay. Let's say three, maybe four, hours to do the work. When do you want to come over?"

"How about tomorrow afternoon? I need to catch the 21:25 train from Bristol Temple Meads."

"No problem. I'm in all day."

Next, Lauren called Natalia.

"I've got him," said Lauren. "He's in Wiltshire and I'm meeting him tomorrow night."

Chapter Fifty-Five

Natalia wasn't easy to convince.

"I told you not to contact him!"

"I had to! You said you'd call back. You didn't. What was I supposed to do? Sit on my hands when I had the chance of luring the killer into a trap?"

"I was *going* to ring you. I just didn't have good news. I put your plan to DCI Terrell and he shot it down."

"Did he even listen?" asked Lauren.

"He doesn't trust you."

"Did you show him the message boards?"

"Of course I did. He thinks all the posts are yours. He thinks it's a publicity stunt for your next prime time interview."

"That's ridiculous!"

"Look, he's under intense pressure. The Chief Constable wants results yesterday. The press are ready to turn on him for lack of progress, and we just haven't got the manpower to follow every lead. He's convinced our killer's going to be found by going through the list of all the people who own the right model Ford Transit and have worked in home security. He's not going to sanction taking people off that to boost your career."

"Do *you* think I'm making all this up?" asked Lauren. "I've shown you the message boards. I've just sent you the emails between me and the killer. Mathew can vouch for the fact that the killer's emails weren't sent by me. He was here, watching, all the time."

Natalia sighed. "I want to believe you, but you don't make it easy with all your Honey Badger interviews."

"I didn't do any interviews until the Chief Constable called me a suspect. I was in danger of losing my career. I had to fight back. After that it was a matter of using my position to put pressure on the killer – to get him to make a mistake."

"Look," said Natalia, "I'll show the DCI the emails and see what he says."

"Tell him I'm not asking for personnel. All I need is equipment. A hidden camera and microphone so I can film the killer and everything he says. Recording equipment so Mathew can monitor everything as it happens. A GPS tracker so you'll know where I am. And maybe have Bob and Kofi reassigned from guarding Laburnum Cottage to watching over me?"

"I can't equip you then leave you to fend for yourself."

"Then help me. It won't need many people. The potential benefit way exceeds the cost. You know that's true."

I could feel Natalia wavering.

"Natalia," said Lauren. "Last week you told me that DCI Terrell wasn't the only one who can make decisions. Was that true? If it is, we can end the killing tomorrow."

~

With Natalia onboard everything changed. We weren't alone. We had someone who'd run similar operations before. We had proper professional equipment. We had back-up.

I even got my car back. Natalia arranged for Devon and Cornwall police to deliver it later that day.

I think I actually felt happy. I had hope. I had a future I could look forward to. I could even see my reputation being restored. If the killer confessed to tricking me with directional speakers, then no one could question my behaviour last year.

Lauren spent most of her time fleshing out her character, DianaPrince1941. She decided her real name would be Diana Collins.

"Nice common name," she said. "Bound to be several in the Bristol area if the killer tries to find me online."

"Do you think he'll vet you?"

"No idea. I'm hoping this isn't an audition, but I've got to be prepared for anything. I think I'll have Diana just coming out of a difficult relationship with a coercive controller. That'll give me a good reason for not wanting to talk about personal stuff. And a good reason for making Diana into a loner. The killer likes loners, they don't have people asking questions when they go missing."

"Have you agreed on a safe word with the police?"

"Not yet. They'll be watching the output from the camera, so they'll see what's happening."

"You know they're not going to want to intervene until they have something incriminating on tape?"

"I wouldn't want it any other way. My job is to draw him out. And stay alive long enough to get a conviction."

~

The next day we were both up bright and early. For once the Dollhouse Murders wasn't the main story on the TV news. That honour fell to a government minister caught up in a corruption scandal. I imagine he was cursing fate for having the scandal break on a slow news day.

I made us both a full English breakfast – part celebration, part last supper. Succeed or fail, this could be the last meal we ever had together. Lauren kept her laptop open throughout the entire meal, glancing at the screen now and then, watching out for the killer's email to arrive.

Natalia rang just after eight to check in. Everything was arranged. She'd send a car to pick up Lauren at noon and take her to Keynsham police station, just outside Bristol, where Natalia and another officer would hand over the surveillance equipment and show Lauren how to use it.

From there an officer would drive Lauren to her friend's flat and then return later to take her to the train station.

"The officer will remain at the station," said Natalia. "Keeping well out of sight, until you've boarded the train without incident."

"What about Warminster station?" asked Lauren.

"We'll have an officer in the taxi rank. We've made an arrangement with one of the taxi firms to have one of our officers stand-in for a two-hour shift. So make sure you head for Woodcock Taxis."

"Got it. Woodcock Taxis."

"All we need now," said Natalia. "Is the address."

~

At nine thirty I almost had a heart attack. Someone was knocking on the front door. My first thought was Terrell. It wasn't his knock, but who else could it be? Had he got wind of Natalia's off-book operation with Lauren and was about to put a stop to it? It would be just like him to insist on doing it in person.

It wasn't Terrell. It was a uniformed constable, presumably one half of our protection detail. And he had a ripped open parcel in his hands.

"Sorry about the parcel," he said. "But we were told to open any package and check for wires and stuff. It's clean."

He handed over the remains. Well, we had mentioned our fear that the killer might try and plant a bomb. We hadn't thought he might use the Royal Mail though.

I took the package through to the lounge. "It's the pet tracker you ordered."

I didn't think Lauren would still be interested now that she'd been promised real surveillance equipment, but we had time on our hands. It was pretty easy to use, and it worked. The receiver was the size of an old Nokia mobile phone – small and compact. The transmitter was smaller, but it wasn't something that could be easily concealed. It would have to go in a pocket or a bag, but even a rudimentary search would find it.

"What do you think?" I said after we'd tried it a few times. "Too bulky?

"It's bulkier than I thought, but I can have it in reserve."

Just after eleven, the long-awaited email arrived. The message read:

Meet-up address confirmed.

Friary View, Moorleaze.

We'll keep an eye on the place throughout the day. Check your emails frequently in case we need to contact you again.

"Where's Moorleaze?" asked Lauren.

I had no idea. I was about as far removed from a fount of local knowledge as you could get.

Lauren typed the address into a map site. Moorleaze was a small village about eleven miles to the north-east of us. And Friary View was a large isolated property two miles outside the village, set well back from the road.

It was the ideal location for the killer. Remote. Quiet. The nearest neighbour was two hundred yards away down a winding road.

~

Lauren rang Natalia, forwarding the email with the address.

"It sounds like he's going to be monitoring the property all day," said Lauren. "He could have cameras outside."

"Don't worry," said Natalia. "We'll drive past once in an unmarked car, but that's all. We'll find somewhere nearby, invisible from the road, to set up a base. We'll be close enough to get to you quickly, and far enough away not to draw the killer's attention."

Natalia sent Lauren a picture of the officer assigned to drive her to Keynsham.

"His name's Jermaine," said Natalia. "He's already on his way. Should be with you at twelve."

Natalia appeared to have thought of everything. As had Lauren.

"I think I'll back up my phone and laptop just in case the killer decides to wipe them before he tries to kill me."

As noon approached, I started getting more and more nervous. I wasn't sure what Lauren felt. Maybe being an actress prepared her for these moments waiting to go on stage. Me? I was a dry-mouthed wreck.

And then she was gone, disappearing down the road in the passenger seat of Jermaine's car. And it definitely was Jermaine. Both of us checked his face against the picture Natalia had sent.

The end game had begun.

Chapter Fifty-Six

It was a long, long afternoon and early evening. I tried to fill in the time doing useful things. I even cleaned. And cooked a meal without using the microwave.

When my phone rang at six o'clock, I almost knocked it flying off the kitchen table such was my rush to answer it.

It was Natalia. Everything was fine. She was coming round at nine to show me how I could receive the audiovisual output from Lauren's camera. I hadn't been expecting that, but, apparently, Lauren had insisted.

I put my alarm on for five to nine and watched some old sitcoms, dipping into the news channels whenever the adverts came on. Still nothing new about the murders.

Natalia arrived just before my alarm went off. She'd brought one of her technical people with her to connect me up.

"How's it going?" I asked Natalia.

"Everything's proceeding as planned. Lauren's on her way to Bristol Temple Meads at the moment. She's unrecognisable. Her friend has done a stellar job."

"How's she holding up?"

"Like a pro. You have nothing to worry about. She's in good hands, and she's extremely capable."

An image appeared on my laptop. Sound too. A view from the front seat of a car in busy urban traffic.

"The camera's in Lauren's glasses," said Natalia. "It's almost undetectable. The GPS tracker is in her left earring."

"Can she hear us?" I asked.

"No. It's one-way communication. We can hear her, but she can't hear us. Here's my phone number. If you lose the live feed, call me. Or tell your protection officers outside. They've got both the live camera feed and a radio link to me and the forward base. We're half a mile from Friary View and very well concealed."

When Natalia left, I made myself a cup of coffee, placed the laptop on the dining table, and pulled up a chair.

~

I watched Lauren arrive at the train station. I watched her board her train, the screen swinging left and right as she observed her fellow passengers. I couldn't see anyone behaving suspiciously. I couldn't see anyone with a big bushy beard either.

Time slowed down. My initial excitement replaced with a desire for the train to speed up and get to Warminster.

I fetched a packet of biscuits from the kitchen. And some cheese. Apparently I'd become a nervous eater. Stations came and went. People got on. People got off.

Then, as the train was approaching Warminster, Lauren suddenly looked down at her phone. She'd received an email.

Change of plan. This is a training exercise.

Turn right out of Warminster train station, after 100 yards turn left onto West Street, after fifty yards turn right into Taunton Place. You'll see a blue bike padlocked to a railing on your right. The combination is 1927.

There's a map showing best route to Friary View taped on the handle bars. Don't worry, you can't get lost. We'll be watching. Volunteers need to be flexible and fit.

I did not like this at all. What did he mean by training exercise? Was this turning into an audition with several candidates being vetted? Or was this part of his grooming routine – like telling Susan and Mark to break their journey at a different train station?

And how would Natalia and her team react? They had an officer outside the station in a taxi. Was he now going to follow Lauren? Surely that would be too much of a risk with the killer saying he was going to be watching her?

Lauren left the train at Warminster, hanging back to watch the other passengers disembarking. No one appeared to be watching her. She passed through the barrier then out onto the street. The screen darkened as the camera adjusted to the change in light levels. The sun had set hours ago.

She looked towards the taxi rank. I couldn't see any cars with a Woodcock Taxis logo. Perhaps the driver had gone on ahead to Moorleaze to join Natalia?

Lauren followed the route she'd been given. It looked like it had rained recently – shop lights reflecting off countless small puddles on the pavement. It was twenty past ten on a wet Wednesday in Warminster – very little traffic and hardly any pedestrians.

Lauren found the bike. It was chained to railings just as the email had said. I thought the map might have been sodden and unreadable, but it had been wrapped in clear plastic. Lauren peeled it off the handlebars and stowed her bag on the luggage rack behind the saddle.

She unlocked the padlock, switched on the front and rear lights and set off.

I checked the distance between Warminster and Moorleaze on a map. It was eight miles. I wondered when Lauren had last cycled eight miles.

Lauren peddled into the night. It was really dark. No moon, no stars, and no streetlights now that she'd passed the outer edge of Warminster. Just the faint cone of light illuminating a small patch of road in front of the bike. Luckily the camera appeared to cope well in low light. The colours had gone, but the contrast was good.

It didn't like the sudden appearance of car headlights emerging from a blind bend, though. It took a short while to compensate.

"I think I'm being followed by a slow car," said Lauren. "I'm going to look behind me."

Lauren turned. I held my breath. It was a large van. I

couldn't make out the driver's face. The van's headlights drowned out the rest of the image. Then the headlights flashed twice. The van accelerated, braking hard as it pulled alongside Lauren.

The passenger side window slowly opened. The driver turned his face towards the camera. He was wearing a mask and dark glasses.

"Diana Prince?" he said in a slight West Country accent. "Hi, I'm GyGaX76. Cwarrior14B told me to fetch you. The forecast says rain. There's no point you getting wet. Put your bike in the back. It's open."

Chapter Fifty-Seven

He sounded harmless and friendly, but he could be the killer. Or the killer could be in the back, waiting for the side door to open. The police were seven miles away. This wasn't supposed to happen!

Lauren got off her bike and let the camera take in the entire length of the van. It looked like the van the killer had been driving in Brixham. It was white – or a light grey – and to my untrained eye it looked like a Ford Transit.

I wanted to scream 'Don't get in!' at the laptop, but she had to get in. This was her job. To go undercover. To gather evidence. All we had at the moment was a soft-spoken man in a scary mask.

Lauren slid the side door open and loaded the bike, taking a little longer than perhaps necessary, slowly panning the camera over the contents in the back. I couldn't make out too much, most of it was covered in white sheets, but I thought I saw part of a number plate poking out from beneath.

Lauren climbed into the front passenger seat. I could see the driver better now. He was wearing sunglasses, a full facial mask, gloves, a woollen hat, a black turtle neck sweater and black chinos. There wasn't an inch of skin visible.

He handed an identical mask to Lauren. "Here. Take it. You'll need it. They have facial recognition cameras everywhere. You'll need these sunglasses as well. They'll block the iris recognition software. Go on, I'll put your glasses in the centre console. Don't worry, you'll get them back once we reach Friary View."

Lauren reluctantly complied. The audio kept transmitting as clear as before, but the image was now the underside of the car roof, vibrating slightly as the van sped off.

Seven miles to go. Seven miles with only the audio to tell

us what was happening.

"How many of us are going on tonight's mission," asked Lauren using a slight Liverpudlian accent.

"Just the three of us," said the driver. "Me, you and the boss."

"Cwarrior14B is the boss, is he?"

"Yeah, this was his idea. He's good at ideas. Me, not so good. But I'm a quick learner. I'll show you in a minute. We've been practising night driving. We can show you how to do it if you want."

"Isn't this night driving?" asked Lauren, sounding as confused as I was.

"*No*. Proper night driving. No lights. Just night vision goggles. We use it when we're on missions. No one can see us, and we can drive real fast."

I wasn't sure what to make of GyGaX76. He sounded a lot like his onscreen persona – helpful and friendly – but he was coming across as almost childlike at times. His voice didn't sound young, but he was wearing so much disguise I had no idea how old he was. He could be a teenager. He could be the killer playing mind games.

"This should do," said the driver, a few minutes later. "It's always quiet here. I can't see any lights ahead. Are you ready for some night driving?"

"Definitely," said Lauren.

The car stopped. The onscreen image darkened as, presumably, the car's lights were switched off. Then the car lurched forward.

"The only danger with night driving," said GyGaX76. "Is if you suddenly meet an oncoming car with its headlights on full beam. You've got to anticipate. Scan ahead all the time looking for the slightest hint of a light flickering through the hedgerows."

I wasn't sure how fast the van was travelling but the image of the car roof was vibrating and jumping.

"How you doing?" asked GyGaX76.

"Fine," said Lauren. She didn't sound fine.

"Another thing to learn is never drive directly from A to B. Always go the long way round. Always check to see if you're being followed, and vary your route from day to day. Do you know why there's so many more potholes in the roads today than there used to be?"

"The government elite?" said Lauren.

"Exactly. All the money that used to go on road repairs now go on facial recognition cameras. Every road sign has one."

The driver went from potholes to traffic calming measures, speed cameras and smart motorways. All of them were ploys to install surveillance devices.

"That's why the government are dead against people working from home now," he continued. "They can't monitor you if you stay at home. They want you on the road so they can see where you go, who you meet and when."

The journey ended abruptly a little while later with a sudden screech of brakes.

"We're here," said GyGaX76. "Keep your mask and sunglasses on until we're inside the house. I'll bring your glasses. Did you have a bag?"

"Yes, it's on the back of the bike."

"Okay, grab the bag and follow me. Keep your head down and vary your gait. There could be a surveillance drone overhead."

Once inside the house, GyGaX76 handed Lauren's glasses back to her. They were in a large open plan lounge kitchen. Lauren slowly panned around the room. It was a huge, rectangular room with windows to the front and back of the house. The lounge took one half, the kitchen the other. The latter dominated by a floor to ceiling kitchen island. Every curtain was drawn.

"I'll take your bag," said GyGaX76, holding out a hand. "I'll put it on the hall table."

Lauren handed over her bag. GyGaX76 took it. He still hadn't taken his mask off. He walked over to the kitchen island and sat down on one of the bar stools.

"You're not taking your mask off?" asked Lauren.

"Not yet. The boss says we should get used to wearing our masks as often as we can. Make it second nature. You never know when someone's watching you. See that coffee machine over there? It could be one of those smart ones transmitting all our biometrics to GCHQ."

"Should we disable it?" Lauren asked.

"Do you know *how* to disable it? I don't. 'Off' switches stopped being 'off' switches years go. They're all 'stand by' and 'sleep mode' now. Some of them you can't even unplug. They suck up electricity using Wi-Fi."

"So," said Lauren, pulling out the end bar stool. "Where's the boss? Is he upstairs?"

"He might be. I thought he would be down here to greet you."

"Should we check?"

"No, best not to. He doesn't like being disturbed. He's a … he's a private person."

I couldn't see Lauren's reaction, but if I'd been there, all my alarm bells would have been ringing.

"So," said Lauren. "What's the plan for tonight. Have you got the addresses of the two possible substations?"

"No. The boss has them. He's going to brief us when he gets here."

"You think he might not be here? I didn't see another car outside."

"You wouldn't. It would be in the garage. I'm sure he won't be long. He could be checking the two addresses again. He's very thorough."

My gut told me that GyGaX76 was the killer, stringing Lauren along, but I wasn't sure. He could be an innocent acolyte. He could even be tonight's victim.

"When was the last time you saw him?" Lauren asked. "You said he sent you to fetch me. Did he do that from here?"

"Yes, he did. He's probably upstairs doing last minute checks on the EMP device."

"The Russian EMP device?" asked Lauren. "In a dollhouse?"

"That's the one. The boss left the bedroom door open yesterday and I saw it from the corridor. Didn't go in though. The boss doesn't allow anyone in his room."

"But there's no rule about the corridor, is there?" said Lauren. "We could nudge the door open and have another look from there. I'd love to see one of those Russian EMP devices."

"No, best not to. We'll see it soon when he brings it down. Sorry, where are my manners? Do you want a coffee? You must be parched after the train journey."

"No, thanks. After what you told me, I don't think I trust that coffee machine. I prefer to keep my biometrics secret."

He laughed. An odd, nervous laugh. "A drink then? We've got everything here. Orange juice, grapefruit, beer, wine, brandy. It's one of our traditions to toast a new recruit."

I waited for Lauren to say 'no.' It was top of our list of things to avoid at all costs. *Never* accept a drink.

"Okay," said Lauren. "Do you mind if I have tap water? I'm on a course of antibiotics and have to be careful what I drink."

"No, no, no!" I shouted at the laptop. "What are you playing at? Just because it comes out of a tap doesn't mean he can't put something in it. He could doctor the glass."

GyGaX76 took a glass out of an overhead cupboard and took it to the sink. He had his back to Lauren. I couldn't see what he was doing. I could see him reach for the tap, and I heard the running water, but I couldn't see what his other hand was doing.

What the hell was Lauren playing at? Why didn't she just refuse?

Lauren's gaze dropped. She stopped watching GyGaX76 and looked at her left wrist. She slipped a couple of fingers under her left sleeve and pulled down a bracelet. A date rape bracelet. She was going to test the drink.

Could she do that unobserved? Wouldn't he be watching her like a hawk?

GyGaX76 came back from the sink and handed Lauren the

glass of water. He then turned his back on her as he walked to the fridge. What was *he* playing at? She could have poured the water into the nearest houseplant! Not that I'd seen a houseplant.

Lauren used the opportunity to dip a finger into the water and dab a droplet onto the bracelet's test circle.

I remembered Lauren telling me that if it turned blue in two minutes it was spiked.

I checked my watch.

GyGaX76 returned from the fridge with a bottle of beer and a straw. He wasn't even going to take his mask off to drink. There looked to be a small hole over the mouth area of the mask, just large enough to take a straw.

"Cheers," he said, raising his bottle to Lauren.

"Cheers," said Lauren, raising her glass.

"Don't drink," I said at the screen. "There's another minute and a half to go! Stall somehow."

I couldn't see what happened next. Lauren's head appeared to dip and I could make out a partial hand and glass appear in the bottom right of the screen, but it was out of focus and almost out of shot. She might have drunk from the glass. She might not have.

I couldn't see if GyGaX76 was watching her either. His head was facing the camera, but his eyes were obscured by the sunglasses.

"It's great to be fighting back at last, isn't it?" said GyGaX76. "We're going to make a real difference. And when the truth comes out – which it will – the people will rise up and join us. They will. I *know* they will. You can't trust elections any more. They're all rigged anyway. The only way to gain power is to seize it. That's what the boss says."

Lauren didn't say a word, but the screen nodded. I suspected she had a mouthful of water and was waiting for an opportunity to spit it out.

Two minutes passed. She checked her bracelet. It hadn't turned blue.

I was surprised. Did that mean the drink was safe? Was

GyGaX76 an innocent? Was the killer this elusive 'boss' character?

~

I had no idea what Lauren was doing with the water. I didn't see her spit any out, but she was talking again, asking if the boss lived in the house. He didn't live anywhere according to GyGaX76. He moved from house to house 'liberating' them from the idle rich.

Meanwhile, Lauren had left her bar stool for a slow tour of the kitchen.

"So, none of this is his?" she asked.

"No, he doesn't believe in possessions."

I hoped Lauren was using this opportunity to get rid of her drink. She had her back to GyGaX76, but she kept dipping her head and raising the glass to her mouth. If she *was* getting rid of the drink, I had no idea how she was doing it.

And I couldn't see the glass well enough to gauge the level of the water.

"How long have you known the boss?" she asked.

"Months. He's one of the *real* warriors. Lots of people talk about fighting back. Very few do anything about it."

"Was all that online or have you been on real-life missions with him?"

"I haven't been on any live missions with him yet, but we've been training together for the last two days."

Lauren continued her slow stroll around the kitchen, picking up ornaments and admiring the decor. All the time keeping her back to GyGaX76.

"What time's the mission tonight?" She asked.

"He hasn't said, but I *do* know that he likes to wait until everyone's asleep. Two o'clock to four o'clock are the golden hours, he says. REM sleep is at its deepest. People are at their most vulnerable."

There was a sudden noise from the lounge. A loud hissing sound. Lauren spun round.

"What's that?" she asked.

"I don't know," said GyGaX76.

They both hurried over to look.

A television had come on in the far corner of the lounge. I couldn't see the picture at first as the angle of the screen was too acute. All I could see was a bright aura of light.

But then it became clear.

"Is that a QR code?" asked Lauren.

That's what it looked like to me. A large QR code that took up most of the television screen.

"It must be a test," said GyGaX76. "The boss is a big believer in changing things at the last minute. He says we've got to be quick on our feet. No plan survives first contact with the enemy. We've got to adapt, and get used to surprises. That's what this'll be. I'm sure of it."

"We better scan it then," said Lauren, moving closer to the TV and holding her position so the image remained stable. "I definitely think we should scan it now."

I pointed my mobile phone at the QR code on the screen, wondering where it was going to take me, hoping it wasn't to some black hole on the dark web.

A picture appeared. A bird's eye view of a room. *The* room. The room Lauren was in. It was a live camera feed with audio.

Lauren was unrecognisable. For a second I wondered if it was someone else. That this wasn't a live feed but a recording made earlier with another woman. But everything was in sync. The killer's feed, Lauren's feed. They were the same, just shot from different angles.

GyGaX76 showed Lauren the image on his phone.

"The camera must be over there," he said. "In the kitchen ceiling above that wall light."

They checked. Lauren climbed onto a chair and examined the wall light. In doing so her face filled the screen. I would never have recognised her. Her blonde hair was now dark brown and long with a fringe. And her face was fatter. Was she wearing prosthetics? Her nose was different too.

The camera on the wall light was minute. A tiny black dot at the base of the light fitting. Lauren put her finger over it.

The camera feed went dark.

"That's it," said GyGaX76.

Lauren jumped down. "What now?" she said. "Was that the test? Scanning the QR code and finding the camera?"

"I don't know," said GyGaX76. "The boss told me the art of a good test is for no one to even know they were being tested."

Lauren's body looked different too. She looked heavier. Her friend had done an amazing job. I expected her face to be different, but I hadn't expected a total transformation.

"Maybe he wants us to find him?" said Lauren. "Let's search the house."

"No!" said GyGaX76. "The test is in this room."

"How do you know?" asked Lauren.

"I just do."

I was baffled. What was the killer playing at? The only thing that made the slightest sense was that he was testing how compliant Lauren was. A gullible, compliant victim would be easier to control. He might be assessing Lauren's suitability as a victim.

In which case, Lauren should dial back the questions. I could see she was itching to search the house.

But then again, if she ignored GyGaX76 and ran upstairs she might find a dollhouse and a waterboard. Would that be enough to secure a conviction?

Not if the killer was parked a few miles away in his other van watching the camera feed. GyGaX76 could be his designated fall guy if the evening went pear-shaped.

I was still going around in circles when the screen on my laptop went blank.

Chapter Fifty-Eight

I stared at the screen, unsure what had happened. I refreshed the screen. Nothing.

The feed from the wall light continued unaffected. I turned the volume up. Lauren and GyGaX76 were still talking.

"Can't you phone him?" asked Lauren.

"He won't have it switched on."

"But you do know his number?"

"You ask a lot of questions."

"That's because I'm committed. I want to pass this test."

I tried the laptop again. Still nothing. The battery was at ninety percent so it wasn't that.

I decided to check with the officers outside. Natalia said they had the feed from Lauren's glasses. I grabbed the laptop and ran outside. It was Bob and Kofi. They had the same problem.

"Lauren's feed dropped out for everyone," said Bob. "There's a technician working on it, but it looks like the fault is at her end. It might be a fault in the glasses. It might be someone jamming the signal."

"You can still get a good feed from that QR code," said Kofi. "Have you tried it?"

"Yes, I've got it on my phone."

"She's doing well," said Bob. "Can't work out the GuyGax bloke. Kofi thinks he's the killer. I'm not so sure. I think the killer's upstairs waiting to make an entrance."

I went back inside. I thought Bob and Kofi were too complacent. The only feed we had came from the killer. He could turn it off whenever he wanted. He could splice in another camera, pause it, replay it. We could end up not knowing if the feed we were receiving was live or twenty minutes behind.

I kept the laptop switched on just in case. And went back to watching the feed on my phone.

Lauren and GyGaX76 were still talking. At times it sounded like sparring. I agreed with Bob, I couldn't work out GyGaX76 either. Some of the things he said convinced me he was the killer. Then he'd pass up an opportunity that I thought the killer would have leapt upon.

As for Lauren, I wasn't sure how long she could keep her natural instincts in check. It wasn't that I doubted her acting ability. I just doubted her decision making at times. If she thought she could wrap everything up with a risky manoeuvre, she'd be tempted to take it.

What I wasn't expecting was a loud thud. I couldn't work out at first where it came from, but the way both Lauren and GyGaX76 were looking up at the ceiling made me think it came from the room above. It sounded like something heavy had hit the floor.

"There's someone up there," said Lauren, moving towards the door to the hall.

"No!" said GyGaX76. "Stop. We're not allowed to leave the room."

Lauren stopped and turned.

"What are you talking about?"

"We have to stay. It's part of the test."

Lauren looked confused. And then a door started rattling. It sounded like someone was desperately trying to pull open a locked door.

GyGaX76 put his hands over his ears. "Don't react," he said. He sounded terrified. "It won't last long. If we stay where we are no one will get hurt."

Then came the screaming. A young girl.

"Help!" she screamed. "He's going to kill me. Help me, please."

Sophie's words. The killer's taped impersonation of Sophie. I was immediately transported to another time, another place. Lying in bed, reading a book. The last seconds of peace about to be blown apart by that scream, those words. They'd haunted me for months. And here they were again.

I was shaking. Those familiar feelings of dread and despair rising up around me. Bleak and black and all-pervading.

But I was stronger now. The screams weren't real. The accusations weren't real. I was a *good* man.

I took several deep breaths, lowering my pounding heart rate with each breath. Concentrate, Mathew. Concentrate!

Lauren hadn't moved. She would have recognised the words the girl had shouted. She'd know it wasn't real.

"Let's wait here then," she said. GyGaX76 still had his hands over his ears.

But not for long. It was like someone had thrown a switch. One second he looked distraught, the next he was smiling, and … I couldn't explain it. He just *looked* different.

"Congratulations, Diana," he said. "You passed the test. Obedience is crucial to the smooth running of an operation. There will be times when you'll be given an order that makes no sense at all. Like staying in this room when there's a girl screaming upstairs. In the field there's no time to stop and explain orders. Obedience is essential."

"So you knew this was going to happen?"

"He did it to me yesterday."

"Are there more tests?"

"Two more. The first is observation. How observant are you, Diana?"

"Reasonably, I think."

"You see, I've been observing you and I notice you're wearing one of those drug testing bracelets."

That made me sit up.

"Force of habit," said Lauren, unfazed. "A single girl has to be careful."

"Oh, I agree, but you do know there's a problem with them?"

"Is there?"

"Yes, they work brilliantly on GHB and that family of drugs, but they can't detect Rohypnol."

Shit! Rohypnol was another date rape drug. The killer had used GHB before. Had he changed his MO? Lauren had recommended date rape bracelets on TV. Of course the killer would have looked for a way of circumventing the problem.

Which begged two questions: 'Had GyGaX76 drugged Lauren's water?' and 'How much had Lauren drunk?'

Lauren still looked unfazed. I tried to locate her glass on the feed. She'd had it with her when the TV came on. Had she left it in the kitchen or taken it with her? She certainly didn't have a glass in her hand when she climbed on the chair to find the camera.

There was a glass on the end of the kitchen island. I zoomed in on the area, trying to make the image as large and as crisp as I could.

The glass looked empty.

"The final test is more a lesson in tradecraft," said GyGaX76. "You use the handle DianaPrince1941. Do you use that anywhere else?"

"No."

"What about Diana? That's not your real name I hope?"

"Actually it is."

"Change it. Delete all your DianaPrince1941 posts and make sure you use a new one for all your subsequent posts."

"Okay." Lauren appeared to sway slightly before quickly regaining her balance.

Shit! Was it the Rohypnol?

"You can choose a real name," said GyGaX76. "But not your own. And no members of your family or their maiden names."

"Got it," said Lauren.

"If you want any suggestions," said GyGaX76. "You could call yourself 'Lauren.'"

Chapter Fifty-Nine

My first instinct was to call Natalia. Lauren had to be pulled out now! He knew her name. He'd as good as said he'd drugged her.

But how could he have known her name? There was no way in hell that he could have recognised her. It had to be a freak coincidence. He was obsessed with Lauren. Her name would be on the tip of his tongue.

Wouldn't it?

I clung to the possibility. More hope than reason. Natalia would be watching this. She'd know what to do. She'd know when to send her team in. She wouldn't risk Lauren unnecessarily.

Would she?

Lauren had sat down in one of the lounge armchairs. She didn't look that steady on her feet.

"Another piece of tradecraft advice," said GyGaX76. "Is to thoroughly research surveillance equipment, and always assume there's a bug you didn't find."

GyGaX76 was a completely different person to the excited acolyte who'd picked Lauren up on the outskirts of Warminster. He was more measured, assured. It felt like he was savouring every word.

"Take this room for example," he said. "If I were a government agent, I wouldn't just install a camera. I'd install a microphone as well. I'd place it where it would be most likely to pick up the kind of conversations I was interested in. Maybe the kitchen island. Maybe here in front of the television. And I wouldn't only install one microphone. I'd install two. Do you know why?"

"No," said Lauren. She really didn't look well.

"Insurance. So many people have bug detectors these

days. We have one. But bug detectors only detect active bugs. If a bug isn't transmitting on one of the frequencies you're scanning for, it's undetectable. So I'd install one active bug to give me twenty-four-hour surveillance, and one passive bug that recorded all day but only transmitted twice a day in short, compressed bursts. There'd be a twelve-hour delay in receiving those recordings, but unless someone was running a bug detector during those few seconds when the bug was actually transmitting, no one would ever find it."

He turned to look directly at the camera.

"You might even have one in your plug socket by the television, Mathew."

I stared at the screen open-mouthed. And then at the plug socket. No one had looked there. They'd checked the alarm buttons, and everywhere we thought the killer had gone, but no one knew he'd been anywhere near the plug sockets.

He'd been listening to us all that time. Lauren's plan, the 6G message boards, everything we'd talked about was compromised.

Natalia had to go in. Now! The operation was blown. Lauren was in danger.

"Are you feeling okay, Lauren?" said the killer. "You look tired."

"It's just a headache. I'll be fine in a minute."

"I'm sure you will. So, you see, I knew all about your plan to infiltrate my band of followers. You don't think I chose you on merit, do you? You're good, but you're not that good. I saw your fishing expedition, trying to get noticed. A bit too eager, I thought. But exactly what I wanted. You will be the perfect hors d'oeuvre to the main course."

He turned his head to look directly into the camera again.

"This is all for you, Mathew. Your little girlfriend being waterboarded for your delectation."

Where were the police? Natalia must have sent them in by now! She'd said they were only minutes away. What was taking them so long?

"What *is* your obsession with Mathew?" asked Lauren.

"It is an obsession, isn't it?" said the killer. "From the beginning it's always been about Mathew. He is so much fun to play with. So uptight, the way he bottles everything up. You can see him being eaten alive from the inside out. Marvellous entertainment. I can watch him for hours. For such a tightly-wound man he has such an expressive face, don't you think? Everyone else were just pawns or useful idiots. Plastic puppets, every one of them."

"Is that why you dressed them as figurines?"

"I knew you'd understand. Deep down, you're very like me."

"I'm nothing like you!" She said, wincing in pain from the effort.

"If you say so. I'm doing the world a favour really – cleansing the gene pool. Did you see all the crap they believe? Some people really do deserve all they get."

"Did Sophie deserve..." Lauren was slurring her words. "Did she deserve what she got?"

"Ah, yes. Poor Sophie. I didn't set out to kill her, you know? She was just an extra in my little game with Mathew and her father. When I saw her fall in the river, I ran over to save her. Yes, me, the Good Samaritan. She was hanging onto some reeds. I held my hand out and ... stopped ... and watched instead. I was surprised at how thrilling it was. Watching her struggling, and shouting, and crying."

He was enjoying himself, smiling at the memory.

"She almost climbed out once, but I nudged her back in. Technically, I don't think it can be called murder. It was more 'letting nature take its course.' Who'd ever have thought drowning could be so entertaining?"

"Why wait ... wait so long ... to kill again?"

"As I said, technically I hadn't killed Sophie. Sophie was an unexpected bonus in my examination of Mathew."

"Examination?"

"I think that's the best word for it. He was my project. My subject that I was studying. A bit like dissecting someone while they're still alive. It was a fascinating project, and he was superb. I have months of footage. I first encountered Mathew when he was being harassed by a gang of young kids. They were being their usual obnoxious selves, climbing all over his car, trying to rip his windscreen wipers and side mirrors off. And Mathew comes out of his house and just stands there, watching. He doesn't say a word. He doesn't do anything. He just stands there by his front porch, disapproving. He must have stood there for two minutes. And then a neighbour comes out and chases them off, and Mathew turns on his heels and walks back inside his home as though nothing had happened."

I remembered the incident. I had gone outside to tell them to stop, but I didn't know what to say. You hear so many stories of families having their lives made unbearable by gangs of kids who wouldn't leave them alone. I didn't want to make things worse. I was hoping my presence alone would convince them to leave.

"That's when I knew he'd make the perfect subject," said the killer. "I'd fill his home with cameras and see if I could break him. Not that I wanted him to break. I wanted to push him to the point of breaking, and then pull back. It's far more fun."

I listened, unsure if this was a conversation I wanted to hear, but knowing I had to. I'd often asked myself 'why me?'

"Several times I thought he was going to kill himself," the killer continued. "I was ready to intervene. I only lived around the corner from him in Rayford. I'd have cut him down, or phoned for an ambulance. Death should be savoured, never rushed."

Lauren's head dropped forward. It sprang back up again, but it was another sign that the drug was taking hold.

Where were the police? What more did they need? He'd confessed on tape to the murders. Even Sophie's. Lauren would be next. Another ten minutes and he'd be able to carry her upstairs to the bathroom!

I wasn't waiting any longer. I ran outside. Bob and Kofi would know what's going on.

They didn't.

"It's the wrong house," said Kofi. "The officers broke into Friary View. There's no one there."

Chapter Sixty

"What? How? Where did they go?" I couldn't believe it. We'd watched them every step of the journey.

"DI Lipinski thinks this was the plan from the start," said Bob. "All that business with the sunglasses, the night driving, the taking the long way round to avoid detection. It was meant to make sure that Lauren never got a good look at where they were going."

And the camera spent the entire journey pointing at the underside of the van roof.

"Didn't she have a tracker?" I asked.

"It stopped transmitting when she got in the van," said Bob. "We think the van had a scrambler fitted. The same goes for the house."

"What about her phone? Can't you get a fix on that?"

"No. Wherever they are there's a scrambler blocking all radio signals."

"So how's the killer's camera feed getting out?"

"Our expert reckons the camera must be wired directly to the internet hub," said Kofi. "If it was connected wirelessly the scrambler would block the signal."

He really had this all thought out. I thought he was being remarkably calm chatting to Lauren about how he'd known what we were planning when, if that had been true, he'd have known the police were less than a mile away waiting to pounce.

Now it made sense. He'd been calm because he was miles away in a different house.

With Lauren, drugged and vulnerable.

Someone had to *do* something!

I ran back into the house. I had the dog tracker. I grabbed it. I grabbed my phone, and ran back outside.

"I've got a dog tracker," I said. "Lauren's got the transmitter. I don't know if it'll work, but it's got to be worth a try. It's got a nine-mile range. They can't be far. It's not picking up a signal now, but If we drive north east and circle around we might pick something up."

"It'll be blocked like the camera on the glasses."

"It might not. If there's the slightest chance I'm going to take it. What else can we do?"

"Let the police deal with it. We've called in a helicopter."

"No. I'm not waiting any longer. Please come with me. There's no point you guarding an empty house."

"We can't leave our post," said Bob. "Not after last time. We were told whatever happens, we weren't to be drawn away."

"This is different!"

"DI Lipinski made it clear. 'Stay put,' she said. 'The killer's devious and obsessed with this house.'"

"The killer's miles away!"

"There could be two of them. He's used accomplices before."

"I'm going," I said. "You can either follow or stay here. I've got my phone on. You can track me if needed."

"Wait," said Kofi, unclipping his police radio. "Take this. Keep in contact."

I put my phone, dog tracker and Kofi's radio on the front passenger seat of my car and sped off into the night. I had no expectations, only hope. Lauren was resourceful. If there was a way of signalling her location to us, she'd find it.

The killer was still talking about me. Boasting how he'd manipulated my neighbours by suggesting plans of action, whipping them up, planting stories he'd heard from 'friends' in the police. Everything calculated to make sure I had no safe place where I could shut the world out and heal.

He'd been behind everything. The excrement pushed through my letterbox, the hate sprayed over my car and windows, the gangs of drunken teenagers screaming at me in the early hours.

And then he was talking about how he'd cool things down if it looked like I might get sectioned or slit my wrists. How he'd graciously give me a few days respite before he started again.

I listened, and I seethed. A part of me, a distant part, wanted to pull over, switch everything off, and curl up into a tight, protective ball. But I *wasn't* that man any more. I would *never* be that man again. I gripped the steering wheel tighter, took a deep breath, and pressed on.

Eventually the killer stopped talking about me. "Lauren?" he said. I glanced over at the screen. Lauren had hardly spoken for over a minute. Her head was slumped forward.

"Wake up, Lauren," said the killer, putting on a singsong voice. "I have your clothes laid out on the bed upstairs. Shall I help you put them on?"

Lauren didn't move. She didn't answer.

"Come on, Lauren. I know you want my special room service."

I felt like vomiting, but pushed the car faster instead. The sat nav showed a spidery labyrinth of winding roads up ahead, none of which consistently pointed north east. I chose the straightest. At least I could put my foot down now and then.

Suddenly, the dog tracker lit up.

I nearly swerved into a hedge.

I braked hard just in time. The arrow on the dog tracker was pointing to the right. Eight-point-seven kilometres. I checked the sat nav. The road I was on bent round to the right. I set off, accelerating hard, my mind awash with questions. Should I call Natalia? But what could I tell her? Lauren was 8.7km to the right of me, but I had no idea where I was.

I had to find a signpost.

I drove as fast as I could, my eyes darting from road, to dog tracker, to phone. And all the while the killer droned on and on about what he was going to do to Lauren.

A signpost appeared up ahead. I stopped the car and

switched on the police radio. I wasn't sure I had it on transmit, but I was ready to press every button until I found one that worked.

"Hello? Can anyone hear me?"

"Who's this?" said a female voice.

"Natalia? It's Mathew. I think I've found Lauren."

"How have you found Lauren? And what are you doing with a police radio?"

I told her about the dog tracker.

"I'm on the junction of the B32347 and the B12245. I'm pointing down the B12245 and Lauren's 4.7km in front of me."

I started driving again. The road was wider and straighter. I put my foot down.

"Looks like it's near Clinton Deverill," said Natalia. "We're ten minutes out and on our way. If you get there first, drive slowly past, and confirm the presence of the van. Do *not* stop. Do *not* engage."

An oncoming car almost blinded me with their headlights on full beam. I slowed down, cursing and shouting at them. And then I was flying forwards again.

Lauren was still not moving. The killer was on his feet, walking towards her, looming over her, bending down. He was gong to carry her upstairs.

No, no, no, no, no!

And then everything changed. Lauren grabbed him, pulled him down hard, and rolled. Suddenly it was the killer on the floor with Lauren on top of him, swinging wildly with her fists, but connecting. He took most of the punches on his arms, but some were getting through.

He grabbed her arms, pulled her close, the two of them wrestling, rolling across the floor. Lauren was thrown off, her glasses flying through the air.

The killer ran to the kitchen island – Lauren in pursuit – a kicking, flailing, gouging ball of energy. He fought her off – momentarily – reaching up to open one of the kitchen cabinets. He got a hand inside, but Lauren was on him again, smacking his head hard into the cabinet, grabbing his mask and ripping it from his face, doing the same with his glasses and woollen hat.

He tried to break free, but Lauren was pressed tight against him, her right hand digging into his hair, yanking his head back, and swinging his face round to point directly at the camera. She held him there, unmasked and visible to everyone receiving the camera feed.

"Smile, you fucker!" she screamed.

The killer was incensed. He threw his head back trying to make contact with Lauren's face. He flailed and heaved, leaning back against Lauren and using his legs to push against the kitchen island. Lauren toppled over backwards. The killer was first to his feet, running to the open cabinet. He pulled something out, something small and white. He pointed it at the ceiling.

Lauren was just getting to her feet when the gun went off.

I looked at the dog tracker. Five hundred metres to go. I was almost there. He wouldn't shoot Lauren. Not this killer. Death had to be savoured, not rushed. That's what he'd said.

"Get up!" shouted the killer, the gun now pointed at Lauren. "This may look like a toy, but it isn't. It's a six-shot, state-of-the-art miracle of 3D printing. The choice is yours – do you want to be drugged and waterboarded, or slowly bleed out as I shoot you in a succession of non-critical places."

"Let me think," said Lauren. "Am I allowed to phone a friend?"

~

Fifty metres to go. I slowed down. It had to be the house coming up on the right. I couldn't actually see the house, but I could see a gap in a tall, well-maintained hedge.

Please, let the signal be real and not another trick planted by the killer.

Nearly there. Drive slowly, Natalia had said. Look for the van. I drove slowly, peering at the house and grounds. There was a plaque by the open gate. The Old Rectory, it said. The house itself was set well back from the road. There was a light coming from two downstairs windows. I glanced at the camera feed on the passenger seat. The lounge had two windows.

And there was the van. On the lawn about twenty yards from the house. Was it the same van? It looked close enough to me.

I stopped the car once I'd cleared the entrance and grabbed the police radio.

"I'm outside the house," I said. "There's a van on the lawn that looks like the killer's. There are lights on in the house that correspond with the camera feed. The house is called The Old Rectory."

"Got it," said Natalia. "We're seven minutes out. "Drive to a safe distance where you can keep an eye on the entrance."

"You really are an annoying bitch, Lauren," said the killer. "Haven't you realised yet that no one's coming to help you? Your police friends have raided the wrong house. They have no idea where you are. All your tracking devices have been jammed since you climbed into the van. You have no hope. I can take all the time I want, and the more you annoy me, the longer I'm going to take."

Lauren laughed. "The police know exactly where we are. We had a drone set up to follow me from the station. You were too obsessed with yourself to look up and notice. The grounds are teeming with police snipers waiting for the word."

"I don't believe you."

"Then why is there a red laser dot on your chest?"

He looked down, and in that moment, Lauren put her head down, and charged.

Chapter Sixty-One

She almost got to him, her hands outstretched, reaching for the gun. Two shots rang out. Lauren was thrown backwards by the force of the impact. She staggered, looking surprised, clutching her chest, then falling, blood seeping through her top. She'd been shot twice in the chest.

I threw the car into reverse, shooting backwards, braking hard the moment I'd cleared the entrance, and then flying forwards, turning into the drive, racing towards the house.

I switched the car's headlights to full beam. I hit the car horn again and again. If Lauren was still alive, I had to show her she wasn't alone. Help was on its way!

I hit the brakes, the car skidding to a halt just short of the lounge windows. I checked the camera feed. The killer was motionless, looking towards the lounge windows. Lauren wasn't moving either, her lifeless eyes staring into the camera.

Then the killer was moving fast, running towards the lounge door. The lounge lights went out. The camera feed died. The whole house fell into darkness.

I jumped out of the car. The killer could come flying out the front door any second. I sprinted to the side of the house. The kitchen had French windows. I'd seen them when Lauren was investigating the room. If I could get into the kitchen, I could check on Lauren.

I reached the back of the house, found the French windows. They were locked. I rattled the doors. I kicked at them. They wouldn't give. I couldn't see anything heavy to throw at them. Then I heard a noise from the side of the house. Someone running. It had to be the killer.

I set off in the opposite direction. I'd run around the house, dive in the car, and reverse the hell out of there. I could slew my car across the entrance to the property and throw away the keys. He wouldn't be able to get out. He'd have to try to escape on foot.

I rounded the far corner of the house. I couldn't see anyone. My car was less than ten yards away. I went for it, running round to the driver's side, jumping in, pressing the start button.

That's when the front passenger door opened and the killer climbed in.

He was pointing that white plastic gun at me. "Hello, Mathew," he said. "What a wonderful surprise."

I didn't move an inch. I just sat there. I hadn't seen him at all. He must have been hiding in the front porch.

"Empty your pockets," said the killer. "All of them. Throw everything onto the lawn. Including your personal alarm."

I did as I was told. The killer threw my phone, the dog tracker and the police radio out of his window.

"Now drive. Head out the gate and turn left."

I buckled myself in, and drove off.

"How did you find the house?" he asked. "I didn't see anyone following. And you haven't brought the police with you. Are you acting alone?"

I kept quiet. *Don't engage. Don't give information. Let him worry about how you found him.*

"Still the same old Mathew. Bottle it up. Keep your head down and hope it all goes away. You never learn, do you?"

I drove slowly and carefully. I didn't want to get too far away from the house. The police would be there soon. They'd search for me.

"Did you see me kill your girlfriend, Mathew? I bet you did. Feisty little thing, wasn't she?"

Don't engage. Think. What would Lauren have done in a situation like this?

"No one's going to save you, Mathew. The police hate you. Even *you* hate yourself. And as for Lauren. She hated you too. You were just too stupid and needy to notice. What could a girl like that see in you? A tongue-tied no-talent coward. She used you from the get go."

I let the words wash over me. I'd seen so many similar scenes to this in films. The gunman hijacking an innocent's car, climbing into the front passenger seat, pointing a gun at the driver, and ordering him to drive. Everyone assumes the gunman has all the cards. No one considers the driver, sitting quietly at the controls of a two-ton killing machine.

Until he puts his foot down on the accelerator. Then there's only one card. *Who wants to live the most?*

I started to accelerate, slowly at first, nudging the car faster, accelerating again as we came out of a bend.

"Slow down," said the killer.

"Or what?" I said, all emotion drained away. "You're going to shoot the driver doing eighty on a bendy, country road? Which tree do you want me to hit? I don't care. What have I got to live for? You won. No one cares if I live or die, least of all me. I'm the most hated man in Swindon. And you killed my only friend."

"Slow down!"

I nudged the car faster.

"You should know me better by now," I said. "All those hours you've watched me. How fast do you think I can drive before I lose control?"

"You're too scared to crash a car."

"You think?" I turned slowly to look at him with empty eyes. Smiled an empty smile.

Then, still looking at him, I took my hands off the wheel.

"Look, no hands!"

The killer grabbed for the wheel. I grabbed it too. We tussled, the car weaving left and right.

He let go. I laughed. And locked all the car doors. *This ends tonight. There will be no more victims of the dollhouse killer.*

"What are you doing?" There was real panic in his voice.

There was no panic in mine. No panic, no emotion, nothing.

"I'm keeping you inside," I said. "If I'm dying, I'm taking you with me."

I nudged the car faster one time too many.

Chapter Sixty-Two

I must have turned the wheel too sharply. Suddenly we were spinning. Up. Down. Rolling over and over. Metal squealing and banging. Pain shooting. Consciousness fading...

I woke up. No inkling of how much time had passed. Something was hissing, and my vision was ... disturbing. I could see flashing lights. Not flashing emergency vehicle lights, but flashing pinpricks of light. Everywhere. And was I upside down?

I tried to move but I was stuck fast. Or paralysed. And I had a headache like nothing I'd ever experienced before.

I slowly checked my body. My legs were pinned. One arm too, but my left arm was free and uninjured. I didn't think anything was broken, but I felt like my entire body had been squeezed tight by a giant hand.

As for my headache, I wasn't sure if the pain was made worse by me being upside down with all the blood rushing to my head.

I tried to turn my head left to check the passenger side, but the pain was too intense. The killer must have fared worse than me. I had a seat belt on. He didn't.

I could feel a breeze on my face. All the windows had been closed. The windscreen must have gone. He must have gone with it. I couldn't see too well. The car's lights had packed in, and my vision was littered with my own personal meteor storm.

Was that a body? Lying on the road, five yards in font of the car? It looked like a body. The killer thrown free to die in the road.

Except, this body was moving. He wasn't dead.

Shit! He was moving and I was immobilised, hanging upside down in an overturned car.

He had to be too badly injured to get up. Surely? He had to.

What if he still had his gun?

I tried to free my right arm, my legs - straining, pulling, pushing - nothing worked. I was held in a vice. All I could do was watch as the killer raised himself to a sitting position. One arm hung limp, but his right arm was working fine. He was trying to get up!

How far away were the police? Would they even bother to look for me? They had a major crime scene to secure. A murder. They wouldn't automatically think that the killer had made his getaway in my car. They'd be checking the grounds first.

I was on my own with an obsessed serial killer who wouldn't die!

I felt for a weapon with my left hand, patting blindly, unable to turn my head. Maybe he dropped his gun in the car? It could be lying here, next to me. I just had to find it!

The killer had got to his knees. He was pushing with his good hand, bringing a foot under his body, then a second foot, now pushing with his legs, staggering, getting to his feet.

And looking around. Back towards the car. Our eyes locked. He smiled. His face streaked in blood. His clothes torn, tattered and bloody.

And, in his right hand, something small and white.

How the hell did he still have his gun!

I pushed against the driver's door. I tried to drag my feet out of the well. Nothing budged.

And then I heard it. In the distance, a car engine. A car driving fast. There was no siren, but it had to be the police, and it was closing fast. The killer could hear it too. He looked up, his smug smile replaced with concern.

Suddenly, I was concerned too. I was in the middle of the road, hanging upside down in an overturned car with no lights. Were we on a bend or on a straight stretch of road? I had no idea. The car was approaching fast. Would they see us? Would they plough into the back of us?

I tried to find the car horn, desperately patting and pressing. And then there was a long squeal of brakes behind me, going on and on. I braced for impact.

The car rocked as a pale van flew past alongside, its tyres still locked. It screeched to a halt ten yards in front of the car, slewed at an angle, half on the road and half on a grass verge.

"Don't get out," I shouted, my voice surprisingly hoarse. "He's got a gun."

The killer had steadied himself. I'd thought he was going to fall, but, of course, he didn't. He raised his gun to point at the driver of the vehicle.

"Get out the van," shouted the killer. "Leave the keys."

He was going to get away. After all we'd been through, he was going to get away.

I heard the driver door open. I couldn't see the driver. I couldn't hear them either. Were they hiding behind the van? Preparing to make a run for the trees?

And why couldn't I see any headlights? The whole time the van had been braking, I hadn't seen a single arc of light.

A shape appeared at the back of the van. They were crouched down. There was something odd about their face. Were they wearing a mask? And something was flickering in their hand, or was it my eyes?

Then they were moving fast, darting out from behind the van, the hand with the flickering light raised high in the air ... and then brought down with force. The killer was still turning to face the threat, when glass exploded at his feet, flames racing up his lower legs, engulfing them.

He dropped his gun. He needed two hands to beat at the flames. The shape ducked down and scuttled back behind the back of the van.

It was a woman. I could see her better now she'd ripped off the night vision goggles. Lauren? It couldn't be, but ... who else would charge an armed murderer, and have a petrol bomb handy?

How could she be alive? I'd seen her shot. I'd seen the blood.

She was moving again, crouched low, and running fast. This time she had a large can in her hand.

The killer didn't see her. He was still frantically trying to beat out the flames. Weird flames. They weren't yellow and flaring. They were blue and burning evenly.

Lauren was on him in an instant, spraying his face, shaking the can, and spraying again. The killer was flailing and screaming, trying to protect his eyes. Lauren swept his legs from under him and shoved him hard to the ground. She scooped up the gun, and pointed it straight at him.

"Lie down on your belly, and put your hands behind your back," she said.

"Or what?" said the killer, breathing hard. "You're going to shoot me?"

"That's an idea. I'm just like you, remember? Shall I start with your non-critical organs or would you prefer I move straight to my special room service."

"You haven't got it in you."

"Are you sure? You've spent the last week trying to break me, and failed every, single time. Me, I had you screaming like a frightened little baby in under a minute. Roll over, snowflake. Assume the position."

Chapter Sixty-Three

I don't remember much after that. I kept dropping in and out of consciousness. I remember a lot of sirens and I think I had to be cut out of the car. I also remember waking up several times convinced that the killer had escaped, but everyone assured me that he was locked away.

I think I even saw an apologetic DCI Terrell at my hospital bed, but that may have been a dream.

As for my injuries, I had severe concussion, cracked ribs, and extensive bruising, but my prognosis was good. My brain scan hadn't been as bad as they'd feared. I'd make a full recovery.

In the meantime, I slept a lot. Lauren came to see me the next day, but she wasn't allowed to stay for long. I was dosed up with painkillers, and suffering long bouts of confusion, so I don't remember too much about what was said. But I do remember that Lauren was looking like Lauren again. She still had dark brown hair, but she'd removed all the hair extensions and prosthetics.

She told me that the killer was safely locked away. That his real name was Michael Garston, and he'd worked in the home security business for twenty years. Until he inherited a large, expensive house in Surrey from his father. He'd then quit his job, sold the house and used the proceeds to finance his new life of doing whatever the hell he wanted.

I'm sure Lauren told me more, but I couldn't remember.

It wasn't until the next day that I started to feel like I had a working brain.

I remember that day very well. It started with a nurse waking me up.

"How are you feeling today, Mathew?" she said.

"Fine," I said.

"I thought you'd be watching the television," she said. "Your friend Lauren's on *Morning Everybody*. She's very good. Shall I switch it on for you?"

"Yes, please," I said.

The nurse switched on the television and helped me with my pillows so I could sit up in bed.

Lauren was talking to one of the female presenters. I'm useless with names. I think she was called Ashley.

"What I find fascinating," said Ashley. "Is the trick you came up with to make it look like you were drinking from the drugged glass."

"It *was* clever, wasn't it?" said Lauren. "Of course, my first thought was to refuse all offers of a drink, but the problem with that is you're putting the ball back into his court. He's not going to give up. He's going to find another way of subduing you. Like tasering you, or pointing a gun at you. Better to solve the problem you know about than wait for the one you don't."

"You really thought it through."

"I had to. My life depended on it. So, first of all I had to make him think I had no suspicions whatsoever. If he thought I was on to him, he'd watch me like a hawk. So, I took a sip from the spiked glass."

"You knowingly took a sip from a drugged glass of water?"

"I had to. It wasn't a large sip. I made it look like a large sip, but I used my hand to hide the water level from him. After that I went for a little walkabout, pretending to drink and keeping my back to him as much as I could. He could see me raising the glass to the area around my mouth, but he couldn't see the tiny funnel I was pouring the drink into."

"We have your homemade drinking device here," said Ashley, holding what looked like a siphon out to the camera for a close-up.

The camera zoomed in on a tiny clear plastic funnel attached to a two-foot-long plastic tube that ended in small pouch.

"I had a turtle neck jumper on," said Lauren. "So I could

hide it well. I'd use my left hand to pull the funnel out a little, then pour the water into it. If Garston had got suspicious, I would have tucked the funnel back down out of sight. The tube went under my arm and down to a small pouch on my side. We muffled any sound by filling the pouch with a super-absorbent pad."

"Brilliant. So, he thinks you're drugged, and you're playing along. What happens next?"

"I started acting drugged. I'd read up on all the symptoms, and how long everything takes. All I had to do was convince him that I was slowly going under. He lapped it up, and did exactly what we hoped he'd do. He started boasting about his crimes, telling me all about the sick, disgusting things he'd done to his previous victims. And how he was going to take even longer with me."

"That sounds horrific. You had to sit there, pretending to be drugged while he mentally tortured you?"

"I had to get him to admit to as many crimes as I could. It was all on camera so it was absolutely critical."

"Of course, what you didn't know at this time was that the killer had taken you to a different location, and jammed all the signals between you and the police."

"That's right. I'd been told that once we'd gathered enough evidence to get a conviction then the police would come rushing in and arrest him."

"When did you realise they weren't coming? That you were on your own?"

"When he was cataloguing all the ways he'd tortured Mathew. He'd already admitted to killing the others. He'd waterboarded them, drowned them to within an inch of their lives, gave them a few seconds to recover, then started it all over again. And again. He'd done the same to Mathew. Not physically, but mentally. He'd psychologically waterboarded him for six months. *Six months!* Taking him to the point of suicide, making him into a hate figure, planting fake stories about him, inciting hatred, whipping up his neighbours, pushing excrement through his letterbox."

It was a hard watch. The camera had zoomed in on Lauren's face. Tears were sliding slowly down her face. Her voice almost broke several times, but she carried on.

"Mathew never fought back. It wasn't in his nature. He bottled everything up and hoped it would all go way. That was why Garston had chosen him. He was an interesting subject to break. To torture. To push to the brink, relent for a few days, then start the process all over again. And again. And again!"

The camera panned to Ashley. She was also in tears.

"When the police didn't arrive after hearing that," said Lauren. "I knew I was on my own."

Lauren wiped the tears from her face.

"So, I knew I was going to get one chance. Drugged victims might be easier to control, but they can't walk upstairs on their own. Garston was going to have to help me to my feet. And when he bent over me, he'd be vulnerable to a surprise attack."

"You knew he was bigger and stronger than you?" said Ashley

"I did. Which was why I had to use surprise and go full-on honey badger on him. No quarter."

"And you did."

"I did. It's all on camera. If there'd been a referee on hand, he would have intervened to save Garston from taking further punishment. I had his mask off, I grabbed him by his hair, and shoved his face into the camera for a close-up. No need for EFit."

"Is it true he fired a gun at you?"

"He didn't just fire a gun *at* me. He *shot* me. Twice. I have the dents in my bullet proof vest to prove it."

"So, how did he manage to shoot you?"

"I got overconfident and relaxed too soon. He wriggled out of my grasp, and suddenly pulled a gun on me. There were no reports of him ever having a gun. So, it was a bit of shock."

"But you had a bullet-proof vest?"

"By sheer luck. Agnetha, my brilliant make-up artist, told

me I could borrow it. Her boyfriend's an armourer in the movies. I thought 'why not?' I was going into danger. A vest could probably absorb punches. And, if I was taking the vest, I thought I might as well take some blood bags too. I love blood bags. When it comes to dying on stage, I'm the girl. And when the killer shot me, I put in the performance of my life – staggering backwards, the disbelieving look on my face, the perfect pressure on the blood bags to burst them without it looking fake. I'm sure there wasn't a dry eye in the police control room."

"Why did you decide to play dead? He could have kept shooting?"

"I really don't know. Instinct, I think. I'm so used to being shot in my acting career that it's second nature for me to play the death scene. But I soon realised it was the clever thing to do. The killer didn't want me dying quickly. He'd told me a few minutes earlier that death should never be rushed. It should be savoured. So I played dead, waiting for Garston to come over and check on me. I was getting ready for honey badger part two, the one where I shoved his gun up his lower GI tract."

"But he didn't check on you. He ran off. Why?"

"Because Mathew, the one-man rescue party arrived, drove up to the house, headlights flashing and horn blaring."

"How did he find you? You said all the radio signals in the house were jammed?

"They were. But me and Mathew, when we thought we were doing the whole undercover sting on our own, had bought a pet tracker. I was the pet. Naturally. And had this transmitter and Mathew had the receiver. I took it with me just in case. You can never have too many trackers. Then, as Garston was driving me to his house, I had second thoughts. He was bound to search me when we got inside. The glasses and the earrings would probably be okay, but there's no way the pet tracker would pass any inspection. So I dropped it on the lawn on the way to the house. It was far enough away from the house that the jammer had no effect on it. Pure luck."

"So, Mathew's making a distraction out front. What did Garston do?"

"He killed the lights and camera feed, and got the hell out. Me, I went looking for weapons, rifling through all the cupboards and drawers in the kitchen. Then I ran to the window to see what Garston was up to."

"This is where he abducted Mathew?"

"That's right. Mathew didn't have any weapons with him. All he'd been thinking about was finding and saving me. He knew Garston had a gun. He knew Garston had shot me. But that didn't stop Mathew. He drove his car straight at the house making as much noise as he could to draw Garston away from me. That's real bravery."

"I heard that you chased after Garston wearing night vision goggles. Is that true?

"It is. I saw Garston force Mathew to drive him away. I had to follow, but I didn't want to alert Garston that I was following him. Which is difficult in the middle of a night in the countryside. Headlights can be seen for miles. Then I remembered the night vision goggles. Garston had left them on the driver's seat of his van. I put them on and drove away with all the lights turned off."

"What was that like?"

"Interesting. It was a bit like driving through an enchanted wood. I could see all these pairs of eyes looking at me from the roadside."

"Then you found the upturned car."

"I did. That was a shock. Mathew's such a careful driver. He doesn't like speed. But the car was a mess, and I almost ran into it. I braked just in time."

"That's when you came face to face with Garston again."

"It was. He was standing in the middle of the road pointing a gun at me."

"What did you do?"

"I ducked down, opened the van door, and rolled out onto the verge. Then I grabbed my box of weapons that I'd found in the kitchen."

"Is it true you threw a petrol bomb at him?"

"No, it wasn't a petrol bomb. If I'd found petrol in the kitchen I'd have made a petrol bomb, but all I found was cognac. So I made a brandy bomb. Much smaller flames, and a very pretty shade of blue. So, he wasn't petrol bombed. I just mildly flambéed him."

"You mildly flambéed him?" said Ashley, smiling.

"Yes, and, believe me, if someone sets fire to your trousers, you tend to forget about most other things. Which made it easier to fly spray him."

"You fly sprayed him?"

"Yes. I'd grabbed anything in the kitchen that looked remotely useful in a fight. And *he* didn't know it was fly spray. All he knew was the crazy lady who'd set fire to his trousers was now spraying chemicals into his face. That's when I duct taped him to a luggage rack."

"A luggage rack?"

"I *know*. Where did that come from? I suppose it must have been torn off Mathew's car roof. All I know was that it was big and unwieldy. So, if he did get to his feet, he wouldn't be able to move far."

Ashley was giggling.

"I think I may have overdone the duct taping," said Lauren. "But, at the time, how do you know how much duct tape you need? I was more concerned about immobilising him. I wasn't looking to optimise my use of sticky tape. But he did look a little comical. A bit like a singed silver robot."

Ashley was trying to stop giggling. "I believe we have a picture," she said.

"That's right," said Lauren. "I took a selfie of the two of us, as I knew he'd want the moment recorded for posterity."

A picture of a blood-stained, but beaming Lauren, giving the thumbs up sign as she lay on the road next to an equally bloody, but pissed off, Michael Garston, filled the screen. Only the circle of his face wasn't covered in silver duct tape.

I envied Lauren's ability to find humour in the darkest of

places. Not everyone would agree. But men like Garston were impervious to hate. They fed on it. They craved being both feared and admired. *Look how clever I am. Look what I can do to people. Your rules don't apply to me.*

What they couldn't take though, was ridicule. That picture with Lauren would hurt far more than any prison sentence.

Chapter Sixty-Four

Lauren arrived later that morning.

"You're awake," she said. Her powers of deduction were truly astonishing.

"I am," I said. "I saw you on TV."

"I was good, wasn't I?" she said.

"You were."

"Did you see the bit I did about you?" she asked, her voice tentative. "The psychological waterboarding?" she continued. "I hadn't made the connection before. I hadn't realised the extent of what he put you through."

I listened. There wasn't much I could say.

"I really don't know how you survived," she said. "I wouldn't have. Have you thought of … getting help? You know, talking to a professional a couple of times a week, processing what happened to you?"

"I don't know," I said.

"People are going to be queuing up to help you now. There's so much guilt out there. No one had a clue what was going on. Talking is good."

I wasn't sure about that. Talking to strangers was frightening enough as it was. All I really needed was time. I was slowly getting better.

"Natalia told me about the accident report into your car crash," said Lauren.

"Did she?"

"Yes, the report said the car was doing over ninety when it crashed."

"Was it?"

"Yes, they didn't find any evidence of the car braking either."

"It was wet," I said. "I expect the tyres leave less of a trace when it's wet."

She looked at me. She knew I was lying.

"I expect that's it," she said. "I'd tell the insurance people that you were in fear of your life – which you were – that Garston had a gun on you, and was taking great delight in telling you all the different ways he was going to kill you."

"That sounds like a plan," I said.

"You know that they've found Garston's home?" asked Lauren. "I told you yesterday, but I don't think you were fully awake."

I had no recollection. "Did they find the recordings?"

"The house was full of them. Discs, memory sticks – all of them neatly filed, indexed and backed-up. All the murders documented in great detail. But mostly it's about you. He has a year of recordings of you, of commentaries about you, musings, thoughts, plans of what he could do to you next."

I listened. Garston's obsession with me was worse than I'd even imagined. Why? All because I'd been too frightened to tell a bunch of kids to get off my car?

"It looks like he might have murdered his wife too," said Lauren.

"He was married?"

"For fifteen years. Then she disappeared – just as he was moving to Rayford. He told his new neighbours he was a widower, but the police have found no record of his wife's death. His old friends and neighbours back in Surrey thought she'd moved to Rayford with him."

"Didn't any of her friends or family try to contact her?"

"She was estranged from her family and didn't have any close friends. Sounds like Garston was a coercive controller as well as a sadistic serial killer. All his old neighbours saw him as the uncomplaining husband of a woman who had chronic fatigue and depression. She barely talked to anyone."

I could imagine what she'd been through. I'd had less than a year of his attention. She'd had fifteen. And when he tired of torturing her, he went looking for someone else. That was the trigger.

"Georgia and I are going to make sure that these recordings are seen by the people who need to see them," said Lauren. "Maxton's going to see them. Terrell's going to see them. Sophie's coroner's going to see them. Every journalist, every pundit, every podcaster who delighted in your vilification are going to see them. We promise."

"I don't want them broadcast."

"They wouldn't be. We'd make sure of that. We'd just make sure they saw the kind of monster he was and what he'd done to you."

"Thank you," I said.

"Georgia says you could sue Swindon Council for wrongful dismissal if you want. You could get your old job back. You could sue everybody for that matter. No one's going to want any case to go to trial. A jury would award you millions."

I wasn't sure I could do my old job. Not yet. That man had left the building. But it would be nice to be able to go outside without the fear of someone yelling abuse at me or chasing me down the street. To be able to shop in a supermarket without keeping my head down, rushing from item to item on my list, afraid to browse or stand in the queue at the cheese counter for too long.

It was always the little things that got to me the most.

"I'm not sure I want to sue anyone," I said. "That would throw me back into the spotlight. I just want to be normal again."

"You could use it as leverage, though," said Lauren. "To ensure that everyone goes on record to exonerate you. And does so. Now. Not next week or next month."

She was right. No one liked admitting they were wrong. And, in a strange convoluted way, they were victims of Garston, too. He was a clever, manipulative, obsessed sadist who even made me doubt what I'd seen and heard. He was the real guilty party in all this.

"They'd pay for counselling," said Lauren. "They'd pay for the top people. I know you think you don't need counselling now, but the option would be there. You'd only have to go the once. If you didn't like it, you wouldn't need to go again. But I really think you should give it a try. For me."

"I know you mean well, but, really, all I need is time."

And to forgive myself.

Even now, knowing what I know, there was still a part of me that felt guilty. The killer may have manipulated me, but I was the one who walked into the police station, and turned a missing child investigation into a possible homicide. That was on me. I didn't point the finger at Sophie's father, but I gave the police the ammunition.

Perhaps it was time for that man to leave the building too?

"Okay," I said. "I'll try counselling. I'm not promising anything, but I'll give it a try."

"Excellent! You won't regret it."

"No," I said "I don't think I will."

Tears started to fall down my cheeks. I hadn't cried in years. I wasn't hurt or unhappy. I just couldn't stop myself. Twelve months of self-hatred and guilt came spilling out of me.

Acknowledgements

Thank you to my editors: Patricia Rice,
Rachel Neumeier and Michele Dunaway.

About Chris Dolley

Chris Dolley is a *New York Times* bestselling author and a former teenage freedom fighter. That was in 1974 when Chris was tasked with publicizing Plymouth Rag Week. Some people might have arranged an interview with the local newspaper. Chris created the Free Cornish Army, seized the Torpoint bridge, sent an army into Truro, and persuaded the UK media that Cornwall had risen up and declared independence. As he told police at the time, 'It was only a small country, and I did give it back.' The magazine *Punch* described the events as, 'A splendid hoax,'

He now lives in rural France with his wife and a frightening number of animals. They grow their own food and solve their own crimes. The latter out of necessity when Chris's identity was stolen along with their life savings. Abandoned by the police forces of four countries, who all insisted the crime originated in someone else's jurisdiction, he had to solve the crime himself. Which he did, and got a book out of it – the *New York Times* bestseller, *French Fried: one man's move to France with too many animals and an identity thief.*

About Book View Cafe

Book View Café is an author-owned cooperative of professional writers, publishing in a variety of genres including fantasy, science fiction, romance, mystery, and more.

Its authors include New York Times and USA Today bestsellers as well as winners and nominees of many prestigious awards such as the Agatha Award, Hugo Award, Lambda Literary Award, Locus Award, Nebula Award, RITA Award, Philip K. Dick Award, World Fantasy Award, and many others.